A LOVER'S TOUCH

"They would not sell anything to me in Swanston," she confessed quietly. "They turned me away."

"Aye, Robbie told me. What will you do about it?"

"Why nothing." She turned her eyes upon him, surprised by such a question. "There's nothing I can do."

"You can go back to their shops again. Right now. I'll go with you."

His eyes were serious as they looked into hers, and she shook her head. "Nay, I can't do it."

"Yes, you can. Here, take my hand." He clasped her fingers and drew her up. She did not move, and slowly, gently, he pulled her close, drawing her so near that her cheek rested against the ridge of his shoulder.

His shirt felt warm with the sun and with his own coursing blood. Never had Chaynoa been held close to a man in tenderness, and she did not shrink away now, but remained still, smelling the pine resin upon his skin, seeing the dark hair against his nape, feeling the slight pressure of his hand on her spine.

She let her head rest against him for long moments and closed her eyes, quivering with tangled emotions, but one thought was clear: through some whim of divine grace the best man in all of Christendom held on to her.

FILIGREE

DEBRA HAMILTON

ZEBRA BOOKS
KENSINGTON PUBLISHING CORP.

ZEBRA BOOKS are published by

Kensington Publishing Corp.
850 Third Avenue
New York, N.Y. 10022

Second Printing: May 1996

Printed in the United States of America

"I do desire we be better strangers."

—Shakespeare

Chapter 1

June 15, 1774

Like an arrow released by the magic bow of some heavenly warrior bent upon whimsy, a bird soared through the sky and pierced its azure canopy, then, losing velocity, glided downward on wide-stretched wings of immaculate white. It dipped, shrieked a wild cry, then dipped again.

A man observed its flight with envy, while, with an involuntary wince, he rolled his shoulders against the tightness of his uniform. He held a pair of reins, and although his fingers were scraped from a recent brawl, they possessed the peculiar, long-jointed dexterity often found in artists' hands. He flexed them and stared more intently at the gull, which circled the topsail of the graceful man-of-war anchored in the river. At the sight of the ship his fingers tightened until the scratches on his knuckles stood out in raw, red lines. His belly knotted, and he turned his head away lest anyone read the emotion that crossed his face despite his effort at appearing expressionless.

Astride a steaming horse, he drilled his troops on Boston Common while the sun beat down upon his tricornered hat. After three days of rain the sky had brightened and the temperature had soared, so that the woolen uniforms of His Majesty's army were a bane. The soldiers' boots half sank in the muddy ground, but the weary men obediently plodded into formation while he trotted among their ranks and barked drill commands. They were too proud to show their discomfort in front of the hostile spectators; they wanted to be good soldiers; they wanted to be like him.

With a critical eye he regarded them in their white cross-belts, black cocked hats, and light-colored breeches bespattered now with mire. They were one of the nimblest companies in the whole of His Majesty's army, aggressive fighters, many able to load and fire their muskets in remarkable time, although none had ever come close to matching his own record of thirteen seconds. Despite the fact they were the dregs of British society, former beggars and felons some, he held an odd regard for them—odd because most of the other officers despised the scum they were ordered to mold into men.

"Cock your firelocks!" His voice rang loud as he gave the exercise command. *"Present arms!"*

With the sound of countless moist hands clapping against the walnut and metal of countless muskets, his men performed the maneuvers, the faint rattle of their bayonets blending with the clatter of ox carts on the adjacent cobbled streets.

Courtland was not the only one who watched the disciplined performance of the newest arrivals from London. Merchants, jacktars, and apprentices lounged on Beacon Street, sweating in their oilskins with their hands shoved in their pockets, while old women peeked from behind lace curtains with hard, sullen eyes. They despised the British troops who had come to close their port. They wanted the redcoats gone—except for the strumpets, of course, who hung out of the tavern windows in gaudy gowns and boldly issued invitations to any soldier who had a handful of shillings or a bottle of English brandy to share. More than a few had already propositioned the handsome captain with the silver-laced hat and restless eyes, whose notice they could never catch.

"Captain Day!"

A young lieutenant galloped recklessly toward him over the mincemeat green, and Courtland tipped his hat back a notch, waiting until the officer drew rein in a splatter of muddy water. "If that nag dumps you in the muck on your backside, Lieutenant Eastham," he observed, "these colonials will be hooting like jackals for days."

The lieutenant ignored his jab and spoke with excitement. "The Old Woman wants to see you!"

Courtland arched a black brow. The Old Woman, as he was called in the officers' mess, was none other than General Thomas Gage himself, the English appointed governor of Massachusetts and commander-in-chief of all the British forces in America. "You don't say?" he muttered. "What does he want with me?"

Jeremy Eastham eyed him incredulously, for to be summoned by Gage would have paled the face of any other officer. Envy pricked the youngster like a dart. "How the devil should I know?" he said, affecting his own bland air. "He probably wants to lecture you on keeping your men in line. You know how particular he is about not offending the townspeople here. 'Watch your drunkenness and gambling, don't create disturbances, and by no means offend the virgins.' Damned stick in the mud, he is, if you ask me."

"We're sitting atop a powder keg. Gage know 'tis best not to ignite it with some petty incident. He'll act in his own good time." Courtland pivoted in his saddle to instruct a subordinate to take command of the drilling before turning back to survey Jeremy through discerning eyes. A spoiled aristocrat, he thought, new to the military and already bored with its routine. His manner verged upon insubordination, and during the long sail to Boston Courtland had been tempted more than once to punch him in the jaw.

"I'm not as patient as you are," Jeremy declared with concealed asperity, wheeling his horse around to fall in beside the captain. "Nor do I seem to have your nerves of steel—indeed, sometimes I believe you have no nerves at all. The ladies say you have no heart."

He regarded the hard-jawed officer askance, and receiving no answer to the taunt, judged it best to change the subject. "The general is at his favorite tavern, by the way. Maybe he'll treat you to a dish of kidney pie and a tankard of rum while he sermonizes."

Without answering, Courtland scanned the low townscape. It was a simple one of warehouse roofs, jutting wharves, and a dozen needlelike steeples rising to a taffy sky. It made a crude picture, not rich in gold pigment and ancient ornamentation like those scenes in Venice and Amsterdam he had enjoyed, nor was it even quaint like the mist-veiled villages of his beloved England.

A few drops of water left over from the earlier rain trickled from Courtland's hat, and the sun sharpened the odors of dead fish and tar drifting from the docks. "Hell of a place," he muttered in a rare expression of personal sentiment. "Now that you mention it, I could use a glass or two of rum—if not a lecture."

"Aye." Jeremy gave the inelegant homes they passed a condescending stare beneath heavy-lidded eyes. "I'll take London any day. And fashionably turned ladies instead of Puritan misses."

Not above needling the fresh-faced lieutenant, Courtland replied, "You wouldn't know what to do with a fashionably turned lady if you had one."

Jeremy reddened and glanced at the uncommon profile of the other. Day was neither well-born nor wealthy like himself, but he suffered no dearth of women clamoring for his arm. If Jeremy did not dislike him so much, he would have asked for pointers.

"Just as well to stay away from them," Courtland went on, as if reading his thoughts. "The last thing you need is a camp follower clinging to your coattails while you march all over the colonies."

Some said Boston had the most narrow and crooked streets in the world, and the pair of dashingly clad riders wended their way through a maze of white clapboard houses and red brick artisans' shops clogged with horsemen, wagons, and gliding coaches-and-four. The lanes were filled with pedestrians who splashed gingerly about in patens and spatterdashes in order to protect their shoes from the water pooled along the walks. Ox-drawn drays loaded with kegs of rum from the manufactory rumbled down King Street, and a coach driver yanked upon the lines of his team in a struggle to extract a wheel from a pothole. Women poked kerchiefed heads out of doors and children who were eager to play in the sun rolled barrel hoops over the cobbles and skimmed stones across glistening puddles. Occasionally one of their stones skittered in the path of the redcoats, but the officers ignored the missiles as they had been sternly instructed to do, and finally arrived without incident at the designated tavern.

Their luck was not to hold. As they tethered their horses and approached the entrance, three bearded colonials sidled together and barred their path.

"Step aside." Courtland spoke in a short but civil tone, in no mood for a confrontation with a group of surly colonists bent upon mischief.

The trio made no move to comply. Instead they shifted until their shoulders created a barrier against entry into the public house. "Damned lobsterback," one growled. "Bloodyback! Go to England where you belong!"

"And you go to hell!" Jeremy reached for his sidearm, but Courtland grabbed his arm to stay the disastrous action. "Eastham! Let it pass! 'Tis not worth the trouble." Turning his eyes from Jeremy, he pinned the brash colonial with a steady stare that had caused more than one man to quaver in his convictions. "Now you've had your say, mister, let us pass."

The fellow sized him up, standing for several seconds with his fists clenched. Then, deciding not to risk a fight, he wheeled about to leave, but not before snarling a threat over his shoulder. "We'll be sending you back to London soon, ye interferin' redcoats, have no doubt of that!" For emphasis, he extended his middle finger and ran it rudely over the royal cipher embroidered on the saddlecloth of Courtland's horse.

"Traitorous bastard!" Jeremy exclaimed. In a flash he raised his pistol and aimed it at the colonial's back.

Courtland stepped in front of him. "If you fire that

pistol, Eastham, I'll see you court-martialed before the day is out."

Jeremy stared with hatred into the wintry eyes of the captain. For several seconds the two men stood with locked gazes, and then in a surly gesture, Jeremy shoved the pistol into its holster and remounted his horse.

After a brief, considering stare at the lieutenant's retreating back, Courtland ducked his head and entered through the low portal of the tavern where smoke from clay pipes made the air thick and blended with the smell of meat pies and rum. A crowd of jovial patrons stabbed at their trenchers with wooden-handled forks or threw dice for wagers, and Courtland's red coat earned from them no glowering looks, for the public house was a renowned haven for Tory gentlemen loyal to England.

The captain asked the proprietor to direct him to the private room of General Gage, and found the esteemed gentleman sipping claret while two expressionless sentries stood at attention behind his wingbacked chair. At the governor's cordial greeting Courtland stepped forward, and, tucking his hat under his arm, appraised the features of the man who was the highest official in the land.

The bony nose, hawkish eyes, and powdered hair were unprepossessing, but his uniform shone with such an abundance of gold epaulets and polished brass buttons that it seemed to weigh down the narrow shoulders. As a complement to the splendor of the general's regalia, the room was finely appointed, its rich paneled mahogany ornamented with oil paintings that gleamed with sunlight filtered through Holland lace drapes.

Courtland shifted his gaze back to the governor's face and puzzled over the reason for this private interview. An unpleasant thought struck him: perhaps he was to be disciplined for some infraction. The ship bound for Boston had been so hot and overcrowded that tempers had flared, and he had knocked the first mate senseless for cheating at cards. Perhaps word of it had reached Gage's ears.

Courtland considered silently, deciding that rowdy brawls were too common in this high-spirited army—which was shamelessly prone to drinking and gambling—to merit the notice of a general on any single occasion.

"Captain Day!" Gage began conversationally, setting his glass upon the elegant gateleg table pulled before his knees. "How was your voyage here from London?"

"Uneventful, sir."

"You arrived in Boston only yesterday?"

"Correct, sir."

The governor assessed the tall well-conditioned frame of one of the most intrepid officers in the infantry, and formed a first opinion: *too independent, too shrewd, and too handsome, but, at the same time, too valuable not to be used to his fullest potential in order to serve the Crown* . . .

A dossier containing the personal and military life of Courtland Day had been delivered to him that morning, and he mentally reviewed its contents. The captain was reported to be an aloof and solitary man, more interested in reading than gambling, and the few women with whom he had recently associated were clean and modest, not soldiers' whores. His behavior was above reproach—outside the usual scrapes, of course, and interestingly, Day had not purchased his present rank with cash like most officers. He had earned it through an uncanny ability to be in the most advantageous place at the most advantageous time.

After a moment more of silent scrutiny which did not seem to unnerve his guest, Gage asked, "How do you find Boston, Day?"

Courtland's eyes followed the governor's hands as they drew out a handkerchief and mopped a flushed brow. "Rather hot, sir."

The older man smiled at the astute, noncommittal answer and nodded. "Temperatures in the colonies are extreme, and we're only halfway through spring. Wait until July. But then"—he eyed the captain keenly—"you've lived here before, of course. Has your return elicited any nostalgic memories, Captain?"

Courtland stiffened, so taken aback by the remark that his usual glib tongue abandoned him momentarily. *The damned army knew everything. They had been looking into his past, ferreting out information* . . .

"I've been told that you once resided only a few miles from here in a little village called Swanston," the general went on, satisfied with the telltale tensing of the captain's jaw. "Is that true?"

Although Courtland's thoughts churned, he answered evenly. "Aye. When I was sixteen my mother married a Boston merchant—my father had been dead several years. Her new husband uprooted us from our home in England, brought us here and established a residence in Swanston."

"But you stayed in his home a bare two years. Why did you leave?"

Courtland's eyes flickered at the question, but his face remained blank in the way of a good soldier—an ambitious soldier who would be damned before he allowed a superior to rattle him, even a general. "My stepfather had my brother and me impressed into service aboard a merchant ship."

Gage frowned and shook his head as if surprised by the information. "Forcibly impressed?"

"Aye. Forcibly impressed."

"Why would your stepfather do such a cruel thing?"

"My brother and I rebelled against his authority. He was not a tolerant man. Nor did he hold any particular affection for either of us." The words were toneless, and the direct gray eyes hard.

"Oh? In what way did you—er—rebel . . . ?"

"We refused to be apprenticed as coopers."

Gage leaned back and toyed with the stem of his glass. "And your brother died upon that merchant ship, I believe . . . ?"

Just behind the governor's head, as if it were deliberately placed there, a painting of a great sailing ship hung upon the wall in an ornate gold frame. It was quite detailed, so that even the coils of rope upon the deck were delineated. Courtland fixed his eyes upon it and for a brief second felt himself transported to another place and time . . .

He strained against the bonds upon his wrists, filled with dread as he laid his temple upon the capstan's bar to which he was lashed. The cold sea wind whipped his naked back, stirred the hair upon his neck, and billowed the loose duck trousers about his body, which was too lean from poor rations. He could hear the monstrous ivory sails above his head, that energetic flutter and *whoosh* he had grown so accustomed to hearing, yet would hate until he could hate no more . . .

To shake himself free of the horror he took a breath and made his answer controlled. "Aye. They flogged him to death." *And nearly did the same to me.*

"I see," Gage intoned. "Satisfy my curiosity. If you didn't want to be apprenticed as a cooper, what *did* you want to do with your life?"

"I wanted to return to England."

Gage affected a paternal smile that did not touch his eyes. "But you were only a boy, Captain. What would you have done there? Where would you have gone?"

"I beg your pardon," Courtland replied with brittle civility, "but I don't believe that has any bearing on matters now."

"Doesn't it . . . ?" Gage waved his hand, prompting one of the sentries to cross the room. The man opened a desk drawer, removed a portfolio engraved with the general's initials, and passed it to Gage before stepping back into place.

The general took a pair of spectacles from his pocket and, after wiping them on his sleeve, hooked them over his ears. With exaggerated slowness he then unbuckled the flap of the portfolio and removed a stack of watercolor paintings, which, one by one, he lifted up and turned this way and that to catch the best light. Occasionally, as he appraised the details and found a particularly well-rendered line, he muttered, "Hmm . . ."

When he had finished with his little ritual he removed his spectacles and reordered the pictures into a neat pile. Then he made a steeple of his hands and raised a brow.

They were all paintings of a simple stone house that could have graced any farm in Devonshire. Each view was different and meticulously drawn; in some angles the sun shone upon a white door, and in others clouds hovered above an ivy-cloaked stoop; in one study a small boy kneeled beside a dovecote, and in another the same boy smiled beneath a tangle of rusty autumn leaves.

As Courtland saw the paintings slowly revealed, like pieces of his heart ripped out for anyone to see, rage boiled within his chest and his talented hands snapped into fists. He had to shut his eyes and breathe deeply in order to control himself, for he wanted to thrust out his fingers, close them about the heavy neck adorned with its gold medallion, and squeeze.

"These are paintings of a farm in Devonshire, I believe . . . ?" Gage said, looking up at him. He thumbed through the pictures in a careless way as if unaware of the captain's enmity. "I've been told this is the house in which you were born and raised, the house where your father and grandfather died." When Courtland failed to answer, the general lifted a brow. "Eh, Captain . . . ?"

Courtland looked away from the paintings. He had never shown them to anyone, they were too personal, a part of himself he did not want to reveal. They had gotten him through countless hellish days and nights, they had helped him to survive. When he was on board ship he had hidden in order to paint them, and he had painted them feverishly, desperately, as if to make them real. He had wanted nothing but to go home, back to that house, and the ever-present, driving desire to return there had never dimmed, not even during these last years in the army. If anything, it had only burgeoned until it was a dull, harrowing ache beneath his breastbone. He was tired of being commanded and disciplined and shipped about. He wanted to be his own man. For once in his life he wanted to be the master of his own destiny.

He raised his eyes, and through perfect teeth delivered a chilling reply. "I wasn't aware that British policy condoned the confiscation of an officer's personal belongings. *Sir.*"

"It is our policy, *Captain,*" Gage drawled succinctly with glittering eyes, "to do whatever is best for England. And you *do* want whatever is best for England, don't you?"

Courtland returned the stare. "Any officer would."

"Good. What of your remaining family in Swanston? What sort of relationship do you share with them now? Do they know you are attached to the British military?"

"They know nothing at all of me. I have made no contact with any of them in the past fifteen years."

"Are you quite certain that they know nothing?"

"Quite." The word was a harsh sound that bordered on disrespect.

Gage examined the officer with a shrewd eye, measuring every inch of his physique as he might a piece of horseflesh being considered for its useful function to the Crown. He sighed, thinking it a shame that the captain had not lost his temper a moment ago; a court-martial hanging over his head would make him more cooperative. Well, the interview was not yet over . . .

"I intend to send you upon a mission," Gage snapped. "A rather important one. How accomplished are you at spying?"

The question was unexpected. Courtland knew he was being set up, but he could not fathom the reason why. His stomach knotted but he answered with a glib sarcasm. "I hardly know. I've never had a particular reason to try my hand at it."

"You will."

A pause ensued, during which the general waved

his hand to prompt a sentry to refill his glass of claret. He sipped, allowing Day's nerves to stretch a bit more tautly.

"I want you to take up residence in Swanston again, Captain."

"What?"

"As an ordinary colonial, of course. We'll establish a trade for you so that you can become a part of the local society there."

"And what will you expect me to do—exactly?"

The general noted that Day had dropped the respectful "sir" long ago, and it annoyed him. "You will invite confidences," he retorted, "find out what's being said at the Sons of Liberty meetings. The colonists are plotting rebellion against us, of course, and we know they're stockpiling arms—muskets and cannon are hidden all over the damned countryside. Find out where the caches are. I'll expect you to send me maps and drawings, and any other information that will enable our troops to seize the stockpiles at a moment's notice. That shouldn't be too difficult for an intelligent soldier like yourself." He raised the claret to his lips, and, in the process, spilled a few drops over the stack of paintings. "Do you think you can manage it?"

Courtland wondered if he had a choice. Gage must have studied every particular of his past to have plotted this scheme so well. He glanced at the two sentries standing at attention behind the general's chair, but their eyes seemed to stare straight past him as if he did not exist. "I can manage it," he said through his teeth.

The governor set his glass aside and regarded the officer. Day's jaw throbbed, but he was managing his temper well. It was time to fire the next salvo. "You may be interested to know that your stepfather,

Simon Peebles, is an active member of the Sons of Liberty in Swanston. I want you to gain his confidence."

At the dismaying command Courtland fought to keep his expression blank. He hated Simon Peebles, for God's sake, and would prefer to kill him than befriend him. Hadn't Gage been able to deduce that through his damned babbling informers?

"And you have a sister there, too," Gage went on. "Virtue is her name, isn't it?"

A little girl in pigtails and a white lace frock with an angel's grin. The image was old and fleeting but achingly sweet. Courtland nodded with fury in his eyes.

"She's betrothed to a man named Jack Bretton," the general commented. "He's active in the secret society here in Boston. You're to make friends with him, as well."

"You're asking me to betray my own family?" Though he fought against it, incredulity marked Courtland's voice.

Gage shifted his hand so that it rested atop the collection of watercolors, a lifetime's labor of love. "This house in Devonshire—" He tapped a fingernail upon a painted gable. "I believe your mother sold it after she married Simon Peebles . . . ?"

Courtland inclined his head curtly and waited for the stinger.

"Well, it's for sale again. Surprisingly enough, I know the fellow who owns it. Of course, one would need a bit of money to purchase the place—not much, since it's in disrepair and the soil is poor. Perhaps a . . . bonus for a job well done would be enough. And then a major's salary would help keep up the property." The general glanced at Courtland and smiled mechanically. "I always like to lend a

paternal hand to my officers who have no wealthy
fathers to buy their promotions for them.''

When the young man did not reply, the general
gathered up the paintings and tamped them against
the table to make the edges straight. Then he held
them out with a steady hand. "What do you say to
that, Captain Day? Do we have a deal?''

Chapter 2

Up over the headland rose the scent of the dismal sea, drifting landward like a cloud, wending through the secret paths of a woodlet long forgotten. The sea's vapor dried upon hart's tongue and moonwort, and its tang mingled with the mysterious odors of things both rotting and renewing life, blossoming and withering away. Its damp breath pricked the noses of the creatures hiding in the copse and alerted them to danger. In the space of a moment a fox fled, a hare burrowed, and a curlew's song died in its throat.

Strangely, their signals of fear went unnoticed by the girl moving in the green filtered light. In a curious rhythm she stooped, straightened, and stooped again, pushing aside leaves with frantic fingers.

"Where is it?" she despaired. "It must be here, I remember it as if it were yesterday. My memory never lies to me." She knelt down, and, gouging with her bare hands, hollowed out a hole in the spongy earth. But her efforts were to no avail; she failed to find the thing she sought.

In frustration she leaned back and rested her elbows on her knees. "Another ill-starred day . . . how many more will there be?"

As always her search had proved a fruitless task.

How long had she been hunting? She glanced about through eyes as wary as those of a yearling doe just emerged from its covert. Repeatedly her gaze scanned the landscape, noting the elms framing the river and the crooked oak shading the bed of unripe strawberries crushed beneath her toes.

It had been *here*. She remembered her mother standing in this place frenziedly wielding a trowel. Years had passed, of course, but nature's landmarks did not change so soon, trees did not uproot themselves, rocks did not shift. So why was Mother Nature proving so covetous and sly?

Suddenly a chill wind blew off the river, ruffling the hare's fur and the curlew's feather. A twig snapped and all the birds winged upward in one quicksilver arc. The girl cocked her head to the side and listened. Her delicate nostrils flared with a scent, and in a flash she lifted her frayed skirts and bolted through the underbrush no less swiftly than the other creatures.

When sunshine winked at her from a cracked windowpane, she whimpered in relief. The cottage was near and its magic would keep her safe. She slapped aside trails of ivy, using her shoulders to negotiate a path through the forest's wildness before disappearing beneath a curtain of dappled foliage. Behind her, the parted branches swayed back and resealed their emerald veil. Then, after the settling dust drifted through a straying sun ray, the leaves hung still once more.

And the river coughed up its danger.

In the form of a man it heaved itself over the side of a pinnace, plunging into water so murky even the fish disdained it. The fluid force dashed the breath from his lungs, and with his head lolled back and his legs sprawled, he appeared no more than a piece of flotsam orphaned by the waves.

When the river cast him toward the shore, his feet found purchase on the bottom, but he could not stand. He raised his head above the surface, and, gasping, spat out a stream of water while crawling farther up the bank. His arm jerked like that of a marionette pulled by a string, and with vague surprise he glanced down at the rope still clenched in his hand—at the end of it, the pinnace bucked in the current.

Courtland tried to stand again, failed, and with an ungraceful splash fell back into the shallows. The sandy water invaded the ragged wound on his arm, and with a groan he rolled to his stomach, heaving to cast up a measure of the river. "God save me . . . I have to get up, have to. Have to . . ." He mumbled the words with conviction but made no move to rise.

Loss of blood had taken a toll upon his strength, and weakly he opened one eye to view the foreboding trail of red flowing down his sleeve. He must get up, seek assistance quickly, else the scavenging birds would find themselves with a dainty dish for breakfast.

After he pushed himself up on all fours, he rose and staggered forward, putting the bowline over his shoulder in order to tow the pinnace in.

Once the boat was dragged to higher ground, Courtland braced himself against its hull and caught his breath before retrieving his belongings from the water-logged bottom. With excruciating slowness he collected his boots, pistol, ammunition, a spy glass, and a notebook that contained a few folded papers. Then he shoved all but the boots inside a drawstring bag.

Shivering with cold even while perspiration rolled off his temples, he thrust his wet feet into the boots, never believing the task could be so difficult. Next, cursing the garment for its tailored fit, he eased his injured arm from the sleeve of his bloodied uniform jacket and damned the provincials who had taken potshots at him before he could follow plan and don civilian clothes. What a bright target he must have made sailing down the river!

With regret and a strange sense of loss he tossed both his scarlet tunic and waistcoat into the water, and through dazed eyes watched them swirl to the bottom, sucked down by the current. The pistol he thrust in his waistband before raising his eyes to survey the landscape.

It had been years since he had last glimpsed this shoreline, but its rippled dunes and crooked willows he would always know; they were fixtures in his heart. The piercing northwesterly wind he well remembered too; in the past it had coaxed him to sleep in the place of a mother's good-night.

He pushed aside ugly memories and made his way through the bullrushes toward the bank, his dragging feet instinctively finding the path. Through unfocused eyes he scanned the view, seeing swampy fields and the fringes of a woodlet.

Its tangled depths he did not know well, for as a child he had been warned away from their lost paths, and from the deep pools that nestled like deadly mirrors among the fern. Once or twice, however, ignoring warning, he had ventured inside only to find the place impenetrable, too dense for riding and too boggy for exploration. But today he must pass directly through its wild and unsociable heart. To circumvent it would add miles to his destination, miles he could never make now. How long had he lain senseless and bleeding in the boat?

Dizziness caused him to reel as unpredictably as a

drunken sailor when he plunged into the wood. His blood dripped a steady trail, and tiny creatures scattered in all directions beneath his crashing, zigzagging pace. He squeezed his wounded arm above the elbow in an attempt to staunch the flow while swearing at the misfortune that had jeopardized his important mission. "Hell of a thing to happen . . . come this far only to die in a godforsaken colonial hamlet, have my body spat upon by some blasted backwoodsman . . ."

Barely conscious, he stumbled on in his mud-caked boots, nearly falling headfirst into a pool choked with waterweeds. He stared at the water and licked his dry lips, but still possessed enough wits to know it was too brackish to drink. Through blurred eyes he gazed about in the green gloom, searching for a path to follow through a landscape so wild it appeared no man had ever breached it.

When he finally glimpsed a tiny crouched dwelling through the trees, he was so surprised that he shook his head to clear it. The house was overcome by nature, almost indistinguishable as a thing once constructed by human hands.

He squinted and stared harder. Willows stood guard around it with their boughs draping its gable, while serpentlike ivy crawled over its walls and wreathed a window that would have gone unnoticed had not a sunbeam glinted off its panes. Likewise, the door was nearly invisible below its awning of curling greenery. Birds nested under the eaves and scolded a pair of squirrels scurrying up the side of a half-crumbled chimney.

Courtland would have assumed the place abandoned and moved on, except that he noticed an impression in the sand beneath his boots. A small footprint it was, with the toe more deeply etched than the heel, as if the owner had sprinted quickly over the ground.

He gripped his pistol, knowing himself in danger now that the country hovered so close to war, for even though he had shed his uniform jacket, the cut of his breeches would reveal to a sharp-eyed man the nature of his profession. His life depended upon gaining assistance, but that assistance might come only with a threat, for few in these parts would willingly save the skin of a "Jack-pudding" as they so contemptuously called the British officers.

Letting his bag drop, he stumbled toward the crude residence with his pulse pounding so loudly he feared the occupant would be warned. When he reached the door he almost fell against it, and had to brace a shoulder on the jamb to keep from keeling over. Pistol ready, he put his hand upon the latch, shoved the door open, and staggered inside.

The place was dim and he could scarcely see anything at first. Adjusting his eyes, he glanced around to discover that he stood within the meanest cottage, so tumbledown as to provide scant shelter for a savage. He blinked. Was that a figure . . . someone crouching in the corner . . . a girl . . . ?

To keep from toppling over, he widened his stance and tried to focus upon the dark feminine features of the figure.

It was a girl, but one so wild-looking as to resemble a creature come in from the woods. Her masses of thick hair hung as tangled as the brush outside, and her eyes peered through the locks with the same mesmerized fear of a rabbit caught in a snare.

With his pistol aimed, Courtland barked, "You here alone?"

She said nothing, only crouched lower with her arms crossed at her midsection in a defensive posture.

"By your silence you tell me that you are." He jerked the pistol. "Bring a piece of linen and bind up my arm."

But she remained frozen, rooted in her corner.

Having no time to lose, desperate for her assistance before his blood flowed away and left him dead, Courtland took a step in her direction. "Do what I say!"

At the violence in his voice the girl started and straightened her posture. She was tall and slight, almost gaunt, garbed in a tattered rag with her feet bare in the chilly spring morning. Without taking her eyes off him, she skirted the wall inch by inch, her back pressed against its planks and her hands splayed behind her hips. Pausing, she seemed to consider her direction for a moment, then sidled to an old wooden trunk squatting beside the unlit hearth. On shaking legs she knelt down beside it, and still watching him with alarmed eyes, eased open its lid as if she feared that any degree of haste would prompt him to pull the trigger.

With maddening unhaste she withdrew a roll of linen, and, holding it between her quivering hands, stood up to regard her intruder with undisguised dread.

"Come here!" he ordered, his voice cracking on the last word. "Tie it about my wound, tight enough to staunch the bleeding."

She stared at the injured member, following the long line of it down to his hand, from whose curled fingertips a continuous stream dripped onto her earthen floor. Then she scrutinized his face with quick assessing eyes as if judging the length of time he could remain conscious.

"I've got at least an hour or so left in me," he

informed her unsparingly. He cocked the pistol in warning.

She clumsily slipped the end of the fabric between his ribs and biceps, twitching in distaste when her fingers made contact with his damp shirt. She stared at him as if he were some wounded beast about to strike out, but her hands were dextrous as they wrapped and tied off the bandage ends, only faltering once when Courtland winced in pain and bobbled the pistol.

After she had finished, he glanced at the wooden settle placed behind him and, grunting with the strain, dragged it a few feet back to bar the doorway. With a long, low moan he then collapsed upon its seat before ordering her to get him something to drink.

His unwilling hostess backed her way around the room again in slow degrees, and at the weathered table she retrieved a cup carved from a gourd, her grip so shaky that half the brew sloshed onto the floor.

With one hand clutching the pistol and the other out of commission, Courtland could not take the cup from her, but he salivated at the sight of it. "Put it to my lips. And be quick about it."

Her eyes widened as if she would refuse, but when he glowered, she took a hasty step forward with the cup cradled between her extended palms. He bent his head, too thirsty to wait for her cooperation, and drank greedily, thankful that she at least managed to tilt the vessel enough to aid him in the ungraceful endeavor.

He had no idea what he consumed, but when he had swallowed the last measure he leaned his head back in exhaustion. His arm throbbed and his brain was muddled. He observed the girl, who stood petrified with the empty cup still clutched in her hand, and in agony laid his head back and drew up a knee so he could prop his wrist across it and keep the pistol directed at its target. He knew he was close to being at the mercy of this wild-looking girl, perilously close to relinquishing his fate into her trembling hands.

His papers . . . what had he done with his papers? Had he left them in the boat, dropped them in the woods, or brought them with him inside this place? It wasn't like him to be so negligent . . . not to remember . . .

"What's your name?" he asked the girl in a slurred whisper, inquiring just to concentrate, just to prevent the tempting darkness of senselessness from creeping over him and leaving him subject to her power.

Refusing to answer, his hostess regarded him through the tangles of hair straggling over her brow in brown skeins.

Courtland grunted in frustration and closed his eyes for a few seconds before introducing himself in a tired drawl that revealed a trace of the wit he possessed under better circumstances. "Courtland Day . . . at your service. Now that we've got through the social pleasantries, have a seat. Yonder. And don't get up. My aim is hardly up to scratch at the moment—as you have doubtless noticed through that mane of yours. But I daresay . . . 'tis still damned tolerable for a dying man . . ."

Chapter 3

Warned by some inner sense of danger acquired during years of misadventure, Courtland jerked in his unrestful sleep, and the movement caused the pistol beneath his palm to teeter upon the edge of his knee, then topple to the earthen floor with a dull but disturbing thud. He realized he had closed his eyes, but he did not know for how long.

Like a drowning swimmer fighting to resurface from murky depths, he struggled up out of unconsciousness, and even as his eyes opened, he caught the sly, quick movement of the girl as she kicked the pistol and sent the weapon spinning far beneath the settle and out of his immediate reach.

He stared at her, startled by the emotion he saw in the face that loomed over him in the weird half-light of the cottage. The wildest, most wrathful passion stretched the hollows beneath the girl's cheeks and glowed like fire from her eyes. At the same time, as if in a nightmare, he saw her raise the wicked blade of a jackknife and arrow it down toward his throat.

Her action was so quick, and his own awareness so beclouded with pain that Courtland believed his life was to end in that instant. And yet, the girl paused for a fraction of time. Her arm remained poised, atremble with furious emotion, just a hairbreadth from his artery. He stared back, and thought if eyes could do battle, theirs surely did in that spinning spell of indecision. Narrowed and fierce, his gaze challenged hers, dared her to seize her advantage quickly and employ it to the fullest.

Her glittering stare did not waver, did not blink, and he likened her eyes to mirrors, reflecting hurt, reflecting a hatred so deep that he himself recognized it as the same bedeviling thing that had driven him to past desperate acts. He read clearly the malice in her eyes, saw it upon her curled lip and in the fingers that clenched the knife hilt with every ounce of strength she owned. He had the odd notion she saw someone else as she glared at him, saw transposed upon his features the eyes and nose and mouth of some other man.

During her second of hesitation Courtland could have reacted, knocked her arm aside in a vicious swing or captured it and snapped the wrist in two; even in his incapacity his strength would be superior to hers.

And yet, he allowed this dreamlike contest of wills to go on, not knowing why he did so, except that he was vaguely curious as to its outcome. Perhaps he did not really believe the girl had the courage to spill his blood and end his life. Or, perhaps some twisted sense of battlefield honor made him relinquish to her, the weaker contender, the next fateful move of confrontation.

The portentous moment hung suspended, resting upon the tip of the poised blade as Courtland continued to dare the girl with his stare. "Go ahead . . ." he whispered when the seconds whirled into a moment. "Take your chance. 'Twill be the only one

I'll give you. Besides, they would call you a heroine in town if you were to show them what you'd done. There's one gentleman who may even reward you for laying my body at his door."

Courtland watched while she considered his words, saw her chest heave with a killing passion, and some sprite of humor deep within his consciousness laughed at him, laughed at the realization of what he had survived only to die beneath the hand of a mysterious girl—an enemy nothing more than happenstance had created. And yet, after a few seconds more she lowered her arm, shakily removing the knife from its threatening pose inch by resigned inch.

Courtland scrutinized her, wondering what had made her merciful. He did not believe it was any lack of courage; but, possibly, in an odd, equal act of honor she had surrendered her opportunity to kill simply because he had given her the choice to do so. At any rate, whatever demon had seized her seemed to have fled, leaving her white-faced and subdued. Perhaps he could drift into oblivion again and rest unmolested . . . perhaps not. Perhaps she would change her mind in the way of women and put an end to him before the night was done.

Hell of a place to have stumbled across . . . hell of a strange girl. Courtland closed his eyes, and with a slight, whimsical half-smile, muttered, "I knew I should have taken that post in Afghanistan . . ."

When he next awoke he found himself staring at the sky, and yet, not a wide blue canopy of sky as one would see out of doors, but a circular hole through which a ribbon of light streamed. At first he thought he had died, been transported to heaven, and now limelighted by some divine ray, awaited judgment.

But unless there were ravens in heaven, he reasoned, he was yet a breathing resident of earth—if a damned miserable one.

The bird fluttered to the edge of the hole above his head, cawed raucously and sent dust motes drifting down in the sunbeam. As the raven flew across his line of vision Courtland realized he stared at a raftered ceiling—or what remained of one. The roof had deteriorated with the elements to such a degree that strands of ivy hung down through it in gnarled braids.

Courtland regarded his surroundings with a clearer head than yesterday, taking in all he had missed before: the damp-stained walls sprouting with weeds; the hearth of native stone, sooty but glowing faintly with the embers of a fire banked hours past; and above his head, strung bunches of drying herbs crisscrossing the rafters in a strange pattern of plaid. He fancied he could smell them—basil, mint, sage, thyme—all scents from memories collected long ago but never quite forgotten. Dried rings of apple and pumpkin dangled on twine, too, strung like shriveled necklaces for a hag's neck.

"Where in God's name have I landed?" he murmured to himself, running a hand over the back of his stiff neck and glancing again at the denlike habitat.

A movement caught his attention. From the stool, a squirrel watched him with the same curiously hostile stare he had seen last evening in the girl's eyes, and he wondered if his hostess had not been human at all, but some crafty witch who had transformed herself into this bewhiskered beast at the midnight hour, while he had slept blissfully unawares.

Reaching beneath the settle, he felt about for his pistol, remembering the slender foot that had kicked it there last eve. But the weapon was nowhere to be found.

"Sly little witch," he mumbled, punctuating his words with an oath. "And my papers . . . where did I mislay those blasted things? God Almighty, if the girl has happened upon *them* . . ."

He stood up, only to find himself assaulted by nausea, which thankfully passed with a few deep breaths. Dismayed, he saw that his wound still bled; the flow was not substantial, but the bandage was sodden. If he attempted to walk and make his way through the woods, the stream would doubtless increase and leave him dead long before he could make his destination.

But where was the deuced girl who had almost plunged a knife in his throat last night? Investigation soon supplied his answer. She had moved the settle even while he had slept upon it, inched it away from the door a foot or more, and slipped out the exit to make her escape.

Courtland groaned his thoughts aloud. "Likely she's gone to bring half the town down upon my head. Probably decided having my throat slit was too good for me . . . would rather see it stretched instead. Or have me rot in some stinking provincial jail. Well, I can't blame her, can I?" he said to the squirrel. "If some wild-eyed fellow dripping blood had shoved his way into my house and waved a pistol at me, I would have put an end to him in short order."

Wondering if he should attempt to make his way to the pinnace again and try his luck at another landing downstream, he eased open the door, braced his weight against the frame, and peered outside. But before he could get a foot across the threshold, a loud crack rent the air.

Fifty yards distant, moving in the eerie green light,

the girl wielded an ax. A fallen tree was her target, a monstrous oak she had obviously hacked upon bit by bit over time. She could scarcely lift the heavy tool, and yet she managed to heft it, bringing it to the height of her shoulder and clumsily swinging it downward.

In some fascination Courtland continued to watch her arms strain with effort, watch the dance of ankle-length hair as it swayed with her body's motion. His mouth twisted in a fleeting smile, for he realized he had never seen a woman employ an ax before; indeed, recently, he had seen feminine hands lift nothing heavier than a silver tea service and a platter of scones.

After a few minutes the girl managed to hack off a piece of the oak and split it into fire logs. She gathered the wood and, walking barefoot over grass spiked with dew, approached the cottage. Gallantly, Courtland dragged the settle away from the door to clear a passage for her, and, leaning against the jamb, awaited notice.

When she glanced up and saw him looming in the entrance to her home, the girl dropped the logs and backed away, poised for flight like a skittish animal.

He moved forward and held out a hand in an effort to reassure her, just before he heard a shuffling movement behind him. Suddenly a monstrous body sprang out of the bramble and leapt upon his back, its weight so great that Courtland lost his balance and crashed to the ground. He rolled over and grunted with the pain, managing to escape the jabbing fists of his attacker while landing a punch of his own.

"Hahnee!" The girl screamed the name and threw herself over the two furiously wrestling men. "Hahnee!"

Twisting free of the other's weight, the captain staggered to his feet and, with astonishment, stared at his assailant.

The fellow crouched behind the girl and peered over the top of her shoulder through small, birdlike eyes set in a curiously vacuous face. He was short but brawny, and his hair, though shorn close, was hardly less wild than the girl's, except that it stood on end around his head. Ragged brown clothes hung from his burly body and he wore no shoes, only stockings so riddled with holes it was a wonder they stayed on his feet. He straightened and raised his face above the girl's shoulder, revealing the slack jaw and gaping mouth commonly found in feebleminded persons.

"He is my brother."

The words came softly, a melody of husky feminine sound, and Courtland stared at the girl in some wonder, for hers was the most beautiful voice he had ever heard. He looked at her, then again at the childish fellow of indeterminate age she called a sibling. Although disgruntled over being blind-sided, Courtland could scarcely denounce the fellow without feeling like a lout. "Your brother, eh . . . ?" He eyed the extraordinary pair while holding his injured arm. "Ask him to go easy on me next time. Damn if I'm not bleeding like a stuck pig again."

He glanced down at his wound and shivered. He was freezing and weak and wanted nothing so much as to lie down beside a fire before he collapsed. With a wince, he knelt to scoop up two of the logs that the girl had dropped and balance them in the crook of his sound arm.

Declining to say anything to her or her brother, who still hovered behind her back, he reentered the cold hut and built up the fire, thankful that the embers were still hot enough to catch the wood alight.

He hoped his hostess would creep in soon. He had need of her. She would have to tend his arm again and give him food and drink.

After a moment he knew she stood in the doorway, not because she had made the slightest noise, but because her form blocked the light. He turned his head to glance at her.

She stood with the sun creating a halo behind her hair, a reed basket dangling from her hand. He thought she looked unreal, like a dryad fashioned from all the wild and mystical components of her tangled forest.

"I won't harm you," he said.

She continued to stare. Her eyes blinked with the same long-lashed guilelessness as a fawn's, but she said nothing. He grew frustrated, for he not only wanted to hear her voice again, he wanted her to trust him.

"If I intended to hurt you," he went on, "I could've done it last night when you hesitated a second or two with that pigsticker aimed at my throat." She did not answer and, deciding on a change of tactic, he flashed a smile that had dazzled many. "You would have given me a respectable fight for my trouble though, wouldn't you? 'Twould probably have been the end of me in any case. Now that I think on it, perhaps *I* should be the one watching my back. Between your jackknife and my pistol, you're rather well armed, while I"—he glanced at his wounded arm and affected a helpless expression—"have little more than one bare hand with which to defend myself."

She ignored his cajoling, her liquid gaze flickering over his wound. "You'll bleed to death ere long, moving about like that."

His imagination had not exaggerated the beauty of

her voice, and fascinated in spite of himself, he moved obediently to the settle.

The squirrel leapt on the table, and the girl produced a nut which the creature took directly from her hand. Then with her usual wariness, she approached Courtland, seemingly satisfied for the moment that he did not intend to harm her. He noticed that her feet were long and slender and that she almost glided over the floor. Her drab gown was clumsily patched with white thread, and like yesterday, her hair was an outrageous tangle, adorned now with a crumpled leaf or two. He had never seen locks so long. Where he had previously viewed her only as some strange, half-savage girl, he now observed her through purely male eyes, and realized she was older than he had first surmised, with a mature figure. He wondered how she had come to be here, where her people were, what she was called.

"I have something to stop the flow of blood," she stated, indicating the contents of her basket with a nod. Her tone was curt and bullying, as if she had calculated the best and speediest way to remove him from her cottage and was proceeding without delay. "Untie the bandage from your arm."

Courtland eyed her and the rough-made basket with suspicion, unsure whether he wanted medical ministrations from a backwoods colonial girl who had nearly murdered him a few hours ago. But he hardly had a choice; the wound still bled, and he needed to get to a proper doctor and have the ball removed.

Giving the girl another doubtful glance, he began to unwind the soggy linen.

She thrust back her hair, and spoke as if testing the extent of his gratitude. "I could have abandoned you while you slept. Left you to die or survive on your own like any dangerous beast wounded in the woods."

He raised a brow and gave her an ironic smile, glad that her previously mute tongue was loosened now, even if it was sharp. "You could have killed me, too. Why didn't you?"

She raised her chin. "Because I haven't a shovel to dig a grave."

Courtland stared at her, thinking she had made a poor attempt at humor, but, after further consideration, realized her sincerity. He said, "You could have always tossed me in the river if it was such a colossal problem."

She ignored the sarcasm. "Now that you've survived and will be making your way to the village, I wish to strike a bargain with you."

Her cold tone indicated she found the proposition distasteful, and she clutched the basket possessively as if prepared to withhold from him whatever dubious benefits it contained if he refused to concede to her deal.

Reaching into his pocket with a knowing sigh, Courtland withdrew a guinea and held it out to her, assuming she desired money like most other females of his acquaintance.

"Nay!" she hissed upon spying it. "I'll not accept your coin! 'Tis something else I want."

Courtland observed her high color and indignant posture. He slid the guinea back within his pocket and raised a brow. "Just what might that be?"

"In exchange for my tending your wound," she said tightly, "and my giving you food and drink, you shall leave here on the morrow. Not only that, but you must tell no one, *no one,* that you were here. You must say naught about the cottage in the woods. You must say nothing about . . . about me."

Courtland wondered why she seemed so agonized to protect her isolation, and the mystery surrounding her grew deeper. "If you had asked," he declared quietly, "I should have honored your request even without the exchange of assistance."

She eyed him doubtfully. "I suppose I shall have to take you at your word."

"Galling, isn't it?"

Although obviously loath to touch his person, she approached. "I shall have to rend the sleeve of your shirt."

He nodded, and she removed the knife he had seen at close range the previous evening, wielding it with skill as she ripped the sleeve in half with one deft slice.

He winced and sucked in a breath when the fabric pulled loose from the raw and jagged flesh.

The girl wasted no time on sympathy, but produced a ball of some material, which Courtland could only liken to spun white thread. "What's that? Wool? Flax?"

"Webs of spiders." While he looked on with vague horror, she pressed the mass to the bleeding wound.

"Hold it for a moment," she instructed, and he reluctantly obeyed, putting a hand over hers before she could slide her fingers free.

At his inadvertent touch, she jumped back as if stung, upsetting the basket and backing away from him while fear darkened her eyes again.

Courtland regarded her quizzically, and after a moment she seemed disconcerted, as if she had expected him to spring at her and was confused when he did not. She wiped her fingers on her skirt as if to remove the traces of his touch, then backed to the oven, which was built inside the stone hearth. With a long-handled shovel she removed two small clay pots which were obviously warm rather than hot since she carried them to his side with her bare hands. Before he could protest, she dribbled the contents of one pot directly over the wound.

It burned Courtland's flesh like fire. "Aah! For God's sake, have you decided to murder me, after all!?"

" 'Twill clean the wound."

"I have little doubt it will!"

Ignoring his ill-temper she sliced a piece of coarse-spun linen from the roll in the basket, dipped it in the second pot containing a thick grayish poultice, then after pressing another wad of cobwebs upon the wound, bound up his arm again.

Courtland watched her with dread, not knowing what sort of witchery she practiced upon him, and frankly afraid to inquire.

Obviously relieved to be done with the intimate contact, the girl gathered up her odd assortment of remedies and put them away. Then she brought Courtland a handful of dried apples and a bowl of drink, but when he would have taken them directly from her hands, she evaded him by setting them down on the edge of the settle.

" 'Tis all I have," she said as if daring him to complain. "The strawberries are not yet ripe, and I did not have time to fish last eve." She glanced at him. "I—I only go to the river at night—after darkness falls."

"So you'll not be seen?" He was beginning to understand her behavior even if he did not know the reason behind it.

"Aye. Boats and other fishermen are often upon the water by day."

"That they are," Courtland replied slowly, scrutinizing the elfin face that was gaunt with hunger, and turning a thought over in his mind. Then, both ravenous and parched, he consumed the meager fare in no time. "How did you come to be in this place?" he asked.

She answered with a shrewd glance, "Shall I ask you how you came by the ball in your arm?"

A smile curved Courtland's mouth. "You could ask, but I'd probably only tell you a lie you wouldn't believe."

"No doubt."

"Will you tell me your name, if nothing else?"

"Chaynoa," she said.

An Indian name, Courtland thought. "Just Chaynoa . . . ?"

"Just Chaynoa."

He was gratified to see the fear had left her eyes, if not the suspicion, and set out to make her more at ease with a charm he knew well how to utilize in feminine company. "What do you call this drink you've served me? I've tasted nothing like it."

"Mead, a brew I make of honey, water, and yeast."

" 'Tis very good. I could grow to like it. By the way," he continued smoothly, hoping to catch her in a charitable moment. "Where did you put my pistol?"

She almost smiled while mimicking his previous words. "You could ask, but I'd probably only tell you a lie you wouldn't believe."

Courtland was good-natured enough to laugh. As he did, he noticed that Hahnee peered through the open door. Chaynoa's brother stood like a huge, sheepish child with his finger crooked in his mouth, while his vacuous eyes darted from his sister to her guest and back again. To add to the odd picture, the squirrel sat atop his shoulder with its tail flicking.

Chaynoa spoke gently to her brother in an Indian dialect, and he lumbered forward and sat down in a corner upon a three-legged stool. Removing a piece of wood from his tattered jacket, he began to whittle it with a knife produced from his pocket.

"He does not speak," Chaynoa told Courtland. "A demon took his tongue when he was born."

"And you take care of him by yourself?"

"Aye. By myself."

Courtland thought the occupants of the cottage, both human and beast, were the most curious menagerie he had ever seen. Leaning further back and stretching out his long legs, he watched Hahnee carve the bit of pinewood from which long whorls of shavings fell until the shape of a fantastical bird with outstretched wings emerged.

Across the room Chaynoa dumped the contents of two wooden pails into the enormous black kettle hanging from the crane above the fire, and Courtland contemplated her, wondering how complete she and her brother had made their isolation here. He asked, "What do you know of recent events in Boston?"

She set down the heavy pails and shrugged. "I have a friend, a—a woman who comes here to see me on occasion. She told me that there is a new governor in Boston, a General Gage. He has brought with him many British soldiers. She says everyone in town is scared of the redcoats, saying that they are a scurvy lot, and that they drill all day as if they plan to attack the citizens."

Courtland managed to mask a grin. "Well, 'tis true what they say. They *are* a scurvy lot and their officers *do* keep them drilling till they drop. But I don't believe an invasion is imminent."

"Then why are they here?"

"Because King George is put out with having his tea dumped in the harbor and has closed the port of Boston until someone decides to pay for it."

"My friend says it will throw the people into hard times now they cannot trade."

"Aye." Courtland agreed. "Times will be hard indeed outside your woodlet. And I fear they will get no better before they worsen." He held up a sliver of dried apple peel and examined it with a rueful expression. "Count yourself fortunate that you depend upon no one's bounty but that of Mother Nature."

"Hahnee and I would have starved long ago without the charity of these woods. The trees and the animals are our sisters, the sun our brother, and the moon our grandmother. They are all we need."

While Courtland gave her a skeptical regard, she retrieved a set of candle rods from beside the hearth, and, after propping them upon long poles placed horizontally across the stool and the table bench, added in a low tone, "In town, we've already been warned off once."

Courtland frowned. "Warned off . . . ?"

She nodded, still going about her task. "Many of the smaller towns don't welcome those who can't support themselves. The citizens feel obliged to provide from their own pockets, and resent it."

"Ah. And so if no employment is to be found, one can be routed out of town like a stray cat?"

"My mam, Hahnee, and I arrived here half-starved in the dead of winter, and were asked to leave by the constable until—" Chaynoa hesitated. "Until someone offered Mam a position."

"And where is your mother now?"

"Dead."

The words were uttered with such coldness that

Courtland let the subject drop. He watched her in silence, noting that the candle rods were tied with crudely twisted wicks, which she began to submerge, slowly and with skill, into the melted tallow of the kettle. She dipped, hung them to cool, and dipped again in a smooth cycle she had obviously done countless times before.

Courtland was intrigued by the homey chore. He had never had occasion to linger about a kitchen hearth before and follow feminine hands at their simple tasks. His world had been filled with foul-mouthed ships' crews, boisterous soldiers, and heavy-handed masters, and, in better times, blowsy widows in stuffy parlors whom he used awkwardly and without emotion.

Through narrowed eyes, he scrutinized the girl, deciding that she was as earthy as nature, unlike any other female he had ever known. He watched her fingers dip, watched steam from the kettle dampen the hair at her brow, watched the pale candles grow longer and thicker on their twisted stems until the air grew heavy with the smell of wax as it was stirred by the swaying motion of the girl's young body. Embarrassingly, he felt his vitals quicken in a way they had not done since he had first stood upon the pruriently adventuresome threshold of early manhood.

The girl suddenly froze with a candle rod dangling from her fingertips, then whirled about and pinned him with a keen, suspicious stare. Something of his thoughts must have revealed themselves upon his face, for her eyes grew wider and darker in the eerie way he had seen before. With a soft thud the candles fell from her hands, their pliant forms crumpling in the dirt. Breathless, she backed away from him, skirting the wall all the way to the door. And then she fled, no less nervous than a young animal catching its first scent of man.

Across the room her brother threw down his carving, seized the squirrel, and galloped after his sister like a faithful hound.

Courtland rubbed a hand over his jaw. He had not meant to frighten her again. What unseen and forbidden boundary had he overstepped by his inward and essentially innocent glance of natural male longing? More intriguingly, how had she divined it so astutely?

Chapter 4

She and her brother did not return to the cottage that day, nor had they reappeared when night fell and made their strange, burrowlike dwelling cold and black.

Courtland sat alone, staring at the bright hunter's moon framed by the hole in the roof, and wondered where the devil they had gone, although he did not particularly worry for their safety, figuring they were as at home in the woodlet as they were sitting before their hearth. But he did experience a twinge of guilt that he had driven them away to spend the night in the open air—that is, until he glanced heavenward again and viewed the stars from his seat in the uncivilized parlor.

The next morning he awoke well before dawn, and, after making a sling for his arm out of a strip of Chaynoa's linen, rubbed his cramping abdomen, feeling like a bear emerging out of a long and nightmarish hibernation. His wound had stopped bleeding and his head was clear; Chaynoa's treatment—much to his surprise—had been effective.

He searched the cottage but found nothing substantial to eat, so he wandered outside to look for his misplaced bag of belongings, which he finally remembered dropping near the hut. After a lengthy search through the thick undergrowth he threw up his hands with a mumbled "needle in the haystack," and conceded that he had lost not only his papers on this unfortunate wilderness detour, but his pistol.

He judged himself strong enough to make the journey to the Tory household, whose members would be discreetly aiding him in his mission. Wanting to reach their house by early afternoon, he set out, giving the little wildwood house one last rather brooding glance.

He had not gone a hundred yards when he saw his bag straddling the path, placed conspicuously there, as if to encourage him to retrieve it quickly and keep on walking. He searched its contents, finding the papers undisturbed, but no spyglass. And the pistol was not there; his hostess had obviously decided to keep that for herself.

His strength was not as restored as he would have liked it to be, and by the time he reached the outskirts of Swanston, his steps were flagging and a small stain of red seeped through the bandage on his wound. Fortunately the Saunderson house was not difficult to find, and as he climbed over a turnstile and approached the clapboard home, large and rambling, with its brick chimneys and slatted green shutters, he could not help but think what a contrast it was to the crude little hut he had lately left.

His welcome was made warm by the Tory family, and he received the promised change of clothes and a meal while a servant was dispatched to fetch a doctor. The fellow proved not only competent at removing musket balls, but carefully incurious as to how Courtland's injury had occurred.

The following week, with his arm on the mend and

his strength rejuvenated, Courtland set off for town outfitted in a plain dark coat, waistcoat, knee-breeches, and black tricornered hat. As he breached the rise where the cemetery lay adorned by rows of simple headstones, he gazed down upon the village of his troubled adolescence with eyes made hard by the sharp remembrance of his stormy departure from it. The sound of harsh oaths seemed to echo in his ears, and he recalled not only his stepfather's rage, but his own wrathful vows; he recalled, too, how his younger brother had stared at him during the furious scene with eyes that were bewildered but infinitely trusting of his older sibling's judgment.

A soft breeze sighed in the trees behind him and Courtland's expression changed, his turbulent thoughts turning to softer yet more confounding recollections of his mother. It had been nearly fifteen years since he had seen her and his sister Virtue. The little lass had been weeping then, distraught and confused over Courtland's bitter departure and the shattering of the family, but his mother had been as cold as marble during the episode, her arms folded over her lace-draped bosom in a posture of detachment and her eyes enigmatic.

She had never been maternal. It had been Webster Day, Courtland's father, who had done much of the child rearing, for although Susannah had found a transient interest in her daughter, she had left her pair of sons to run like wild colts over the farm. When she had married Simon Peebles, she behaved as if Courtland and Toby were little more than nuisances. Courtland supposed they had been, especially after she sold the land they loved and transported them to the colonies in the care of a resentful stepfather. They had been rebellious and unmanageable adolescents who quarreled bitterly with Peebles and kept his house in constant turmoil.

He wondered if his mother would smile to see him now as a man. He hoped she would, he desperately hoped she would, for although it had taken him more than a decade, he was beginning to discover that a man could not live the whole of his life without the affection of another human being, no matter how determinedly he attempted to deny it.

His step quickening, he descended the hill and scanned the unpretentious rural scene spread like an unfurled canvas of needlepoint before him: the mown village green, the fenced gardens, the houses neatly kept and shuttered. He remembered the plain little parish church with its bell tower and delicate steeple, the tavern, the grist mill, the picturesque wooden bridge spanning the silver ribbon of river.

Upon seeing it all again he had expected to feel the same violent dislike he had as a rebellious boy just arriving from the folds of Devonshire, but as he viewed it now through the eyes of a man, he found the loathing gone. Only dispassion filled him—that, and the realization that this colony town still compared no more favorably than before with the village of his birth.

His progress took him past modest houses where kerchiefed women swept wooden porches, and apple-cheeked girls knelt in flower beds tending vegetable gardens. He passed stacks of fresh-cut lumber in fields that were dotted with spring colts grazing on sweet grass. People paused in their toil as he went, some shading their eyes to give the unremembered traveler stares of curiosity. He nodded and met their regard directly, feeling a prick of regret for them when he realized their peaceful world would likely soon be shattered by the clangor of war.

At last he paused to view again the stately Georgian home his stepfather had built upon a hill. What changes had been wrought! No longer was it a modest home. Now it appeared as a plantation complete with abundant outbuildings, carriage houses, and quarters for outdoor laborers. The sight of it after so many years and the consequent reminder of the misery suffered inside its walls gave Courtland a moment of swift rage, which, with conscious effort, he quelled. Nevertheless, at the thought of seeing his stepfather again his hand curled reflexively over his pistol, for when Toby had died with his young body flogged to ribbons, Courtland had wanted to kill Simon Peebles, and since then he had dreamed of committing that satisfying act a thousand times.

He smothered his temper and walked up the drive. A black servant answered his knock, and, after ushering him quietly inside the cool house, took his hat and inquired his name, which Courtland refused to supply.

As the servant bowed and left, Courtland's eyes flickered over the familiar commodious reception hall with its new fleur-de-lis wallpaper and polished hardwood floors. Beside the imposing staircase an elaborately carved grandfather clock tolled the hour of ten, its brass pendulum swinging inside a case of beveled glass. He found himself listening for the feminine tones of his mother's voice, but instead he heard the thud of what proved to be a pair of silver-buckled shoes.

A gentleman of short stature wearing a bottle-green coat and white hose halted at the threshold of the adjoining library. His powdered hair was precisely curled and tied, his nose bulged beneath narrow-set eyes, and his black brows were lowered in a scowl of impatience, as if he had been interrupted at an important task. He did not recognize the man who stood in his vestibule.

The burn of an old hatred caused Courtland's fists to clench, but when he spoke his voice held the composure of a man accustomed to commanding companies of soldiers. "Good day, Stepfather."

He was rewarded by the look of utter astonishment, then the grimace of stunned dismay that paled Simon's fleshy cheeks. The old man stared at the visitor as if he beheld an unfriendly apparition. With incredulity his gaze traveled the length of Courtland's tall frame, scrutinizing it, before fastening a second time upon the manly face.

Finally certain of his stepson's identity, Simon coughed, and blood returned to his face in such a swift rush that the vein in the center of his forehead throbbed. With considerable effort he recovered himself and reordered his features into the haughty, disaffected ones more befitting to his nature, while clasping both fists behind his back and strolling forward. Contempt curled his short upper lip. "So, the prodigal has returned."

"Shall I expect the fatted calf?"

Peebles opened his mouth as if to make some scathing retort, then snapped it shut. With icy control he said, "I hope you expect no welcome. For you will surely receive none from me. You—" He stopped in mid-sentence and glanced behind him toward the drawing room.

Repositioning himself, Courtland followed the direction of his gaze.

In the middle of the rich Oriental carpet, with astonishment upon her face, an elegantly dressed woman stood staring at Courtland, her figure flanked by curio cabinets packed with blue and white Delft. Behind her, two matrons in equally fancy attire and calash bonnets sat leaning forward upon a striped sofa, their coffee cups suspended while they regarded the new arrival with barely contained curiosity.

"Courtland . . ." Susannah Peebles breathed.

He looked into his mother's eyes, eyes that were so like his own clear gray ones, and knew he searched them imploringly. He could not help doing so, perhaps because it was an instinctive urge to desire a mother's welcome after so many years away.

She had scarcely changed at all; indeed, she was quite beautiful with her rich brown hair piled high upon her head, and her clothes were no less fashionable than any he had seen in London. He smelled again her lilac perfume, heard again the high chime of her voice, and the clear memory of her winged back to him in a swift rush of confused emotion.

With a rigid posture Susannah glided forward amid a swish of silk, and spoke low enough so that her guests could not hear the words delivered to her only son. "Courtland . . . well, I'm stunned. Why have you come back? I don't know what to say . . . We thought—we thought—" She put her hands to her cheeks and whispered, "Well, you can imagine what we thought."

She stared at him as if she did not know what to do next. Courtland had expected her to cry or to embrace him after so many years, but she made no move to stretch out her arms, and he was not certain she would welcome such a liberty from him. He had never been certain.

"Aren't you going to introduce me, Mother?" he asked quietly, smothering the disappointment that rested like a stone in the pit of his stomach. With a nod, he indicated the pair of matrons ogling him from the drawing room sofa.

The remembrance of her guests seemed to spur

Susannah into action, and she looked grateful for a way to break the awkwardness. "Oh, yes! Of course!" She clapped her hands, feigning brightness. "Mrs. Dove, Mrs. Higginbotham, this is my son Courtland Day, just arrived from—"

"Boston," he supplied smoothly, smiling at the gaping matrons who likely knew well the tale of the two disgraced sons. But he would have wagered his horse they did not know the true story, the one in which the upstanding Mr. Peebles had consigned his stepsons to hell upon the high seas. Undoubtedly some carefully worded story had been spread about the village—two unruly rascals running away from Simon's generous, paternal guidance to seek adventure—that sort of thing.

"Er—can I serve you coffee, Courtland?" Susannah asked. Her voice was so stiff that he might have been an unwelcome stranger rather than a son she had not seen since his boyhood.

He had sat down upon a delicate silk-covered chair.

"Cake?" she quavered.

He declined, and as she passed a cup and saucer to him with a rattle of porcelain, he assessed the furnishings with a quick eye. The panelled walls were painted pale green and hung with a collection of English landscapes; plenty of silver candlesticks and mahogany vied for notice. Peebles had done well for himself. Susannah must be very pleased, Courtland thought, for surely such wealth gave her the social position she had always craved. He had no allusions concerning his mother's nature; she had always been a grasping woman.

"Tell us where you've been since we saw you last," Peebles said, affecting the thinnest, most unctuous smile for the benefit of the guests. "I'm certain we are all most interested to know."

Courtland declined the sugar from the silver box his mother offered and gave Peebles a direct glance. "I've been doing a bit of sailing."

The matrons, probably mothers of eligible daughters, regarded him with burgeoning interest, sensing no dark undertones in his carefully toneless reply.

"Oh, of course!" Mrs. Dove said, "Susannah told us you and your brother had become sailors. What a pity that Toby—was that his name?—succumbed to that dreadful fever abroad."

So that had been the story.

"And where have you sailed?" Mrs. Higginbotham asked, her polite smile revealing a set of protruding teeth.

"Almost everywhere, ma'am."

"What a grand adventure! You must have seen many fascinating cities."

"Quite a number."

"And all of them so much more exciting than Swanston," Mrs. Dove sighed.

The conversation was proceeding to his advantage, and Courtland answered with the appropriate touch of earnestness. "Indeed. But that excitement only seems to have given me more of an appreciation for the peace of Swanston."

"Do you mean to take up residence here then?" Mrs. Dove cocked her bonneted head to one side as if to better catch his answer.

"As a matter of fact, I do."

The matrons beamed while Simon set his plate of spongecake aside with a clatter.

"T-this is quite a surprise, Courtland . . ." Susannah stammered. "Why, we had no idea, no letter . . ."

"I hope the surprise is not distressing."

"Oh, no, of course not."

Her answer did not convince him. "I'm anxious to see Virtue," he said. "Is she here?"

Struggling to maintain her composure, Susannah busied her hands by stirring the sugar in her coffee, apparently disturbed over her son's intention to reestablish himself within the bosom of the family. "She's in Boston visiting friends. She won't be returning for several days."

"Is she married?" he asked, knowing through Gage's information that she was not.

"Betrothed. And to quite a fine young man." Susannah lifted the cup to her lips with a trembling hand. "His father is a wine merchant, and young Jack is assuming the business. A profitable one I understand. That is, until that despicable King George ordered Gage to close the port. Now, we're all suffering with the lack of trade."

"Having just come from Boston, Mr. Day," one of the matrons asked, "how do you feel about Gage and his regiments of British soldiers?"

"Indeed," the other lady cut in, "do you think we should send them packing?"

Courtland grinned with sincerity. "I believe we should send the redcoats back to England for a very long holiday."

The matrons tittered and nodded their heads in agreement, thoroughly pleased with the answer without appreciating its underlying humor. Courtland had not expected such a convenient opportunity to establish himself so soon within the good graces of the community. Doubtless the matrons would rush home and tell not only their husbands, but the gossips on the other side of their fences about the recently arrived gentleman who was sympathetic to the patriot cause.

Of course, gaining the confidence of his stepfather would prove far more difficult, for even if Courtland could swallow his own hatred long enough to curry favor, Peebles would be wary of friendly overtures.

"And were the redcoats the unsavory band of gamblers people say they are?" Mrs. Higginbotham asked, leaning forward as if to hang upon his every word.

Courtland whispered in a grave voice, "You have no idea, ma'am."

She clapped her hands to her cheeks and exchanged a smug look with her crony. "I just knew it!"

From his place beside the tea trolley Simon cocked his head and addressed Courtland suavely. "Does that mean you're a proponent of armed insurrection?"

"I'm a proponent of fair rights for the colonists," came the careful reply.

As if unwilling to allow the conversation to turn to a discussion of politics when personal tidbits were far more intriguing, Mrs. Dove intervened. "Where in Swanston will you be living, Mr. Day?"

"I've purchased a house on Queen's Road."

"Oh, that would be the widow Foree's old home! Poor dear. She died of a lung ailment last summer."

"And will your wife be joining you soon?" Mrs. Higginbotham inquired.

"Alas, ma'am." He smiled charmingly. "I haven't a wife."

Mrs. Dove attempted to conceal a delighted grin behind her coffee cup. "Then I shall have to organize a little gathering to introduce you to some of our young ladies," she said, bestowing a sharp glance upon her peer as if daring her to steal the privilege.

"You mustn't trouble yourself, ma'am—"

"Oh, but it shall be my pleasure, Mr. Day. And now, Prudence and I must be taking our leave so that you can reacquaint yourself with your family." Mrs. Dove set aside the Delft cup she had so daintily balanced upon her lap, her body fairly quivering with the need to toddle out into the streets and shrill that she had been the first to meet the handsome, long lost son of Susannah Peebles who had sailed the world— and who was conveniently unattached.

After the matrons had been ushered out in a flutter of black taffeta, Courtland reseated himself. His mother sat to his left upon the striped sofa and Simon stood beside the window with one hand upon the drape. The silence in the room was palpable.

A black maidservant glided in over the waxed hardwood to remove the cold coffee and soiled cups, and when she had floated out again, Simon broke the hush. "Why did you return to Swanston, Day?" he demanded. "I should like to have a truthful answer this time, not some asinine palaver about the quaintness of the colonies."

Courtland's eyes hardened in a dangerous way, and he almost informed Peebles that he no longer spoke to an adolescent boy but to a man who would not tolerate condescension. But a cool head was essential if his mission here were to succeed.

"Answer me!" Peebles barked.

Despite caution, Courtland came swiftly to his feet at the insult, prompting Susannah to rise from her seat and step between them. "Simon!" she cried. "He is my son, after all! We must remember that."

Courtland regarded his mother. Her eyes were wide and alarmed and her hands clenched the folds of her skirt, crushing it into wrinkles. Now that he saw she intended to defend him, no matter how temporarily, he knew he must make the most of it. He must act now, before the tension accelerated into irreversible hostility and caused him to lose the moment.

He walked to within a few feet of his stepfather, and staring into the eyes he hated, stretched out a hand. "Shall we let bygones be bygones, Simon?"

The moment hung in silence. A bird soared close to the window and its flight broke the beam of sunlight slanting between the two men, making it quiver for a fraction.

"Simon . . ." Susannah said with a trace of warning in her tone.

Peeble's eyes moved to her face, flickered, then moved back to regard his stepson. A visible battle raged within his wolfish eyes while his throat struggled to swallow an enormous lump of pride. He held out his hand and spoke under his breath. "Very well. If Susannah wishes it."

Courtland grasped his stepfather's hand in an insincere seal, nearly recoiling before he could decently release it. He turned to face his mother. "I must go now, but I'll call again when Virtue comes home."

"You've . . . been well?" she asked awkwardly, belatedly.

"Yes," he said with no warmth, feeling suddenly dispassionate with the knowledge that the two of them might never be more than polite strangers. "I have been well."

"Your stepfather and I . . . we're glad you've returned from your travels safely." She forced a smile, but as if to belie the words, retrieved his hat from the huntboard without delay.

A moment later, as Courtland walked down the graveled drive he was certain she and her husband watched him from the window; he could feel their eyes upon him. And he could feel their perturbation.

He wondered if they had believed him dead, and now found the unexpected return of his ghost annoying.

He strolled alone through the village to the sound of chiming, for it was noontime and the bell in the steeple tower called the townfolk to dinner. Women garbed in ruffle-edged caps and starched aprons gathered their broods or bustled past with baskets of vegetables hooked over their arms. Men bumped wheelbarrows over the green or trudged in from the fields wearing rough homespuns soiled with earth. Hens and pigs and cattle roamed about the streets with no regard for the human industry and browsed through the tall grasses sprouting on either side of the road.

Just as Courtland remembered, the houses built along the common were the finest in town. Constructed of warm red brick with white or green enameled shutters and sparkling dormer windows, they sported yards perfectly clipped and well shaded by stands of beech and hazel. Pink or white begonias bordered every pebbled walkway, and old crones in stiff bonnets gossiped over wicket gates while their striped tabbies tiptoed behind flocks of wandering geese hoping for a catch.

Beyond the huddle of homes a variety of shops offered services or wares. Courtland passed a cobbler, a tailor, a saddler, and a potter's establishment, responding with a polite nod to everyone who gave him curious regard. They would all know his name soon enough—by nightfall he guessed—unless he had seriously underestimated the garrulousness of the matrons Dove and Higginbotham.

As he strolled past the blacksmith's shop, the clink of a hammer reverberated through the air, and he smelled the pungent odor of singed hooves and woodsmoke. A few more modest homes ridged the straight road, then, at the edge of a stream, he saw the water wheel of the gristmill as it churned the river. The town looks so new, he thought. It possessed none of the ancient stone ruins and timeless history of that faraway village he loved in Devonshire. There was little history in Swanston, or, at least, no history recorded in tomes resting dustily in a Roman church, no gravestones encrusted with the moss of centuries, no ageless walls stacked by an ancestor's hands. The edges were harder in the glare of the New World sun, the grass less venerably verdant and lush.

Mentally, he shook himself, for he had unconsciously slipped back into the attitude of his adolescence that had so colored his outlook of the world. But the thoughts of England had reminded him of his purpose here, and he increased his pace until he reached the end of the lane. There, enveloped in neglected shrubbery and ringed by apple trees, the house Gage had purchased in Courtland's name stood awaiting its new tenant.

He opened the gate, which hung forlornly upon one hinge, and stared at the place which was two stories with a dormer over the peeling front door. "In need of paint," he murmured. The house had obviously suffered neglect since the death of the Widow Foree. The garden, trees, and shrubbery were as wild as . . .

Courtland stopped, his mind suddenly filled with images of a cottage in the woods. Until now, the girl had been far from his thoughts.

With her image still in his mind he went around the east end of the house, past the well to the commodious barn whose doors were boarded up, and whose water trough was clogged with stagnant water. Two turtles sunned themselves upon its edge, blinking in reflected light. A dovecot had been built beside it, and several pigeons strutted about, all of whom scattered in a rustle of pearl-colored feathers when he walked past and pried away the lumber holding the barn shut.

The portals swung away to reveal a dim interior smelling of musty straw, and he assessed the space, judging it adequate for his purposes. Gage had decided that his spy should establish a livery stable during his stay in Swanston, for a newcomer who idled his time away with no occupation would arouse suspicion among townspeople who toiled from dawn to dusk. Since Courtland had no trade, but did possess a knowledge of horses, the livery would provide an adequate foil. Gage's informers had said that the neighboring tavern did a lively business, and it often could not accommodate the increasing numbers of travelers and their horses. Courtland's enterprise should function well enough.

He fished about in his waistcoat pocket for a key and forged a path through the tangle of lilacs to the garden entrance of the house. The door proved stubborn and he had to access it with a thrust of his shoulder. Once inside, he discovered a residence in dire need of cleaning. The furnishings had been sold along with the property, and a film of grit lay across every surface. Coughing amidst the rise of dust, he climbed the narrow wooden stair to the three bedchambers on the second floor, both furnished with four-poster beds, and then inspected the tiny attic space with its dormer. As he flung the casements wide in the stifling spring heat, he noticed that mice had found themselves cosy quarters in which to live.

When he inspected the kitchen he did so with a baleful eye; he had never cooked for himself, for on board ship and in military encampments others had been hired to perform that task. Of course, he could hire a woman to cook and keep house for him, but he was loath to have a gossip underfoot who might report his every move to interested village ears.

He tapped an egg beater with his finger where it hung on a peg beside the hearth, then examined a long-handled waffle iron, and decided that there was no alternative but to stock the empty pantry shelves and have a go at feeding himself.

After donning his hat again, and letting the kitchen door slam behind his back, he strolled down to the merchant who sold general commodities, having earlier noticed a swinging sign painted with the words HODGE SUPPLIES.

Its door stood open, and he entered, the thud of his boots upon the wooden planks arresting the attention of a young thickset woman standing behind the counter. She wore a frilled white cap with a kerchief pinned across the bodice of her gown, which stretched over enormous breasts of a size to match her hips.

"May I help you, sir?" she asked with a smile full of crooked teeth. "Oh! You must be Mr. Day, the gentleman who bought the Widow Foree's house."

"I am," he acknowledged, marveling at the efficiency of the matrons Dove and Higginbotham. "And glad to find a lady here to give me some advice—"

"What kind of advice? I'll be pleased to give it."

He glanced with the proper amount of male helplessness at the stores of sugar, flour, spices, oats, molasses, and coffee ranged about the place. "It's just that I need to stock my kitchen, and—"

"Oh, allow me to help you then," she said, batting her lashes and waddling on tiny feet to the coffee bin. She scooped out a measure with such eagerness that half the beans spilled on the floor. "My father will deliver everything in his cart tomorrow, Mr. Day. If you'd like, I could accompany him and establish the kitchen for you. Oh, my name is Miss Hodge," she added, with emphasis upon the title. "Miss Molly Hodge."

Although less than enthused over suffering the flirtations of an overeager maiden, he decided it could do no harm to have her put things in the proper place, for he would have enough to do without bothering with the kitchen. When he consented, she almost fell over herself, and a few raisins joined the coffee beans as she once again overloaded the big brass scale.

Courtland wandered about inspecting the merchandise, giving Miss Hodge's slightly fuzzed cheeks a chance to cool while he selected sacks of feed for the horses Gage would send. As he turned to examine a penknife, his eyes alit upon a bin full of dried apples, and the sight of their thin, curled shapes caused him to rub his chin in thought.

Coming to a sudden decision, he turned to face the merchant's daughter. "Miss Hodge, could you double every measure you've set aside for me? And if you've a hammer and nails, I could use them too—and a shovel. Do you have a shovel, by any chance?"

When she brought it out from behind the counter, he grinned and stroked the rough wooden handle thoughtfully. "Aye, that'll do. That'll do just fine."

Chapter 5

The next day his horse was brought round from Boston, along with two other mounts and a wagon that he would keep in his livery for hire. Mr. Hodge delivered the supplies ordered the previous day, and his infatuated daughter sailed into Courtland's kitchen and began to organize it with an industrious alacrity surely designed to impress any bachelor. He feared he would never manage to get her out. After she had contrived to spend half the morning pouring flour into his bins and stowing coffee in his cannisters, her father finally took hold of her plump arm with an apologetic glance at Courtland and towed her outside to the cart.

As soon as she left, Courtland unpacked more than half of the stores she had just put away, bundling cornmeal, flour, and oats into sacks, and, together with a few pieces of lumber and the new shovel, lashed them to his saddle. He had decided that Gage's business could wait until tomorrow; today he wanted to see the girl in the woodlet again. Both she and her brother wore the same pinched look he had seen on the faces of innumerable London beggars, the look which most well-fed English citizens had chosen to ignore, but which he had found unconscionable. He would supply them with food, telling Chaynoa his gesture was payment for her help.

He made certain no one saw him leave the village, choosing a narrow cattle path that wended close to the river through a maze of bull rushes, leading his heavily laden horse over swampy ground rimmed by wild cranberries until he reached the fringes of the wood. Its green interior seemed even darker and more intricately knotted than it had during his previous visit, as if it had resented his trespassing and sought to bar his reentry now.

Before long, after he had pushed his way through blackberry bushes and dense pines, he became lost in a world of primeval harmony, and wondered suddenly what it would be like to abandon his regiment, to forget war and all the boorish, complicated trappings of society, and reside in a simple world like Chaynoa's. Musing, he breathed in the pureness of the resinous air, relished the birdsong and restful colors in a way he had not relished them since the earliest days of his youth. There had been no opportunity during his turbulent adulthood to take pleasure in much of anything, for marching through the countryside in a scarlet coat with a musket and sword did not lend itself to the enjoyment of nature, especially when bullets flew. He had spent time upon the sea, of course, and seen radiant sunsets floating atop the curly waves of exotic oceans, but his young eyes had been far too beclouded in those days to appreciate simple scenes of beauty.

He had not gone far when he spotted Chaynoa in a clearing. Her figure was chameleonlike, scarcely discernible in the brownish gown, and he would not have noticed her, except that her quick movements

contrasted so startlingly with the languid stillness of
the forest.

He watched the sun escape through the tree
branches around her, ethereal and nebulous, in the
way light filters through the stained glass of a centu-
ries-old cathedral window. In the midst of its aureole
she knelt upon the ground and dug a hollow in the
earth with her thin, bare hands. Her fingers were
covered with soil, and lines of concentration fur-
rowed the smoothness of her brow.

Puzzled, Courtland observed her for a time,
watched her frustrated, almost frantic digging while
noting that she had already excavated and abandoned several other holes. He wondered what in the
devil she was doing, and a whimsical grin touched his
mouth as he imagined the possible fate of some wayward traveler who had not been fortunate enough to
escape her jackknife.

While he observed, she glanced up at the trees and
studied them as if suddenly distracted from her purpose. Then she removed Courtland's stolen pistol
from her gown, and, crouching down, zigzagged
stealthily through the underbrush as if stalking prey.
A few seconds later she put both hands upon the
weapon, and, sighting a target above her head, aimed
and fired.

As if hoping something would fall down from the
sky, she waited with her head tilted back, then, disappointed reloaded the pistol from a powder horn slung
over her shoulder, and began creeping through the
trees again.

Courtland left the horse and strolled along after
her, but in the sensitive way of a forest creature, she
heard the sound of his passage before he had even
closed the distance to a hundred yards. She stepped

back in alarm, and with her eyes carrying a clear warning, swung the pistol at his chest.

He raised up his hands and laughed at her serious intent. "You haven't a shovel, remember . . . ?"

His attempt at humor did not lessen her vigilance and she kept the weapon trained, but having faced far more formidable foes in his career, Courtland proceeded toward her, glancing up at the high branches of the maple above her head and pointing. "There's a curlew perched up there. Want to try your luck with that, instead of me?"

She eyed him consideringly, then turned her gaze to the bird, and after a pause of indecision finally changed the direction of the muzzle. But her hands shook so badly upon the weapon that Courtland knew she would never hit the mark, and moved to steady her aim.

He had scarcely touched her hands when she reacted with a quick and astounding violence, striking his chest and face as if he were some fiend bent upon murder. Caught off guard, he cursed, and with difficulty seized her wrists. But his rough handling only caused her to grow more ferocious. As she struggled, he began to realize her reaction was that of a cornered animal spurred by an instinct for self-survival, and certain that she would continue to do battle with him until she had exhausted every ounce of her strength, he abruptly released her.

She fell back, her eyes fastened to his face, her chest heaving with the remnants of fear and exertion. When he made no further threat to touch her but simply stood his ground in silence, her agitation gradually began to subside and her shoulders drooped, the muscles relaxing. Without a word he bent to retrieve his pistol from the ground, and, at the sound of her harsh and erratic breaths, raised his eyes and, for a fugitive and almost painful minute, regarded her with a dawning flash of empathy. He had understood fear like that himself once, long ago. He had understood it well.

Up above, the curlew returned to the fretwork of leaves, and in a movement as automatic as breathing, Courtland lifted the pistol and fired. His prey fell through the branches and landed with a soft feathery plop beside his boots. Glancing at Chaynoa, he grinned and said, "Supper."

She stared at him in her characteristic wary way and made no reply. With a shrug, he picked up the bird and retraced his steps to the clearing where he had left his horse, then set off in the direction of her cottage. After a moment, as he had expected, Chaynoa fell in with him, her steps nearly as long and easy as his. He marveled that her bare feet were not scratched and bleeding from the underbrush, but she seemed to know instinctively where to step in order to avoid the thorniest vines, and the fact that the hem of her frazzled skirt snagged repeatedly on brambles until it was nearly a fringe seemed not to bother her feminine vanity at all.

When they arrived at the cottage and he began to untie the supplies from his saddle, Chaynoa stared at the sacks of flour, sugar, raisins, and barley with candid distrust. But her hunger seemed to override her skepticism of his motives, for when he began to unload the stores and set them inside her cottage door, she sidled closer, hovering over the tantalizing goods.

He slid the new shovel from the saddle and, suppressing a smile, said, "This should help you with your grave digging."

She paled at his words, then glanced down at her hands as if the soil of the forest, which still stained them, had betrayed her somehow, had given away some long-kept and excruciatingly intimate secret.

"I saw you digging in the clearing," he explained, watching her closely. Her face had grown shuttered suddenly, the eyes veiled by fanned lashes, and even though she looked askance at the shovel as if she desperately wanted to take it, she clasped her hands behind her back to restrain a wayward impulse.

"I—I haven't the means to pay you," she said at last, and although her voice was so soft he could scarcely catch it, its tone was full of dignity.

Hearing it again stirred Courtland more than he had expected, and being a man unaccustomed to soft emotions, he made a business of adjusting his stirrup strap. "You've got it wrong, Chaynoa," he said quietly. "I've brought these things to repay you. I owe you a debt, and I wanted to even up the account." He raised his eyes to meet hers across the flat seat of the saddle, and smiled with a kind of honest but inoffensive playful humor. "For the spiderwebs, you know."

After a slight hesitation, when he held it out a second time, Chaynoa reached to take the shovel, but she was particularly careful that her hands did not touch his.

"You're not partial to that hole in your roof, are you?" he asked.

Her mouth curved in perplexity. "Nay."

"Then I'll repair it for you. The birds will have to find another way in."

An ancient beech tree grew beside her cottage, and after testing a lower branch, Courtland climbed it, favoring his still sore arm as he crept out on a branch and accessed the roof. Chaynoa still stood below, and behind her, squatting half hidden behind a holly bush, her brother watched the proceedings raptly. Thinking to befriend the fellow, Courtland called down to him. "If you could fetch the lumber I brought, and the hammer and nails, I'll get started. Climb atop my horse and hand it up."

Hahnee made no move to do as suggested, but Chaynoa agilely mounted the horse and stood in the stirrups to pass the items to her benefactor's outstretched hands.

"Do you know how to make thatch?" he asked her.

"Aye."

"Good. Then you can finish the job off later—unless you're afraid of heights."

"I'm not afraid."

Courtland gave her an amused look. "I didn't suppose you were. I don't think you're afraid of much of anything in these woods except me."

She was not shy with her answer. "That's because you are not a part of them."

"I have no reason to be a part of them. I'm not hiding from anyone."

"Mam used to say that everyone hides from something. I suspect you are no different, Mr. Day." She handed him another nail, then gently rubbed her arm in an obvious reference to his injury.

Courtland laughed and sketched a mock salute. "You have bested me. I surrender."

In no time he had completed the repairs and shimmied down the tree again. Chaynoa still sat astride his horse and he moved close, dusting his breeches while making a casual comment. "I'll pluck that bird for you if you'll invite me to supper."

He was so near he could smell the wild mint that clung to her clothes, and he could see the translucent flecks of amber that, gemlike, ringed the black pupils of her eyes. In a progression natural to any interested young man his gaze moved downward to study the neckline of her ragged gown.

But in a self-conscious gesture she laid her arm across her chest as if to shield it from his view and, while her eyes held his unswervingly, spoke in a low virulent tone. "Don't *look* at me in that way. And don't touch me again like you did in the clearing— not for any reason at all."

With a serious mien Courtland observed the deep color which spread across her cheeks in a slow stain; her mouth firmed, and her strong, thin hands quivered as they curled into fists at her sides, and although her lashes were lowered now, he knew her eyes would be dark and clouded with the same kind of fear he had seen in them before. With a sudden unpleasant dawning, he suspected he knew one of Chaynoa's grim secrets; it was a savage and ugly one, and he felt regret for her—that, and a strange sort of male tenderness never before experienced, which included a surprising desire to alleviate with his own touch the shame with which some other man had left her.

But he knew she would not let him. Any overtures he made in that direction would only make her strike out again. And so, resisting an impulse to put a gentle hand upon her shoulder, he spoke to her with gentleness instead. "You have my word upon it."

His promise seemed to put her more at ease, render her less nervous than she had been before, although she still maintained her distance while he hunkered down and plucked the curlew.

Once, she leaned to capture a handful of the feathers, wayward and weightless, which floated on the air like buff-colored butterflies, and, closing her eyes, mouthed a prayer in her Indian dialect. "I don't like to kill them, you know," she said when he gave her a curious regard. "My father's people believe that every creature has a spirit, and when it dies, that spirit returns to the Maker of Souls, just as man's does. It's good to say prayers over any dead being, to apologize and praise it for its earthly sacrifice. If it's not too angry its soul will come back one day and perform favors for us." She sighed and blew a feather off her palm. "The birds are the most difficult for me to kill."

"Why?"

"Because they're put here by the Ancient One for no other reason than to give us joy, to provide beauty and song."

Courtland kept plucking. "It's a little difficult to appreciate either beauty or song when you're half-starved and staring at a potential bite of food. And you, miss," he told her with a straightforward stare, "are half-starved."

A silence fell between them, and the sun slid from beneath a quilted cloud to shine benignly down upon the cottage. Chaynoa felt its glaze wash over her like warm water from the river in summer, and, at the same time, through her lashes, observed the man who had intruded upon her world of tenuous security. As if he were a complicated puzzle, she watched him go about the unpleasant business of preparing the bird for the cooking pot. She noticed the tucks of his shirt as it strained across his back, the way his boots fit against his calves and were rubbed in the insteps where spurs would rest. She remembered his eyes were clear and gray. A cleft marked his chin and his black hair was pulled back in a queue to reveal a neck as brown and strong as those of the warriors she had known and revered in childhood.

She wondered who he was, what sort of profession or trade he practiced. By his attire, he was not a

yeoman; for one thing, his boots were too finely made
and too little worn, and for another, his shirt was of
quality cambric. His features, while harshly chiseled
and dark with sun, bore a stamp of refinement not
found on most provincial miens, which tended to be
broad and plain. As for his character, she sensed he
was a man who had endured more than his share of
suffering, for sometimes a faraway glint came into his
eye that was frighteningly bitter, and therefore easily
recognized and understood by her own wounded
spirit.

Using her hair to shield her perusal, Chaynoa let
her eyes wander over the rest of his masculine person.
He squatted with one knee to the ground and the
other leg bent so that he could rest his injured arm
across its ridge as he worked. She watched his fingers
move; they were strong upon the downy feathers but
not indifferent, not disrespectful of the limp, still
warm body, and a shudder raised the flesh upon her
arms, for thinking of him in such a way brought her
fear.

"Your brother," Courtland said now, "is he afraid
of me? He's been watching me from the bushes since
I arrived."

"He's like the rabbits," she said simply.

"The rabbits?"

She stood up and darted inside the cottage, returning with an example of the species, curled in a fragile
gray ball and no more than a few days old, cradled
in her palm.

"Even though I tell him to leave them be," she
explained, "Hahnee robs them from their nests every
spring. The mother will not take them back once they
have the smell of a man upon them. So I must raise
them until they're old enough to survive alone."

With some wonder Courtland took the tiny crea-

ture and nestled it in his hand as she had done, feeling
its quivering life, the warmth of its flossy speckled fur
as it wriggled against his flesh. "Where do you get the
milk for it?"

"Hahnee steals a bit from the cows of the farmers—never for ourselves—just for the rabbits," she
said as if afraid of his condemnation.

As she took the youngling from his hands he regarded her, then looked over his shoulder at the
spike-haired man who still peered at him through the
foliage. Fishing about in his pocket he found a piece
of toffee wrapped in a twist of paper. "Does he like
candy?"

"Oh, yes."

"Why don't you give it to him."

She accepted it and went to her brother's hiding
place, from which he popped up and snatched the
candy, before divesting it of its wrapper and cram-
ming it greedily into his mouth.

Chaynoa smiled at his enjoyment and picked up
the curlew that was now ready for roasting, carrying
it inside where she spitted it and slid a pot underneath
to catch the juices. Courtland washed his hands in the
pail beside the door and, with all the cringing furtive-
ness of a wild puppy unsure of its welcome, Hahnee
crept up beside him. In his hand he held the captain's
missing spyglass.

"Hahnee!" Chaynoa cried upon seeing it. Speaking in her Indian tongue, she admonished her brother
and snatched the instrument from his tenacious fingers. "He stole it," she told Courtland. "I'm sorry."

Courtland neglected to remind her that she had
filched his pistol; instead, he focused the spyglass on
the pile of feathers outside and invited Hahnee to
peer through. "I can understand how he would find
it a fascinating toy. Let him play with it awhile."

The young man continued to examine the workings of the instrument and to gaze through both ends of it with an inexhaustible fascination while Courtland watched Chaynoa prepare griddle cakes studded with raisins. They all three shared in the simple meal, and although Chaynoa would not sit close to Courtland, she did not seem averse to his conversation.

"How did you learn to shoot and load a pistol?" he asked, consuming his food with unself-conscious relish. "Have you owned a gun?"

After sucking grease from her fingertips in a manner that was indecorous but delicate, Chaynoa set down her wooden trencher and, opening the battered trunk, removed an ancient musket wrapped in oilskin. "It won't fire anymore," she said, holding it out to him.

"I'm not surprised." He inspected it and grinned. "Good Lord, I haven't seen one of these since I was a lad, and even back then it was a relic. Where did you get it?"

" 'Twas my father's."

"He taught you to shoot?"

"Nay. I watched him at it."

He gave her a considering glance. "Was your father from Swanston?"

Chaynoa took up her plate again and shook her head. "My father was Delaware. But my mother's people were from Swanston, from an old, respected family. She ran away to live with him, stayed with him and lived the life of his people for nearly twenty years, until he died. I was twelve, and my brother thirteen, when Mam brought us back here to her people."

Courtland could imagine a young girl from Puritan roots running off with an Indian brave, living with him in the wilds, then returning destitute with a couple of half-breed children in tow. Little wonder the three of them had been "warned off," as she had termed it, by the townspeople. "Did your mother's folks welcome her back?" he asked quietly.

She lowered her head. "No."

At the sadness in the word, he ran his hand over the musket and withdrew a penknife from his pocket, changing the subject. "This could use a good cleaning."

Chaynoa watched his movements in her observant way and, wanting to give him plenty of space to work upon the table board, removed his empty trencher. Her brother at last grew tired of the spyglass, and set it close to their guest's elbow, where a stray beam of sunlight clearly illuminated the words engraved upon the polished brass base: 4TH REGIMENT OF FOOT. She wished she knew what the letters spelled, but she had never been taught to read. Perhaps she could remember the shape of the words, copy them out, and ask Sadie their meaning.

Her eyes shifted back to Courtland, and full of sudden curiosity, she asked, "What of yourself? How do you live?"

He thought it an odd way to phrase a question. "How do I live . . . ?" he echoed. For a moment his eyes stared at the flintlock of the musket, and then he shrugged, answering with a few words of insightful honesty that he had to reach down and find somewhere in the deliberately unanalyzed, usually unplumbed depths of his heart. "Rather desperately most of the time, I suppose. Marching up the cannon's mouth, as they say."

She turned from her place at the hearth to regard him with a quizzical expression. "Marching up the cannon's mouth? It sounds like a foolhardy notion. Why do you do this?"

He rubbed his thumb over the barrel in an absent rhythm. "I don't know. I've been at it so long I guess I don't remember how to live any other way. Courting danger provides excitement, I suppose."

"Courting danger? Do you mean that you *like* to be afraid, that you enjoy it in some way?"

He laughed, not at her, but at the innocence that left a mind untouched by the perplexingly insane, and yet gloriously noble reason that made men long to go to war. "It has nothing to do with fear. It has to do with feeling alive, really feeling alive. When a man is in mortal danger all his senses are heightened to a peak, engaged upon surviving. His blood rages through his body."

Surprisingly she stared at him as if his words touched some chord in her understanding, one that was elusive and could not be fully grasped, but that lay at the fringes of her own past experience. "But I want a tranquil life, tranquil like the blue ponds on the edge of the wood," she said.

"Even the forest trembles with the winds of a storm from time to time, Chaynoa—experiencing passion in a sense."

She gave him a glance that warned him that he was on the verge of overstepping the bounds she had earlier laid out for him, and he changed the subject rather than risk losing what little ground he had gained. "Where is the powder and shot for this thing?"

She brought him a leather pouch filled with ammunition, a flint and a tinderbox packed with linen patches. The powder horn was carved with the figure of a rearing bear, and he admired it. "Your father's?" he asked.

"Aye."

He measured the powder and, upending the musket, poured it into the barrel, then dropped in a ball with a patch of linen and rammed them both down. After setting the hammer at half cock, he tapped a finer powder from another, smaller horn into the flash pan and closed it.

Chaynoa was amazed at his deftness; the whole procedure had taken him less than fifteen seconds. With avid interest she followed when he walked outside carrying the musket, and saw him squint his eyes against the brightness of the sky, then scan the landscape, and in the space of a few seconds, raise the musket and fire.

When his quarry plummeted to the ground some distance away he nodded toward it and handed her the weapon with a sportive smile. "Tomorrow's breakfast."

She stared at the plump partridge he had targeted in a distant oak, amazed that he had been able to hit it, for she had believed the musket to be inaccurate beyond twenty-five yards.

"And now," he said, looking up at the sky to judge the time, "I must take my leave."

When he began to walk away, she trailed behind, twisting her hands, realizing that he was taking with him something that she needed, although she could not decide what it was. Her contact with people had been too limited, too cruel, to fathom this new and bewildering feeling, and when Courtland turned his head to speak with her, she lowered her lashes lest he read her eyes and understand it better than she.

"Do you need anything else?" he asked, untethering his horse. "Is there anything I can bring you from the village?"

His offer of generosity increased her discomposure. "No," she said. "B-but you are kind to offer."

"Could you show me the shortest path out?"

She nodded and, while he followed with his horse, set off northward at a fast pace. She wanted the parting to be over quickly so that she could sit alone in her cottage with her knees drawn up and her head bent low, and begin to forget him—even though the act of forgetting had never been easy for her. Every scene she had ever witnessed, every sound and feeling, were rooted firmly in her memory, and some of them, like weeds in a springtime garden, plagued her dreadfully. But she knew that memories of this man would be more like the first blossoms after the harshness of a long winter; she would cherish them.

As Chaynoa walked, Courtland watched her straight back, and the heavy uncombed hair as it brushed her ankles. He did not deny that he had become fascinated with her during their short acquaintance, his maleness roused by a need to protect her, his mind driven by a desire to understand her complicated allure. He attempted to speak to her as they tramped along, but she proved uncommunicative the whole way, and it was not until they paused at the edge of her private wilderness that she finally deigned to turn about and address him.

"That swamp—see it yonder? You must cross over it. 'Tis not deep, but watch for vipers. If you keep on this course you'll come upon the east side of the village before the sun has touched the treetops."

While she spoke she refused to look at him, keeping her eyes downcast and fixed to the wild green grass beneath her feet. Courtland was reluctant to leave and abandon her to her strange and isolated life. He felt like a man sailing away from some mythical, forgotten isle, taking the only seaworthy ship, and leaving behind a castaway who seemed too vulnerable to weather either loneliness or hardship very long. Even now, as he hesitated, wanting to say something meaningful but uncertain how to express himself on an emotional level he had heretofore never reached, she continued to keep her eyes down in a studious avoidance of him. He found he wanted to look at her face again, brush the hair aside with his fingers, study her features in the sunlight so he might remember them. Odd, he thought, the way a person briefly met, and under desperate circumstances, can leave an enduring stamp upon a man's life.

He put out his hand in farewell, held it suspended beneath her nose, so that she must look at it through her lowered lashes. "If you should ever need anything, Chaynoa," he told her, "I live at the end of Queen's Road. Don't be too proud to ask for my help. And don't fear that I'll betray you. As long as you choose to remain hidden here, I won't speak your name to anyone. You have my word on that."

When she did not reply, he added, "Keep the musket handy. You may have cause to use it in the months to come. Here—" He drew out his pistol and slipped it into the pocket of her skirt. "You might as well take this, too. 'Tis more accurate than the musket."

She said nothing and he put out his hand again in farewell, and although she did not move a muscle toward touching it, he kept it poised, one more moment, beneath her eyes.

Chaynoa stared at the long fingers so patiently awaiting the clasp of her hand in parting. At first, she had feared he would seize her hands in an aggressive manner, and she had hidden them behind her back to discourage him. But he was bestowing upon her the choice to touch him or not, and she found suddenly that she wanted very much to touch him, just once, just to say goodbye. After all, in the end, he had been kind to her; he had understood.

Her heart hammered as fast as that of the nestling rabbit she had earlier held between her palms, and she squeezed her eyes shut, then lifted a trembling hand. She felt it encircled by the grasp of another. The flesh was warm and hard and very sure. At its feel something within her loosened just a bit, seemed to melt away like the snow banks beneath her window ledge at the first pale sun of spring. She had always believed that her cottage possessed a sort of magic that kept her safe, but there was magic here, too, in the grasp of this man's hand.

And yet, as if a piece of her was determined never to thaw, the ice-shard of her past arrowed across memory, and she jerked her hand free, severing the sweet contact her loneliness begged to hold. Wheeling about in a reaction more instinctive than reasoned, she fled, and once more became a creature of moss-painted oaks and timeless seasons.

"Godspeed, Chaynoa," Courtland said. And he watched her, followed the flash of her ill-made skirts until the forest conspired to conceal the last trace of them from his eyes.

Chapter 6

His first attempt at breakfast was edible, but little more than that. He had attempted to make waffles, but lacking any recipe, had mixed a batter that when cooked could have done double duty as ammunition for his musket. After drowning it in molasses and butter he managed to consume it, but determined in future to purchase pastries from the bakery and save himself a sore jaw.

The red dawning sun streamed in through the window of the kitchen, which he had flung wide to catch the morning air, and it touched the molasses pooled upon his plate so that it glowed red-brown and clear. The luminous hue reminded him of the eyes of the girl, and he had a sudden vision of her long hands kneading a mound of barley dough on the scrubbed table board of her cottage.

He shook his head and told himself he was mad. She had no place in his life. He would be in Swanston only a short span of months to do his duty for England—or for his farm in Devonshire, however one chose to view it—and Chaynoa was an eccentric creature of the woods, an exile with a cloudy and probably brutal past she obviously did not intend to share. It would be folly to involve himself too far, for nothing could come of it. A dalliance she would never be—his interest was more complicated than that—and his short stay here and the nature of his mission forbade any deeper involvement, even if he were inclined to seek it.

Pushing away the plate of molasses, he thought of the work he must begin. Since Gage had requested detailed maps of the area, including the layout of roads, bridges, and landmarks, Courtland decided to stroll around the confines of the village and take notes, then return to his desk and sketch the charts.

He would have to use caution in his efforts. In such a small village, where each resident made everyone else's business his own, his journeys around the environs would be noticed and discussed. And since he was a newcomer, their eyes would watch him with more scrutiny than normal, and news of his movements would be passed from wagging tongue to wagging tongue.

Today he would chart a section of the western perimeter, including the river. Gage wanted to know possible encampment sites, the most accessible roads in and out of town, and the shallowest point of the river for the fording of his regiments. Courtland had earlier paid the saddler's son a few coins for a fishing pole and creel, and now, tucking a notebook in his pocket, he plopped a hat atop his head and went out. He would appear to fish for his supper like any colonial might do, and tonight, he would go to the tavern, drink with the locals, and let it be known that his livery was open for business. If a few of the hotheaded patriots wanted to discuss politics there, he would be more than agreeable to join their heated conversation, and even fan it a bit if opportunity arose.

In the afternoon he returned to town, toting not

only pages of detailed notes, but a fine pair of shad that he planned to clean and roast for supper if his culinary skills could be stretched so far. He made a point of strolling down Main Street for the benefit of the gossips, tipping his hat at every lady in sight, and, when asked about his luck on the river, humbly displaying his catch to the men who sat at the open doors of their shops stitching leather or tying wigs.

Even as he spoke with the residents of Swanston, he regarded them with a certain cultivated dispassion, the sort of dispassion required of any soldier who knew he may be required to raise arms against them one day soon.

"Courtland! Courtland!"

At the sound of the high, excited voice, the captain pivoted.

A young woman ran toward him down the rutted street. She was dressed expensively in a sacque gown that stretched over its hooped petticoat and swayed about her legs like a huge yellow bell. As she hurried forward, she held on to her plumed hat to keep the breeze from snatching it, and with her free hand waved frantically, smiling so widely that he could see the dimples punctuating the soft curve of her full cheeks. His pole and creel slid from his hands. "Virtue . . . ? My God! Is it really you?"

"Yes! Yes! 'Tis me, Courtland!" She came to a breathless halt and tilted her face to let him inspect it.

"You have grown up!" he declared, laughing, putting an arm around her waist. "You're not the girl I left behind!"

As he held her he realized how much he had missed the vivacious, scatterbrained miss who had once dogged his footsteps like a shadow. Drawing back to examine her radiant face and the silvery hair piled high beneath her hat, he added in a voice made husky with emotion, "And you're as pretty as ever. Prettier."

"And you are certainly no eyesore yourself, dear brother." With an impish flick of her hand she tipped back his tricorn to better examine the attributes of his face. "Now I understand why every girl in the village runs to peer out her window whenever you saunter past. I've only been home since yesterday, and already a gaggle of my friends has come begging for an introduction to my dashing sibling—he's *so* charming, with such an earnest grin, they say. And they're all jealous as sin of Molly Hodge, who spent a whole morning in your kitchen. Why, Courtland, you *would* choose the plainest girl in town!"

"I've not chosen her!" he protested, laughing again, holding up his hands.

"Well, she believes she has a head start over the rest."

"Then for God's sake, tell her—and the rest of the gaggle—what a blackguard I am and stave them off."

"That would only intrigue them more. Oh, Courtland! There is so much to talk about!" she cried, squeezing his arm in affectionate delight. "How have you been, how have you fared? I never stopped thinking of you."

"Was no one else about to keep you out of trouble?" he teased.

"Oh, you! As if you were my rescuer more than once or twice. There was only the time I got stuck straddling the tree, and the time I got marooned on the raft in the river. Oh, and you came to the rescue when Toby and I—" Her round eyes grew moist as she searched his face. " 'Twas such a tragedy about Toby. I wept for him. And for you, because I wanted you to come home. And now you are here, and I'm aswim with tears." She pulled a lace handkerchief from her sleeve and dabbed at the corner of her eye. "See, I'm no less silly than when you saw me last."

Courtland smiled fondly and touched her shoulder. "Walk home with me so we can catch up on the news of the last fifteen years. The place is a wreck but I can serve you some cold cider."

She made a moue of disappointment. "Oh, I do wish I could, but I came to meet Jack—he's my betrothed, in case you haven't heard. He went to have his pocket watch repaired at the goldsmith. But tomorrow . . . ? Could I come tomorrow to your house? I think it would be much more relaxed there than meeting at Stepfather's house and having him and Mother—" She broke off with color rising to her cheeks.

"You needn't feel awkward," Courtland drawled. "I'm fully aware that they're less than enthused about my return."

"Oh, you know how they've always been." Embarrassed for him, she cast her eyes down and toyed with the satin bow at her waist.

"Aye, I know. I know." No self-pity marked his tone, only resignation.

Virtue said, "They've become pillars of the community in the last years. Simon has grown wealthy, and on the heels of money comes respect, of course. You'll soon find you can do no wrong in this village, simply by being connected with them. Where your looks will make the female population swoon, your link with the Peebles' name will gain you the esteem of the menfolk."

"And to think I planned on earning their respect through good citizenship." He gave her a wry smile and she giggled. "But tell me about this young man of yours. Will I approve of him?"

"You certainly shall. If you don't, I'll pout for

days and days. And I've never known a man yet who doesn't surrender to a little coy petulance. I've got it down to an art so that Jack, poor dear, is a slave to my moods. But there, now you know what a sly miss I've grown into."

"Forewarned is forearmed."

"Such an insolent tone you use with me, just like the old days. But Courtland," she said with sudden hopeful excitement, "have you *really* come back to stay?"

Her question caught him unawares, and he looked into her eyes, which were the same innocent and gullible shade of blue as Toby's had been, and realized that lying was going to be a far more difficult task than he had previously imagined. Odd, that a few simple words should require more courage than a foray upon a battlefield. He smiled in order to make the deceit more convincing, but the syllables came stiffly through his lips. "Aye, Virtue. I have come back to stay."

She did not have a chance to reply with more than a glad cry, for a disturbance suddenly broke out upon the lane. A gentleman attired in a red curled wig and high white stock stepped out to cross the street, followed by his servant, who trotted behind lugging a basket filled with items purchased from the market. The servant paused, and after putting a hand feebly to her brow, swayed on her feet dizzily. A second later she swooned and dropped the basket, so that a bottle of wine and an earthenware jug tumbled to the ground and smashed together. Dark red claret spilled over the dirt and mingled with oozing molasses, while custard tarts plopped in the midst of the mess.

"Clumsy fool!" the bewigged gentleman snapped. Ignoring him, Courtland went to aid the woman,

who lay like a rag doll in the midst of the street.
Propping up her head, he knelt and chafed her wrists.
A crowd gathered and the presence of so many gawkers seemed to make the gentleman forget his expensive wine and adopt a more benevolent attitude toward his fainted servant.

"Sadie," he said, not touching her, but leaning
over stiffly and arranging his pinched lineaments into
an expression of concern. "Ah, you seem to be recovering yourself now. Whatever happened? Was the
heat too much for you?"

She mumbled a few words and opened her eyes,
struggling to sit up with the support of Courtland's
arm. She was close to middle age, frailly built and
pale.

"I'm fine now . . . really," she breathed, passing a
wrist across her eyes before attempting to crawl forward and gather up the ruined contents of her basket.

"Allow me," Courtland said.

The irritable gentleman in his clock hose and sil-
ver-buttoned knee breeches impatiently took hold of
his servant's arm in an attempt to haul her to her feet.
When she staggered and sank back to her knees,
Courtland scooped her up in his arms, and asked the
gentleman where she lived.

"She resides under my roof, of course," he replied
arrogantly, assessing the captain from beneath blue-
veined lids. "I suppose she should be taken there and
put to bed."

Courtland gave him equal regard, and as he contemplated the cold thin mouth and sallow skin which
stretched over protruding cheekbones, he experienced an immediate dislike. This was not a man to
turn one's back upon. "Shall we go then to your
house?" he asked.

Wordlessly, the fellow turned, and Courtland followed this towering, slope-shouldered figure, whose black clothes and mincing gait brought to mind the image of a raven wearing a fancy red wig. The crowd parted to let them pass, and Courtland shifted the limp figure in his arms, thinking that, unless he was far off the mark, the woman would soon require the services of a midwife. Not that her state was obvious, but now that he held her, he could see her waist was a bit too thick for one of such slender build.

Virtue trailed behind as they crossed the common and entered a large brick home, whose furnishings rivaled the expensiveness of those in the Peebles estate. Although the windows were open, no breeze lifted the curtains, and the spacious rooms crammed with walnut and silver were stuffy.

"In here," the gentleman directed, indicating a chamber off the kitchen, where Courtland gently deposited the servant upon the feather tick. "Her name is Sadie. And I am Julius Twiggs, the local magistrate. You must be Peebles's stepson."

"I am."

"I hear you're establishing a livery close to the Stirrup and Iron Tavern. Is that so?"

"Aye. I'm opening for business tomorrow."

"You'll likely not go long with an empty stable. The traffic to and from Boston is growing by the day. Indeed, last year at a town meeting I predicted we would need another liveryman to accommodate the flow of travelers through Swanston." He drew his thin lips over his teeth and gave Courtland an assessing look. "And my judgment is rarely wrong."

While Virtue went to fetch water and a cool compress for the maidservant, the magistrate escorted Courtland out of the house to the iron front gate. Their vantage point gave a clear view of the common, where a flock of geese honked furiously and flapped their wings at a group of children throwing sticks in a puddle.

" 'Tis a pleasant village," the magistrate remarked in casual conversation. He regarded the captain and rocked upon his wide, flat heels. "Have you decided to end your travels and settle down here permanently?"

"A man needs a home after so many years at sea."

"Indeed. But it may not be a peaceful home before long. Were you surprised to return and find the colonies so tense? Of course, I could have predicted our current state of affairs, for I know the temperament of the colonists. Ah, yes, even during the fifties and sixties, I knew 'twould come to this. The King is going to have a difficult time maintaining a tight rein on his American subjects."

"No doubt you're right."

"I'm certain I am."

Courtland glanced at the magistrate, whose sharp, thin-jowled visage was framed by a set of paste curls rolled over each ear. The captain had met many men like him, mostly high-ranking military officers, ruthlessly ambitious, who would go to any lengths to maintain for others the high opinion they held of themselves.

"The records show that you paid cash for the widow Foree's old place," the magistrate said now. "You are a fortunate man to afford it. Not many in the county have cash these days, not since the port at Boston was closed. Most of the citizens are forced to buy on credit."

"I was able to save a bit during my years at sea," Courtland said smoothly. "A sailor has little on which to spend his pay."

"Aye. I hear that even in foreign ports the whores are cheap."

Virtue's light soles sounded upon the pebbled path then, and both men turned.

"Your maidservant is resting peacefully," she told Twiggs.

"I am obliged to you, Miss Day." His eyes swept her figure in the automatic way of a man who is preoccupied with the charms of women. "And to you, of course, Mr. Day."

Courtland nodded and, taking Virtue's elbow, swung the gate wide.

"Viper!" she said under her breath when her brother had escorted her beyond earshot of the magistrate. "He treats that wretched woman who works for him abominably. I don't know why everyone has such a high opinion of him here. Who cares if he's a magistrate? To my mind he's nothing more than a snake in the weeds."

"In the grass."

"What?"

"A snake in the grass." He steered her around an old grizzled hound who lay dozing in the street. "Is it Twiggs's child that the servant carries?"

"What?" Virtue faltered in her step and stared up at her brother's face, which was half shaded by his hat. "What did you say?"

"You didn't notice?"

"No!"

Courtland kept walking, nodding amiably at a man in woolen hose and buckled shoes who sat weaving a basket in front of the joiner's shop. "I'll wager you a guinea that she'll give birth within the year," he said beneath his breath.

"You seem very certain of yourself." Virtue raised her brows coyly, falling into the ease of their old relationship. "How is it that a bachelor like you noticed such a condition, when I did not?"

"Sharper eyes?"

She tapped him with the end of the folded fan that dangled from her wrist. "You have come back to us a worldly man. Dry under the chin."

"Behind the ears."

"I suppose what they say about sailors is true."

He smiled. "Every bit of it."

"Don't tell me that you're a libertine."

"I wouldn't dream of telling my sister such a thing."

She tossed her head. "Old Twiggs must have begun life as a sailor. I swear he is a womanizer of the worst kind, although he's careful not to touch any of the village girls and cause a scandal. You can be certain he *looks* at them, however. Disgusting, he is. And him a magistrate, too, whose sworn duty it is to be a 'father' to the people. Ha! Poor Sadie is like his slave, and always has been. And then . . ." She broke off and thoughtfully tapped her teeth. "Years ago, there was that other poor woman and her children."

Courtland glanced at her sharply, and, after an ox cart rumbled past and left the street quiet again, asked, "What woman?"

"I don't recall her name. But she had two children—both half Indian. There was some scandal . . . at any rate, the poor woman was found killed, strangled to death, and her children gone. Twiggs swore that their Iroquois father had done the vile deed—even though he was supposed to be dead. The magistrate insisted that the Indian had stolen the children away in the dark of night after murdering their mother."

"Quite an interesting tale."

"Yes. Afterward, Twiggs spoke very ill of the woman, spreading it about that she had been of loose virtue, and her children half-savage. He swore the little girl had stolen some piece of jewelry—a necklace, I believe. To his credit he went to extraordinary lengths to find them after they vanished, sending out search parties in hopes of following the trail of the father. But you know Indians—if they choose not to be found, they won't be."

"And no one has seen or heard from the children since?"

"Nay. Vanished, they did, like smoke. Oh, look!" Virtue cried, her attention diverted. "There's Jack coming out of the goldsmith's. You must come and meet him. Jack! Halloo!" She patted her hair in a hasty gesture of vanity and yanked Courtland forward by the arm.

The young man strolled toward them with an eager step. Reed-thin with a loose-jointed stride, he sported conservative brown clothes and wore his hair in an unpowdered queue. His generous mouth was the most remarkable feature in his countenance, which was plain and honest.

"Jack," Virtue said. "This is my brother, Courtland. And he has given me the most marvelous news—he's come here to stay!"

After the introductions were accomplished, Jack displayed an eagerness to grow better acquainted with his betrothed's brother, and graciously issued an invitation. "I'd be pleased to have you come and join me at the tavern tonight, Day. But I must warn you that the two of us will likely be the center of attention since we're recently from Boston. The locals are often without news, and now that Gage is stirring up trouble, they'll be especially avid to learn of developments there."

"I should be pleased to join you," Courtland answered. He regarded the young man whom Gage had reported to be actively involved in the secret rebel society of Boston, and judged him to be a typical member of the new emerging breed of colonial—fervent, idealistic, and pugnacious. The combination of those qualities made for a formidable force, and Courtland suspected—not for the first time—that Gage underestimated it.

Nevertheless, contemplating Jack's expressive, readable eyes as the man gazed at his sweetheart, Courtland judged there would be little difficulty in gaining the rebel's confidence. The difficulty would be in meeting Virtue's trusting eyes in the uncertain and troubled days to come.

Chapter 7

Evening's veil shrouded the magistrate's house of dark, blood-red brick, and the breeze blew tree shadows over its shuttered facade in a way that resembled the dance of a hundred specters. The air smelt of rotting pine bark, and made cool the damp grass that squelched beneath Chaynoa's soles as she darted along the shrubbery. She noted that only one window in the magistrate's abode glowed with candlelight— the one downstairs—close to the huge, copper-hung kitchen.

She remembered that kitchen, that house; every item of furniture, every piece of silver, every ornament in every room had been locked in her mind since the moment she had fled them nearly a half score years ago. As she stared at the house through the blackness, it seemed to be a crouched dragon-beast about to spring up and wrench from her heart the secret she knew about it.

She took a deep breath to quiet herself, knowing she had become too much a part of nature, wary of society—of man. Even the refinements of civilization, the simple manners and conventions taught to her by her mother were almost forgotten now with lack of use. The knowledge disturbed and confused her, just as it might a sparrow who saw its feathers gradually evolving into fur, or a deer who watched its legs slowly transforming to one long scaly form. There were times when she stared down at her own bare and calloused feet, her own sinewy brown limbs and tangled hair, and wondered if she were metamorphosizing into some being other than the one that God had intended her to be.

Even as she sat in her hiding place, the scent of clove wafted on the air, and she imagined some goodwife baking a cake in a cheery kitchen where children gathered to listen to a father reading tales from a book. How she yearned to be a part of a such a setting! How she yearned to wear petticoats layered like rose petals beneath a pretty gown, and dainty slippers, and lace at her wrists the color of milk froth.

But such a life was not to be hers; instead, through a twist of destiny, she must reside among the woodland creatures with only Hahnee as her family—and with Sadie as her friend, her last and only link with the society of safe houses and fast fences and neatly raked rose gardens.

In Sadie's room a candle now burned, and Chaynoa prayed that the maidservant was alone. It had always been the habit of Julius Twiggs to visit the Stirrup and Iron Tavern on Friday evenings, and if routine held true this night, he should be there swilling rum and telling ribald jokes to attentive villagers, who, if they did not venerate his character, respected his office. None of them, of course, knew the truth about him.

Chaynoa was worried about Sadie. For the first time in six years, the servant had not come to visit the woodland cottage as she was won't to do at the end of every moon cycle. She had not come with her news of the world and with her basket of bread stolen from

Twiggs's kitchen. Chaynoa had waited fretfully for a fortnight, and finally, anxious for her friend's well-being, had decided to creep into the village after the streets had quieted and approach the hated house of the magistrate. The decision had taken every ounce of bravery she could summon.

She moved close to the window now and, pressing her face against a pane, peeked inside, discerning Sadie's reclining form upon the bed. She thrust her head through the window and hissed, "Sadie! Sadie!"

The maid sat up. "Chaynoa!"

"Is the magistrate in the house?" the girl asked, poised to climb over the sill.

"Nay, he's gone to the tavern—but, 'tis so dangerous for you to be here! Why ever did you come?"

"Because you didn't venture into the woodlet as usual, and I was plagued with worry for you." Chaynoa moved close to the four-poster, and, examining her friend's drawn face, cried out. "You're ailing!"

The maid lowered her pale lashes and sank back against the pillow, her hand sliding down to her belly in an unconscious gesture. "I'm breeding," she confessed. "It has made me a bit weak."

Early on, Chaynoa had learned to accept both the unpredictable courses of nature and inescapable ironies of life. She showed no shock at the news, only chagrin for the consequences surely to be suffered by her friend. With quiet suspicion she asked, "Is the father of the child Julius Twiggs?"

Sadie nodded in humiliation.

"That man is a spawn of a demon! How I would like to see him sent back to the dark pit from which he must have crawled!"

"Oh, Chaynoa, I fear that must be left to the judgment of God. I only pray that I can endure this confinement. The worst of it is, I can scarcely keep down food, and when I get out of bed, my dizziness causes me to fall. Why, a few days ago I swooned in the street and a stranger had to carry me home. Mr. Day was his name."

"Mr. Day . . . ?"

"Aye. He's the stepson of Simon Peebles. Years ago—before your Mam brought you here to live—he left to go to sea with his brother. He's only just returned. Every marriageable girl in the village dreams of snatching him," Sadie went on, oblivious to her friend's agitation. "And 'tis rumored that he's sympathetic to the rebel cause. The men are impressed by that—at least those who are not staunch Tories, and there aren't many taking the side of the King these days. I suspect Mr. Day will become a great favorite in Swanston before long."

Chaynoa said nothing. She did not want to tell Sadie of her acquaintance with Courtland Day, for it would require an explanation as to how the two of them had met, and she suspected Courtland wanted to keep the circumstances surrounding his injury from the busybodies. She would not betray him. But his popularity dismayed her unexpectedly, and she imagined him taking a wife, forgetting the woodlet, and venturing in the direction of her cottage no more.

She forced her thoughts back to her friend's concerns. "I'll bring you a special brew tomorrow night, Sadie. One that will help your sickness."

"A recipe learned from your mother?"

"Aye. Mam learned cures from my father's people, many of which are more effective than those the white doctors use. But Sadie, does Twiggs know you are breeding?"

The maid's mouth firmed. "I was forced to tell him when the sickness came so hard upon me. Though he would surely like to throw me out upon the street, he won't dare, for I've threatened to tell the villagers the truth about his character. And most would believe me, for they know I have always been an honest, chaste woman."

"I've already cursed him a thousand times," Chaynoa said through her teeth. "And I'll curse him a thousand more."

"But you should not come back here." Sadie clutched her friend's sleeve, and as she regarded the unusual face framed by its wild wreath of hair, she experienced a shudder of forebodement. When the faint noise of a creaking board broke the hush she started.

" 'Tis only the house settling, I think," Chaynoa whispered.

Sadie looked doubtful and her hands fluttered in agitation. "What if Julius were to return home early tonight? You must go now and not come back. Heaven knows what he would do if he discovered you."

Chaynoa laid a gentle hand atop over the quilt where the other's belly swelled. "No. I shall return tomorrow eve and bring a potion. You must regain your strength before delivering the babe."

"You're a good friend. A brave friend."

"You're braver, living here with *him.*"

The night was still. Chaynoa crept through the neat rows of shadowy houses and weedless gardens, hearing a woman's laughter float through an open window and mingle with the thin wail of an infant. The back door to one dwelling banged shut just as she darted past, and a man stumped out upon his stoop to smoke. They were all homely sounds of habitation which would have comforted any other passerby, but Chaynoa heard them as alien noises, startling and unfamiliar.

Thoughts of her own secret, cloistered cottage urged her to run faster, and she scurried from the purple hedges to the lane beside the river, whose familiar green smell beckoned like a friend. She paused once, fancying that her footsteps were echoed by another set, and suddenly every shifting shadow masked the lurking presence of a man with evil intent. She wondered if the deer and the rabbits lived with such imaginings, if their shyness was a result of their constant fear of danger.

She began to run again, and before long realized she had turned upon Queen's Road. Had some instinct to seek safety led her toward the house of Courtland Day, the last one in the lane? Without admitting the answer, she hurried on, trotting beside the ghostly beech trees that lined the road, smelling wild onions, feeling the texture of the sand beneath her soles, and hearing the faint tattoo of hoofbeats at the end of the road.

The hooves pounded the earth at a brisk clip, and within seconds Chaynoa knew the horse and rider would be upon her. Unwilling to be seen, she glanced about for a place to conceal herself, but between the lane and the woodlet several acres of plowed fields stretched, providing no cover, and she dared not cut across in the open lest she attract the attention of the horseman. She tried to convince herself that he only traveled down the lane upon his own business and would have no interest in her; indeed, even if he spied her flitting shape in the blackness, he would not know her identity. What reason would he have to follow?

But her emotion had risen to the irrational panic of the gentle creatures with whom she had so long resided, and she began to run with all her speed, feet flying and arms pumping while she searched for a place to hide. The hoofbeats behind her increased from a trotting rhythm to the four-beat clop of a canter, consuming ground so quickly that Chaynoa soon heard the horse's breaths. She did not turn about to look at the rider, but sprinted faster through the trees, seeing ahead the dim shape of a house surrounded by a dense circle of shrubs.

The horse swift upon her trail, she dashed for shelter and skittered through the deepest knot in the hedge, where she burrowed and lay still with a pounding heart.

"Chaynoa!"

The rider checked the horse and swung his leg over the saddle to dismount. Cautiously, as if approaching a startled deer on the verge of bolting, he walked forward through the undisciplined hydrangeas, pausing several feet away.

She peered through the branches and saw him fold his arms across his chest.

"You've not gone back to being sheepish with me now, have you?" he asked in frustration. "I hate to think of starting at square one all over again. Tiresome business, having to repeat all the little social pleasantries. I swear it would test even the patience of Job. Take pity on me, will you?"

For a moment she said nothing, for the queerest sensation had beset her all at once. She felt as if two different selves dwelled inside her breast, and each of them tugged at her, encouraged her to make opposing decisions. One advised her to avoid the man, wait until he gave up and went on his way so that she could scurry safely back to her covert. But the other self begged to stay, to listen to his voice, to be close—not too close—but near enough to see his face in the night.

The horse snuffled and lowered its head to nibble at the untrimmed lawn, and Courtland bent down to

retrieve its dragging reins. Suddenly afraid that he
might give up his coaxing and abandon her, Chaynoa
stood up. "Who was Job?"

He laughed. "A fellow with extraordinary forbear-
ance who got bad advice from friends. Come on.
Have a look at my livery. You like horses, don't you?
I'll wager you have a way with them."

Without waiting, he led the animal around the
back of the dark house toward the barn, and she
followed.

A lantern hung upon a wall, and its flickering candle sent out a meager glow, outlining rows of loose
boxes and a stack of straw, whose fresh smell combined with the hot scent of horses. Chaynoa observed
Courtland as he uncinched the girth, slid the saddle
from his mount's back, then rubbed down the sweaty
patch of hide where the pad had rested.

"There are oats in the bin," he said, indicating with
a jerk of his head the container topped by a slanted
lid. "Would you mind scooping out a measure and
dumping it in the first stall—there?"

As if confident that she would do his bidding,
Courtland resumed his grooming of the horse, hoping to put Chaynoa at ease and discover why she had
ventured into the village at so late an hour. He had
been astounded to see her flitting amongst the trees
like a tattered fugitive, running through town as if
terrified for her life. It angered him that she must live
in such fear, and he intended to do something about
it.

After glancing at the gloomy corners of the barn
she ventured forward and went about the chore he
had suggested. The sweet odor of oats soon filled the
air as she poured the grain into the trough, and his
horse nickered, pulling at its tether in eagerness to
eat. Courtland led him into the stall, and, after draw-

ing the bridle over his ears, closed and latched the half-door while Chaynoa stood aside.

She reached a hand over the gate to touch the silky hide. "He's the color of the cinnamon Mam used to grind up and sprinkle over our bread when . . ."

"When she was working for Julius Twiggs?" Courtland quietly finished.

"You know about her? About what happened to her?"

"A bit." He draped an arm over the top rail of the stall. "Will you tell me more?"

She looked uncomfortably at him, at this man who had entered her lonely life and unsettled its unstirred surface like a stone cast into a stagnant pool. The brim of his hat threw a shadow across his face, but the lantern illuminated the angle of his clefted chin and the brown skin of his neck above the linen shirt. The gathered yoke of the garment stretched across his shoulders and the shirttail was tucked neatly into a pair of breeches inset with leather. She could not see his eyes clearly now, but she could feel their observation as if all her senses had come alive. Her mind churned. Did she want to tell him about Mam, about the reason for her exile in the woods? Whatever bits of gossip he had gleaned in the village would likely be distorted or false, and she wished for him to know the truth. But honesty would require the revelation of her own shame and she could not relinquish it. It was too private, too terrible. "Nay," she murmured. "I don't care to tell you any more."

A disappointed smile, glib and candid, lent his face a blatant charm. "Spoken straight up and down. But then, that's the colonial way, isn't it—honesty to the point of bluntness. In England, people lie through their teeth rather than risk the merest social blunder."

"And what do you consider yourself?" she asked. "A colonial or an Englishman?"

Courtland found that he could not lie to her as he had done to Virtue; the brazen falsehood would not come again to his lips. And yet, he could hardly admit the truth of who he was and what he was doing here; he could hardly say that he detested the colonies and loved England, and would defend his native land with his life before he would spill a drop for America. With a self-derisive smile that was engaging in spite of its wryness, he said, "At the moment, I consider myself somewhat of a scoundrel."

She looked at him with clear and guileless eyes that shone almost amber with the lantern light. "I don't find you so. At least, not anymore."

Her words were a gift from a heart that did not easily put faith in human honor, and they were so earnestly uttered that Courtland did not know what to say in response.

Suddenly the thud of hooves sounded on the drive, sparing him a reply.

"Courtland Day! Are you about?"

Chaynoa darted into the shadows, and, annoyed to see her crouching there like an animal, Courtland spoke brusquely. "Go into my house—the back door is open. If you keep beside the hedges on the way, you won't be seen."

Chaynoa slipped past the barn doors just as the stranger called out Courtland's name again.

"I've brought a horse from the tavern, Day. McNair hasn't room to stable him tonight. Can you put him up?"

"Certainly."

"Obliged to you."

Chaynoa heard the voices drift through the open window of Courtland's house. The place was dark, and she had to grope her way about to avoid the trestle table and bench seats arranged in the center of the kitchen. The glow of the moon slanted through the panes and, after insinuating itself through the table legs, spread silver light over the planks of the floor. The iron utensils hanging on pegs over the hearth glinted, and the faint smell of molasses wafted on the air to remind her of a long forgotten taste. She felt uncomfortable. Old, almost buried lessons on propriety floated back to her memory suddenly, and she wondered if it was shameful to be here alone in a gentleman's house.

But she saw Courtland then, walking down the path carrying the lantern, which, once he had stepped inside and shut the door, he used to light the candle on the table. Soon its gold lustre chased away the murk, and she glanced about the room again to see that it was ordinary in its homeliness, furnished with a cupboard lined with pewter, and with a hearthside rocking chair positioned on a rag rug. The chair was made of cedar, its back and seat caned, and its arms curved like the back of a smooth-gaited horse. She admired it, thinking that she would like to rock in it awhile, sway to and fro on a day when the air was sweet with summer. There would be bread baking in the oven and a bowl of snap beans in her lap . . .

"Are you thirsty?" Courtland asked, raising a brow at the museful expression on her face.

"Yes. Yes, I am," she answered shyly, still standing near the open window, where the cool air blowing in off the river seemed to lend her courage, or remind her that she could jump through to freedom at any time.

Removing his hat, Courtland tossed it negligently onto the bench seat, then retrieved two pewter mugs from the cupboard shelf and filled them to the brim from a small wooden keg. He set them on the table and, extending his hand, invited Chaynoa to seat herself.

She met his gaze, knowing through instinct that she should leave, seek the safety of her home. But she did not want to go; she wanted to look at his face and hear his voice for a few moments, even though she sensed that the pleasure of indulging such an urge would put her upon a treacherous path. Life's largest lesson to her had been that human relationships were painful and best avoided.

I'll give myself one or two minutes to enjoy this stolen treat, just a brief spell to connect with someone outside my shuttered world, then I'll go.

Slowly she eased onto the bench, and Courtland took a seat opposite, waiting until she had taken a sip of her drink before tasting his. She liked the coolness of it, she had forgotten how sweet cider could be. Her host seemed to relish it as well, for he drank heartily, and she watched the Adam's apple in his throat move up and down with each swallow. Her perusal seemed not to give him the least twinge of self-consciousness, and when he had put aside his cup, he rested his forearms upon the table, made a steeple of his hands, and spoke to her in a conversational tone.

"Did I tell you that I used to be a sailor? No? Well, I was. Once, when we were sailing the Atlantic, our ship was buffeted by a storm and it broke apart at the stern. We launched the long boats and no one was drowned, but our stores of water and rum were lost. We were three days off the Barbary Coast, and the weather was beastly hot that time of year. By the time we made our way to shore, the other men craved nothing but a glass of water. But I dreamed only of cold cider."

He grinned and put a finger to his mug where

beads of condensation gathered upon the pewter like pearls. "I swear there wasn't a drop to be found in all of Africa. I had to wait almost six months to get any. And the apples in Spain aren't as sweet as they are here."

She smiled at him and said, "When I dream of food, I dream of fresh cream—of pouring it on top of strawberries."

He looked at her, and the extent of her deprivation, which she seemed to endure so stoically, struck him anew. No one should be forced to live like an animal, no matter what the circumstances. He had learned a part of her secret through Virtue's unwitting revelation, but he was determined to learn more, for he would not be satisfied until he had paved the way for her to be a part of society again. Although he was worldly enough to know that she may always remain outside the pale to a certain degree, owing to her parentage, he was stubborn enough to force the issue.

"Why did you come to the village tonight, Chaynoa?" he asked directly.

She looked down at her hands where they cupped the mug, and as if ashamed of their roughness and ragged nails, hid them in her lap. "To see after a friend. Her name is Sadie."

"How long has it been since you were last in Swanston?"

"Almost seven years."

Although Courtland was vaguely surprised by her reply, he did not betray it. "Sadie must be quite a friend."

"Aye. Aye, she is."

"I never expected to find you skittering along my lane. Good lord, you behaved as if I were the Prince of the Bottomless Pit himself, brandishing a pitch-

fork at your heels. I could have been offended. Who
did you imagine I was?"

He posed the question casually, knowing the answer—knowing, too, that she would not confirm it;
the darkening of her eyes told him so. He looked at
her abundant, twining hair, which was the color of
walnuts, and at the firm smooth arms, and at the rise
and fall of her breasts beneath the pitiful gown, and
felt as if he had managed to coax inside his kitchen a
wild creature of the most rare and elusive kind. He
recalled a tale he had read about an adventurer who
had captured a unicorn, and how, when the adventurer had touched it, his soul was filled with magic.

A scratch from the shrubbery marred the smooth
roselike curve of Chaynoa's cheek, and it bled
slightly. Courtland stared at it while she gazed at the
candle flame, and realized he wanted very much to
wipe the blood away; he wanted to touch her face.
But with her uncanny ability to sense his thoughts,
she turned so that he could no longer see her profile,
fastening her gaze upon a framed piece of needlework hanging beside the cupboard.

Courtland had not given it particular notice until
now, but seeing Chaynoa's interest, he studied it, and
its whimsical irony made him frown.

Wrought in threads of gray and brown and cream,
it depicted a wolf and a sheep, each wearing the
clothing of the other upon its back, so that the wolf
appeared to be a sheep and the sheep appeared to be
a wolf. Both animals grinned, but the grin upon the
face of the sheep stretched wider. Below it, a verse
was stitched.

"What does it say?" Chaynoa asked.

Courtland glanced at her, faintly surprised that she
could not read, although he knew that many women
in the colonies were unable to commit their names to

paper. He raised his eyes again to the sampler and quoted, " 'Tis double the pleasure to deceive the deceiver.' "

" 'Tis double the pleasure to deceive the deceiver . . ." Chaynoa repeated the words with serious thought, then scrutinized the embroidery a moment more as if fitting the picture to the wisdom. Her mouth slowly curved.

Courtland had never seen her smile so widely, and the gesture made his mouth twitch as well. Their eyes met, and she reached to brush a strand of hair off her cheek, which caused the scratch to bleed again.

Taking a handkerchief from his breeches pocket, he reached out a hand, extending it so slowly that the flame of the candle scarcely fluttered over the table.

But Chaynoa flung his fingers away and drew back, arising so hastily that she upset her tankard and sent cider splashing over the floor. She backed against the window and, with her eyes dark and challenging, wrapped her arms about her waist in the usual defensive posture.

Without a word Courtland pushed back the bench and circled the table, approaching her purposefully, almost angrily, in a determination to have her accept his touch. She stepped back until her hips pressed against the windowsill, but still he came forward, and, when he was close enough, lifted his hand and placed it along the edge of her jaw, cupping it so that the tips of his fingers touched her ear.

She pulled back and twisted her head away, but he kept his hand in place, undeterred by the shivers of fear that passed in palpable waves through her body. Her breaths came so fast that her nostrils dilated, and he could feel the blood pulsing in her veins beneath his fingertips, see in her eyes the same apprehension of a creature held at the mercy of a greater strength.

He raised his other hand, and with the handkerchief, gently blotted the quivering blood drop.

"Perhaps I do you a disservice, after all . . ." he murmured.

His words confused Chaynoa. She thought he spoke as much to himself as to her, and in his voice there lurked a regret she did not understand. It chilled her, but the touch of his flesh counteracted it. She felt her fear dissolving into a strangely painful need, one that made her feel like the being she was meant to be. She wanted to grasp the feeling and hold on to it, but his fingers had begun to slide down the curve of her throat, and even though the gesture was not meant to be a liberty, but a tenderness, the intimacy brought on terror.

The terror constricted her throat, made her gasp for breath, for life. She thrust out her hands, shoved him, wrenched free. Then, seeking the haven she had made for herself in the woods, she threw open the door and ran.

She heard him call out, his voice hoarse, impatient. But she did not heed it, and much to her relief, he did not follow.

Chapter 8

Courtland sipped his brandy and conversed with a farmer seated across from him at the scarred tavern table. The man drank a potent brew of ale blended with molasses and bread crumbs appropriately nick-named "whistle-belly vengeance," and the more he drank the looser his tongue became. He had already let drop several comments that indicated his harsh disdain for King George, and of course Courtland had taken the opportunity to offer suitable sympathetic responses to earn his confidence.

"Are you a tea drinker?" the farmer asked now.

Courtland hid a smile, knowing that this was the fellow's way of determining his political leanings. Several years ago King George had lowered the tax on tea in order to encourage the colonists to consume more, and thereby increase British revenues. But the Americans, tired of being taxed, had boycotted the consumption of the beverage in a most dramatic way. Now only Tories bought it from the handful of pub-licly scorned merchants who had been commissioned to sell it by the near bankrupt East India Company.

Courtland leaned back in his chair and grinned. "I haven't touched a drop of it since I set foot on Ameri-can soil."

His comment merited an enthusiastic whack upon the shoulder and another half hour of discussion on unfair taxation.

Jack Bretton was not at the Stirrup and Iron this evening. Virtue's betrothed had cut short his stay in the country and returned to Boston, although Courtland had hoped to have more time to solidify the friendship. If he could infiltrate the Boston branch of the secret society through Jack, he might glean the large-scale plans of the Sons of Liberty, or even obtain a list of local munitions stores. That would make his task here easier, and enable him to show the streets of Swanston a clean pair of heels before the year was out.

He smiled convincingly at some crude jest the farmer made concerning King George, and decided he would have to be content for the time being with worming his way into the local organization—if his stepfather did not blacklist him from membership.

He was certain Peebles was a member. The colonials were pathetically incautious. Last night two dozen of them had met in the private parlor of this tavern behind closed doors, and the company had been so diverse that Courtland was certain no other business than that of politics had brought them together. And if that diversity had not been enough to convince him, the sight of their angry, fierce-eyed faces as they had stalked out of the tavern had been ample proof.

Much to his surprise, Julius Twiggs had been amongst them. Last night that self-important gentleman had been the last to arrive at the meeting and the first to leave, slipping unobtrusively past the locals in the parlor. Now he stood across the room fingering the ribbon fob of his pocket watch, at the end of which dangled several small gold seals. His paper-lidded eyes continually roamed to the door as if he expected someone in particular to arrive, and occasionally he lifted a finger to tap the sheep's tooth that was cleverly wired to replace his natural cuspid.

Two town selectmen entered the parlor, and, pulling up Windsor chairs, greeted Courtland with enthusiasm, immediately turning the conversation to news of Boston, for the town leaders could not get enough talk of General Gage and his scurrilous deeds.

"How many redcoats would you say have defiled the fair city of Boston, Mr. Day?" the Selectman McCracken asked. He leaned back in his chair and scratched his ribs beneath his unbuttoned waistcoat. "I hear they're crawling like flies over Boston Common."

Courtland looked properly concerned. "Two regiments were encamped there when I left. But I've heard rumors that four or five thousand redcoats—eleven regiments and four companies of artillery—will be arriving over the course of the summer. Of course," he added with a touch of innocence, "I don't know if that number can be trusted. You know how people are prone to exaggerate when they're panicked."

"I've heard Gage is weak-willed and doesn't want to fight. He believes war is too messy, too expensive. What do you think?"

Courtland picked up a shilling that had been left upon the table and rubbed it between his thumb and forefinger. "Gage will fight."

"Then he'll be sent back to King George in a box!" the drunken farmer declared in a voice so slurred that the edge of its bravado was lost. "We have veterans from the last war who'll be happy to raise their muskets against the lobsterbacks and send 'em all to hell!"

The selectman ignored the outburst. " 'Tis predicted that the folks in Boston will be starving by winter."

"I've heard the same," Courtland said. "Have you thought of collecting supplies and sending them there? Each family in Swanston could contribute whatever it could manage to the cause."

The response to Courtland's plan was enthusiastic, and Selectman Hullover said, "I'll wager Simon Peebles would be willing to donate considerable stores to the cause. Perhaps he'd grind the flour for us at his mill without charge. Good man, Simon. In spite of his wealth he hasn't forgotten his roots." He raised a brow at Courtland as if to prompt an agreement.

"Indeed he hasn't," came the dutiful reply, and the words were scarcely out of Courtland's mouth when the door opened and the subject of their conversation strolled in.

Garbed in a mustard-gold jacket, white stockings, and black pumps with silver buckles, he made a vivid picture if not a handsome one. Courtland met his stepfather's eye directly and gave his regards, but the man's face seemed to pucker into lines more sour than ever. Without acknowledging the greeting, he joined Julius Twiggs beside the pipe rack.

The magistrate appeared relieved to see him, for the tenseness in his tall, rawboned frame relaxed. The pair exchanged a few words while Peebles selected a clay pipe from the rack, clipped off the end, and filled it from the wooden tobacco box at the bar. While Twiggs paced impatiently, Simon went to the hearth, retrieved a hot coal with a pair of smoking tongs and lit the pipe. Puffing on it, he motioned for the magistrate to come and join him at a table set apart from the rest.

Courtland eyed them consideringly for a moment and then spoke again to the selectmen. "If you could use a wagon and team to transport the supplies you collect to Boston, I'd be pleased to offer mine."

They expressed their appreciation for his generosity heartily, unable to know that the more food Captain Day hauled into the city, the more the British army would be able to confiscate for its hungry soldiers.

As the landlord bustled out of the taproom with a tray of ale a while later, Courtland insisted upon paying for the round. "Pour another one for the magistrate," he said convivially, intending to get the lot of them as drunk as he could. "And make my stepfather a glass of flip. I seem to remember his partiality for it."

"Aye, sir." The smiling landlord drew a tumbler of cider, added ale and spices, then took a long-handled loggerhead from the hearth fire and thrust it into the drink to mull it. "Compliments of your stepson," he announced, setting the steaming beverage before Peebles.

Simon appeared taken aback, and glancing over his shoulder to regard his stepson's mocking expression, made to push the tankard away until he saw the selectmen watching the exchange. A look of annoyance crossed his face before he finally raised the drink in a forced salute of thanks to Courtland, then sipped tentatively as if he would strangle upon the offering.

A while later Courtland noted that Peebles and Twiggs were once again deep in conversation, so absorbed that they seemed oblivious to the bustle in the now overflowing public parlor. Buckskin-clad travelers with muddy boots clomped in to boast of recent

Indian fights in the Alleghenies, apprentices in country homespuns enjoyed meals of cornbread and fish, and a Philadelphia schoolmaster sat alone reading a dog-eared copy of *Ovid* and nibbling parched corn. The newest arrivals, a florid-faced merchant and his wife from Baltimore, stood close the hearth drinking cider and laughing at the turn-spit dog.

Courtland had been watching the curious little animal as well, and, taking a slice of gingerbread from a platter, strolled over to join the others with an ulterior motive for changing position. Although the hearth was installed with a modern clock jack which rotated a roast on its spit over the fire, the landlord occasionally employed the turn-spit terrier for the entertainment of his guests. It ran round and round a specially constructed wheel, and the action caused the spit to rotate. Seeing Courtland with the gingerbread in hand now, the dog sprinted faster, then hopped off the wheel and sat down to await its reward with the stub of its tail wagging.

Kneeling, Courtland fed it and rubbed its coarse-haired ears while listening intently to the snatches of conversation that floated intermittently from the nearby table.

"You're suffering from delusions if you believe the chit has returned to Swanston after all this time," Peebles was saying, his voice raised louder than normal after three tumblers of flip. "It's been seven years. Why would she show her face here again? And what can she do, besides? She has no power over you. Who would dare to believe a word she said, even if she were bold enough to open her mouth? Julius, you are fretting for naught."

"I tell you, 'tis a sense I have that she's come back," his companion argued. "I would swear upon my mother's grave 'twas her I spied last eve."

Peebles's reply was lost in an off-key rendition of "Old Dan Tucker" performed by the drunken farmer, and Courtland returned reluctantly to his seat with a frown of consternation. He lingered there for a time, and, when Twiggs finally took his leave, laid down three shillings to settle his tab and followed. On the stoop the storekeeper Hodge delayed him in order to brag about the new supply of Spanish lemon juice he had bought from colonial smugglers, who, after having eluded British harbor patrols, were selling it all over the province.

As the conversation lengthened Courtland found himself distracted, making mental notes to be included in the next dispatch to Gage. A half hour passed before he was able to bid Hodge good night and mount his horse.

Although some sixth sense warned against it, Chaynoa once again stole through the magistrate's garden. Overhead, the clouds flitted like scraps of smoke across a blue moon ringed with gold, and the air was filled with odors of decaying leaves and newly turned soil. Chaynoa believed such signs were omens, who, like friends, warned her to beware of danger. But her loyalty to Sadie was too strong to be denied tonight, and so she hurried along the path to Twiggs's house with her fingers curled over the pistol hidden in the pocket of her skirt. It was Courtland's pistol, and she clutched it firmly as if some of his own confident skill could be transferred to her hands. When she arrived at Sadie's window, breathless and edgy, she was surprised to see the maidservant waiting expectantly beside the lace curtains.

"Chaynoa!" Sadie hissed, seizing her arm before

she could climb over the sill with her medicine basket. "You mustn't come inside!"

"Why?"

"Because I fear Julius will not tarry long at the tavern tonight. He's been restless all day, pacing about and muttering to himself. Twice he burst into my room and glared at me suspiciously. I can't fathom what his odd behavior signifies, but I'm frightened by it."

Chaynoa glanced behind her at the impish face of the moon, whose pallor cast an eerie glow upon the garden statuary, and her uneasiness increased. A storm approached from the north, threatening to cloak the light of heaven, and she did not take the sign unheedfully, for at an early age she had been taught to trust nature in all situations.

"Perhaps your caution is wise, Sadie," she said, wavering, and from her basket retrieved a small jar stained with a thick blue liquid. "Here's the restorative. Drink it in equal portions five times tomorrow and the sickness in your belly will be lessened. Rest as much as you can and lift nothing heavy. And don't eat any pork or your child will be born sickly."

"God keep you, Chaynoa! No one could have a truer friend than you. I know how you must have loathed this journey through the village. Please go now and keep yourself safe."

"I'll return again." Chaynoa patted the maidservant's thin arm, but shivered even as she made the promise and bade goodbye.

She scurried headlong into the storm-scented garden whose tossing oak branches groaned. Above, the mouth of the moon formed a moue of chagrin. On the common, wandering cattle lowed in plaintive voices, and the church steeple pointed an accusing finger at the boiling clouds.

Evil was afoot, and Chaynoa hurried past rows of
dark shops and darker windows thinking of nothing
but the safety of the cottage. The gravel in the road
cut her feet, but she did not slow her pace, and after
awhile, when the wind died for a brief spell, she knew
with certainty that someone followed her footsteps.
Glancing about, she searched for a safe place to cut
through the rows of houses and strike for the woods,
but too many townspeople were about. As if restless,
they smoked on their stoops, bade good night to
neighbors, or stepped out to ponder the moon and its
unusual ring. She feared to trespass and call attention
to herself.

While she stood indecisive with her heart pounding, rain began to splatter the road, and the wind
gusted, carrying with it the acrid odor of the coming
storm. She heard doors bang and windows thud as
they were hastily shut against the wet, and sheets left
to dry upon clotheslines were speedily yanked free by
rescuing wives. People moved all around her, and yet
she could ask not a single soul for help.

She spied her pursuer hovering beneath the apoth-
ecary's porch across the street. With his hat pulled
low over his brow and his hands thrust in his pockets
he appeared no more than a gray column propping
up the backdrop of an ebony night. But she knew he
watched, knew he waited.

Struggling to keep her wits about her, she darted
past the peruke maker's shop, where a flash of light-
ning illuminated a dozen bewigged and disembodied
heads displayed in a window next to the plumed hats
of the milliner. Rain cast an eerie veil over their
ghoulish shapes and cascaded over the road in long
silver swords. With all the speed of a panicked deer
Chaynoa bolted toward Queen's Road, and by the
time she discerned the gables of Courtland's house

through the rain and trees, she was drenched and terrified. If her pursuer still followed, the drumming of the rain now masked his tread, and the possibility of a silent stalker was doubly horrifying.

With dismay she noted that no light glowed from the windows of Courtland's house, and, veering toward the barn, she nearly exclaimed in relief when she saw the doors standing open. Inside, she stopped to orient herself in the dark musty place, and the sound of her gasping breaths blended with the restive stamping of the horses, who appeared as little more than shadow shapes with silver blazes and white-rimmed eyes. Made nervous by the storm, they crooked their necks over the rails and snorted at her intrusion.

The rain pounded the roof and streamed from the eaves while wind whistled through the doors and eddied wisps of hay. Mud covered Chaynoa's freezing feet, but she was so consumed with fear she scarcely noticed. She decided to hide and wait until Courtland came home, but as she turned, one of the horses shied in its stall and alerted her to an ominous sight.

As if he had materialized from a sheet of rain, a figure appeared in the doorway, his dark attire superimposed over the black of night. Chaynoa knew him well. He embodied every horror she had ever imagined, every evil spirit she had ever been taught to dread, and was the monster who had kept her exiled in a forgotten woodlet for nearly seven years.

He took a leisurely step forward, then another, extending one hand as if to beckon her, to lure her to his side. She backed away and whimpered, and in a plaintive, passionate voice wild with memory, begged him not to come closer.

He paid no attention, moving forward in a slow,

sinister tread, and she stumbled toward the rear of the barn, searching frantically in the darkness for an exit. With a cry she fell against the rough planked door leading to the paddock, then recovering herself, groped for the bar that held it locked until her fingers bled with splinters. Behind her the magistrate's shoes rasped over the straw, and she knew he closed the space.

In one great lunge he hurled himself toward her, grasping her skirts, but she pulled free and shimmied through the rails of a loosebox. She collided with the muscled haunches of its occupant, who wheeled in a flurry of hooves and kicked out just as Twiggs vaulted over the rail. He cursed as he was struck, and using the animal to shield herself, Chaynoa released the bar of the stall gate. Then, clasping a handful of mane and heaving herself atop the horse's back, she dug her heels into the animal's flanks to escape.

But the magistrate grabbed her ankle, and with brutal hands dragged her to the ground. She landed on her back with such a jolt the air left her lungs, and for a moment she lay stunned, hearing the vibration of the mare's hooves as they pounded an escape. Burrowing beneath the hay rick, she raised her eyes and saw Twiggs loom above her like a towering pillar of black.

The sound of her breathing rivaled the beat of rain upon the roof. Through the slats of the rick she could see no more than the lower half of Twiggs's face, but she discerned clearly his white hands where they dangled beside the black shanks of his legs. The fingers opened and closed, opened and closed, and she remembered the untrimmed nails, the knuckles protruding like knobs from the freckled skin. She remembered how they had looked around Mam's neck, she remembered how they had felt sliding over her own young flesh.

The magistrate stepped closer, and she slid a hand into the pocket of her gown. When his defiling fingers stretched out, thrust themselves through the slats to touch her face, she aimed Courtland's pistol and fired.

Its spark flashed in the darkness and spewed smoke, and with a soft thump, Twiggs fell backward into a cushion of straw.

Seconds passed, counted by the rain as it descended in a furious deluge. Afraid Twiggs would prove indestructible and leap up to attack again, Chaynoa stayed beneath the rick, watching, waiting. Finally, never taking her eyes from his body, she crawled out of her burrow and stood up, staring down into the face of the man she had slain, only vaguely hearing Courtland's entrance into the barn a moment later.

Courtland had scarcely dismounted when he caught sight of Chaynoa poised beside the open gate. Leaving his horse behind he sprinted forward, halting abruptly, focusing his eyes on the unsavory scene. He could smell death, could smell the fear surrounding Chaynoa's rigid, motionless figure. "Are you hurt?" he asked, and when she made no response he took down a lantern, lit it, and held it high.

In sharp relief it illumined her trembling form and the pistol in her hand as if they were both props in some weirdly staged tragedy. The long, sprawled body of the magistrate lay beneath her, appearing oddly shrunken, as if its flesh had already decayed away and left only bone beneath the covering of broadcloth and satin. He lay face up with his red wig knocked awry upon his head, revealing in an obscene way the few sparse hairs sticking up like boar's bristles on his balding pink pate, and his white satin waistcoat glowed with its gruesome splotch of blood.

Chaynoa turned her eyes to Courtland's face, feeling in that instant as if he were the only thing real in a world turned upside down. She saw every detail of his face: the beads of water upon his nose, the deep hollow at the base of his neck where his collar was unbuttoned. Rain dripped off the creases of his tricorn and, as if he had donned it in haste, his double-caped surtout lay unclasped across his shoulders. How calm and substantial he seemed. She wanted to lay her head against his shoulder, feel the woolly dampness of his coat on her cheek. She wanted to rest within his arms for a long, long time, until all the exhaustion and bewilderment of the night faded away.

Courtland knelt to examine the body, taking care not to bloody his fingers. "Well, you did a proper job of it," he announced grimly. " 'Twas a quicker death than he deserved." Raising up, he searched her face, expecting her to dissolve into hysteria. Her features were so statuelike that the quivering of her lower lip seemed childishly exaggerated, heartbreakingly sad. A tear trickled from her lashes when she read the bleakness in his own gaze, the bleakness that told her he knew as well as she did the inescapable seriousness of her deed. "Chaynoa . . ." he whispered, his voice breaking with the dread he felt.

"Hallo in there! Day? Are you about?"

Hullover's voice echoed around the vast space, and Courtland pivoted to see the two selectmen stamping mud off their boots as they milled about the entrance to the barn looking for him.

"Day!" McCracken called. "Did we hear a shot fired?"

Courtland cursed under his breath, and, yanking

the weapon out of Chaynoa's hand, leaned to remove
the small dueling pistol from Twiggs's belt, which he
placed beside the curled white fingers. "Say nothing,"
he hissed.

"But—"

"Say *nothing*."

"What's happened here?" Both selectmen stalked
forward to investigate, their steps unsteady from the
ale Courtland had generously supplied all night.

"God in heaven!" Hullover exclaimed upon seeing
the bloodied body of Julius Twiggs. "Who has done
this?" His eyes alit upon Chaynoa, who stood with
dripping hair and muddy feet in a gown that was no
more than a frayed wet rag. "Did you shoot this man,
girl?"

Courtland stepped between them, his face set, his
bearing calm. " 'Tis me you'll want to address," he
said quietly. "I killed the magistrate."

In disbelief Chaynoa turned, fixing her gaze upon
him, opening her mouth to deny his confession until
his narrowed eyes flashed a warning.

The selectmen seemed not to notice the soundless,
furious exchange and demanded an immediate explanation. "My God, man!" Hullover exclaimed. "This
is a damned serious offense."

"Don't you think I'm aware of that?" Courtland
threw him an insolent look. "I heard this woman
scream as I rode up the drive, and when I came in,
Twiggs was struggling with her here—trying to have
his way with her. Like any gentleman would do, I
ordered him to stop. But the blackguard pulled his
pistol on me—I swear he would have killed me had
I not been the quicker one to draw."

Chaynoa could not fathom his reason for taking
the blame, nor his self-possession as he fabricated the
story. How coolly and spontaneously he lied, she

thought, so coolly that no one could doubt the reasonableness in his voice, the honesty in his intelligent gray eyes.

"For God's sake, Hullover," he went on, as if offended by the selectman's silent stare. "You must see that I had no choice in the matter. I couldn't allow the girl to be ravished in my own barn."

"Do you know this young woman?"

Courtland did not glance her way. "No."

McCracken, slightly less inebriated than his companion, fastened his eyes upon Chaynoa with unmasked contempt. "What's your name?" he demanded. "And what were you doing here?"

She was so confused by the turn of events she could scarcely speak. "Ch-Chaynoa. I—I came here to—to find shelter from the storm."

"What sort of name is that?" Hullover stepped closer and eyed her rudely, his eyes asquint with growing suspicion. " 'Tis a heathen one, isn't it? Aye! I'll be damned if you ain't the thieving brat of that sluttish maidservant Julius employed several years ago! Fathered by an Indian savage, and as dirty as any I've seen. Look at her, she—"

"Gentlemen!" Courtland cut in, struggling to hold his temper. "Let's see to the body now, for God's sake. Surely your interrogation can wait until morning."

"There'll have to be a hearing tomorrow." Hullover glanced with distaste at the body again. "Just as soon as another magistrate can be summoned to conduct it. I'll take that pistol, Mr. Day, and you'll have to spend the night in jail. And this young miss shall join you—"

"Join me? There's no need for that," Courtland argued. "After all, she's the one wronged here—"

"That remains to be decided."

Knowing further protestation would cast suspicion, Courtland offered his horse for the transportation of the body, then stepped aside while the selectmen clumsily draped it across the saddle. Leaning close to Chaynoa, he whispered, "When we leave the barn strike for the woods as quickly as you can. These two have too much ale in their bellies to follow. Go back to your cottage and live just as you've always done if that's what you want—"

"No!" she shook her head with vehemence and hissed the words. "I must stay to bear up your tale now you've told it. Why did you take the blame? I've yearned to kill that monster since my mother's death—even before that. Don't you understand?"

"I understand nothing except that 'tis time we sorted through your past and made these people behave respectfully toward you—"

"They'll never accept me," she retorted bitterly. "Don't waste your efforts."

He glanced at the town leaders, then turned back to meet a pair of dark, unnerving eyes that gleamed with the shine of unshed tears. "Yes, they will." He swore under his breath, taking her by the arm. "By God, they will."

Chapter 9

After rousing the young constable from bed, the selectmen escorted Courtland and Chaynoa through the drizzly darkness to the village jail. A crude, fifteen-by-twenty frame structure constructed of rough planks, it possessed an earthen floor and a window inset with bars, but no furniture, not even a cot.

Hullover had sobered, and perhaps that sobriety was due in part to the realization that he was incarcerating the stepson of the town's wealthiest and most influential member.

"My apologies for—er—locking you up, Mr. Day," he blustered, setting down his lantern in the center of the cell as if to make its roughness more presentable. "But I can hardly neglect my official duty. I'm certain that circumstances occurred just as you say they did tonight, and that no charges will be filed against you when the facts are put before the officials. I myself saw Julius leave the tavern, and he had drunk his share of ale."

He shifted his eyes to Chaynoa, then tried and failed to meet Courtland's unwavering stare. "Er— you'll have a good meal brought to you in the morning—the constable's wife is a fine cook. In the meantime"—he pointed to a gloomy corner—"there's a bucket of water yonder and a chamber pot."

"Most accommodating," Courtland muttered, listening to the key scrape in the lock. With a resigned sigh he watched the selectmen and the inofficious little constable splash homeward through the mud with their knee-length jackets flapping in the breeze like bat wings.

He shook his head, knowing Gage would be roaring mad when he got wind of this escapade. The methodical governor had advised discretion and circumspection in all things when dealing with the colonials, and now his carefully placed spy had just claimed responsibility for murdering a magistrate.

Well, Gage could go to the devil if he squawked. The blasted mission would not be jeopardized, for Courtland was experienced at extricating himself from tight circumstances and emerging unscathed, and this circumstance would prove no exception. At least Gage had been meticulous in his precautions; if the officials decided to do an investigation into Mr. Day's past they would find no history of military service and no connection whatsoever with the British government. It would look as if Peebles's stepson had been doing nothing more than sailing the seven seas since his departure from Swanston years ago.

He glanced at Chaynoa. She had gone to stand at the window and stood so silently and still, that had he not known her better he might have thought her serene. But he could tell by the way she pressed her face against the bars that she yearned to be away, safe within that queer little dwelling she had made her hermitage. She possessed a rare dignity he had seen in few others, for in spite of the scarecrow clothes and bare feet her carriage remained erect. Even now, knowing the ordeal she would face on the morrow, she had not succumbed to hysteria in the way of most women.

"Will your brother be able to manage on his own for a day or so?" he asked to interrupt the hush.

Chaynoa did not answer immediately, giving the impression that Courtland had broken into a contemplation so deep that she had to reorder her thoughts in order to speak aloud. "Aye. Now that spring is fully upon us the forest will be bountiful and provide him with much food. But he will fret for me in the way of a child, and fear that the Ongwe Ias has spirited me away."

"The what?"

"The Ongwe Ias. 'Tis an evil ogre who snatches people and eats them."

Courtland smiled. "In Devonshire we called it a barghest."

She twisted her head to look at him, curious, and he elaborated. " 'Tis a fiendish hound with four huge paws, slavering jaws and the most horrible red eyes you can imagine. Not a pleasant creature to meet in your travels—it attacks from behind and tries to do you in."

"Did you ever come across it?"

His mouth curved. "Many times."

"And does it really resemble a dog?"

"Nay," he scoffed. "Every time I see it, 'tis in the shape of an ordinary man."

For a moment Chaynoa studied his carefully expressionless face, and then pronounced, "I think you are very cynical, Courtland Day."

He grinned but did not deny it, bracing a shoulder against the wall so that he could better view her dusky profile. She hugged her arms, and her dark, uncommonly long hair hung down her back in a soaking mass while the wavy ends dripped water on the earthen floor. Occasionally she shifted her bare feet, so thin and fine-boned where they emerged from the fringe of her gown, and Courtland surmised they were half-frozen. Doffing his surtout, he shook the rainwater from it, and, although he would have liked to have placed it about her shoulders himself, simply extended it in offering.

"Oh, n-nay," she said, shaking her head as if loath to accept anything so personal as a garment just removed from a man's body.

But he did not intend to be refused. "Take it."

She at last accepted the heavy coat and draped it over her shoulders, meeting his eyes across the space of the room. Neither of them spoke, and the sound of a moth dashing itself in a hopeless circle against the lantern glass seemed disturbingly loud. Chaynoa looked at Courtland long and gravely, her eyes naked with an emotion that both beseeched and condemned. "Why did you do it?" she asked him in a whisper. "Why?"

He did not reply immediately, but removed his tricorn and tilted it so that water trickled from its points and splattered upon the dirt, where the moisture created a glistening stain that spread into the shape of a half moon. He stared at it, and said simply, "Because they would have hanged you."

At his bald honesty Chaynoa gripped the folds of his coat and drew it closer, and he made a rueful expression. "Scoundrel or not, Twiggs was esteemed for his position. From what I've gathered, he made certain no scandal besmirched his name, and he had friends in high places. On the other hand—" He gave her a level glance. "Regardless of any justification you might have had for using my pistol on him tonight, you've no witnesses to the deed. And your past would have weighed heavily against you once it was dredged up. Sentiment would have gone in his favor. You wouldn't have had a chance."

"And . . . you are willing to be hanged in my stead?" she breathed.

"I won't be hanged."

"You sound very confident."

Courtland shrugged and, finding a knotty bole protruding from the log planks, hung his tricorn upon it to dry. "My alleged shooting of Twiggs, rashly done or not, will be viewed as an act of honor and self-defense."

"How can you be so sure?"

"Experience."

She blinked at his nonchalance. "You've been charged with such crimes before?"

He lifted a shoulder and the corners of his mouth twitched. "Nay. But I've learned the difference between what men want to hear and what they're willing to believe."

"Where did you learn such things?"

Courtland slipped a hand inside his waistcoat pocket and retrieved two pieces of toffee wrapped in twists of paper, one of which he tossed to her with an easy flick of his wrist. "In ships' holds and quayside taverns and Italian alleyways. And before that, in my stepfather's drawing room."

His voice was hard, and Chaynoa closed her icy fingers over the round, sticky piece of candy. "I could tell the officials that I shot Twiggs in self-defense."

"Could you . . . ?" He gave her a penetrating regard. "Don't think that I condemn you in any way, Chaynoa. Quite the contrary. I know well what hatred can do. When 'tis planted in a young heart and nourished like a weed year after year it becomes poisonous. Even if Twiggs didn't lift a finger to hurt you tonight I can understand your desire to kill him. More than that, I'm sure he deserved it."

"They'll make you swear to the murder tomorrow at the hearing," she said, still clenching the candy like a talisman. "Will you have no qualms about lying under an oath spoken before God?"

He laughed and leaned back against the wall. "Most women I've known would have no concern whatsoever for the state of my soul under the circumstances, just as long as I saved their pretty necks from being stretched. But the lie gives me no pause. After all, 'tis a virtuous lie, don't you think?"

"My mother was a Puritan. I never thought a lie could be virtuous."

He grinned. "You will tomorrow."

Chaynoa studied him as he idly watched a stream of rain water slither beneath the wall frame. He seemed large in the tiny space—incongruous somehow, as if his vitality and the bounds of the prison could not be reconciled. The curve of his neck was made molten by the lantern light, and the amber glow flickered over his long fingers as they unwrapped the toffee. She could scarcely absorb the fact that he was here on her account, and by his own choice; but his sacrifice gave her a painful distress instead of the relief it should have brought.

She took a breath. "You needn't . . . do it. I wish you wouldn't. Even now you could tell them the truth and leave me to my fate. I'm not unwilling to die for what I did." She raised her chin in a show of moody defiance. "And besides, it's not as if I'm any of your concern."

His eyes turned upon her with such intensity she flushed, and his tone came passionately low through his lips. "But I have made you my concern, Chaynoa."

The words made her heart tremble like the wings of a hummingbird, and no longer able to meet his eyes, she cast her gaze to the ground. But even with her eyes averted, she could remember every feature of his face just as clearly as she remembered the glistening of sunshine on the woodland pools or the shimmering of sand on the river shore; his face remained inside her mind as if enclosed in a crystal dome made for viewing in secret, precious hours. For an instant she could feel his thoughts across the silent space as well, and knew that he was as empty as she, and that he sought to find a way to fill the hollowness. She knew also that he was taken aback by his own words, as if they had come unbidden even as he realized they were true.

Suddenly Chaynoa knew Courtland cared for her in a way greater than she had ever realized or even suspected. The revelation caused her to look at him sharply, and she sensed by the slight parting of his lips and the directness of his gaze that he would like to cross the room and touch her. But she could not welcome such intimacy; some part of her did not want it, feared and dreaded it. That part of her was like the mysterious nettle in the woods that, when brushed by a human hand, curled up tight upon itself and hid from the light of day.

All at once she wished she were someone else—anyone else: an ordinary village lass whose father labored in the fields and whose mother kept a tidy house beside the common. She wished she were not the shoeless, wild creature from the woodlet who possessed not even a ribbon for her hair. For what normal girl would spurn the attentions of this man who stood so tall and straight beside her, and who had, out of some astonishing motive, accepted the blame for a murder she had committed herself? What girl would not want to be held in his arms and rest her head against a pair of shoulders broad enough to carry the weight of the world? Only one such as she.

She bowed her head, and the tightness in her throat made her voice hoarse. "I'm sorry you've come to care for me."

Courtland closed the distance between them, searching her face as if to understand the reason for her regret. Her hair was trapped beneath his surt-out—she had not bothered to pull it free when she had thrown the garment on—and in an impulsive gesture of tenderness he reached out to draw out the long, wet locks.

But she jerked away from his hands. "No. You shouldn't have involved yourself tonight. Now I'm indebted to you, and what you want in return for your kindness is something I can't give. Don't you understand?"

"Are you afraid of me?"

She shook her head in confusion, shivering at his deep, probing tone. "I—I don't know . . . I don't know how to explain. I suppose fear 'tis the only word there is to use."

"And if you were not afraid . . . ?" he persisted.

Her hands clenched inside the pockets of his surt-out and the piece of toffee molded to her palm, hot and pliant. Agonized with the desire for him to understand, she cried, "Even though Julius Twiggs is dead, the *feelings* inside me will never change. Not ever! I—I wish they would. Not a day passes that I don't wish it."

Courtland thought how lovely—and how tragic—

her countenance appeared in the dim but revealing light. As a boy he had always brought home injured animals to patch up and set free again, and he asked himself now if he only meant to do the same for Chaynoa, but his answer was a firm and bewildering "no" that led him to a more disturbing truth: she was not simply someone who needed him, but someone he needed, too. He even understood her feelings, for the tragedies of his own life had made him view the world in a less than trustful way. He understood that there were scars within a heart that would never heal no matter how much time passed, and no matter how conditions changed for the better. It was not difficult to imagine what act Julius Twiggs had committed to make Chaynoa fearful of closeness, and the thought of it sickened him so much that he wished he *had* murdered the man.

"Come here," he bade her softly. "Come and sit down."

He indicated a place beside the wall where the lantern shed its warmest light, and she obeyed, taking care to prevent the hem of his surtout from being soiled on the floor. He sat next to her—not so close that she would be uncomfortable—and rested a forearm across his upraised knee, collecting his thoughts, basking in her nearness while thinking how extraordinarily ironic were the circumstances that had put the two of them here together. "Perhaps you'll tell me about Julius Twiggs now," he said quietly. "There are things I need to know before we go to the hearing."

"It makes my blood run cold to speak of him."

"And yet you must speak of him tomorrow. They'll demand that you answer many questions about your past, about the years that you and your mother and Hahnee lived with Twiggs."

"I know."

"You told me once that he offered your mother employment when the three of you were on the verge of being escorted out of the village by the constable—warned off you called it."

Her eyes grew dark. "Twiggs made it appear as though he were being generous. But he was a user of people. He treated my mother like a slave, for he knew she had no other place to go and no other means to support Hahnee and me. At first I thought he loved her, for to my childish eyes he looked at her as my father had once looked at her. But 'twas nothing to do with love—he was incapable of that. Mam hid her misery from me and kept me away from his notice for as long as she could, but—" She shuddered and put her face in her hands.

Courtland wanted to touch the fingers she pressed to her face. The light played between them and created a shifting tracery of gold over planes of her cheek. He searched for the proper words to say, for he had never been adept at giving comfort, nor even felt compelled to give it often, and platitudes failed him. He wanted to speak of his need suddenly, so she would understand the stake he had in her own emotions, but voicing such a depth of feeling gave him pause, lest it should bind them more tightly than his prudence recommended. "Chaynoa . . ." he breathed in frustration. "Let me—"

"Nay," she interrupted, as if sensing his dilemma. "There's only one thing that I would like to tell you—something no one else knows, not even Hahnee. I have kept it to myself all these years. Julius Twiggs murdered my mother, strangled her with his own hands."

"You witnessed it?"

"Yes."

Courtland's expression fiercened. "My God, what a beastly thing for a child to see."

"The image of it will stay with me forever."

Briefly his eyes clouded with the haunting pictures that dwelled in his own heart. "I know. But you must say nothing of it tomorrow at the interrogation. It would give you a motive for killing Twiggs and they would pounce on it. It would make it difficult for me to convince them of my story. I had no idea of the extent of Twiggs's evil. My sister told me that he had spread the tale that your father had entered his house and killed your mother, then ransacked his house before taking you and Hahnee away."

"My father died before we came to Swanston. He was killed by British soldiers in a skirmish close to Fort William Henry. That's why Mam brought us here, hoping to shelter with her family. But they had gone back to Europe, and only a few cousins remained who would have nothing to do with us."

"And after your mother was killed, you and Hahnee fled to the woods?"

"Aye. And I never set foot in Swanston again until last night. I was concerned about Sadie, who had also been one of Twiggs's servants during Mam's time there. Sadie is in a . . . delicate way, and I was fretful over her health. I returned tonight to deliver a tonic, and Twiggs must have followed me when I left his house, although I can't fathom how he discovered me."

"And you ran to my house?"

She fingered one of the brass buttons on his surtout and nodded.

"Why?"

Her eyes raised to his and in their depths he saw a flicker of what he desired to see. Then they slid away and color rose to her face. "Because . . . because you remind me of the men I lived among as a small child."

"Indeed?"

She grew concerned and stammered, "I—I didn't mean to offend you by the comparison. I know many white men despise the savagery of the Indian warriors."

"No offense taken. On the contrary, I'm complimented. There's no shame in being compared to men who fight for what belongs to them."

"Some people would say there is."

"Then they're fools."

"Fools or not, they'll continue to make war on my father's people until they are all gone—even though they've been here since the ancient days when the Sky Woman descended from heaven. They'll all be conquered. Sometimes I find it hard to understand how God allows it."

Courtland ran a finger over the cuff of his boot and remarked idly, " 'Tis said that God is always on the side of the big battalions."

"Do you believe that?"

He looked up at her. "I'd never be so bold as to pretend to know the mind of God."

She considered him through her lashes and, detecting a twinkle in his eye, said, "You are very glib, Courtland Day."

"Is that a compliment?"

"You don't need my flattery," she murmured.

"Your flattery is not what I want."

At the significance of his serious, softly spoken words, another silence fell between them, and Chaynoa brushed a spot of dirt from the lining of the surtout, then smoothed the wool and closed her fingers over it as if the texture gave her comfort. When she spoke, her voice was deep with feeling. "There are no words to tell you of my gratitude tonight."

Courtland contemplated her face, so innocently open and touching, and did not want to hear her stammered gratitude, for he felt it would wrench his heart just then. "There needn't be," he said. "There needn't be any words."

She met his eyes, but only briefly, as if the communication between his gaze and hers made her too uncomfortable. His hand rested atop his bent knee, and she pondered the shape of it, studied every curve and line and feature: the clean square nails, thin fingers, sturdy wrist emerging from the ruffled white cuff of his sleeve. And then she reached out her fingers, and in a feather touch, laid them over the ridge of his knuckles.

Her hand was thin and very cold. Courtland turned his palm over and clasped it within his own, lent it his warmth. But as if it were no more than a fleetingly captured butterfly, she slid it from his grasp and tucked it between her knees.

Near dawn, after he had invented a tightly woven story and advised her upon which pieces of the past to reveal and which to keep untold, Courtland went to retrieve the bucket of water from the corner of the cell. Morning lightened the retreating night sky to a pallid tangerine, and the first sounds of the village, stirring industriously to life, drifted through the iron bars.

Taking out his handkerchief, Courtland dipped it in the stale water, wrung it out, and handed it to Chaynoa. "Wash the mud from your feet. And then let us prepare ourselves to go and face them. We'll get through. Whenever you feel afraid, just look at me."

And she did. Courtland Day's presence was the only thing that carried her through the long ordeal.

Chapter 10

Courtland sat at his desk and twirled a quill pen between his fingers, absently staring out the window.

A neighboring farmer plowed a distant field, tramping up and back behind his lumbering pair of oxen, whose tan rumps were mottled by the last rays of an afternoon sun. The aroma of the rich earth, newly troughed and warm, wafted through the open window, and the smell brought to Courtland's mind recollections of his boyhood days. He could feel the rough plow handles under his palms, see the soil furrow beneath his feet, and hear the oxen's breaths puff in rhythm to their labored plodding.

Courtland wished he had time to work the few acres of untilled land behind the Foree piece of property. After years of life divided between mending sails and marching over foreign soil, farming seemed like an agreeable profession, and he remembered with a remote wistfulness the farm in Devonshire that he would someday be able to cultivate to his heart's content.

He glanced down. Spread beneath his hand was a piece of dispatch paper upon which not a single word was penned. He was distracted, just as he had been all day, all week. God knew he hadn't time to sit wool-gathering as he was now; between Gage's work and the livery, and the hours he had to spend socializing in the tavern in order to further his mission, he had no leisure to dream.

His hand made an imprint in the film of dust coating the desk, and with a baleful gaze he surveyed the cobwebs that laced the chair and footstool together across the room. When Virtue had come to visit yesterday she had gone about flapping her handkerchief and coughing, imploring him to find a maidservant before the spiders marched away with all the furniture. And yet, as desperately as he needed help in the house, he was loath to have a servant bustling about the rooms and taking note of his activities.

Lifting his eyes to the smudged windowpanes again, he stared beyond the fields to the faraway line of trees separating the earth from the sky. A week had passed since the interrogation, and yet he could not forget it, could not forget his reason for having been there.

The ordeal had gone well for Courtland; he had made certain the officials perceived his actions as innocently gallant, and no charges had been filed against him. Even Peebles had testified at the hearing that Twiggs had drunk enough ale to impair his judgment, although Simon had not spoken directly to Courtland before or after the trial. Nor had Susannah approached him or invited him to their home.

All during the hearing Courtland had defended Chaynoa's position without being conspicuously protective. Before the proceedings he had asked that clean clothes and shoes be brought to her, but his request had been ignored. And so she had stood bedraggled and waiflike before the bewigged magistrate, who, in a scarlet robe and snowy wig, had presided imperiously and with a face soured by doubt even though Chaynoa had managed to answer his questions with quiet and articulate dignity, reciting perfectly what Courtland had coached her to say.

Wisely, she had not besmirched the name of Julius Twiggs in any way, but had related the truthful circumstances of her journey into Swanston on behalf of her friend Sadie. She said that she had been caught in the storm, and seeing the doors to Mr. Day's barn agape, sought shelter there. Deviating only slightly from the truth, she insisted that Twiggs had followed her inside, and in his drunken state, attempted to force himself upon her.

Only she and Courtland knew that Julius had been clearheaded enough to stalk her. Whether or not the magistrate had really intended to murder Chaynoa, Courtland would never know—nor would he discuss the subject with her. He did not care why had she killed the man—revenge, fear, and hate were all the same to him.

Chaynoa supported Courtland's part of the story admirably, and when queried about her past, professed to know nothing about the circumstances surrounding the murder of her mother. With concern, Courtland had noticed the unsteadiness in her voice as she was forced to lie, but fortunately the magistrate seemed to attribute her faltering to nothing more than nerves. She had ended by saying that she had taken her brother into the woods to live because the two of them had nowhere else to go after her mother's death.

Outside the meeting house, the townspeople had milled about all day, avid for a glimpse of the girl who had led such a reclusive life, a life socially unforgivable by its very strangeness. "Just like a savage," they had declared in unkind whispers, straining to see her when the interrogation ended.

But the object of their curiosity, skilled at evasion, had slipped quietly out, eluding them all, including Courtland.

Since then he had ventured into the woods only once, for Chaynoa had not been at the cottage, and although he had searched hours for her, even sensed that she was aware of his presence, she never showed herself.

The increasingly rife gossip he heard in the streets disturbed him, and more than once he had had to quell an angry response in defense of Chaynoa's honor. For days after the interrogation the busybodies of the village huddled at shop fronts and garden gates and whispered that the half-savage girl had probably seduced the unsuspecting Julius Twiggs after luring him into the barn. Likely, she had meant to steal from him again and took advantage of his drunkenness. All the old suspicions that Twiggs had so cleverly planted years ago about Chaynoa and her mother were revived and embroidered and magnified, so that the magistrate's words became more damaging after his death than they had ever been before it.

Conversely, in the perverse way of human nature, the villagers not only forgave Courtland for his act of murder, but applauded his action, and his already respectable reputation evolved into that of a sentimental hero. Every village maiden dreamed of having her virtue defended by the romantic Mr. Day, and even the men approved of his gallant but uneffusive regret over the slaying of the town father.

Now, shrugging off his reverie, Courtland dipped the nib of his pen into the pot of ink only to realize that twilight had cast a wash of violet over his paper. He sighed, annoyed that he had wasted the last hour in useless rumination, and, pushing back his chair, moved to the window to contemplate the darkening landscape. It was supper time and hunger gnawed at his belly. Glowing windows dotted the distant lane as wives lit candles and prepared meals, and Courtland felt a sense of exclusion from the human circle. His untidy, rented house seemed more solitary than ever beneath the pall of evening, and with vague surprise, he realized he was lonely.

Another feeling plagued him as well. He knew it caused his lack of concentration and his restlessness, and he knew the cure for it. In the way of any healthy young man he had felt it often before, most acutely on sea voyages that grew too long. But since he had been in Swanston he had kept himself away from finding a woman for those purposes, and the reason for that avoidance now troubled him almost as much as the need.

"Thank God I'll be gone soon . . ." he murmured to himself, starting to turn away. But at the distant edge of the woods, pinpricks of yellow light danced like fireflies and caught his attention. He stared at them curiously, then left the window and pushed open the back door to get a better look. The lights had vanished, but a young boy crossed the corner of his property with a fishing pole in hand.

"Did you pass the edge of the woods on your way from the river, lad?" Courtland called.

"Aye!" Excitement raised the boy's voice to a high pitch. "There's a group of men out looking for that half-Indian girl."

"What?"

"They say they don't want her living hereabouts. Some of the womenfolk sent their husbands out to find her shack, and they've been searching the woods for nearly three days now. Tom Shandy thinks he knows where it is, and he and his friends have decided to pay the girl a call tonight."

Leaving the boy, Courtland sprinted toward the barn, slipped a bridle on his horse, and rode out of the yard bareback. Not bothering with the paddock gate, he put the stallion to the rails and spurred it toward the black fringe of Chaynoa's world, and although he knew he risked the beast's legs on the stubbly dark fields, he did not slow until they penetrated the wooded depths. Only when the beast could no longer forge a passage through the tangle did he dismount and leave the steed to find its own way home.

Courtland had snatched a lantern on his way out of the barn, and he paused to light its candle, thankful for the illumination when he began to shoulder his way through the cloying underbrush knotted with grapevines. He searched for familiar landmarks to orient himself, and hoped to God Tom Shandy had not found the shortcut to Chaynoa's clearing.

When he came to the swampy acre of ground that meandered through the northeast quadrant of the wood, he did not hesitate, but plunged through the snake-ridden water with the lantern held above his shoulder, its light casting eerie patterns that sparked off the mesmerized eyes of forest creatures. For over a half hour he jogged through the airless vegetation, slapping away vines and branches, and only his natural sense of direction kept him from getting lost in the maze. A familiar towering spruce pricked his memory finally, and he realized the cottage lay only a few hundred yards away. Pausing, he searched the darkness ahead, glimpsing a sudden bright and ominous flash through the trees.

He lunged forward at the sight, sweating, gripped with dread, his fear confirmed by the smell of smoke,

which blended with the resinous odor of pine. Hazy
gray wisps began to curl through the branches, and
Courtland dashed toward the clearing, finding the
cottage enveloped by fire. The flames were spreading
from the interior of the structure to the roof, where
the dry thatch ignited like tinder while the drooping
willows on either side of the door trembled with the
heat. A half-dozen men ringed the house with torch-
lights in their hands and their faces twisted into
devils' masks by the reflection of the orange glow.

Courtland charged into their midst and, seizing
Tom Shandy by the shoulders, slammed his body
against a tree. "Where is she? *Where is she!*"

Startled by the unexpected attack, Shandy could
only stutter.

"*Where is she?* Did you trap her in there, damn
you? Is she in the house?"

"For God's sake, man, let go! I can scarcely
breathe—huh!" Air left Shandy's lungs as Courtland
dashed him against the tree again. "I don't know—I
didn't see her! She didn't show herself!"

Letting him drop, Courtland sprinted toward the
blazing cottage, yanking his shirt up over his head to
protect it as he went. Wisps of thatch swirled through
the air and the heat from the conflagration was so
great he was almost driven back. He sucked in air as
he crossed the charred stoop, threw an arm over his
eyes and searched through the smoke, bellowing
Chaynoa's name repeatedly. The hearth, the trunk,
and the table board were all licked by flames ignited
by sparks showering from the roof. "*Chaynoa!*" he
cried.

In the space of a few seconds the thickness of the
smoke forced him back, but not before he had completed a stumbling circuit of the cabin, assuring him-

self that neither Chaynoa nor Hahnee were trapped inside.

Staggering out, he bent over and coughed, drawing fresh air into his lungs while sweat dripped from his brow. His eyes streamed and his shirt smoldered in several places. As he pulled the scorched garment over his head and cast it aside, he glanced at the group of young men who still stood in a loose circle a safe distance from the heat.

They stared sullenly at him. A moment later, without a word, they all turned away and melted into the woods like guilty shadows, leaving him alone against the roaring, flaming backdrop of their handiwork.

"Cowardly bastards!" he growled before another fit of coughing seized him. Still wheezing, he retrieved his ruined shirt and, slinging it over a shoulder, went in search of his lantern.

While the cottage burned behind him he carried the light through the woods, forging a path, avoiding treacherous bogs and pools in his hunt for Chaynoa. His initial relief over her escape from the fire had given way to a new concern that she had fled the area with her brother, and even now trudged a dark road away from him.

After an hour of desperate searching, he struck out in the direction of the river, raising his lantern high enough so that it cast a feeble blanket of light over the bullrushes and the frothy shoreline. The ground near the bank was overrun with grapevines, wild cranberry, and dwarf willows, and Courtland had to wind his way through them in a tedious, zigzagged route. As he slid down the muddy embankment, he heard the cattails edging the water rustle suspiciously.

"Hahnee . . . ?" he called, swinging the lantern forward to investigate.

At the sound of his name the stooped young man slowly rose up to reveal himself, but when Courtland lifted the light to better see his face, Chaynoa's brother covered his eyes and disappeared in the dense stalks again.

"Where's your sister, Hahnee?"

The head popped up once more, and with a leap the awkward young man scrambled out of his hiding place and lumbered along the river bank, covering the dark, slippery ground with such amazing nimbleness that Courtland had difficulty following.

Before they had gone very far, he spied Chaynoa. She sat upon a knoll with the river spread before her like an undulating band of silver thrown atop a sleeping landscape. The lantern reflected off the poplars quaking behind her, and off the strands of her hair which the breeze lifted in long gossamer threads. She sat with her knees drawn up to her chest and her arms clasped about them, her body curled as tightly as a corkscrew, and she never glanced his way, not once, even though he knew she heard him approach.

Hahnee stood beside his sister and looked from her face to Courtland's as if wondering why neither of them spoke. Finally, with his mouth hanging open in bewilderment, he went to sit beside the water's edge, dangling his stockinged feet in the current like an ignored child.

The direction of the breeze changed and the sharp odor of smoke permeated the fresh scent of the river air, prompting Courtland to glance over his shoulder at the distant glow mirrored on the dark sky. He set down the lantern.

"Are you all right, Chaynoa?" His mouth was so parched from smoke and thirst that the words sounded hoarse. "Had I known, I would have been waiting for them on your stoop with a pistol in my hand. The lot of them should be strung up."

"It wouldn't have mattered," she said, staring at the river. "It wouldn't have made a difference. Not in the end." She glanced at him, saw the broad span of his naked torso, the muscles of his chest and arms where they were delineated by the lantern's glow, and wished he had not come tonight. His appearance, so assured and solid, and the fact that he had cared enough to search the woods for her half the night caused the dark thing within her chest to twist and melt and try to burrow deeper. She had thought about him endlessly since the hearing. How brilliant he had been, his testimony a balance of remorse and earnestness that had easily gained the sympathy of the magistrate. He had been so convincing, in fact, that more than once she had had to shut her eyes and force herself to remember that *she* had been the one to murder Julius Twiggs.

"You shouldn't have come," she murmured. "There's nothing you can do."

He eased down beside her and, pulling his shirt down over his head to clothe himself, spoke in a short tone, impatient with her loss of spirit. "On the contrary, I can do a great deal."

"You went inside the cottage?" she exclaimed suddenly, appalled. She had noticed that his sleeves were scorched, even burned through in places.

"I did." He brushed a few wisps of thatch from his shoulders. "But nobody was home."

At first the utter absurdity of his remark, his light treatment of the tragedy, took Chaynoa aback. Then his own humor in the face of disaster infected her, and the night's strain suddenly floated out of her body like the air bubbles beneath the shallows of the river. A little smile touched her lips, then stretched wide. "You're very disrespectful."

"I know."

"Was everthing lost?"

"Aye."

"There wasn't much," she said with a sigh. "But I would have liked to have saved the things in the trunk."

He searched her face with concern. "What will you do now?"

Shrugging, she plucked a blade of grass, listening to the sound of its roots tearing loose from the ground. "Hahnee and I will go away at first light."

"Just like that? Where will you go?"

She closed her eyes and held on to the sound of his voice, for its deep strength seemed to chase away all the fearful things of the night. When she realized that in another few hours she would hear it no more, she felt a smarting behind her eyelids, and spoke quickly lest her throat constrict. "Boston. Or another large town. I'll find work someplace."

"What sort of work, Chaynoa? What can you do? And what about Hahnee?"

"I'll care for him just as I've always done. I don't except anyone will hire him because of . . . the way he is, but he's really a helpful fellow when the tasks are simple. And he's strong."

"Times are hard in the colonies now that the port in Boston is closed. People will come near to starving this winter. There's little work as it is. Before long there may be war."

"I'll manage."

Her tone was obdurate and Courtland's jaw hardened, for he had no intention of letting her go. "You'll come back to Swanston with me."

At his command Chaynoa threw him a challenging

look and shifted away, and Courtland knew that he
had not constrained the forcefulness in his voice well
enough. If he did not proceed more carefully she
would grow stubborn and bolt. "I could use Hahnee
in the stable," he said less coercively. "I've too much
to do now that the livery business is picking up. And
I've decided to plant the few acres behind my house,
put in some corn."

He paused and gave her a sideways glance to judge
her expression, and seeing that her interest was
piqued, affected a more appealing tone. "The worst
part of it is, my house is a calamity. I'm not much
good at keeping it. My cooking is so deplorable I've
taken to eating at the tavern regularly, which is in-
convenient. I'd be grateful to have a woman put
things in order for me, cook a meal now and then."

For nearly seven years Chaynoa had survived by
her own wits and resources, managed to exist with no
more human contact than Hahnee's mute presence
and Sadie's occasional visits, but now she had received an offer of much more, of a decent existence.
She bit down upon her lip and considered, knew that
if she were to allow Courtland Day to go out of her
life she would be lost, unable to withstand the grim
picture of her future. And yet, if she were to return to
Swanston with him, she would be forced to face the
villagers, and how could she endure their scorn?

Every scrap of pride she possessed suddenly
shrank against the thought of living in their rigidly
conventional and condemnatory society, even while
in an inexplicable way, she yearned passionately to
be one of them, to be included in their warm, tribelike
circle. If she were to return, they would whisper when
she walked down the street, they would stare when
she entered a shop, and worst of all, their disparage-
ment would spill over to include Courtland Day be-

cause he had gone against the grain of their resistance and chosen to help her. Their opinion of him would alter. He had already risked much—even his life—to defend her, so how could she bear to let him risk his reputation as well?

Her stomach knotted as she stared at the moon, which had finally shed its cloudy beard and emerged as a perfect pearl. "I can't accept your kindness," she said.

Not bothering to hide his anger, Courtland picked up a pebble and hurled it into the river with a violent sideways flex of his arm. "That's the difference between us. I'd be damned before I'd walk away."

Taken aback, Chaynoa averted her head while he continued harshly. "Do you think people in Boston or Philadelphia will treat you and Hahnee any differently than they treat you here, Chaynoa? Do you think you can simply walk to some city street, rap on a shop door, and be promised a job? Don't bet on it. That's the odd thing about folks—they're the same the world over. They'll mistreat you, malign you, exclude you just as long as you let them."

"What am I to do then?" she cried, turning on him. "I don't know what to do, I don't know how to change them!"

"You won't change them. But if you walk away from the people of Swanston, you'll be walking away for the rest of your life."

"Why do you defend me?" she shouted, angered over his dogged defense. *"Why?* I don't understand!"

Courtland released a short breath through his teeth, then swore before laughing in an unpleasantly caustic way. "I know you don't. Hell, I know you don't." Flinging himself backward upon the grass, he laced his fingers behind his head and stared up at the sky.

Chaynoa craned her neck to read his shadowed face, but he only shook his head surlily as if to discourage her regard. She felt a great remorse, and as her gaze flicked over the length of his body, looked at the beauty of it, strong and raw, she wanted to lay down next to him, and just for an instant curl up and be very still, like the deer who crept into the open meadow to catch the warmth of the sun on early spring days. As she looked at him, at the square flap across the front of his breeches and at the thin white shirt, visions of intertwined limbs and straining faces flashed behind her eyes, and they were her limbs and his, her face and his. Perspiration gathered between her breasts and rolled down to wet the gown where it stretched over her stomach. All her life she would remember sitting beside him for the last time on a flawless spring night, the last night of the world.

"Will you come home with me, Chaynoa . . . ?"

His voice had come from deep in his throat, and she closed her eyes, concentrated very hard upon the virile timbre of it, which still lingered passionately on the wind, wishing she could hold on to it forever like a treasured talisman. But . . . she *could*—if not forever, then for a little while.

A tiny soar of joy winged its way through her heart as she reconsidered her decision. She thought of the future, and for the first time it was a straight road, removed from all the danger she had ever known. She imagined what life would be like with Courtland Day at her side; she believed in him, trusted his ability to make all things right. She turned her head to look at his profile, fiercely sculpted in the lantern light, and wondered about him, wondered what had made him so faithfully noble, so protective of a girl no one else cared to know.

He watched her intently, waiting, and she touched

his ruined sleeve, the sleeve of the man who had made himself her soldier. "I will go home with you, Courtland," she whispered softly. "For a little while, I'll stay with you."

And so, when dawn spread itself like apricot jam over a new morning, she and her brother emerged from their woods. Just as if they were a pair of well-dressed friends newly arrived from the city and invited home for breakfast, Courtland directed them through the main avenue of the village. As people stepped out to sweep stoops and unlock shops, as sleepy-eyed girls ambled out to squeeze a fresh pail of milk from a complaining cow, they witnessed the curious spectacle.

The handsome and admired Mr. Day, who met every eye unflinchingly, strolled along in scorched clothes and muddy boots, and next to him walked the strange girl with no shoes and tangled hair. She looked neither right nor left but straight ahead toward the end of the road, fixedly, her eyes glowing as if they saw a perfect vision there.

And behind them, with his thumbs hooked beneath his armpits in a comically cocky way, marched an awkward young man with wildflowers stuck in his pockets, pickerel weed trailing from his ankles, and a chattering squirrel perched atop his shoulder with its tail flicking.

Swanston had never seen such a sight, nor was it ever likely to again.

Chapter 11

Chaynoa had never seen the house by day. She paused for a moment as Courtland opened the gate, and stood staring at the shingled roof and high gables of the plain white clapboard in need of paint. A profusion of untended flowers, creepers, and shrubs spread from the foundation of the house over the yard, spilling beyond the fence to the road like a frayed tapestry of brightest color. Sunshine dappled every leaf and patch of untrimmed grass, and daffodils with dewy heads twisted heavenward, bathed in the golden glow while purple pansies hid shyly beneath the scented foliage of lad's love.

Chaynoa breathed deep of the fragrance and glanced at Courtland, who held the front door open waiting for her to enter—Hahnee had already vanished to explore his new surroundings. She had never been invited to enter a house by the front door before, and as she walked into the tiny vestibule, the walls seemed to enclose her as if she were a long-awaited guest. For a moment she fancied they actually vibrated with warm welcome, although she knew it was only the interplay of light filtering through the window that made their pale green panels quiver.

The house has a soul, she thought in sudden wonder. Most did; even the house of Julius Twiggs had claimed one, but it had been a cold and hollow spirit that had left the rooms like caverns full of frost. But this home had the sun of the New World fields at its heart, and its warmth radiated through the diminutive rooms and increased itself with light borrowed from the windows. It fell upon the floors to make the rough grained planks liquid gold, it transformed the plain rails of the bannister to ochre ribbons, and a square of its heat knelt upon a parlor footstool needlepointed with cream-colored spaniels. She likened it to a sheltered island upon which she had landed after a tumultuous sail at sea, and her heart, which had grieved over the loss of the woodlet cottage, now soared with the knowledge that she was to live in this warm place and care for it.

For a moment she stood silently beside Courtland in the golden hush, glancing up at his face to find him contemplating the tiny parlor and adjoining study with a scowl. She followed his gaze, and in that instant, saw the place as he must see it—an untidy house in disrepair with cobwebs in the corners, dust on the tables, tracks imprinting the unswept floor, and the windows so oily they blurred the landscape view outside.

"Maybe you'll decide to turn around and go to Boston after all," he said dryly.

"Oh, no. No!" How could she explain that the little house suited her, enchanted her, and that to be with *him* in a place safe and dry, and with plenty to eat, was like being dropped in the midst of a paradise?

She looked at his scorched shirt and water-stained boots, at the dark hair tumbled over his brow, at the face that was unshaven and drawn with fatigue, and knew that despite the dishevelment, he was more than commonly handsome. Why would such a man be so kind to her?

"What are you thinking?" he asked unexpectedly, laughing, watching her intent expression.

Flustered, she cast her eyes down, unable to speak of her emotion. She was afraid of closeness. For too long she had put faith in nothing at all but nature, for its cycles and seasons were always predictable, whereas man and things of man were capricious, often failing faith either through neglect or deliberate cruelty. With dread, she suddenly knew Courtland Day would try and unlock her feelings, just as he might open an intriguing chest with a long-lost key, and she was not sure she wanted him to try, for she sensed that with any unlocking a great surge of pain would follow.

"I was wondering about . . . about sleeping arrangements," she finally improvised.

"There are two bedchambers upstairs. Hahnee can share one of them with me, and you—"

"My brother and I will sleep in the attic, which is proper for servants to do," she declared, keeping her eyes averted. "I can make my own way up to explore. You needn't take time to show me."

Courtland regarded her keenly, then glanced at the dusty, unkempt parlor again. "Can you manage it all, Chaynoa?" he asked.

"My mother was raised a Puritan, taught all the skills a woman needed in order to run a household. And she was a dutiful servant. I worked alongside her, cooking, cleaning, gardening, and sewing."

At her straightforward, almost offended, recitation of her accomplishments, Courtland cleared his throat, a smile tugging at the corners of his mouth. "Well, then. I'll leave you to take it all in hand—very capably I'm sure—and go up and change my clothes."

After he had climbed the stair Chaynoa went to inspect the kitchen. The window stood open and a breeze blew through the muslin curtains, swaying them gently to and fro before stirring the ashes in the grate. Hanging in neat arrangement around the hearth were utensils of all kinds: waffle iron, toasting fork, egg beater, apple parer, copper warming pan, a few iron pots, and a long-handled peel. Sun streamed through the window and slanted across the cupboard, gilding the pewter noggins lined across its shelves. On the table board a blue pottery jug sticky with molasses attracted the attention of a lazy honey bee.

The rocking chair still rested on the rag rug, and she eased down into its smooth seat, leaning back so that the piece of furniture swayed. With her feet on the rungs she rocked forward and back, forward and back, smiling with the delightful motion.

The sun crept over the walls plastered with oyster-lime and reminded her of all there was to do. She would not be idle here. Courtland had hired her to work in his house, and she would labor hard, never disappoint him or cause him to regret his kindness to her and Hahnee. Besides, she wanted to care for the house on Queen's Road just as if it were a living, breathing thing.

With excited but careful hands she began inspecting every item in the kitchen, opening the bottom doors of the cupboards and pantry, unlidding bins and cannisters to peer inside, then stepping out the back door to search for the entrance to the cellar. Moving aside its wooden door, she descended the little ladder into the earthen hole shored with stone, and discovered apples, potatoes, onions, carrots, and more. She gathered what she would need, dashed into the kitchen again, and in her noiseless, nimble way, began to work.

Upstairs, Courtland washed himself, shaved, and changed his clothes, then went down to the kitchen, where he paused in surprise.

Upon the table board a single place was set, perfectly arranged with linen, a knife and fork, and pewter from the cupboard. Beside it were a platter of sliced ham, bread, an opened jar of peach preserves, apple wedges sprinkled with cinnamon, and a pot of steaming black coffee.

Seeing him, Chaynoa hastily wiped her hands upon her skirt and stepped back in the impulsively skittish way Courtland knew well—and which he feared might never leave her. Such a naked look of apprehension tightened her face that he knew she agonized over his reaction to her hasty effort at breakfast. " 'Tis a feast you've made for me," he said, smiling.

Relief brightened her eyes. " 'Tis all I could do in such a short time."

"And better than anything I could manage if I took all day. But you've set no place for yourself."

"Servants don't eat with people they serve. Hahnee and I will breakfast later." Giving him no time to argue, she slipped out the back door, and Courtland bit into the delicious meal even as he shook his head at her stubborness.

Outside, Chaynoa explored the kitchen garden which, although overrun with chickweed and thistle, still sprouted with plenty of sage, basil, parsley, cabbage, and pumpkin. Squatting, she began to clear the fertile patch with enthusiasm, imagining the future as she worked, deciding that the house would be a beautifully tended refuge, made alive and homey by her nurturing hands. Courtland would be proud of her, and the townspeople would stroll by and tell him what a talented servant he had.

At the sound of footsteps she looked up to see a most curious person hobbling toward her through the hydrangeas. An ancient woman she was, bent and frail as a willow bough, her hair white beneath a straw hat, her wrinkled features translucent in the radiant light. She wore a black gown, and its voluminous folds rustled like river reeds as she crept through the lush green foliage.

Chaynoa stood up and stared at her warily.

"Your hands needn't be idle because of me," came the soft, creaky greeting. "Go on, kneel again and work. Don't let time flee."

The words were kindly said, and, after giving the strange personage another questioning glance, Chaynoa obeyed.

"My name is Iris," the elderly visitor said. "I live in the house next door—over yonder through the oaks. My grandson Robbie lives with me, and he is such an active, wandering imp, you shall surely meet him soon."

Shy and socially unaccomplished after her long sojourn in the wilderness, Chaynoa found herself taken aback by the ordinary kindness of the stranger.

"I have seeds you can plant here," Iris went on unaffected, regarding the straggling swatch of garden. "Flower seeds as well as vegetable. I shall send Robbie over with them later."

The simple offer of neighborliness moved the girl, and she spoke with warmth. "I'm Chaynoa. Housemaid to Mr. Day."

"Ah . . . Mr. Day," Iris sighed, leaning more heavily upon her cane with her gnarled hands. "I have met him. A fine man. A hard outer shell, but tender and wounded inside. Wouldn't you agree?"

" 'Tis not my place to speak in such a way about him," Chaynoa answered, ill at ease with the topic.

The old one bent low to peer into her face. "Ah. And you are a wildflower turned in upon itself, aren't you?"

"Why, I don't know, I—"

The back door banged and Courtland strolled out, setting his tricorn atop his head and shrugging into a brown, knee-length jacket of the kind worn by colonial working men. At sight of the two women he grinned and tipped his hat. "Good morning, Mrs. Oakchurch. Have you become acquainted with Chaynoa?"

"Indeed. I wasted no time."

"Good. Perhaps she could call upon you if she needs advice."

"Any time. I have a good deal of that, if little else."

"Your modesty is charming, ma'am."

"And you are what we used to call a rogue."

Courtland laughed and, bidding them good day, went about his duties in the stables. When his chores were finished there he tucked a leather pouch into his jacket and informed Chaynoa he would be away until late, then mounted his horse and set out. He planned to map the southern roads for General Gage, and afterward spend his evening in the tavern learning what he could from the rum-drinking patrons. The day passed rapidly, and after his journal was well lined with notes, he proceeded to the Stirrup and Iron where he was met by a rowdy gathering of men whose tempers seethed over news that the 5th and 38th Regiments of His Majesty's Army had landed at Boston harbor.

Sitting back with a tankard of rum in his hand,

Courtland relaxed and, with a rueful though private enjoyment, listened to the fiery spurts of conversation. Patriots in both drab homespuns and silk waistcoats thumped their fists upon the tables and cursed Gage and King George for their audacity to rule.

"Britain is forcing us pay her debts!" one declared hotly. "The French and Indian War cost her a hundred and forty million pounds, and now she thinks to tax us in order to recover the loss. Well, we'll be damned rather than be used in that way!"

"Aye! And her treasured East India Company can go bankrupt with her!"

"Or go to hell!"

Only a handful of men dared to disagree with the tide of sentiment that was slowly gaining strength not only in Swanston, but throughout the colonies. William Saunderson, the loyal Tory who had aided Courtland upon his arrival—and discreetly pretended no acquaintance with him now—argued that America could not stand to forgo British protection and economic aid. His neighbor, Benjamin Jay and a few others, agreed, which prompted a shouting match with the patriots.

Courtland calmly ordered another rum and fixed in his mind the names of the staunchest patriots, encouraging their confidence whenever the opportunity presented itself. His affairs were going so well he surmised he could make himself a member of the secret society before the first frost hardened the Massachusetts earth.

Not surprisingly, every resident of Swanston now knew that he had taken Chaynoa and Hahnee into his home, and upon his arrival at the tavern tonight he had received a few speculative glances which he answered with studied unconcern. He mentioned that he hired the pair as housekeeper and stable boy, and the gentlemen in the tavern, more interested in politics than domestic matters, seemed perfectly satisfied with the explanation.

When the gathering of rum-filled patrons finally dispersed after exhausting their evening's conversation, Courtland quitted the place with relief. He was tired and eager to return home and, as he neared the well-lit house, found himself stirred by the notion that a woman moved about his rooms, warmed them with her care.

Guiding his horse around back, he dismounted at the barn where a lantern had been left alight for him. He unsaddled his mount, rubbed it down, and strolled briskly up the path, catching sight of Chaynoa through the window.

She stood over a huge wooden wash tub, steam wending up from the hot soapy water to curl the wisps of hair about her face. The contents of the tub proved to be his dirty laundry, including the scorched shirt he had worn the previous night, and he watched her transfer it to a pan of rinse water before wringing it out and tossing it in a basket. She was weary, he thought, noting the droop of her thin shoulders; she has worked hard all day.

He opened the door and, quietly entering, said, "I didn't intend for you to work like a slave in my house, Chaynoa. 'Tis very late, and you had no sleep last night."

She stood holding his damp shirt to her bosom, staring back at him with glistening dark eyes. "Nor did you."

"This is not a contest of endurance," he said, smiling, tossing his hat on the peg beside the door. Besides, I'm accustomed to late nights. Leave this and go to bed."

She defied him quietly. "When I finish I shall go."

"Which one of us is the most stubborn, do you think?" A tiny smile curved her lips in answer and he laughed, bending over to pull off his muddy boots. "Is Hahnee abed?"

"Yes. In the barn—he refuses to go to the attic."

"Why?"

"Because he likes to be near the animals outside," she said. "He misses the cottage, I think."

Courtland glanced over his shoulder. "Do you?"

For the first time since she had entered his house, she met his eyes directly, and her voice was warm and shy. "Nay."

He looked at her hair tumbling down her back and thought how warm and feminine she was, how young. "I'm glad," he said huskily.

"I—I baked a pastry for you," she told him then in some confusion, indicating the pie with a nod of her head. "In case you should be hungry."

Courtland glanced at the offering. He had eaten at the tavern and was not hungry, but realized that if he sat down and ate he would have an excuse to enjoy her company awhile. He looked at her face, still flushed from the steam, and at her gown, dark and wet from his dripping shirt, which she still clutched to her breasts with long, water-roughened fingers.

"Here," she said quickly, as if to change the direction of his masculine and clearly speculative thoughts, "let me cut the pie for you." Throwing down the shirt, she took up a knife and cut the pastry, which oozed with sweet, spiced mincemeat.

Still regarding her with a burgeoning absorption, Courtland began to eat while she turned away to refill a kettle. He wondered—not for the first time—what it would feel like to hold her in his arms, to touch her, to unfasten her gown and slide his hands over her softness, over the place between her breasts, the place between her thighs . . .

She dropped the kettle suddenly, and, when he made to get up and retrieve it for her, waved him brusquely away. Her cheeks were pink and her hands fluttered as she mopped up the water, and he knew she had sensed his passionate imaginings.

"Your family," she blurted, as if hunting for something to say to break the train of his thoughts. "I—I saw you speaking with them at the hearing. Are you close?"

Her question caught him off guard. He was not eager to discuss the awkward subject. "My sister Virtue and I were close once," he said uncommunicatively. "Years ago when we were children."

"And your stepfather?"

"We prefer to avoid each other."

She dropped the last article of his laundry into the rinse tub and swirled it with both hands before squeezing the water out. "And what of your mother?"

He stopped chewing and stared at his fork. "We're strangers. We always have been."

Her expression grew softly compassionate all at once and she whirled about to face him, speaking quietly. "I guessed correctly then."

"How do you mean?"

"Well," she said earnestly. "All during the hearing your mother sat so calmly in her seat—she never fidgeted or twisted her hands as if she were nervous about the outcome, about what would happen to you. I—I wondered at it."

Her astute observation hurt Courtland, and the intensity of his hurt surprised him, for he had thought himself beyond caring about his mother's lack of affection long ago. In silence he finished the pie, the mincemeat tasting less sweet as he thought of Susannah's indifference and his own despicable vulnerability to it, a vulnerability that seemed to linger still, from boyhood, in some dark part of his heart.

Chaynoa glanced at him from beneath her lashes, her full, luminous gaze locked with his, reading clearly what was written in his expression. His face grew ruddy and his jaw tensed with pique.

"I—I'm sorry," she stammered. "I—"

"Don't say anything more." He looked down at his plate and made a business of stabbing the last bite of pie, adding brusquely, "It doesn't matter."

Chaynoa wrung the water from his shirt, and when drops trickled off her elbows and onto the floor she stooped to blot them nervously with a piece of linen. Throwing the last shirt in her basket, she lifted the container by its handles and, after hesitating with a stricken look upon her face, backed out the door into the darkness without saying anything more to him.

Through the window Courtland could see her shadowy form as she hung his wet garments along the length of twine she had tied between two branches. He had not meant to put a strain between them. God knew there was enough strangeness in their relationship already. In a thoroughly ill temper he threw down his napkin, picked up his boots, and headed upstairs, pausing on the first step to survey the house in astonishment.

The parlor and study were transformed, immaculate, their furnishings dusted and polished, the floor scrubbed with fine sand, flowers crammed into a cracked vase and set upon his desk. With dismay he realized he had said nothing to Chaynoa about the work she had done all day, he had failed to mention it and compliment her.

Disgruntled, he went on to his bedchamber and

undressed, throwing himself down upon his bed and wondering why on earth he had installed Chaynoa in his home; she had done nothing but complicate his life, and considering his circumstances, their life together could only grow more snarled. Nevertheless he found himself listening for her with studied engrossment. A half hour had passed and still she had not come in from the yard.

With impatience he padded to the window and thrust aside the curtain, and, failing to find her shape in the gloom, assumed she had gone to the barn to see Hahnee. Waiting with his hip braced against the sill, he stared into the darkness until she finally reappeared, flitting between the trees of the yard like a graceful dryad. Oddly, she did not come from the direction of the barn, but from the river, and when she stepped into the circle of light cast from the kitchen window, he saw that her hair was dripping wet.

"Good lord," he muttered. "She bathed in the river rather than use the washtub beside the hearth." With inexplicable chagrin he realized that Chaynoa was still inherently a part of the wilderness, and he wondered if she would ever be anything else, ever be completely comfortable with the ways of civilization. Did he want her to be?

The kitchen door creaked, and he listened as she washed the soiled plate he had left on the table. He heard her set it on the cupboard shelf, then negotiate the stairs in her graceful way, passing his door rapidly before closing the attic door with a firm thud.

He continued to listen, hoping to hear the sounds of her undressing, but the floor above remained silent. For a while he roamed about his room restively, feeling like an animal penned up too long, and it was not until the moon glanced off the chest where his pocket watch lay, reminding him of the hour, that he sought his bed again. With his hands behind his head, he stared up at the ceiling, plagued with turbulent thoughts, and then with a growl of confused thought tossed aside the quilts and climbed the attic stair.

Chaynoa lay upon a pallet curled on one side. Her hair, darkly wet against the paleness of the pillow, fanned out like a peacock's tail about her head, and he knew it would be full of river scents. There was nothing remarkable about her in the usual feminine way, no dainty beauty to her features, no sophistication. On the contrary, she was unusual, full of fears and haunted by past sorrows. She wore the shabby, tattered gown, the only one he had even seen her wear, and with a troubling belatedness he realized that she owned nothing else. The thought made him feel ashamed suddenly, made him feel tender in a way he never had before, and, frowning concernedly, he retreated down the stairs to seek his bed alone, and to ponder the circumstances that were beginning to alter his life in a disturbing way.

Why had Chaynoa taken hold of his mind? Had he changed, intellectually or emotionally, to be so taken by such a woman? And more significantly, what was he to do about it?

The questions plagued him long after dawn came to quiver upon the horizon and melt there like a liquid tangerine ball.

And up above his head, in the attic space, Chaynoa lay sleepless, too, watched the light creep across the rough raftered ceiling. She wondered why Courtland Day had come to stand beside her pallet, so silently, so still, as if something there had caused him consternation.

Chapter 12

Just as the first breath of dawn blew through the kitchen window, Courtland laid a handful of guineas upon the trestle table where Chaynoa had set a single place for breakfast. The coins clinked together as he put them down, and she watched while he used his forefinger to divide the sum of cash in half.

"You'll be needing money for kitchen stores," he explained. "All of this is yours to manage. Half is for supplies, the other half is to be spent upon yourself and Hahnee—buy clothes and shoes with it, and whatever else you need."

Chaynoa stared at the pieces of gold, whose edges reflected the soft hues of dawn. She had never been entrusted with money before, and it was on the tip of her tongue to argue that the offer was too generous, that she would prefer not to spend any on herself. But as she raised her eyes to meet Courtland's, some communication in the gray depths arrested her, and in a terrible rush understanding smote her.

In the way of some dumb animal who was unaware of anything but the need for freedom and survival, she had been oblivious to her appearance these many years, having neither need nor reason to consider it or its effects upon others—until now. And how wrenching to her latent femininity was the realization of how she must appear to this man! Struck by self-consciousness, she glanced down at her bare feet and stained gown, lifting a hand to touch her tangled hair while a flush crept to her cheek. Although Courtland had been indirect and delicate about the matter, her embarrassment was no less acute than had he told her outright that her appearance was pitiable.

If he understood the extent of her distress he made no comment upon it, but merely told her politely that he would take no breakfast except coffee and the bread she had earlier toasted over the fire.

"I plan to cut firewood today along the edge of the woods," he commented as he sat down and spread preserves over his toast. He kept his eyes away from her flaming face and seemed not to notice when she sloshed coffee over his mug. "We've only a cord or two left in the wood pile. I've offered to cut some for Iris Oakchurch, too—she's lending me her team of oxen and a cart."

"Will you be returning for the noon meal?" Chaynoa murmured, managing a steady voice.

Courtland sipped the last of his coffee and set the cup aside, contemplating her as she fidgeted with an apple parer and a pile of green apples. It annoyed him that she worked so hard, so single-mindedly, and he spoke firmly. "Don't concern yourself with cooking today, Chaynoa. Enjoy the shops." Gulping the last of his coffee he bade her good morning, and satisfied with her softly murmured reply, went out to the stables.

After watching him disappear down the path, Chaynoa dropped the apple parer and sprinted upstairs to his bedchamber, which she had avoided except to gather laundry. The mirror hanging above the washstand compelled her this morning. Since the days when she had lived in the magistrate's house, she had not gazed at her reflection once, except by chance in murky pools, and now she wanted to see her features clearly, as *he* must.

She stared into the honest silver depths, and saw that a stranger stared back, a girl whose brow was so obscured by unruly hair that her eyes peeked out. Her lips, as dark red as berry juice, were parted with dismay, and a pair of roughened hands with ragged nails slid up to cover cheeks made rosy by unflattering self-discovery. Her gown hung like an ill-made sack, the hem unraveled, the sleeves rent in several places, and the poorly patched seams conspicious.

Chaynoa's eyes slid from the mirror to the ordered pile of masculine shirts she had earlier brought in from the line. She had folded and stacked them upon the oak chest that contained Courtland's clothes. The shirts were finely sewn and made of quality material, as were all his garments, even those things he wore to work or ride in. They were neither expensive nor elegant, but well cut and neat, a reflection of their owner's person.

Her gaze returned to the glass, and as she stared critically at the stranger there, her perception of herself changed, and her long buried female vanity emerged and spread its fledging wings.

She hastened from the room, nearly flying down the narrow stairs to the kitchen. Taking up the pile of guineas in her hands, she grabbed a basket, then scurried through the back door and out into the budding day. She could scarcely wait to enter the shops, to buy something respectable and clothe herself. Yesterday she had thought of working hard to make the house a place of beauty, but today she yearned to be a complement to it. She wanted the people of Swanston to look at her with approval, she wanted to be a credit to Courtland Day—more than that—she wanted to find admiration in his eyes.

She was rounding the corner of the house when he called out to her from the stable yard. Acutely concious of her appearance now, her first impulse was to elude him, pretend that she had not heard his voice. But he called again, and she stopped to glance questioningly across the yard.

He stood beside a team of oxen yoked to an old cart with large wooden wheels, and perched upon it was a little boy with hair so red it shone copper in the sun.

"Come and join us, Chaynoa," Courtland said when she continued to hesitate. "This is Mrs. Oakchurch's grandson, Robbie. He brought over the oxen this morning."

Chaynoa smiled at the freckled child garbed in patched brown stockings and butternut knee breeches, guessing his age at nine or ten.

He hopped down from his seat like a sparrow from a perch, dusted the back of his pants with the cap in his hand, and greeted her with a gap-toothed grin. "My grandmother said you can have all the eggs and milk you want from our place. We've a dozen laying hens and a cow that needs milking every morning. If I don't come over, you can help yourself. Sometimes you have to hunt for the eggs. The hens like to lay them under the porch."

"That's very kind of your grandmother," Chaynoa said in her quiet way, liking the boy.

Courtland had been standing with his hand atop the yoke, and his voice was full of good humor as he asked, "Have you ever driven a team, Chaynoa?"

"Nay. I—I've never had reason to."

"Well, then, you'll have the honor today." He handed her a hickory whip with rawhide thongs.

"Now, carry the whip in your right hand and stand here—that's it—to the left of the oxen. Make them walk, just flick their necks lightly with the end of the thongs."

Loath to put herself on display but anxious to please, Chaynoa did as he instructed, scarcely touching the hides of the beasts for fear of giving them pain. But to her delight they obeyed her, lumbering forward while the cart trundled behind over the rutted ground.

"Now, turn them to the right," Courtland instructed. "Crack the whip over the ox on the off side, and say 'Gee off!'"

She did as he explained, but her voice came so low and unsure that the animals continued plodding forward, ambling toward the lane.

"You've got to holler at them!" Courtland called, laughing as she trotted alongside the pair. "Go on. Try it again or you'll find yourself following them all the way to Boston."

Determined, she raised her voice and wielded the whip again, and this time the oxen veered. She laughed with pride and repeated the command again and again until they had turned a full circle in the yard.

"Perhaps we should make her the ox master, Robbie," Courtland said with a wink.

"Aye. And then come springtime next year, she can do the plowing for me."

"What would your grandmother say to that?"

"Mayhap she wouldn't care. She's threatenin' to send me to the schoolhouse this year. She says she'll not have a dunce about the house."

"Learn your letters and I'll lend you my copy of the *Iliad* to read," Courtland said. "You like adventure stories, don't you?"

"Aye!"

Turning his eyes back to Chaynoa, Courtland made a suggestion. "Why don't you take Robbie with you to the shops? If you buy him some peppermint at Hodge's, I bet he'll be more than happy to escort you."

Robbie crowed his pleasure at the mention of such a treat, and over the top of his bright head Chaynoa met Courtland's eyes, understanding his motives perfectly; he intended to connect her with society again, beginning with the friendship of this innocent and unjudgmental child.

"Very well," she conceded. "Robbie can come with me."

"Get some peppermint for me, too," Courtland said with a grin.

A few minutes later, as Chaynoa and Robbie walked down Queen's Road, Hahnee materialized beside them, and together they all strolled toward the shops of Swanston, which were just opening for business. Chaynoa consumed every detail of the neat lime-washed buildings, the rumbling carts laden with straw, and the picket-enclosed yards, for not since girlhood had she strolled the streets freely this way, and then it was skipping along behind Mam's skirts.

At the blacksmith's shop the bellows fanned the charcoal fire and filled the air with smoke, while two draft horses awaited new sets of shoes. Next door the potter pounded a fresh batch of clay, while his neighbor the saddler carried out a newly sewn harness with shiny brass rings and buckles. Robbie waved his arms to scatter a flock of geese from the road, and Chaynoa smiled when one of the ill-mannered specimens refused to be intimidated and nipped at his sagging breeches. Skittering out of its way, the boy laughed in his blithe way.

Above their heads, the sky spread a splendrous cobalt canopy, and Chaynoa's spirits soared high with hopefulness. She was beginning a fresh existence today, and although such a prospect frightened her, it freed her, too, for she was in exile no more. The earth felt warm with promise beneath her feet, and she thought that the leaves of the chestnut trees seemed greener than ever, and the birdsong sweeter than it had on any other day of her life.

But her optimism was quickly dampened, for as she entered the heart of Swanston where the close-knit society of housewives and servants went about their morning tasks, she realized she was not to be allowed to blend unnoticed.

With baskets dangling on their arms and children trotting at their starched skirts, they stopped one by one, scrutinizing the approaching trio with open mouths. Some nudged their companions with their elbows, and all delivered bold, rude stares.

Hahnee, too simple to be intimidated—perhaps even misinterpreting their stares as flattery—enjoyed the attention. Picking up a fallen willow switch from the ground, he tied its ends together to make a wreath which he lifted on and off his head in deference to each lady he passed. His clownish antics and crooked smile caused ripples of tittering laughter to run through the crowd of bonneted females, and Chaynoa's distress over such embarrassing attention increased with each step, especially when she noted Robbie's anxious brown eyes.

She cursed her own optimism. Had she thought that simply by being Courtland Day's servant, by spending a night beneath his respected roof, that she would have a new identity, a protection from an old disdain? Had she thought the past could be erased with such ease, along with the suspicions raised during the hearing? The townspeople had called her a squaw, a seductress like her mother, and spread gossip that she had lured Twiggs into Courtland's barn in order to rob him.

She gripped the basket handle, and the quaint street scene shimmered through her tears. Neither time nor circumstances, it seemed, would change opinions that had been so long ingrained in the minds of people who did not care to understand. What a fool she had been to hope otherwise!

Squeezing the moisture from her eyes, she walked with her gaze fixed ahead, ignoring the stares directed at her brother's ridiculous capers. Every eye in the street was turned upon them, and she felt that she and Hahnee walked down a long and narrow courtroom whose benches were filled with unkind judges. An aproned woman emerged from the baker's shop, and when Hahnee gamboled closed to admire the toddler at her side, the mother snatched it to her chest as if he were a monster out to steal it. Two young girls put their hands over their mouths to smother giggles, and Chaynoa yearned suddenly to throw down the basket and run, take Hahnee and retreat to the woods where they belonged.

And yet, a strong need to please Courtland, a desire to hold on to her dignity above all else, kept her feet upon their straight and determined path. Holding her head high, she crossed the common with its circle of shuttered homes, at last spying the painted sign of the milliner, which like most colonial signs included a picture above the words for the benefit of those unable to read. Even as a child she had admired the artful drawing of a lady's plumed hat with a pair of gloves tucked in the brim.

In spite of all the staring eyes, she paused for a moment to peer through the shining bow window where calashes, ribands, and sleeve knots tempted a feminine eye. She had forgotten Hahnee momentarily, and he lumbered out to perform for the gawkers gathered upon the street, still wearing the willow wreath on his head. Mimicking a ceremonial dance he had seen his father do long ago, he leapt and danced in a circle, then did a somersault or two.

Chaynoa shouted out to him in the Indian tongue, and, hastily pushing open the milliner's door, bade him follow her inside. Like a chastised child, he obeyed, and poor Robbie trailed after them with his hands shoved in his pockets, exceedingly ill-at-ease.

The shop was wondrously delicate, festooned with ostrich feathers, silk flowers, and lace shawls, which hung from pegs nailed around the walls. Long satin ribbons in rainbow hues shimmered upon the wooden countertops, and a silver-backed brush gleamed beside them, along with a collection of combs carved elaborately of tortoiseshell and ivory. Awed by the dainty, beautiful adornments, Chaynoa briefly imagined herself arrayed in a mauve silk gown stretched upon a dress form, and fingered the guineas in her pocket wistfully before reminding herself that such finery was not meant for a girl so plain and dark and tall as she.

A clerk stood behind the counter but offered no greeting. She merely stared in irritation at Hahnee, who shuffled about the premises with his slack mouth agape and the odor of the barn clinging to his scarecrow clothes.

"I—I'd like some muslin," Chaynoa stated when the woman continued to observe them coldly. "And some thread, along with some—"

"I have none of what you need." The words were as brittle as chipped ice.

Chaynoa's eyes slid to the small selection of fabrics

arranged on a table beside the counter, but she did not bother to argue, for she was intelligent enough to know precisely what was being done to her. Robbie looked up at her face as if seeking an explanation, obviously puzzled and uncomfortable by the undercurrents he could sense but not understand.

"Let us go, Robbie," she said to him preemptorily. "Get Hahnee."

"But—"

"Come!"

Leaving the door hanging open in her wake, Chaynoa led them down the street again at a breathless pace, and the stares they earned were no less insolent than before. The peal of the church bell in its graceful steeple proclaimed the hour of nine just as they arrived at Hodge's rambling establishment. An elderly collie lay soaking up the sun on the porch, barely lifting its head as they stepped past its languidly thumping tail. Several women shopped inside the spice-scented interior, chatting with Molly Hodge while she swept up a pile of spilt tobacco from the floor.

When Chaynoa entered, the others glanced up, their hands stilling upon the brass candle snuffers and tins of English biscuits imported before the closing of the port in Boston, and she knew even before she spoke that her treatment here would be no different than it had been at the milliner's store.

Nevertheless, she summoned her courage and addressed Molly. "I would like some peppermints, please."

Molly's pale eyes slid toward the faces of her patrons, who stood watching her expectantly, and her ample breast heaved as if with a sudden swell of importance. Pursing her full-blown lips, she announced, "We haven't anything for sale today."

Robbie's mouth fell open in astonishment, and before Chaynoa could respond, he put his hands on his hips and argued in the honest way of a child. "Yes, you do! You always do, because your father likes to make money. Everyone knows that."

Titters came from all around and Molly reddened more. "Off with you, Robbie Oakchurch!" she snapped, flapping her fat arms in his direction and raising the broom as if to swat his backside. "What goes on in this establishment has naught to do with you! And tell your grandmother to mind you better. Watch who you traipse about town with!"

"Chaynoa is Mr. Day's servant," he said defensively. "Hired yesterday."

"And I'll wager she serves him well, too!" Molly rejoined, satisfied that her remark prompted a round of half-smothered laughs.

"You're only in a huff because you set your cap for him and he ain't come calling," Robbie charged.

"How dare you!" The shopkeeper's daughter raised the broom as if to wield it in earnest, and Chaynoa grabbed the youngster's arm and dragged him through the door.

Once outside she could no longer restrain her instincts. Ignoring Robbie's fretful questions and Hahnee's vacant smile, she threw down the basket she had brought for her purchases and began to run down the lane, her pace so swift that neither the boy nor her brother could hope to match it. She had no notion of where she flew, no direction in mind, only the need of a private sanctuary where she could hide in the way she had been accustomed to doing whenever hurt or danger threatened. She ran past the blacksmith's shop and past the clapboard homes where women hung laundry in the sun, then beyond the last stake and rider fence that cleaved the fields in a chain of X's.

Across the hump-backed bridge, the gristmill wheel churned the river, sending up clouds of spray whose liquid prisms caught the sunlight and divided it. The scent of crushed grain, damp reeds, and moss pervaded the air, and everywhere along the banks willows danced to the rhythm of the wind. Dragonflies with diamond wings darted from shrub to shrub, and birds glided earthward in search of seed, while, jostling for space, water lilies floated with open petals atop the water's surface.

Chaynoa sank down in the clover blanketing the waterfront, and, drawing up her knees, inhaled great gulps of air while rocking slightly to and fro. Her pain seemed to stretch, balloon, and finally burst, and she buried her face against her knees and wept.

Finally, after the storm of her emotion had passed like a spent thundercloud, she sat and listened to the splash of the river, tasting the salt of her evaporating tears while nature embraced her like a still, enduring friend, soothed her with its old and oft-sung lullaby, hovered above her shoulder like a bruised but faithful angel. And yet, her heart was still sore and mangled, and the hope that had earlier burgeoned like a tender vine had withered.

She heard Courtland approach. She knew his step, it was steady and calm, and out of the corner of her eye she could see his boots parting the tall green thistle. He sat down beside her, and together they listened to the beating wings of a flock of osprey. Chaynoa kept her face turned away, loath to show the traces of her tears, but the awareness of her companion filled her with a new, warm pain.

"I used to come here when I was a boy," Courtland said, his low voice cleaving the silence between them. "When I was angry, or when I wanted to brood awhile, I came. I was here too often, I guess. It was during that time of my adolescence when I suddenly realized life was not fair—and never would be. That's a difficult and confusing lesson for a boy who's spent his childhood steeped in the lessons of fair play."

Chaynoa turned her head. "You were angry a great deal?"

He shrugged and looked up at the sky as if unwilling to share any more of his past. "It was long ago."

"But it still troubles you."

"Sometimes," he admitted.

"Were you unfairly accused of something?"

"Nay, just misunderstood, I suppose. And resentment played a part as well, which made matters worse. Then hatred took over and made a muddle of everything, put my life on its present course."

Chaynoa looked across the river, and in a wistful voice, asked, "If you could go back now, if you could change things so that they were different—really different—would you?"

"Unravel everything, you mean?"

"Aye, unravel everything. Where would you be, what would you be doing now?"

He released a breath, and for a long while pondered the course of the river, watched the directionless meandering of an unanchored water lily. "I wanted to return to England," he said finally, "to a place in Devonshire. I wanted to live there, study, become an artist and paint for the great London galleries."

Astonished by the revelation, Chaynoa stared at him for a moment, then asked, "But why do you not become an artist now, if that is what you really want?"

He leaned to brush the top of a clover blossom

with a long, fine-jointed hand. "The time for that is past. Long past."

Chaynoa did not know what to say. His tone was edged with bitterness, as if the years—whatever they had held for him—had never quite dimmed disappointment, as if he still yearned for something out of reach, something desperately desired and denied. She wanted to offer him comfort, but was neither adept with words nor uninhibited enough to reach out and touch him.

So they sat on, watching the millwheel revolve, watching the bits of flotsam swirl rudderless in the deep green current, watching feathers eddy like dandelion fluff upon the wind. And all at once Chaynoa realized he had turned her thoughts away from herself, taken the sharpness from her grief by making her aware that the world contained other tragedies than her own.

"They would not sell anything to me in Swanston," she confessed quietly. "They turned me away."

"Aye, Robbie told me. What will you do about it?"

"Why, nothing." She turned her eyes upon him, surprised by such a question. "There's nothing I can do."

"You can go back to their shops again. Right now. I'll go with you."

His eyes were serious as they looked into hers, and she shook her head. "Nay, I can't do it."

"Yes, you can. Here, take my hand." He clasped her fingers and drew her up. She did not move, and slowly, gently, he pulled her close, drawing her so near that her cheek rested against the ridge of his shoulder.

His shirt felt warm with the sun and with his own coursing blood. Never had Chaynoa been held close to a man in tenderness, and she did not shrink away now, but remained still and mute, smelling the pine resin upon his skin, seeing the dark hair against his nape, feeling the slight pressure of his hand on her spine. And suddenly, she no longer heard the churn of the water wheel or the sough of the wind, only his heart beating against her own. When he touched her cheek she regarded his finely made fingers, tough and calloused from hard work instead of smooth from the wielding of an artist's brush. His face was ruddy with sun, his breeches stained with soil, and tiny slivers of bark clung to his forearms below his turned-back cuffs.

She let her head rest against him for long moments and closed her eyes, quivering with tangled emotions, but one thought was clear: through some whim of divine grace the best man in all of Christendom held on to her.

Chapter 13

Courtland sat at his desk the next morning, penning a dispatch to General Gage. He dipped the nib into the ink again and began a second page, writing of the increasingly marked division between those colonials who called themselves patriots and those Tories who expressed loyalty to King George. Heated arguments kept the tavern in commotion, and long-time friendships often dissolved during the course of an ordinary evening that had begun with a shared sixpence worth of rum.

Frankly, Courtland thought the colonials were having difficulty deciding what it was they wanted, for they were not calling for revolution, nor did they seem certain that Britain should be ousted from America. But they did not like to be taxed, and they certainly did not like their port closed to trade. The economic pinch was being felt, and yet Courtland suspected that such coercion would do nothing except drive more good men into the patriot ranks. He wrote:

> The Sons of Liberty organization and those who lead it in Boston will determine the Future of Britain's colonies. Do not underestimate

them, Your Excellency; they are neither ignorant nor apathetic. They are alarmed by the
continued arrival of British troops in Boston,
and there is much speculation as to your Inten-
tions. They are attempting to smuggle stores of
gunpowder from France. As for the Town
Meetings, I have learned nothing of interest—
unless, of course, the hiring of a new schoolmaster and the repair of the Church roof are of
interest to you.

With an amused smile Courtland concluded his
letter and sanded it. Then he looked beyond the door
into the kitchen where Chaynoa sat beside the hearth
sewing.

Her nimble fingers fairly flew over the pale muslin
as her needle flashed in and out, and he smiled, for
she seemed desperate to complete the gown in the
space of one night. He was sorry that she had refused
to buy more than the ten yards required for one
garment, but she had insisted that most women spun
their own flax and wove it, and that she would do the
same when she had saved enough of her wages to
have a loom made. The words had struck him, for he
realized that Chaynoa foresaw as a permanent arrangement her future as his servant. Only he knew
that nothing was permanent; within a few months'
time he would be gone, fighting her countrymen, no
doubt.

Courtland recalled their talk beside the river this
morning, and remembered with a kind of excruciating yet pleasurable unease the moments Chaynoa
had allowed him to hold her. He had escorted her
and Hahnee back to the village, giving warning
glances to any who dared to stare at her unkindly.
The women had not crossed him, and the men had

responded to him with their usual good will—some even grinned and tipped their hats in Chaynoa's direction, a gesture which vexed Courtland because he suspected they assumed her to be his mistress. It was an assumption he would have to dispel.

He had suggested to Chaynoa that they go to the cobbler's shop first, and there the squint-eyed maker of shoes brought out a tanned square of leather and bade Chaynoa set her foot upon it, explaining how he would bore holes in the leather with an awl, then sew them up with thread stiffened in beeswax.

Hahnee proved an enthralled listener, and his childlike visage beamed when he was given a length of the coarse thread. Courtland gave him five pence halfpenny, the price for plain shoes, and let him pay the cobbler himself.

When they returned to the milliner, Chaynoa did not hang back, eager to give Mrs. Finley her comeuppance now that Courtland stood beside her. She swept into the shop, repeating her order for goods in a quiet but dignified way, and the woman complied, seeing by Courtland's steady stare that he had no patience for mean-mindedness.

Molly Hodge proved no less uncooperative, but even though she was transparently eager to appear gracious in Courtland's eyes, he could read her resentment whenever she glanced Chaynoa's way.

Now, from his desk, he scrutinized his maidservant, watching the way her hands moved, the way her foot flexed to rock the chair. Her head was bent low over the froth of fabric, for she sewed by candlelight, and although the glow bathed her lap in warm gold, it was a dim glow by which to work. The early summer evening smelled of the white lilies that budded beneath his open window, and he fancied he could smell the odor of the river mingled with them. All at once, remembered sensations enervated his body, and he shut his eyes, recalling the way her young body had felt against the length of his own on the riverbank today. "Chaynoa . . . ?"

She looked up.

" 'Tis late and the light is poor. Why don't you go upstairs to bed?"

She smoothed the folds draped across her legs with a reverent hand. "I'll remain up until I finish. I want to start cutting Hahnee's clothes on the morrow—although I'm not certain he will concede to wear them. His old things are a comfort to him. I suppose taking them from him would be like plucking feathers from a bird."

Courtland folded the dispatch and placed it within the top drawer of his desk, which he locked before pocketing the key. "Let him be comfortable then." He picked up the quill again, sharpened its tip with a penknife fished from his pocket, knowing very well that he delayed going to bed in order to stare at her a few minutes more. The moist breeze, the warmth, and the rhythmic creak of Chaynoa's chair affected his senses, and again and again he raised his eyes to glance her way. He watched the sway of her body in the chair, the controlled, in and out flourishes of her hands, and thought he would go mad wanting to feel those hands touch his own body . . . For the first time, and with disquietude, he admitted to himself that he wanted to make love to her. Madness, he thought.

"Good night." His words were strained and abrupt, and pinching the candle flame, he shoved back his chair and stalked upstairs alone.

The following morning was the Sabbath, and before the sun brushed the night sky with its wash of violet, Chaynoa snapped the hem thread with her teeth and shook out the gown she had made. Her eyes burned with strain, and for a moment the image of the garment blurred. Plain it was, as a maidservant's attire should be, with square neckline and pointed bodice at the waist, its only adornment the ruffles at its elbow-length sleeves. Nevertheless, to her, the garment was beautiful, whole and clean and new.

Although she was weary from her night of labor, she could scarcely wait to don the gown. But first, hearing the sound of Courtland's footsteps on the floor above, and knowing that he prepared to dress and shave before coming down, she hastily fanned the embers of the fire and went out into the still dark morning to fill the kettle from the well, discovering on her return a pail of fresh milk and a dozen eggs by the stoop.

"Thank you, dear Robbie," she whispered aloud, for he had saved her a trip to his house.

After gathering up the gifts she hastened inside to hard-boil the eggs and make hasty pudding out of corn meal, milk, and maple syrup. Setting out ham and the earthenware pot of coffee, she laid Courtland's place, then crept upstairs with her gown and a bucket of water to wash and rinse her hair.

Courtland found his breakfast on the table, still steaming, as he had the previous day, and shook his head, marveling at Chaynoa's timing. After he had eaten, he grabbed his hat and made for the door, intent on feeding the horses, but the sound of a light step upon the stairway arrested him.

He pivoted and found Chaynoa standing on the third step down, wearing the new gown. It was modest, unembellished, a few shades paler than her dusky skin, and where the old rag she had previously worn had hung upon her body, this garment clung, out-

HERE'S A SPECIAL INVITATION TO ENJOY TODAY'S FINEST HISTORICAL ROMANCES— ABSOLUTELY FREE! *(a $19.96 value)*

Now you can enjoy the latest Zebra Lovegram Historical Romances without even leaving your home with our convenient Zebra Home Subscription Service. Zebra Home Subscription Service offers you the following benefits that you don't want to miss:

- 4 BRAND NEW bestselling Zebra Lovegram Historical Romances delivered to your doorstep each month (usually before they're available in the bookstores!)

- 20% off each title or a savings of almost $4.00 each month

- FREE home delivery

- A FREE monthly newsletter, *Zebra/Pinnacle Romance News* that features author profiles, contests, special member benefits, book previews and more

- No risks or obligations...in other words you can cancel whenever you wish with no questions asked

So join hundreds of thousands of readers who already belong to Zebra Home Subscription Service and enjoy the very best Historical Romances That Burn With The Fire of History!

And remember....there is no minimum purchase required. After you've enjoyed your initial FREE package of 4 books, you'll begin to receive monthly shipments of new Zebra titles. Each shipment will be yours to examine for 10 days and then if you decide to keep the books, you'll pay the preferred subscriber's price of just $4.00 per title. That's $16 for all 4 books with FREE home delivery! And if you want us to stop sending books, just say the word....it's that simple.

It's a no-lose proposition, so send for your 4 FREE books today!

4 FREE BOOKS

These books worth almost $20, are yours without cost or obligation when you fill out and mail this certificate.
(If the certificate is missing below, write to: Zebra Home Subscription Service, Inc., 120 Brighton Road, P.O. Box 5214, Clifton, New Jersey 07015-5214)

Complete and mail this card to receive 4 Free books!

YES! Please send me 4 Zebra Lovegram Historical Romances without cost or obligation. I understand that each month thereafter I will be able to preview 4 new Zebra Lovegram Historical Romances FREE for 10 days. Then if I decide to keep them, I will pay the money-saving preferred publisher's price of just $4.00 each...a total of $16. That's almost $4 less than the regular publisher's price, and there is never any additional charge for shipping and handling. I may return any shipment within 10 days and owe nothing, and I may cancel this subscription at any time. The 4 FREE books will be mine to keep in any case.

Name _____

Address _____ Apt. _____

City _____ State _____ Zip _____

Telephone ( ) _____

Signature _____
(If under 18, parent or guardian must sign.)

LF0596

A $19.96 value.... absolutely FREE with no obligation to buy anything, ever!

lined the curve of her ribs and bosom, which belled
up from a neat waist. Her arms, always lithe, seemed
long and elegant where they emerged from their
fringe of ruffled sleeves, and atop the crown of her
head she wore a white ruched cap. But the most
startling transformation was in her face.

Brushed back in two smooth wings away from her
brow, her hair was woven into a single braid, which
fell across one shoulder in a thick twining of umber,
black, and sorrel shades. He realized that he had
never seen the whole of her countenance before: the
small ears, the full but well-shaped jaw, the temples
with their gentle hollows, and the sinuous curve of
her neck. She gazed out at him through the virgin
eyes of a young doe, eyes set in a face of a woman,
and her cheeks were overlaid with shifting patterns of
light filtering through the leaves beyond the window,
lending her the contradictory looks of both fawn and
coquette.

In response to her womanliness, Courtland experienced a strong physical reaction, the kind he had not
felt since the first flush of youthful manhood when
such bodily sensations where fresh and mysterious
and excruciating. Where he had previously considered Chaynoa an enchanting but eccentric girl from
the woods—an oddity—he now saw her through different eyes, as a part of his own world; and somehow,
that new impression changed his perspective of her in
a forceful way.

"I-Is something wrong with it?"

Courtland realized that he had unnerved her with
his stare, but he did not look away. "No. There's
nothing wrong with it."

With a nervous hand she touched her braid and
bent her smoothly brushed head. "I—I'd like leave to
go and visit my friend Sadie today—Iris Oakchurch

said she was employed now at the Lancaster's big house on the common." She bit her lip and demured, "Th-that is, if you can spare me for an hour or so."

"You need never ask me for leave to do anything, Chaynoa. You're free to come and go as you please. Always."

She took a step down, her fine-boned hand still poised upon the banister. "I'll be back in an hour then. Did you . . . did you get enough breakfast to eat?"

His gaze remained intense. "Aye. You have a talent for cooking."

"Mam taught me. She had a way with things— cooking, sewing, gardening, and the like. And among my father's people she was known for her healing skills."

"It seems you've inherited her abilities."

"Do you like it—the gown, I mean?" she asked awkwardly.

"I like it very much."

She flushed beneath his candid admiration, but her worry lingered. "Do you think the women will judge it too full in the skirt for a servant?"

"Do you really care so much?"

"Yes."

"Then I think they'll be envious."

She laughed nervously, putting a hand to her cheek. "Oh, nay. That could never be." But she seemed pleased with his comment and gave him a shy smile before stepping all the way down the stairs. He did not shift his position, and her skirts brushed his legs as she slipped by to exit through the front door.

Behind her, Courtland stood rooted in place for several seconds, clutching his hat, staring like an idiot at the place upon the banister where her hand had trailed.

Chaynoa walked down the road briskly, feeling as
if she had been refashioned, transformed, as if she
actually belonged on the lane that led to the cluster
of sunny houses and flowered yards. The steeple bell
tolled, calling its faithful flock to Sunday meeting,
and both townsfolk and countryfolk began to flood
the streets donned in their best fashions. Rural residents trundled along in ox-drawn carts, their bonneted, fresh-faced children squeezed together like
pansies in flower boxes. Some came on foot, the men
wearing brown jackets and their wives in faded
gowns dyed gray-pink with pokeberry, all with tattered Bibles tucked beneath their arms. Most of the
town denizens wore a better quality of clothes, with
silver buckles on knee breeches and garnet brooches
on bodices.

As people overtook her on the road, Chaynoa
glanced up, and with a new confidence underpinned
by her respectable clothes, offered them tentative
smiles. But when the women realized her identity,
they raised their noses and turned their heads away
without acknowledgment.

Iris Oakchurch stood in her front garden, and with
a slow step Chaynoa passed her gate. The ancient,
shrunken dame was garbed in her neat black Sunday
gown, gloves, and bonnet, and the ensemble gave her
the look of a little girl dressed up for play in her
mother's clothes. "Going to meeting, child?" she
queried in her tremulous voice.

"No, ma'am. "I'm going to visit Sadie."

"Ah, yes. Growing big with child, that one is. She's
blessed that the Lancasters took her on. Good people, they are. Hello, Mrs. Finley," she called when
that starched-faced matron sailed past.

"Good morning, Iris. Good morning—" Recog-
nizing Chaynoa, the milliner folded her arms across

her meager chest and huffed, crossing the street in a swish of stiff taffeta without completing the greeting.

Chaynoa scoffed. "How is it that people can be uncharitable on the way to church, Iris?"

The old one sighed. "Folks is folks. It takes them awhile to warm up to someone different."

"But I don't want to be different. I want to live as they do, have friends, be invited to their house raisings and their corn huskings and—"

"Then you'll have to make them think including you in their circle is to their advantage—but first, dear, decide if that circle is worthy of you. If you think it is, I'll help you." With a misshapen forefinger she touched the black wooly back of a caterpillar inching its way along a canna stalk. "This ugly wee creature will blossom into a butterfly ere long. Robbie!" She thumped her cane on the ground and looked toward the house. "Come along now, boy, or we'll be late for meeting. A good day to you, Chaynoa."

"Bye, Iris."

Although Sadie was confined to bed, her health and color appeared much improved since Chaynoa's last visit. Before the month's end she would be delivered of her child, and she spoke contentedly of the event, especially now that the shadow that had formerly hovered over her life had been lifted. At first, neither she nor Chaynoa mentioned the name of that cloud—the babe's father—skirting talk of him, each in respect of the other's grievous memories.

But when Chaynoa rose to take her leave, Sadie plucked softly at her sleeve. "I've pondered it for a long time, and I believe I've figured out how it was that Julius came to know you'd been to visit me— how he came to follow you that night."

Chaynoa turned about to stare at her friend. She,

too, had deliberated the puzzle endlessly, but to no avail.

" 'Twas the elixir you made up for me and left here," Sadie explained. "The one that smells strongly of marigold and is the color of blueberry juice. He discovered it in my room, and although I thought nothing of it at the time, I realized afterward that your mother had often mixed it for him when he was ill with his stomach ailments. 'Tis a mixture like no other I know, and it must have struck a chord of memory in his brain."

Chaynoa put a hand upon the bedpost and leaned her brow against it. " 'Tis strange . . ." she breathed, relieved to have the mystery solved at last, "how something meant for good ends up as a tool of evil."

"He always behaved as if he thought you would return to Swanston—or, if he were afraid that you would. But let's speak of more pleasant topics. Tell me about your Mr. Day. Is he a good man to serve?"

"Oh, yes." Chaynoa lowered her eyes. "He—he's like no other man I've ever met."

"You aren't the only girl with that opinion," Sadie remarked with a smile. "They're all envious of you."

"They have no reason to be."

"Are you certain?" Sadie probed. She could have related the gossip that was being whispered over the patchwork quilts the ladies of Swanston gathered to piece on Tuesdays, but she was loath to make her friend ill at ease.

"I'm certain."

"That's grand, Chaynoa. You seem content, and you look well. You did a fine job sewing that gown— look at the stitches. Far better than I can do."

Chaynoa smiled and took her leave. And although Sadie had been silent on the subject of the slanderous talk that was being exchanged from whispering lips to eager ears, those in the streets were less discreet with their tongues. As Courtland Day's maidservant walked home in her new muslin gown, she passed two boys idling on the common, obvious truants from church. They sniggered, then dogged her steps, and, as she turned on to Queen's Road, began singing a loud, crude song.

"There goes the liveryman's piece, the liveryman's piece, off to serve her master!"

A haying had been organized by the farmers of Swanston. It was a long-time tradition that neighbors assisted neighbors in the early summer harvesting, gathering at dawn and laboring all day from field to field, then culminating the event with a scything contest and picnic. Courtland had volunteered to participate and, rising long before dawn, quietly crept down the stairs in hopes that he could slip out of the house without disturbing Chaynoa's sleep.

But she was already at work in the candlelit kitchen, moving about as noiselessly as the breeze. She held the waffle iron over the fire, and when the batter was done, flipped the crisp gold square molded with diamond shapes onto a platter for him.

He glanced at the room, and as his eyes took in the loaves of fresh bread on the cupboard shelves and the gleaming pewter plates, it seemed the most welcoming place he had ever entered. The butter churn sat beside the hearth next to the rocking chair, and a jar of honey, the comb stolen from a hollow tree by Hahnee, rested on the windowsill. More and more each day, Courtland looked forward to this morning ritual of eating breakfast while Chaynoa moved about the kitchen.

"I plan to join the men today at the harvesting," he commented, reaching for the pot of coffee.

Chaynoa's swift hands seized the handle before he could, and while he looked on with a tolerant smile she poured the fragrant brew into his mug.

"If you have no objections," he continued, "I'll try and coax Hahnee to come along with me."

She was pleased with his offer. " 'Tis kind of you to think of him. People tend not to, you know, as if he had no brains or no feelings." Her voice grew sad. "His name means beggar. My father called him that after he was born, predicting that he would always live at the mercy of others and have no blessings."

"Hahnee is innocent—far more innocent than any of the rest of us. Perhaps that's his blessing."

Chaynoa glanced up at Courtland's face, fancying that she had heard a faint note of guilt in his tone, but he continued the conversation casually enough. "There's a picnic this evening after the haying. Will you come?"

She moved to the opposite end of the table and, pushing up her sleeves, began rolling out a mound of dough she had earlier kneaded. "There's washing to be done, and cheese to make. And I haven't got the garden weeded yet."

Courtland wondered why she made so great an effort to affect a flippant tone. Something bothered her today, for her smooth brow was puckered fretfully, and she seemed to roll the pin faster and faster over the dough in nervous energy. "What's the matter, Chaynoa," he asked concernedly. "What troubles you?"

The rolling pin bobbled. "Nothing. Nothing at all."

"Are you certain?"

"Yes."

He sighed and, still hoping to tempt her to change her mind about the picnic, said, "Iris Oakchurch will be there today. And Robbie."

"I'll pack you a picnic meal and bring it to you if you like. But I'll not stay."

Her tone was unusually hard and stubborn, and as she sprinkled coarse brown sugar over the raw pastry, Courtland observed her closely. He wanted her to go with him, wanted to see her laugh and smile as a young woman should, but she had dug in her heels, and he knew that pushing her to comply would do no good. He had to remind himself that he had just plucked her from the woods like a wild rabbit, and therefore would have to be patient with her elusiveness for a while.

Finishing his meal, he thanked her and settled his hat atop his head, then gave her a brief glance, that, had she seen it, would have revealed his wistfulness. "Your name—" he asked all at once. "What does your name mean?"

She looked up at him as if caught off guard, then lowered her eyes to the dough again. "Dove," she murmured. "My name means white dove."

He crossed the floor and, taking up a knife from the table, went to consider the batch of dough she had flattened. It was as smooth and clean as unrolled parchment, and she watched in fascination while he moved the knife point over the pastry and drew a series of fine, delicate lines using no more than a few strokes. In no time a fanciful image emerged from the unlikely canvas. After laying down the knife, Courtland gave her a brief and mischievous smile, then went out the door.

She marveled at the talented hand that had left a picture imprinted upon such an ordinary thing as a piece of pastry dough meant to be an apple tart. It was a picture of a dove, one with a graceful neck and outstretched wings, one that was flying freely.

She ran to the open window, thrust her head through, and followed with her eyes the faint blur of the artist's white shirt until she could see it no more.

Chapter 14

It was late afternoon when Chaynoa packed a basket of some of Mrs. Oakchurch's aged cheese, bread, currants, smoked beef, and the apple tarts she had earlier made. Covering the small feast with a square of bleached linen, she left a pork roast turning on the spit and went out the door.

Basket in hand, she set out for the fields, seeing the distant patches of stubbly landscape where the men had labored all day with their scythes, seeing the stalks of grain bundled and tied into shocks, which sat everywhere upon the fresh-sheared earth like strange, towheaded giants. The scent of the severed stalks drifted across the land in wafts that seemed to hold the smell of life itself, and instead of viewing the earth as ravaged, Chaynoa viewed it as a sort of deity that every year sacrificed its fruit before replenishing and dying again in an endless miracle.

She paused, closed her eyes, and said a prayer in reverence to the miracle, one that began with litanies learned from her childhood amongst the Delaware, and ended with a strictly Puritan amen.

Close to the river she spied a large crowd of people gathered on a hillside, and as she neared, a ruddy-faced yeoman waved his arms to gain attention, and then announced through cupped hands that the scything contest was due to begin.

Chaynoa slowed and shifted the heavy basket on her arm. Loath to attract notice, she then veered north to skirt the group of women and children bearing picnic baskets to be shared with their menfolk when the competition ended.

How lovely the party of women looked, she thought. Their petticoated skirts billowed in the wind, their white aprons flapped, and their huge calash bonnets nodded gently as they chatted in shifting knots. Children executed cartwheels and galloped about the stubble, some gleaning behind their mothers, who collected armloads of fallen grain and stacked it in neat bundles to dry.

Chaynoa searched for Courtland amongst the assembly of men, who were now forming a loose huddle about the contest organizer. He was easy to spot, for he was the tallest of them all. Looking for a vantage point where she could watch him but not be easily seen by others, she hastened along a line of alder trees to an outcropping of rock and, spreading her skirts, sat down to await the excitement.

The contestants of the scything event spaced themselves ten feet apart in a field that had not yet been mown, each preparing to cut his own row of grain. The winner would be the man who finished scything his row first.

Chaynoa watched Courtland carry his scythe to the large grindstone which had been placed conveniently beneath a shade tree for the use of the men. He motioned to Hahnee, who was following the children, and handed him the long-handled tool before demonstrating the way to sharpen it.

Chaynoa's heart was warmed by the kindness, and with pride she watched her brother attempt to hone the blade while Courtland guided him. Between the two of them, the metal was sharpened with no mishap, and Courtland strolled off to rejoin the line of men. The signal to start was given, and with the others, he began to cut his row.

The women cheered, waving their homespun handkerchiefs, and gleeful children jumped up and down excitedly, urging on their favorite. No less thrilled, Chaynoa found herself clenching her fingers in hopes Courtland would be the champion, noting how his body rocked in time with the powerful sweep of his arm, how the blade glinted with sunlight. He was broader of shoulder than any of the rest, and his movements were coordinated in the natural way of one who has learned a skill in childhood and never forgotten its cadence.

Tom Shandy worked almost as swiftly, but could not catch up as the last few yards of grain fell beneath Courtland's flashing scythe, and when the contest ended, the surly young man was the only one not to shake hands with the victor.

Simon Peebles cantered into the midst of the gathering astride the back of an English thoroughbred, and behind him a black servant drove a cart filled with kegs of rum and cider. Magnanimously, with outspread arms, Simon offered drinks for all, and with much laughter and good cheer the townsfolk queued up to quench their thirst with the free libations.

As Chaynoa watched the merry throng, sitting apart in her secluded place, as she followed Courtland with her eyes while he moved easily about the others, she felt a pang of exclusion greater than any she had ever felt before. How she wanted to be among them, laughing, sharing, chatting with the women about gardening, babies, and the price of sugar. Her eyes fastened upon the ringleted girls who clustered about Courtland, and she felt jealous. She wanted to march down and join them, lay a hand upon his sleeve, quietly deflect the attention of the other maids with a claim of her own.

She saw his teeth flash in response to some remark coyly delivered by a fair-haired girl, and she wondered in anguish if before the day was out, he would select a sweetheart, and this year or next, carry her home as his bride.

Across the field a small commotion ensued. Simon Peebles unsheathed a musket which the men lined up to admire, for it was much finer than their fowling pieces or smaller caliber replicas. Even though it was only a common Brown Bess—so called because its barrel was discolored with a brown preservative—and despite the fact that the model had been carried by the British army for more than fifty years, it was still coveted by these yeomen, for none could afford to own one.

Chaynoa noted that Courtland was the only man uninterested in the spectacle; he leaned against the cart drinking cider, and watched while his stepfather took out several lightweight wooden targets and paced off a firing distance.

"Eighty yards!" Simon shouted, setting up the targets. "What man will wager he can hit the mark?"

Several volunteers stepped forward eagerly, and a friendly contest of marksmanship ensued, with only two contestants proving skillful enough to strike the bull's-eye. When the targets were moved back to one hundred yards, the sunburnt farmers guffawed.

"Hope that musket has a straight bore!" one yelled. "Only Tom Shandy has an eye good enough to hit anything that far out! And since his is a Tory eye now, 'tis likely it's half blind!"

Irritated by the condemnation of his loyalty, Tom Shandy was more than willing to display his skill. Reloading the weapon, he aimed and hit his mark, much to the delight of those spectators who had wagered on his success.

"Now a hundred and twenty-five yards!" shouted Peebles with an officious flourish of his hand.

The entire crowd of men told him scoffingly to resheath the weapon rather than shame it.

"Hah!" Jeremiah Hullover hooted. "May as well shoot at the moon! A man would have to have one of those fancy new long-barreled rifles from Kentucky to hit anything at that range!"

The prediction seemed true, for Tom Shandy could not even graze the target, nor could anyone else who tried.

"Give Mr. Day a turn!" Robbie Oakchurch called. "He ain't tried yet!"

Courtland shook his head and smiled, but the boy would not be dissuaded from his purpose, and, tugging upon his friend's hand, pulled him insistently toward the others.

Courtland had won many premiums for being the best marksman in his regiment, and although most men, given the opportunity, would be eager to show their talent, he was reluctant; through his army training, shooting had become a serious business to him, not some evening's entertainment on a hillside of picnicking colonials. Nevertheless, unwilling to appear a poor sport, and surmising that he could win the approval of the locals and therefore further Gage's mission, he accepted the challenge.

Clasping the musket by its barrel, he weighed the weapon, its feel as familiar to his hand as plow handles were to these yeomen. His stepfather eyed him with a curious gaze, and the others quieted as well, as if something in his manner, consciously revealed or not, arrested their interest.

A cartridge was handed to him. He tore it open with his teeth, tasting its saline grittiness, and with the butt of the weapon on the ground, poured the powder and ball into the muzzle, then crumbled the paper and rammed it with the rod. Next, he lifted the frizzen and batted the barrel with his hand so the powder filtered through the touchhole into the pan.

Ready to fire, he raised the gun to his shoulder in one easy gesture, and out of the corner of his eye saw the homely, earnest faces of the villagers; many of them he knew, a few he even liked. He felt a sudden prickling down his spine, a presage, and wondered if he would soon be sighting them with his own musket in hand, firing at them in war.

He cocked the weapon and pulled the trigger.

The target fell, and the report of the weapon echoed round the valley while smoke wended up from the firing pan.

"He hit it, by God!" someone exclaimed incredulously. "A hundred and twenty-five yards, and he hit it on the first try! What d'ye make of it, boys?"

"Hell, let's put him out on the Boston Road and let him wait for the bloody redcoats! He can pick 'em off one by one if that bastard Gage thinks to send 'em up here!"

A tankard of rum was shoved into Courtland's hand, but he could scarcely drink it for the hearty back slapping he received from weathered hands. Simon Peebles strolled close, one hand thrust into the pocket of his expensive gold-colored coat, upon which a few grains of snuff clung. He brushed them away with a flick of his fingers, looked Courtland up and down, and asked smoothly, "With so much of your time spent aboard ship, where did you learn to shoot like that?"

The men quieted to hear the reply, and Courtland regarded his stepfather with cold eyes. "My father gave me a fowling piece on my seventh birthday. I made good use of it."

The yeomen laughed. "Hah," one said, "all of us got fowling pieces when we were lads, but you don't see us hittin' targets at a hundred and twenty-five yards!"

"Who cares where he learned to shoot," Hullover declared, "just so long as he's willing to lay out any of King George's soldiers who think to overstep their bounds!"

Tom Shandy, hanging back from the crowd surrounding Courtland, watched with a sullen expression. He had not forgiven Day for his interference in the burning of the Indian girl's cabin in the woods. To add to his general surliness, he was a Tory loyal to the Crown, and the treasonous talk here angered him, caused him to be more than willing to provoke a fight with Day—who seemed to side with the patriots.

Stepping forward, he shouldered his way into the center of the men and demanded, "Would Courtland Day be foolish enough to murder the very soldiers we depend upon for our protection?"

Murmurs rippled through the ranks, punctuated by a few antagonistic mumblings.

"Protection from what?" Peebles inquired with a scoff. "The French are long gone from here."

Shandy turned on him. "That they are. And 'twas the British army who routed them from the colonies and from Canada. Although England is the richest country in the world, she's now the deepest in debt because of a war that ended to our own benefit. Why shouldn't we pay higher taxes to help bail her out of trouble?"

"Bail out a fat, mad old king who sits atop a throne three thousand miles away?" Hullover roared. "In your eye!"

"You may not speak so rashly if the Indians decide to start raiding us again," Shandy spat.

Courtland judged it a propitious time to add his own remarks, and he did so with a serious mien which covered his amusement over playing the turncoat. "The Indians aren't likely to attack without the French here to goad them. Besides, from what I've seen of the frontiersmen, they're far better able to deal with Indians than any of those London-bred gamblers King George calls soldiers."

Much to Shandy's ire, rounds of hearty agreement followed, and as Courtland glanced at the angry young man, it occurred to him in the wriest sort of irony that the two of them stood on the same side of the political fence.

"We don't have to worry about the Indians," Hullover drawled. "We've got bloody redcoats with guns pointed at us. I've just heard that they seized a whole storehouse of colonial powder over in Cambridge three days ago."

"Maybe that'll keep some of you hotheaded rebels from starting a rebellion you can't possibly win," Shandy sneered.

Fearful that the intensifying argument would spoil the picnic, the women began drawing food out of baskets and begged their men to stop bickering and eat. After a few grumbles, the chastised husbands left off their discussion and obeyed.

Courtland found himself faced with several unattached girls, and each issued charming invitations to join their families. He was deciding how best to handle the situation when he caught sight of Chaynoa.

She was walking toward him with a basket over her arm, crossing in a slow, graceful tread the stubbly field he had earlier cut with his scythe. Her eyes were fixed straight ahead, looking at no one else but him, and as she neared, the others began to take note of her and grow still. Even the children, sensing the adults' sudden interest, paused in their play to stare. The entire hillside seemed motionless in that moment, except for the unhurried progress of the tall, dark-skinned girl in her simple muslin gown. By the time she had reached Courtland's side, every pair of eyes was riveted to her figure.

"I watched you with the scythe and the musket," she said, speaking low so that no one else could hear. "You were the best of them all."

He took hold of the basket handle, one of his hands crossing over hers. "Stay," he said with earnestness. "Stay."

But she shook her head and slid her hand away from his. "You must see that I can't. 'Tis better for us both if I don't."

"Chaynoa—"

But she ignored him, quickly making her way alone down the hillside, where blackbirds scattered in her wake. Courtland watched her slim young back, watched the single braid as it swung back and forth like a rope of woven silk.

Tom Shandy stepped up beside him, tearing into a turkey leg with strong short teeth. "Not bad to look at, is she? All that brown skin and hair. Of course, they say that what's between a squaw's legs is sweeter than what's between a white woman's. That true, Day?"

Courtland threw aside the basket, hauled back a fist and hit him.

The stunned young man reeled and nearly stumbled to the ground, but rabid for a fight with Day, regained his balance and charged, butting Courtland in the abdomen and bringing him down to the ground. The others dropped their food and hastened over to circle the combatants, the men shouting out encouragement while the women shook their heads.

Courtland scrambled to his feet, grasped Shandy by the collar, and hauled him up before sinking a fist into his ribs. In exchange, he received a blow to the nose, then one to the mouth Skillfully, he delivered an uppercut to Shandy's chin which proved so forceful that the man tottered backward and fell. Dazed, Shandy failed to regain his feet, staying on his knees with his head hanging between his shoulders while his wife shrieked and flew to aid him.

Courtland dabbed the blood from his chin and pinched his throbbing nose while several men slapped him on the back and murmured their approval. In no mood to talk, he ignored them, but Hullover sidled nearer and spoke in a tone so low that only those standing closest could hear. "We've all been eager to see Tom Shandy knocked on his backside. Damned Tory, he is, while you're a man who's not afraid to defend our own brand of politics. We like that—matter of fact, there's a meeting over at the Stirrup and Iron tomorrow evening at ten o'clock. Know what I mean?"

"I'm listening," Courtland said, wiping blood off his lip with his sleeve.

Hullover leaned closer and spoke under his breath. "Ever heard of the Sons of Liberty? We'd like you to join us."

Courtland bent to retrieve the basket of food, and

turning to go, answered over his shoulder. "I'll be there."

"Fine. You'll be a good man for our organization."

Walking home slowly, Courtland followed the same route Chaynoa had earlier used, his bruised body weary from his day of labor and aching from the fight with Shandy. If he had not been so tired he would have laughed over the colonials' misinterpretation of the fight. But, the brawl had been the spur that had gained him an invitation into the secret society, so he figured it was well worth the bloody nose, if not the slur to Chaynoa's honor. He growled, and anger burned within him.

Hahnee galloped after him, circling like a faithful puppy, distressed over the sight of blood on Courtland's shirt. Laying a hand on his shoulder, Courtland reassured him, and the young man trotted ahead carrying the scythe, which he brandished above his head like a rapier.

When Courtland pushed open the back door, he found Chaynoa seated in the rocking chair sewing a new pewter button on his waistcoat. At sight of him, she threw down the garment and rose, staring at his face in dismay.

"Courtland!"

Without saying anything, he plunged his hands in the bucket of water beside the hearth and rinsed his face and neck. As the water dripped from his jaw, he thought again of Shandy's crude remarks, and knew that similar insults had likely been bandied about the tavern for days. He could well imagine the vulgarities, the names they had branded Chaynoa over their tankards of rum. Closing his eyes, he felt wrath swell inside his chest again.

"Courtland, what happened?"

"Nothing." Going to the table, he sank down, and in an ill-temper dabbed at his lip with a handkerchief. His face hurt like the devil, every muscle in his body throbbed, and he wished Chaynoa would leave the room, leave him alone to nurse both his injuries and his anger.

But she did not. She quietly fetched linen and salve and came to stand behind his shoulder. "It was because of me wasn't it?" she asked softly. "You fought because of me."

He pressed his handkerchief to his nose and did not reply, but she persisted. "You needn't keep anything secret in order to spare my feelings. I—I know what they say about me—I know the name they call me in the village."

His head jerked up, and with narrowed eyes he demanded, "What name? What name do they call you?"

"The . . . the liveryman's piece."

He swore. "Damned ignorant sods! Has any man dared to offend you? I'll thrash him if he has, by God."

"Courtland, 'tis the way they've been raised to think. Prejudices are passed down. They don't know me yet."

Her defense of them, of the very people who had maligned and exiled her the whole of her life, served to aggravate him more. He would rather see her spit upon them, curse them to their faces as they deserved than make excuses for them.

"Your Puritan mother must have preached to turn the other cheek," he drawled derisively, sneering at her. "Well, she did you one hell of a disservice."

He could feel her eyes fastened to his face, full and wounded by his cruelty, and his emotions grew jumbled. It infuriated him that she made him feel confused, made him feel protective, and because he was discomfited he offered no words to ease her own distress.

She quietly sat down beside him, and he saw that she held the jar of salve and a clean piece of linen, which she had folded into a square. He remembered the time she had tended him in the woodlet cottage, remembered how afraid and repulsed she had been, and knew that she would stretch out her capable hands now, and with no reluctance at all, care for him. But he did not want her attentions. Not now. If she touched him he would seize her fingers and press them to his lips, babble something he would later rue, plead for something she would not give him—now or ever. And so, when she reached to press the cool cloth to his mouth, he jerked his head away.

Her hand fell back. Then, rising from her seat, she ran from the room.

Left alone, Courtland sat staring at the hearth fire with his fists clenched. For several long and seething minutes he stared at it, and then he pushed back the bench and, throwing down the wadded handkerchief, followed Chaynoa up the stairs. The door to her attic chamber was shut, but he thrust his shoulder against the flimsy planks, shoving so hard the portal reverberated against the wall.

Chaynoa started, stared at him through the darkness. Behind her a breeze blew through the open window, making the curtain billow and snap, framing her head with a living white veil.

Courtland stepped close, and, stretching out his hands, settled them firmly upon her shoulders. His fingers closed over her sleeves, gripped them so hard that the fabric wadded beneath his palms. She closed her eyes and sank against him as if there were no strength in her limbs to stand, and Courtland bent his head and swiftly put his swollen mouth to hers, the blood from his lip tasting bitter even against the sweetness borrowed from her tongue. Her arms wrapped around his neck, her hands grabbed his hair, and he responded without restraint. The two of them pressed their mouths together, touched with harsh breaths and ungentle hands, grappled to caress through the hindrance of their clothes.

He put his lips to her ear, her hair, which felt coarse and warm with life, then trailed his tongue along the curve of her smooth throat. She responded with the instinct of the wild creatures she had lived amongst, frenziedly pulling his hips into hers, slipping her hand beneath his shirt to feel the heat of his hard shoulders, whimpering when his hand invaded her neckline and explored her intimately.

At the feel of her firm, youthful flesh Courtland experienced a drive more violent than ever before, and it burgeoned with both his anger and his long-held infatuation. He held her face forcibly between his palms and kissed her mouth, his control slipping, his hands growing rougher on her breasts, more insistent. Aware of nothing but his need for her, he fumbled with her skirts, pushed them up, backed her to the bed with his body, intent upon finishing what he had started.

She began to struggle, cry, and in an instant her own need evolved into senseless terror. She pushed him, slapped his hands away, shoved him back so that his hip collided with a table and sent it toppling to the floor. Amidst the sound of its splintering he stared into her anguished eyes, which she covered with her hands in a gesture of despair. "Don't touch me like that!" she gasped.

The limits of Courtland's forbearance snapped, and he shouted at her. "What do you expect from me? What do you expect a man to do? Look at you every day, live with you, and never want to touch you? Hell and damnation!" He shook his head. "I knew I shouldn't have done this. I can't live like this anymore."

At the hot, strained words Chaynoa's hands slid down from her face. "You want me to go . . . ?"

He gave a short, caustic laugh and ran his hands through his hair. "No."

"B-but, if I don't please you—"

"You please me too damned well."

"How can you say that after—"

"I want to make love to you, Chaynoa!" His eyes burned with anguished desire, and he repeated the words more gently. "I want to make love to you."

She shook her head. "Don't ask it of me, Courtland—"

"I do ask it of you! I'm asking it of you now."

But she put her hands over her ears and would not listen. "I can't be what you want me to be, I can't! I thought you understood—if not before, then now, after—"

"There's plenty of time," he said, spreading out a hand. "We have all our lives."

"You're wrong!" she cried in torment. "You don't understand. My fear will stay with me forever, it will stay with me like a jealous demon I can never purge—"

"It *won't!*" he shouted at her, seizing her arms again in a fierce grip. "It doesn't have to, do you hear?"

"You are many things, Courtland Day," she interrupted in a grave, hard voice, pushing his hands away. "A far better man than most that walk this earth. But you are not a wizard, you cannot reach inside my head, inside my heart, and cast out the memories there, the terror."

"How do you know?"

"I do know. I *do* know . . ."

"Let me try," he argued. "Let me *try.*"

But she turned her back upon him and pressed her palms against the windowpane as if she yearned to push out the glass and escape, run back to the obscure, secret place that had sheltered her before.

Outside, the laughter of the villagers returning from their picnic drifted on the evening air, clear as the steeple bell's peal. Their voices floated toward the heavens, happy and kindred as they exchanged parting words, jests, or called to wandering children loath to relinquish their day of play. Their voices brought to mind the purity of pleasure, the wonder of serenity, and it seemed to Chaynoa that she would never grasp the same bonds of harmony that they possessed.

"Chaynoa . . . ?" Courtland whispered.

She wheeled to face him and, wanting him to understand something she did not fully grasp herself, exclaimed, "I can't give you anything, Courtland! I can't offer you what any one of those girls down upon the lane can."

"Yes, you can Chaynoa."

His voice came so sincere, so warmly hopeful that she shivered in its radiance. Swallowing, she said, "I can make no vows—"

"But you will wed me."

She laid her brow against the window and closed her eyes as if overcome, and outside, the sound of the villagers' footsteps created a lasting cadence against the dark endless road.

At last, very softly, she murmured an answer to the achingly handsome man who stood waiting behind her, rashly offering her a share of his life. "If that is what you really want. If you're certain." And again, making certain he could hear her answer, she repeated, "If that is what you want, Courtland . . . I will be your wife."

Chapter 15

Chaynoa felt painfully awkward and tongue-tied entering the house with him, not only because she was now Courtland Day's bride, but because until yesterday, they had been separated during a long span of weeks.

The morning after he had proposed that they marry, Courtland had departed unexpectedly, traveling south to do some horse trading, as he had put it. His sudden and unplanned leavetaking had unstrung Chaynoa, for she had never before realized how much his presence had come to mean to her, how it reassured her days and made safe her nights; indeed, it was as if the sentry who stood at the harbor of her own fear had abandoned her and left her adrift again.

But even though it might have pleased Courtland, she had not told him of her tender sentiments, nor voiced her grateful dependence upon his strength and attention, for the innermost part of herself she was yet unable to relinquish even in so small a measure.

He had displayed an obvious reluctance to leave, seeming almost angry that he must, and frankly, when Chaynoa stopped to consider, his behavior had been quite mysterious. And as he stood ready to mount his horse on that long-ago day in early sum-

mer, one boot in the stirrup, she had known that he
wanted to kiss her farewell, but he did not. He took
her hand instead and, with a note of constraint in his
voice, assured her that he would return just as soon
as his business was complete.

When he had finally come riding down the lane
yesterday, travel worn and uncommunicative about
his journey, she had been relieved, for she had sin-
cerely, desperately, feared that he would not return
to the house on Queen's Road.

And now, this very morning, Courtland Day had
wed Chaynoa in the meetinghouse just as he had
promised to do; they had been united by the Reverend Reynolds with no one in attendance but Hahnee,
the Oakchurches, and the reverend's two sons, who
had acted as witnesses, and behind them the rows of
plain wooden pews and deacons' seats had stretched
emptily, devoid of any curious eyes or ribbon-tied
posies, for Chaynoa had wanted it that way.

After the ceremony Mr. and Mrs. Day had walked
home in silence, and they had entered the little clean-
swept house in silence, and now stood facing each
other in the vestibule as if neither knew quite what to
do to break the hush.

Chaynoa shifted her feet and fingered the white
satin ribbon tied around the end of her braid, which
Courtland had purchased for her during the course
of their walk to the meetinghouse. A pedlar with a
trunk strapped to his back had ambled past hawking
his wares, and the toothless vendor had eagerly displayed his spoons, needles, potions, ribbons, and
bottles of ink. Courtland had offered to buy anything
Chaynoa chose, and she had selected the ink—for
him, she had said, because he was often at his desk
writing. He had paid for it, together with a white

satin ribbon, which he had insisted she have as an ornament for her hair.

Now she fidgeted with it, feeling its cool smoothness slide through her fingers while she watched him unbutton his black broadcloth coat and drape it across his arm, disdaining it in the heat of the house. He looked younger, negligently handsome in the white waistcoat, frilled shirt, and high-top boots, and she felt all of her old self-consciousness return in a rush.

It was difficult—impossible—to credit the fact that she was bound to him now, and, as she looked at him askance, feeling shy and strange, Chaynoa almost regretted that she had wed him at all. She knew that despite his tolerance now, he would expect her to be a wife to him eventually—as any man would—bear his children, and the time would come when his patience would wear thin, then wear out, exhausted by his inability to understand the strength of the darkness inside her.

She thought he must have read the distress on her face now and attributed it to the unwieldiness of the moment, for he managed a smile even though he surely felt as strained as she in the unconventional circumstances. "I thought I'd dig a new well today," he commented, as if hoping the mention of mundane chores would put her at ease. "One closer to the house so you don't have to walk so far each time you draw water. Besides, the one we use is running dry."

"Oh, you needn't do it for me," she protested.

But he only smiled remotely and proceeded upstairs to change out of his wedding clothes, loosing his cravat with a forefinger as he went.

For long moments Chaynoa remained standing in the little vestibule, staring through the parlor door at the furnishings arranged there like objects in a still-life painting: the unadorned high-backed settle, one upholstered chair, one ladder-back chair, the footstool needlepointed with cream-colored spaniels, a barren mantel above the fireplace. She had scrubbed and sanded the floors early this morning, and every surface was cleaned, polished, or in the case of the wood, rubbed with oil until it shone. And she was mistress of it all, not a servant anymore.

The realization bewildered her, then thrilled her, and where her vanity had been born a few weeks past, pride of ownership was conceived now, a sense of belonging to someplace special. This was to be her home, and *his;* this was to be the house in which they ate, slept, conversed quietly by the fire, and grew old side by side. And along the way, through Courtland's good name and protection, she would become a part of the village, be invited to the homes of her neighbors, invite them to her own for supper, share news over the fences as did all the other wives.

Joy flooded her heart, and she pivoted about so that the skirt of her gown made a wide bell. She moved her feet so that they peeked out from beneath the hem, and saw the soft brown shoes Courtland had bought, and to her they were as fine as any fashioned of satin.

Courtland had already gone out; she heard the thud of a spade striking the ground behind the house, and his low patient voice as he addressed Hahnee. Wanting to be near them, to feel the aura of this wondrous new circle of family and home, she ran through the kitchen, flung open the back door, and dashed out, tying an apron around her gown as she went.

The day was so resplendent it nearly blinded her, and she had to blink several times to focus on the two men, her brother and her husband, as they cut into the earth with their spades. She smiled at Hahnee, for he had at last donned the new suit of clothes she had sewn for him, and the butternut coat and knee breeches made him appear almost dapper. And how proud he was of his new shoes, which he perpetually polished against the backs of his calves.

Energized by her own happiness, Chaynoa knelt down in the overgrown flower garden beneath Courtland's study window and took stock of the new growth. She had almost entirely weeded it so that the purple Canterbury bells had room to breathe alongside the blue delphinium. She thrust her hands in the soil and pulled aside the persistent chickweed, lifting her face so the light could kiss it while listening to Courtland as he, too, labored in the sunshine.

Courtland nursed thoughts of his own, and stabbed at the dirt with far more force than necessary, channeling his physical energies into vigorous activity in order to alleviate the turbulence of his musings. *What had possessed him to marry her?* He asked the question over and over again with each thrust of the spade. Had he been mad? Aye, mad with wanting her. And she might never give herself to him, they might remain polite but awkward strangers the whole of their married life. A sense of being confined, trapped, assaulted him all at once, and when Hahnee unwittingly flung a spadeful of dirt in his direction, Courtland snapped at him in ill-temper. "Hahnee! Concentrate on what you're doing, for God's sake."

The simpleminded young man froze at the sharp words, his face contorting. He seemed on the verge of throwing down the tool and running off, but Chaynoa, hearing the exchange, frowned at him across the yard, prompting him to obediently wield his spade again and carefully throw the dirt away from Courtland.

A feminine greeting invaded the yard just then, and two women peered through the dappled foliage that framed the corner of the house.

"Courtland!" Virtue shouted, parting the hydrangeas and stepping gingerly over the path. "Courtland! Mother and I have come to call!"

Courtland straightened and hauled himself out of the shallow hole before laying aside the spade and dusting off his hands. "What a pleasant surprise."

"What in heaven's name are you doing in that hole?" Virtue asked, frowning at his soiled appearance. "I swear you look just like those wretched chimney sweeps in Boston. Can't you find someone to do that for you? I'm sure stepfather has a man or two you can borrow."

She stepped forward in her brilliant polonaise gown of emerald green, and, careful not to dirty her pompadour slippers, bent over to peek into the earth. "What are you digging to find?"

"Pirate's treasure."

"Oh! You're such a cad to tease me." She lowered her voice conspiratorily and leaned closer. "I convinced Mother to come. We've heard the most astonishing news—Courtland, are you really *married?*"

"Are you peeved with me for not telling you?"

"Yes!"

"I'll make it up to you." Courtland looked across the yard at Chaynoa, who had arisen from her weeding to stare at the two flamboyantly attired women.

Susannah Peebles, so serene, so aloof in her mantle of wealth and respectability, fanned herself in the shade a few yards away, and Courtland knew precisely what she was thinking. *He has married a savage.* "Come here, Chaynoa," he said. "Let me introduce you."

Looking as if she did not know what to do with her

hands, which were crusted with mud, Chaynoa joined the perfumed and bejeweled ladies, and waited in polite respectfulness to be addressed. She had never seen women so sumptuously clothed; Mrs. Peebles displayed a cream striped gown with a teardrop brooch at the collar, and Courtland's sister sported a magnificent straw hat with tiny feathered birds and red cherries clustered around the brim. Both were elaborately coiffed, their hair swept up over heddus rolls to make it high and full at the temples.

Virtue broke the awkwardness in her usual breezy way, for she was aptly named, having nothing uncharitable about her beyond the fault that she was at times innocently condescending. "So you are now Mrs. Day? How delightful! Now my brother will not abandon us again and go sailing off to heaven knows where. Of course, the entire female population of Swanston is green with jealousy over your stealing Courtland out from beneath their noses. Oh," she said, noticing Chaynoa's hands, "have you no gardening gloves?"

Chaynoa shook her head, speechless in the midst of Virtue's chatter, which seemed to include a change of subject with every sentence.

"Courtland," the talkative young lady admonished now. "What are you thinking not to insist that your bride wear gloves? She will ruin her hands. Have you bought her none? I hope you're not going to be one of those loutish husbands who are teetotalers with every single penny. You aren't, are you?"

"I promise I shall never be a teetotaler, Virtue," he said with a grin.

"Good. At least you are open-handed if not rich."

"Virtue," her mother chastised dutifully. Breaking her silence at last, Susannah glided forward from the shade, her stiff underskirt crackling like autumn leaves. In her hands she carried a small teakwood casket, which she held out to Chaynoa even while addressing Courtland. "I always planned to present this to you on the occasion of your marriage," she said. " 'Tis the silver saltcellar your father gave me in Devonshire shortly before his death."

Courtland remembered the piece well, along with the domestic turmoil it had caused. Susannah had all but driven Webster Day mad pleading for a saltcellar that was not only far too grand for a farmhouse table, but far above his financial means. But she had managed to wheedle him into buying it anyway, and now, Courtland thought unsparingly, she likely passed it on only because she had the wealth to buy a collection of much finer ones.

Chaynoa did not miss the expression that fleetingly wrenched her husband's face, and the rawness of his exposed emotion made her feel such malice toward his mother that she barely murmured her thanks, even though she was overwhelmed to be the recipient of such a treasure.

"And I have brought you something, too, Chaynoa," Virtue declared, unclasping a large netted purse and drawing out an object wrapped in white silk. " 'Tis something for your mantelpiece."

Embarrassed to touch the gift with her soiled hands, the bride accepted it clumsily, pushing aside the silk to find a most exquisite ornament: a miniature porcelain lady holding a harp in her hands.

" 'Tis beautiful . . ." Chaynoa breathed. "I've never seen anything like it." She looked first at Virtue, who fairly beamed with the delight of bestowing an extravagant gift upon an appreciative recipient, then her eyes flickered over Susannah's countenance, but that woman's wide unwavering gaze was deliberately absent of expression.

"When is Jack coming back to Swanston, Virtue?" Courtland asked suddenly.

"He'll come soon, dear brother," she said with a confident wave of her fairy-white hand. "He is dying of love for me."

"I've no doubt he is, the poor wretch."

"Are you taking his side?"

"Of course. But he had better treat you like a princess or I shall call him out."

"I'm so glad to have my protector returned," Virtue sighed, tapping him playfully on the sleeve. "Wasn't he always my protector when we were children, Mother? A Lancelot slaying dragons, a David slaying . . . oh, whoever it was."

"If that's how you remember him, Virtue," came the cool reply, "then I'm certain that's how he was."

Courtland regarded his mother, his eyes turned to silver by the sun, and wondered why Susannah could never—had never—been able to approve of him. And he wondered, more bitterly, why he continued to desire even one word of praise to fall from her full, unsmiling lips.

"Oh," Virtue exclaimed, fumbling in her purse again and addressing Chaynoa. "I have something else for you. No bride should go without perfume. It smells so divine poor Courtland will be driven insane."

Color seeped into Chaynoa's cheeks as she reached out to accept the stoppered bottle of amber-colored fragrance.

"Use it sparingly," Virtue advised. " 'Tis the last French perfume we're likely to get for a long while if that odious General Gage and his carousing troops don't open up the port—'tis said they use the most abominable language, such cursing as you've never heard. Anyway, this netted purse came from France, as well—it cost Stepfather forty pounds. I'm told 'tis the rage in Paris. But we shall all be wearing outdated fashions soon, I suppose. Courtland, you really must press Jack and Stepfather and that secret society to get something done. In the town meetings they're talking of raising a big militia—but you know all about that, of course. I'm sure you would make an excellent officer. *Do* get yourself more involved."

"Virtue," Susannah interjected smoothly, placing a hand upon her daughter's wrist. "We've kept your brother long enough from his work. Let us go."

"Oh, very well. But I shall invite them to the house, Mother. We'll have a celebration, and we'll make a toast to their marriage. Bye, Courtland, dear. Enjoy your honeymoon!"

Courtland labored indefatigably all day with Hahnee's erratic help, and Chaynoa regularly brought the men tankards of cold cider and watched while the well deepened.

After Hahnee wandered away to chase a butterfly, she quietly retrieved the abandoned spade and assumed his job. The hole had begun eight feet wide, and halfway down, Courtland dug a smaller aperture within the original one so that a natural shelf remained. He threw dirt upon it, which Chaynoa shoveled off and piled to one side. Often, as she struggled to lift the heavy wet earth, Courtland gave her long looks, but said nothing to discourage her help. She thought it odd that they had been wed just this morning, and yet both pretended it was a day like any other, even while their expressions belied the possibility of any tranquil thoughts.

As the day waned Courtland's strong back at last grew weary. Chaynoa's muscles had begun to ache hours earlier, but she did not lay down her shovel until he had laid down his. When he hoisted himself up and declared their work concluded for the day, he noticed her hands, the palms covered with raw, bleeding blisters.

"Chaynoa," he said in exasperation, "why did you not stop before your hands bled?"

She looked at him with wide, straightforward eyes, as if he should know the answer. "Because you did not."

Her faithfulness made Courtland want to draw her close in the hot, still afternoon, but knowing his bride would not be a bride to him in that way, he declined to make the overture.

"Mr. Day!"

Courtland pivoted to see two men riding round the corner of the house, and, shading his eyes against the brilliance of the setting sun, recognized Hullover and McCracken, their weathered faces stretched with excitement.

"We're riding over to Charleston tonight," Hullover declared, halting his mount a few feet from the well. "Care to ride over with us, Day?"

"Charleston?" Courtland echoed.

"Aye. Hitch up your wagon and meet us at the south end of the village—down by the old tannery. We leave in a half hour, as soon as darkness falls."

"What business do you go about?"

Hullover wheeled his horse around and grinned in a way that was both sly and oblique. "Well, you might say we're going to pick up some supplies there and carry them home."

"Will you go?" Chaynoa asked when the two men had departed again in a flurry of hooves.

Courtland had not forgotten that this was the night of their wedding, and although he did not consider himself a sentimental man, he would have liked for the occasion to hold the usual meaning; yet even if he stayed with her, he sensed the evening would pass in the usual way, fraught with his desire and her avoidance. "Aye," he told her. "I'll join the men."

"You haven't eaten. I'll pack something for you to take along."

If her tone held disappointment he could not detect it, and as he watched her enter the back door, he turned his thoughts away from useless regret and romantic longing. Intrigued by whatever sort of scheme was afoot in town, he harnessed his team. When he climbed up on the seat a while later, Chaynoa hastened from the house with a bundle in her hands.

"There's some bread and ham," she said breathlessly. "And apple tarts, too—the kind you like."

He stared down at her, into the soft dark eyes, and laid a hand upon the smoothness of her hair, thinking that perhaps he had not made such a regrettable mistake after all.

Two dozen men assembled at the designated place, some astride horses, others commanding heavy carts or durable wagons built for hauling logs. At a signal, the train of patriots rumbled down the night-shrouded road where the sound of rattling harness and churning wheels echoed loudly off stands of fir trees, whose straight spearlike shapes resembled helmeted giants standing sentinel. In high spirits the men chuckled and exchanged political jokes, behaving for all the world like wayward adolescents on a pleasure jaunt. Courtland suspected they were up to no good and wondered if they had managed to smuggle French gunpowder through the British blockade and land it at Charleston. But he soon discovered that his speculations were underestimated, and that the daring colonials had a scheme in mind far more significant than a few smuggled kegs of powder.

When they had turned onto the road leading to Charleston, Courtland maneuvered his wagon beside Hullover's team and struck up a casual conversation. "What's all the mystery? Did your blockade runners break through British lines and sail in?"

"Blockade runners?" the selectman echoed while an exuberant grin split his face. "Hell, we aren't picking up smuggled goods, Day. We've found a much more convenient source than the Frenchies. We're dealing directly with the British army."

Courtland glanced at him sharply, thankful that darkness hid his concerned expression. It was becoming common for British soldiers to accept money from the colonials in exchange for arms or ammunition; indeed, recently a private had been lashed to the tripod and publicly flogged until he was half-dead for such misconduct, and Courtland wondered if artillery men, or even high-ranking officers, were dealing secretly with the colonials for large sums of cash.

"The British army?" he repeated with the proper amount of artlessness.

"That's right. They've got plenty of what we need, and we've decided to help ourselves to a bit of it, beginning with whatever we find in Charleston tonight. A few of the local boys invited us to help them hunt. After all, General Gage and his men seized our powder stores in Cambridge last week—why shouldn't we steal a little of it back?"

Courtland kept his eyes fixed ahead and made no comment, but his thoughts were simmering. *God Almighty, wait until Gage got word of this.*

They traveled on through the night, a motley, straggling line upon the road, their horses stumbling over ground as black as pitch while the wooden wheels bumped over monstrous ruts. More than once Courtland had to jump down and extricate his wagon from a pothole or help another man wield a lever while the rest of the compatriots waited restlessly.

When they finally neared the environs of Boston and Charleston, the smell of the sea drifted over the land, and Courtland could discern its briny sharpness underlaid with rot. It filled his nostrils and pricked his recollections, reached down into his soul and touched old rending pictures of yellowed sails and weathered decks and Toby's tender face, too youthfully smooth to grow a beard. He reflected upon his days at sea. At first he had sailed because he had been forced; later he had sailed because it seemed the only thing for a boy without funds and skilled at nothing else. He knew now with the introspection of manhood that the brutality and discipline of the sea had quelled his rebelliousness, his immature and uncontrolled temper; but it had also left him hard in a way that was not an attribute, left him liking solitude too much, and made him prone to see after his own interests no matter what the cost to anyone else.

And yet, he recalled vividly the first time he had forgotten his own self-consideration completely, and felt lifted to a higher consciousness of purpose. It had occurred when he was not more than a score and one, when his ship had sailed into London's harbor and he had seen a company of British soldiers lined upon the wharf ready to embark. Their brilliant uniforms, silver sabres, and gold lace had touched a chord in a part of his imagination that had spawned inspiration, and he had examined their faces with something akin to reverence, thinking it glorious that they would march to foreign shores in the name of a king, sacrifice their lives for patriotism. It was only later that he learned most of them had been scraped from the slums of Dublin and London, or hauled from jails to feed the hungry British ranks. But it had not mattered. And sometimes, he still saw that same glimpse of glory, fleetingly, when his own men marched to his command with their bayonets flashing and their faces fresh with purpose.

He had jumped ship on that significant day, rented a horse and nearly ruined it traveling to Devonshire to see the place of his birth, the place he had immortalized upon so many squares of canvas with careful strokes of paint. And as he had beheld its valleys and hills again, the places tilled by his father and his father's father, he had wept. And then he had returned to London where he had taken the King's shilling and sworn to wear a scarlet coat in service to England. It was the only noble thing he had ever done in his life—up until today, he thought, when he had married a woman who could not love him.

"Now, men," Hullover announced, riding the length of the wagon caravan to issue warning. We're approaching the Charleston common, and after we pass the mill pond we'll head for the British battery on the south end—the one in the navy yard."

Courtland straightened abruptly, scarcely believing what he heard, incredulous that these patriot thieves would be so brazen. He glanced about, and saw that the streets of the town were quiet and dark, the sleepy residents ensconced in their shuttered homes. If any had bothered to crawl out of bed to see why a train of farm wagons rolled past, they did not reveal themselves.

He knew the British army maintained a fort at the mouth of the Charles River, directly across from another battery situated in Boston on the opposite shore. Cannon were positioned at both points in order to defend the river mouth by crossfire. Stores of ammunition were deposited in the Charleston fort, the amount of which had likely increased in the last weeks due to Gage's preparations for a possible rebellion.

With a wave of his hand Hullover halted the train several yards from the north entrance to the battery. The tranquil sound of water lapping at weathered gray wharves was almost drowned by the echoing clamor of snorting horses and hurrying footsteps. With concern Courtland focused his eyes and stared out over the black sheet of water. Although he could not discern the huge hulls in the darkness, he could hear the British warships riding the waves, guarding the port like glowering monsters.

A horse kicked in its traces, and the strike of its iron-shod shoe against the cobbles resounded like a gun report off the battery walls.

Courtland cursed under his breath. Didn't these fools know that the slightest sound carried across water? Pray God that some nervous midshipman on board the *Lively* did not hear the racket and fire in this direction indiscriminately. He scarcely relished being blown to bits by his own navy.

A group of men from Charleston and other neighboring villages were already inside the battery, seizing stores and quietly stacking them so they could be loaded in the wagons. Courtland strolled into the fort and surveyed the extent of the thievery, wishing he had means of sending word to Gage, but there was no possible way—at least not before the damage was done.

"Keep your voice down and go about your business as quickly as you can," one shadowy figure ordered in a whisper. "Load the powder kegs onto that cart there."

Obediently Courtland stooped to heft a barrel. "Where are you boys taking all of this?" he asked his unknown companion. "There's at least ten thousand pounds of musket balls in here, and thirty or so reams of cartridge paper—not to mention tents and food stores."

"We're transferring it to Salem and Concord, mostly. We've got plenty of men offering to hide it for us." The rebel straightened and eyed him curiously in the darkness. "How is it you know what the British have stored in here?"

Courtland hoisted the keg onto his shoulder and made for the wagon. "I keep my ears open."

"That so? You seem a handy fellow. Do you know how to dismantle British cannon?"

Courtland paused and grinned in the night, the irony of the situation arousing his sense of humor. "Aye," he said with a resigned nod of his head. "I know how to dismantle British cannon. Very well, in fact."

Chapter 16

The following evening Courtland sat at his desk detailing the particulars of the raid in which he had been a participant the previous night. Of course, Gage already knew that the battery had been looted; not an hour after Courtland and the convoy of wagons laden with British artillery had rumbled out of Charleston, a colonial rider had caught up with them to report that the general had gotten wind of the theft and dispatched a squad of soldiers to investigate.

"Those dim-witted British fools found nothing but an empty fort!" the rider had exclaimed with a laugh, slapping his thigh. "Good work, boys! I wish I could have been there to hear those pompous redcoats curse when they saw their cannon gone!"

Courtland applied his quill to the paper and wrote.

They transferred everything appropriated from the Battery into wagons purportedly bound for Concord and Salem. Be assured that every last cartridge is by now well concealed. These colonials are serious about arming themselves; every gunsmith and farrier in Massachusetts is busy making weapons and firelocks. Powder is scarce, and hoarded like gold.

He smiled wryly, dipped his pen again, and continued.

Perhaps you will pardon my dismantling of your twenty-four pounders at the Battery when I tell you that I have been accepted into the Sons of Liberty; indeed, I have in my Possession one of their tokens—the medal they give to their members. It is engraved with a Representation of the Liberty Tree, which you are probably aware is an old elm in the center of Boston that the colonials have adopted as a symbol of Freedom. They seem to set extraordinary store by it . . .

Courtland put down his quill and, reaching into his breeches pocket, removed the small medal, which he turned over between his fingers thoughtfully. It was an object of great power. Except for the highly secretive Boston councils, it would give him access to any secret rebel meeting he chose to invade.

He glanced up, his eyes following Chaynoa as she moved about the kitchen. He could see the edge of the table where she poured a hot syrupy mixture onto a platter, and the smell of its sweetness drifted toward him. Not for the first time since she had come to live in his house, Courtland realized how her presence accentuated his days. He found himself studying her minutely as he would a puzzle, which, if he could divine it, would give him an understanding of his own obsession for wanting to decipher its intrigue. And he *was* obsessed with her; he had realized it weeks ago, even before he had departed on a map-making mission for Gage. During that separation his fascination had burgeoned until he had begun to imagine her

face peering at him from behind every window he
passed.

Last night in the plum-blue hours before dawn
when he had arrived home from Charleston, tired
and frustrated with the rebel coup d'état, he had
discovered her asleep on her feather tick in the attic.
He did not know why he had expected her to be
awaiting him in his bed. He supposed he had imagined the feel of her body fitted in the curve of his for
so long that he had expected the reality to occur
through the force of his own fantasies. He wanted to
really see her brown arms flung over his pillow, really
hear her rhythmic breathing while he lay beside her
in the darkness. He had almost become afraid of his
own compulsion, for there were times when he
thought that he might lose control of his reason and
force himself upon her.

"Courtland," she called out in a flustered tone.
"Can you come and help me?"

Shaken out of his thoughts, he arose and, striding
into the kitchen, found her struggling with the syrup,
which she had poured onto a platter in long rows
resembling strings of liquid brown glass. As the mixture touched the surface it cooled and whitened at the
edges, hardening rapidly.

"Quick, Courtland," she said. "Butter your hands
and help me pull up the candy before it gets too
brittle to manage. Not like that, silly. There—that's
it—don't let the skein break. Now double it, twist,
and form it in the shape of a rope."

He frowned, trying to maneuver the sticky sweetness, laughing when the rope elongated between his
juggling hands and almost dropped to the floor.

" 'Twould be the same as throwing gold away,"
Chaynoa teased. "Sugar is worth a small fortune
these days. It may be the last we get for a while—at

least until after those despicable British soldiers go home and let us trade again."

Courtland's eyes shifted to her face as he laid his string of candy onto a buttered board, and he wondered how she would react if he told her that she had just insulted a British army captain. It struck him suddenly that the expanding colonial cause had begun to infect her, too, and he frowned in consternation. Soon, when his mission here was complete, he would have to reveal his identity. As an officer's wife she must join the camp followers and trail the military wherever it went—to a colonial fort or to some foreign country in which England maintained an interest. Chaynoa was so stoical, bred to hardship, that Courtland had not expected she would object to such a life, at least until he could leave the army and make a decent home for her in Devonshire.

But now, as he studied her neatly combed head and starched skirts, a niggling doubt assailed him. Not only did she seem contented here, but her self-assurance had blossomed, nurtured by the security he provided and her own determination to come to grips with society. He had the odd notion that she was leaving behind her woodland persona, shedding her diffidence and furthering an affinity with the community. And although he was more attracted to her than ever, her growing independence worried him.

She brushed against his arm as she laid down her rope of candy, but he did not shift over. Instead he looked down at her until she raised her eyes to meet his. Twilight had fallen and the hearth light created mosaics of amber on her young soft-skinned face, patterning it like the wings of a butterfly. Her eyes were dark and deep, the outer corners tilted above smooth cheekbones that were prominent and round.

His hand moved to touch hers, the gloss of the

butter on their fingers warm and slippery as their fingers entwined, and bending down, he put his mouth on hers, twisting it over the warmth of her lips. He groaned and felt the need inside his body burst.

The front door rattled, and Chaynoa broke skittishly away from his kiss. She gave him a linen towel to wipe his hands, and in an ill-temper he went to find Jeremiah Hullover waiting impatiently upon the stoop.

"That bastard Gage is fortifying the Neck at the mouth of the Charles River!" he burst out. "Can you believe his gall? Our raid of the battery infuriated him, and now he's mounted cannon all around Boston. It's a besieged town!"

Courtland calmly leaned against the jamb of the door, rubbing the last of the butter off his hands. "And the citizens there," he asked, "how are they reacting?"

"They're outraged, by God, accusing Gage of having made a garrison of their town. Huge crowds are meeting at Faneuil Hall and the Old South Church in defiance of his measures. Blast it, Day, he has the waterways so bottled up that farmers can't even ferry a load of cabbage across. The British navy has declared that if so much as a piece of driftwood tries to breach its blockade it'll be blown to smithereens."

Interested to hear the news, Chaynoa moved to Courtland's study, where she stood near his desk in order to better catch the conversation taking place on the front stoop. Like the other villagers, she was daily growing more concerned, fearing that these recent volatile events would lead to some sort of confrontation or that King George would become wrathful over the disobedience of his subjects and order the redcoats to attack. People lived in constant trepidation of a British assault, and some Bostonian husbands had already sent their wives and children into the countryside to live with kin until the crisis passed.

As she listened, her eyes shifted idly to the paper on Courtland's desk. She leaned to scrutinize the flowing, negligent lines which covered half the page, wondering what messages they communicated, and to whom. She had asked him once what it was he wrote so frequently, and he had replied with an obtuse air. "Letters of business," he had said.

His drawer was slightly ajar and inside it she glimpsed the brass spyglass. Pricked by a sudden fancy to peer through the fascinating gadget, she eased it out and, raising it to her eyes, discovered its method of visual adjustment. With much delight she focused upon the parlor mantel adorned with Hahnee's collection of wooden animals and Virtue's porcelain figurine.

Smiling at the cleverness of the spyglass, Chaynoa made to put it away, but not before noticing the inscription upon one of its brass ends, the inscription she had noted once before. *4th regiment of Foot.*

She outlined the letters with her forefinger in the same way one would trace a row of hieroglyphics on an unearthed tablet, and wondered at their meaning before shrugging and sliding the glass back into the drawer, where a stack of watercolor paintings arrested her attention. Unable to resist a closer inspection, she drew them out one by one, and with great reverence for the talented renderings, studied images of a farmhouse built of stone.

She became so lost in imagination, so awed by the painter's soulful artistry, that she failed to hear the front door close and Courtland's footsteps as he crossed the vestibule.

A moment later, with a sudden prickling sensation

she sensed his presence, and, glancing up, saw him
standing at her shoulder, his gray eyes soberly regarding the invasion of his desk.

"F-forgive me . . ." she stammered, hurriedly slipping the pictures back into place. "The-the colors
attracted my eye. They were so lovely I couldn't resist
touching them, taking them out—"

The expression on his face discomfited her. His
features had stiffened into lines of strain, and his
body had grown so rigid she had the odd notion that
her viewing of the pictures had unnerved him in some
way.

She put her hands behind her back and moved
away from the desk in a sidling step. And then she
stopped herself, mustered self-possession and spoke
to him not with her usual anxious spirit, but with a
directness born of growing maturity. "They're beautiful, Courtland, very beautiful. Painted with great
feeling."

His eyes remained shuttered but she could see by
the slight flinch in his expression that she had
touched some deeply private and vulnerable chord
with her honest compliment. "The paintings are of
England, aren't they?" she persisted quietly. "Of that
special place—the one you spoke about when we sat
on the riverbank together."

As if filled with disquietude, he wandered to the
window and braced an arm against the frame. Chaynoa studied his back, watched the hard ripple of
muscle across his shoulders as he reached to close the
window abruptly and shut out the chilling air.

Several seconds passed before he answered, and
when he did, his tone was as distant as the cameo
moon that shone down through the trees and silvered
the motionless yard. "Aye," he said. "The paintings
are of that place."

She stepped nearer. "Why did you not return there? If it means so much, why did you abandon it?"

Courtland thought she spoke as if he had forsaken a living thing, an entity. But then, he remembered that Chaynoa believed every object and creature possessed a spirit and feelings of its own. He was uncertain why he had spoken of Devonshire on that significant day by the river, except that he had wanted to share his dream with her, even in some small measure. He wanted to share it with her now, he realized with surprise, even tell her the reason he was in Swanston, but he was slowly beginning to be wary of, even dread, her reaction to his revelation.

"My mother sold the house when I was a boy," he said flatly, not elaborating. "I have no claim to it." *Not yet, at least, not yet. Soon. After I have earned the confidence of your neighbors and betrayed them.*

" 'Tis a tragedy when the place where you belong is taken from you," she commented sadly. "The place from which you draw life and breath, the place that connects you to yourself."

He turned his head to look at her curiously, scrutinize the fawnlike face which still retained its mystery in the half-shadow of the room. She was wise, he thought suddenly, wise in spirit, and although he had never taken time to analyze his feelings about Devonshire, her words rang true in his heart. He felt himself drawn to her unbearably. " 'Tis late," he said, his voice strange. "Let us go up to bed."

She nodded and went to tidy the kitchen and cover the cooling candy while he snuffed the candles, both of them taking up the natural ritual of a married couple at the close of a day, and both of them acutely conscious of it.

Courtland waited until Chaynoa had mounted the stairs, then followed with a candle to light the way, putting a hand upon her arm to stay her when they reached the door to his bedchamber. " 'Tis hot in the attic," he murmured.

She avoided his eyes. "I don't mind."

"You should."

"But I don't."

Seconds passed and he did not release her arm. The candle flickered between them, its flame made wild by their uneven breaths. 'Tis right that you should sleep in here with me, Chaynoa. I don't expect any more than that now."

"Yes, you do. "I . . . I can sense it."

He glanced at the chase of light and shadow on her flushed face, and in a sharp voice asked, "Are you condemning me for it?"

"No." She regarded him solemnly. "But nor do I condemn myself."

For several seconds he stared down at her, and the commanding side of his nature almost defeated his patience. He could smell the freshness of her skin, feel the warmth that radiated from her body, which he desired to look upon and touch, and mold with in order to ease the needs of his flesh. Even if he were only permitted to lie with her nestled in the circle of his arms throughout the night it would be enough, he told himself—enough for now, just as his dream of Devonshire was sufficient until the reality was seized.

"Good night," she breathed, turning away.

"Chaynoa, we can't spend the rest of our lives like this."

"Good *night, Courtland.*"

With angry eyes he watched the voluptuous, elusive sway of her trailing skirts as she climbed the narrow stair, then watched a bead of wax liquify beneath the flame of his candle, where it quivered slightly before spilling over.

* * *

"I'm hosting a quilting at my home next Tuesday evening," Iris Oakchurch announced. "I'd be pleased to have you join me and the other ladies."

She and Chaynoa stood in the yard behind the Oakchurch clapboard house with goose feathers flying about their heads. All around them the shrubs and the straggling grass appeared to wear a fine, drifting veil of snow, and Chaynoa constantly blew air out through her lower lip to dislodge the feathers clinging to her nose.

It was plucking time, and Iris had offered to give Mr. Day's bride all the down she could collect, which would refill or plump mattress ticks and pillows. The old woman kept a large flock of geese, who usually wandered about the neighborhood devouring seeds and waddling through mud puddles left by summer showers. Indeed, the sound of their clacking had become a familiar, even comforting sound to Chaynoa's ears as she worked in her own house each day.

"That old gray gander is the most ornery of the lot," Iris declared, pointing at it with a crooked forefinger. "I declare he's more alert than a watchdog— and meaner, too."

Chaynoa chased after him nimbly and cleverly, understanding his instincts, and finally seized him by his long neck and slipped a stocking over his head in order to avoid his vicious beak. Tucking his heavy, struggling body under her arm, she knelt and began plucking the down, which she stuffed into a pillowcase. She carefully pulled the underfeathers from the bird's breast and underwings, knowing it would soon grow back again, and that it caused him mortification but little discomfort.

"Where's that man of yours today?" Iris asked

conversationally, sitting down upon a shady bench. Behind her, the tea roses withering on their vine seemed an appropriate backdrop for her ancient frame.

"He's ridden off to do business," Chaynoa said, and although it rarely occurred to her to question the vague explanations Courtland offered, she felt suddenly embarrassed over her ignorance of his whereabouts. She confided in Iris. "To tell you the truth, I don't know where he goes. But I know he rides far afield some days. I can tell by the dust on his clothes and by the mud on the underside of his horse's belly."

"Who manages the livery while he's away?"

"Hahnee. He has a way with animals, and he's able to groom and feed the livery horses responsibly. Courtland and I are quite proud of him. Of course, if someone wants to board or rent a mount, I see to it. Courtland has taught me to handle coin."

Iris plucked a rose and pondered it. "It sounds as if the three of you are managing quite well together. Let's see . . . it's been a fortnight since your wedding, hasn't it?"

"Aye." Chaynoa nestled her fingers beneath the warm goose wing. " 'Tis a life I never thought to have . . . a good life." Even as she said the words she realized that her discord with Courtland spoiled complete contentment in their home. His restlessness, his abrupt leave-takings, and the times when he gazed at her with angry desire distressed her. Often, without uttering a word to her, he would snatch up his hat, stalk out the door, and disappear for hours.

"You're fortunate to have such a man," Iris commented. She had tilted her head back in order to catch the sun, and her posture seemed drowsy, but in her half-closed eyes shrewdness gleamed like a spark off a gemstone. "So fine-looking. So healthy. He needs a good woman."

Chaynoa glanced up from the goose, fancying for a moment that the ancient dame's voice had contained a trace of chastisement. But the old one's bonneted head had fallen sleepily forward to rest between her birdlike shoulders, and Chaynoa shrugged the notion away.

"Hullo, Mrs. Day."

Chaynoa glanced over her shoulder to find Robbie beaming at her, a slim book tucked conspicuously beneath his arm. She smiled and released the gander, who, flapping its great wings with its neck extended, departed in high dudgeon.

"What do you have there, Robbie?" she asked, pointing to the book.

"My primer. Granny makes me go to the schoolhouse every day now." He straightened with officiousness. "I'm learning my letters."

"Let me see."

He riffled the pages, and the printed words and tiny illustrations of animals and landscapes intrigued Chaynoa. She stared at the figures, trying to understand why Courtland would be so fascinated with reading and writing. Often she burned with a desire to read the volumes he perused with such great absorption late into the night.

"My book and heart shall never part," Robbie recited blithely from the open primer. "I can't read the words yet, but they're printed here on this page. The schoolmaster makes us repeat them over and over again."

"Robbie," she asked with a sudden frown, "can you teach me what you learn? Letters, I mean. Can you teach me?"

The idea of educating an adult seemed to delight

the child, and with a deal of self-importance, he closed the primer with a snap and announced, "Of course, I can."

"Let's not tell anyone," she suggested in a conspiratorial whisper. "Let's keep it a secret until I can read well—*really* well. I want to surprise Mr. Day."

Robbie hooked his thumbs in his coarse-spun knee breeches and grinned with three teeth missing. "I won't say a word. Not a one! I promise."

The following Tuesday a select group of Swanston matrons streamed into Iris Oakchurch's house like a varied assortment of cats, some waddling, some gliding, and some mincing, depending up the stature, age, and imagined self-importance of each. They all had attired themselves in their best "everyday" gowns, adding modest accessories, for in the way of women they desired to show off their newest trinket or lace kerchief to a more discerning audience than the male inhabitants left at home.

Soon Iris's small parlor smelled of rose water and powder, and its every corner buzzed with snippets of conversation while the guests peeled off lace mittens and ruched bonnets. Some carried baskets of needlework, whose contents would occupy their never idle hands while they chatted and sipped weak coffee in the crowded, sampler-filled room.

Chaynoa had arrived early, and although she trembled with anxiousness, uncertain how she would be received by these village pillars, she was buoyed with hopefulness. She had devised a plan she thought might merit their admiration and acceptance of her.

They had not noticed her yet. She stood to one side, her eyes moving to the wall opposite the fireplace where a black cotton cloth hung. When she was a child Mam had taught her the art of papyrotamia, a method of creating lacelike pictures upon pieces of stiff paper, and a dozen works of such art were pinned on display now in Iris's parlor.

One evening last week, she had approached Courtland tentatively and, explaining her purpose, asked him to sketch some designs for her—fanciful birds, animals, and landscapes—which he had done indulgently and with a certain flattered pride prompted by her admiration of his talent. He was an ingenious artist, quick with his pen, and after he had completed the dozen sketches, Chaynoa had settled herself by the hearth and cut out the designs by candlelight. Sympathetic to her craving for social acceptance, Courtland had left his desk and joined her, his deft hands taking up a cutting tool and making short shrift of the task. With a wide grin he had watched his wife's face glow as she held the finished products up to the light.

Now the pictures were displayed in the Oakchurch parlor, being noticed by the milling guests.

"Why, Iris!" one matron cried, clapping her hands. "Whoever fashioned these? They are exquisite."

"Did they come from Boston?" another guest asked excitedly. "I'm told there is a Frenchwoman there who sells such pictures in her husband's silversmith shop."

"Do tell us, Iris!"

The elderly hostess trundled forward with the support of her hickory cane. "Someone here has created them. And how lovely they would look framed and hung upon your walls at home, ladies."

As most colonial wives could afford no oil paintings or mirrors or silver sconces, any pretty object that would ornament their simple homes intrigued them.

"But tell us who made them?" Mrs. Higginbotham persisted. She scanned the faces of her friends in puzzlement. "Was it you, Iris?"

"Nay. My hands are too unsteady and old for such delicate work." Iris ambled to the corner where Chaynoa hung back and, laying a deferential hand upon her shoulder, announced, "My good neighbor, Mrs. Day, has brought the art."

A silence descended upon the parlor while a dozen pairs of eyes turned to the tall dark-skinned girl in her plain muslin gown. She stepped into their midst wordlessly and, reaching up, unpinned the design that Mrs. Higginbotham had admired. Holding it out in offer, she said quietly, " 'Tis a gift for you."

The lady's neck stiffened above her fichu, and as if she might refuse, her mouth puckered with perturbation. But the lure of the gift proved too much of a temptation, and gazing at the present longingly she blustered, "Why, if you insist . . ."

Chaynoa moved to unpin all the pictures, and one by one, bestowed them upon the women who had slandered and maligned and excluded her from their circle.

In the way of people who receive unexpected generosity from one they have unkindly wronged, they were uncomfortable, and each matron seemed uncertain how to ease her smitten conscience gracefully. But Iris, hiding a childlike smile, smoothed the awkwardness of the moment by asking Chaynoa to help her serve refreshments, and after a tense interim fraught with polite coughs and hissed whispering, the matrons struck up their high hum of conversation again. Before long, after they had sampled cranberry cake and gingerbread, and after cherry wine had sweetened their vinegary tongues, most even ventured to acknowledge the liveryman's wife with wincing, milk-and-water smiles.

When she had helped Iris wash and dry the plates and set the kitchen in order, Chaynoa slipped out into the cool evening to make her way home. As she walked, she looked up at the stars, pondered the faraway spangles of heaven and Grandmother Moon's face, which smiled down upon her with knowing benignity. She inhaled deeply, so imbued with happiness that she suddenly began to sprint down the road as if she were a creature of the woodlet once more.

She discovered Courtland waiting for her on the front porch, his hip braced against the railing while he polished off an apple.

"Oh, Courtland!" she cried breathlessly, her joy spilling over. When he straightened she reached out to grab his hands and hold them between her own trembling ones. "The pictures were a great success! Mrs. Higginbotham has invited me to her home next week. I believe I have been accepted!" Releasing his hands, she threw herself against his body.

He stroked her hair absently, pricked all at once by a new and inexplicable fear, a sensation that her spirit was slipping away from him like a ghost even while he held her body in his arms. "I'm glad for you, Chaynoa," he said quietly, the words genuine but forced. "If it's what you really want, I'm glad for you."

Held against the solid substance of the man who had helped to right her world, Chaynoa sighed in flushed contentment. "It's what I really want. I want to *belong*. More than anything in the world I want to be a part of them."

"And you are now," he murmured, his voice remote.

With an odd guilt, she drew determinedly away from his tightening, needful arms and slipped into the shadowy house, wondering suddenly why happiness was never complete, never whole and flawless, why its fragile spun-gold circle was ever, unfailingly broken by some fracture, as if the heart had not the tolerance for bliss.

Chapter 17

Chaynoa hurried along the forgotten path with a shovel in hand, directing her steps toward the inner depths of the woods, traveling with such native stealthiness that a covey of quail did not even hear her passage and fly their nest.

She did not know that Courtland watched her. Earlier he had gone to help with a house raising a few miles outside of Swanston, joining a crew of townsmen there to construct a dwelling for a family newly arrived from Ireland. But they had needed an extra team of horses for the lumber, and he had offered to return home for his.

He was just buckling harness when he glimpsed Chaynoa darting through the tall grass that edged the distant fields of grain. His eyes narrowed, and in sudden decision he tethered the team in the yard, then started off after her in a long steady stride. After nearly an hour's hike through thorny brambles and mud, he realized Chaynoa's fleet and noiseless steps took her toward a familiar clearing, the tranquil, humid place of fern and ivy that still retained a mystery. He had discovered her there once before, digging with her bare hands when she was still a daughter of the woods in ragged gown and tangled hair.

For some reason he was glad to see her in the place again.

He checked his pace and observed her activities, his artist's eye unable to ignore the setting in which she moved, for autumn had come to reapparel the forest, change her diaphanous summer gown for one of brilliant fire. Gold and bronze medallions hung from tree branches like pendants dangling from graceful arms of ballroom ladies, and the maples wore plumes of scarlet, and shod in umber slippers danced with formal firs clad in darkest green. Like maidens with ribbons twined through twisted tresses, oak saplings sported threads of ivy, their boughs cloaked with mantuas of yellow and orange. Below them, the grapevines crawled along the earth in trails of gold and green.

Chaynoa stood in the midst of this splendor, taking no time to contemplate the wonder of its eternal performance, instead setting her shovel to the ground again and again. For a quarter hour Courtland watched her as she dug a shallow hole, then paused to lean upon the handle of the tool in an attitude of frustration before choosing another site.

At last he left his post, and making no attempt to conceal his rustling passage through the undergrowth, approached.

At sight of her husband Chaynoa hesitated in chagrin. Then, in silence, she doggedly resumed her task, stabbing and throwing aside soil until Courtland reached out a hand and stayed her arm.

" 'Tis time you told me what this means, what you're doing here, Chaynoa," he said firmly.

Refusing to address his demand, she thrust the shovel into the moldy crust of last year's fallen leaves with renewed industry, and, as she put her foot to it, spoke breathlessly. "The frost god has come. And he will come again tonight, touch the green life and make it wither with his icy fingers. My father's people call him Hatho. He wears a cape of ice, and is fierce, old. He makes the trees barren in winter, and when their branches clack together, 'tis his snowy breath howling over them."

Courtland retrieved a leaf from her hair and turned it over in his hands. "And now that you've told me that story," he said quietly, "tell me your own, Chaynoa. Or do you not trust me to know it?"

She stopped as if his words had struck her, and looked at him with grave and glowing eyes. "I trust you as I would trust the return of spring or the coming of sunset. But 'tis not easy to speak of what's inside me, to open it and let the dark things be seen. You . . . you might see me in a different light than before, and I'm not sure I want to risk that. I'm afraid—" She looked helplessly at the branches overhead. "I'm not certain I want to change the way we are together."

The torn leaf fell from his hand. "The way we are together is a torment to us both."

"And yet . . . the torment could be made worse."

His eyes had not moved from her face, and in their depths, through the faint humid haze rising from the ground, Chaynoa saw a glimmer more bright than usual. "Not for me," he said, his voice so low it was scarcely audible. "Not for me."

She lifted the shovel again and stabbed it down, her arms straining with the effort, the loosened hair from her braid falling over one cheek. "Before I was born my father left his tribe and fought beside the French in the war with England. He saved the life of an officer, one with great wealth—a marquis, I believe, and when the two of them parted, the Frenchman gave him a necklace as a token of esteem. It was fashioned of silver filigree and very valuable. When my father's eyes fell upon my mother's beauty a short time later, he gave the necklace to her in love. She never wore it, for there was no occasion in the wilderness, but she cherished it above all things. She told me that it was to be mine when I grew to be a woman, that Hahnee and I must go away to a city and trade it for coin. She said that money could buy respect, even for people with mixed blood and low birth."

Pausing as if to ponder the strangeness of her own words, she glanced up at him and asked, "Do you believe what she said is true?"

With a jaded smile he nodded. "I fear that I do."

A bird nested in the branches overhead and Chaynoa's eyes lifted to find it. It winged downward and quarreled with a jay, then veered upward to become a dot in the sky. "The night of her death Mam buried the necklace here in this clearing," she went on, "along with a bundle of papers she hoped would prove the dishonesty of Julius Twiggs. Only, I can't seem to recall precisely where she buried the box. 'Twas twilight, and she was frantic, frightened. And her fear affected me."

"How old were you?"

"Twelve."

"And what will you do with these things when you find them? Do you intend to follow your mother's plan? Go away and seek a new life somewhere?" Courtland smiled mockingly as if to smother the sudden twinge of doubt, of dread, that she would do just that.

Chaynoa did not reassure him, but stared at the sky, which was overlaid with autumn leaves as bright as fireworks. "If the papers ruin Twiggs's name, I'll show them to the people of Swanston. Then they'll

know he was not a virtuous man, they'll forget the
lies he spread about my mother."

Courtland thought it an optimistic hope, but did
not say so. "And the necklace . . . ?" he persisted.

She raised a hand to her throat as if the filigreed
silver encircled it and shook her head. "I don't know.
I—I don't need it now for the purpose my mother
planned. By giving me your name," she said, looking
at him, "you've already given me what it could buy.
I doubt I could have bought a better life in the city."

The logicalness of her answer and its unemotional
delivery disappointed Courtland, and with barely
concealed asperity he muttered, "You give me more
credit than I deserve."

She studied the clearing and its mounds of freshly
turned earth and sighed. "Well, my efforts have been
futile again today. 'Tis time to go home."

"Not yet. Tell me first about the night of your
mother's death."

She leaned down and retrieved a walnut from the
ground whose shell was split into halves, the fruit
inside decayed. "I don't know why she submitted to
Twiggs—why she didn't take us and flee, even go
back to my father's people, who would have fed us.
But she would not."

"Was her time with the Delaware unhappy?"

"Nay. But she wanted Hahnee and me to grow up
in a town among her own kind, and for almost a year
endured Twiggs's attentions. Even though I was a
child I knew he hurt her, but she wouldn't leave his
house. At least, not until the day he—" She faltered,
and, after taking a deep breath, spoke with sudden
viciousness. "Not until he forced himself on *me*."

Although Courtland had always surmised the nature of her tragedy, the vision of it sickened him.

"Mam discovered us," Chaynoa went on determinedly. "In rage she attacked Twiggs. But he beat her until she collapsed, and swore that if she attempted to leave he would hunt her down and see that she was tried and hanged for some invented crime. Believing that he had subdued her, he stalked out, and Mam frantically threw the necklace into a metal box, then broke into Twiggs's desk and robbed it of its papers. She had overheard conversations that led her to suspect him of unfair dealings, and although she couldn't read, she gathered as many documents as she could hoping to expose his dishonesty to the townspeople."

"Why didn't she just escape with you and your brother immediately?"

"Because Hahnee was ill, recovering from a fever. She planned to wait until the first light of morning, then find a way to carry him here to the woods where the three of us could hide. She thought Twiggs would give up his search of the roads after a little while and we could safely go to Boston."

"So after she buried the metal box here she returned to the house for your brother?"

"Yes. She ordered me to remain in the woods. But I followed her. Sadie was in the house, but she had fallen asleep and didn't hear my mother arrive. Nor did she hear Twiggs when he accused Mam of robbing his desk. A terrible fight ensued, and he seized her by the neck and began to squeeze. Although I flew at him with a firetool and struck him unconscious, he had already killed her."

"And you were afraid to expose him?"

"Wise enough to know I would not have been believed. My word would never have outweighed the magistrate's. So I fled here with Hahnee, and no one guessed our whereabouts. The winters were hard, and if I had not spent my childhood with the Delaware the two of us would have starved. Fortunately I glimpsed Sadie walking beside the river one day, and she brought food whenever she could, but for nearly seven years I lived in isolation, harboring my secret. And in dreams . . ." she breathed, staring at the green tangle behind her, "the magistrate revisited me again and again. And even now when I lie safe in your house, he comes back, endlessly returns to me."

Her last words were so strangely spoken, the image of them seemingly so *real* to her, that Courtland felt chilled. He stared at her with his hands balled, wanting her imagined, irrational fear of a dead man—the fear that lay between them—to be lifted so that the direction of their future would be clear and natural. Because his own spirit was so strong, so weathered and dauntless, he failed to understand why she let herself be tyrannized by a mere memory, why when *he* touched her she remembered another man's savagery. His frustration burgeoned, and had Chaynoa's memory been a thing of substance, he would have smashed it in utter fury.

He grasped her firm brown arm, which was warm with sun and the energy of her life, and spoke brusquely, hotly. "It's all past. Put it from your mind. It's of no consequence now."

She raised her eyes, and they were colored by the darkness of disappointment. "Nay, Courtland. 'Tis of more consequence now than ever."

"Only because you let it."

"Let us not argue anymore. We've done that already, more than once. 'Tis something you cannot change no matter how hard you wish to. If my fear is ever banished to its proper place, *I* must be the one to do it." She averted her head. "You seem to consider it too lightly."

"And you give it more importance than it deserves," he accused sharply.

She turned on him. "Have you no demons, Courtland Day? Have you nothing in your past that rises up to haunt you, colors the way you think and act? I suspect you do. I suspect there's a whole chamber full of secret, chained ghosts in that mighty chest of yours. Maybe you're just better able to keep them bound up and out of sight than other people."

She threw down the shovel and, ignoring his ruthless stare, ran quickly over the churned earth and its buried secrets.

And Courtland let her go.

"I tell you, 'tis a war we'll have before it's all over! Mark my words. Now that Parliament has had the audacity to forbid our town meetings without Gage's permission, and given *him* the right to appoint our public officials, there will be war."

Jack Bretton, Virtue's betrothed, offered his commentary over Simon Peebles's sumptuous damask-draped table whose variety and abundance of gastronomical delights resembled those of a king's banquet. Duck, lobster, vegetable basins, cheeses, red wines, trifles, whipped syllabub, and candied flowers created a glazed swirl of sweet and sour color while silver spoons and saltcellars, crystal goblets and eggshell plates winked in a complement to the savory delicacies.

This feast reigned in a paneled dining room ornamented with a surfeit of mirrors, whose silver depths reflected servants in white gloves as they filled empty glasses and carried in soup tureens filled with lobster morsels.

The company could have been sitting at some elegant London address, Courtland reflected with a certain merciless humor, for with her expensive furnishings and pretentious manners his mother had created in a backwoods village the world that she had coveted in England but never grasped.

The women present graced the company like three markedly different species of bird, he thought. Virtue, no less decorative than a cockatoo in her white gauze and ruffled lace, chatted in her usual inerudite but endearing way, while Susannah Peebles looked magisterially on in a shimmer of peacock blue, her hair smoothed atop her small head and tufted with silver combs.

Courtland's eyes ranged over the grand dessert conceit, the centerpiece of the table, to find Chaynoa, who sat quietly but attentively in soft beige the color of a dove's wing. The gown had been a gift, delivered this morning by his sister, who, when she was not contemplating her own wardrobe, seemed to concentrate upon Chaynoa's with excessive care. She bestowed cast-off slippers, hats, and stockings as one would strew flowers before a bride. He had endured his sister's charity stoically and in silence, and earlier this evening watched his wife descend the stairs in her finery, a creature transformed beneath Virtue's modish wand.

He looked at her now, at the rich dark hair, braided and coiled and twisted, that seemed too heavy for her neck. In his absorbed study of her appearance, Courtland barely touched his food, for it suddenly seemed to him that Chaynoa had become someone other than the woodland girl he had first met, and in another few months might vanish before his eyes. Why did the possibility bedevil him? Why did he want her to remain as he had found her, shy and eccentric? *Whom had he married?* He looked at her again. If it were not for her hand, uncertain on the polished silverware, and her eyes, wide with the reflection of epicurean dishes and hothouse flowers, he would have feared his wife already lost to him under the swath of dove-beige silk.

"I fear you're correct in your prediction, Jack," Simon Peebles said, idly rotating his wineglass and leaning back in his chair. "We're heading for conflict. Every town in the province is defying Parliament. We'll continue to hold our meetings whenever we please, and if Gage dares to arrest any of our patriots and ship them to England for a sedition trial, we'll go to war. Yesterday we voted to raise a militia in Swanston."

Pulling himself out of his reverie in order to do his duty to King George, Courtland met Bretton's eyes across the table. "And what is the news from Boston, Jack? What sort of preparations are the patriots making there?"

Jack's gaze flickered over the ladies' anxious faces. "We're doling out supplies to every town for the protection of its citizens. Even now there are wagons packed with ammunition and muskets en route to Swanston."

"Are they adequate in number for a sustained battle if it should occur here?" Courtland asked.

"We're not yet finished stockpiling. But by nightfall twenty thousand pounds of musket balls, a hundred reams of cartridge paper, a dozen crates of ramrods, and two dozen medicine chests will arrive here. More will be coming."

"Swanston voted to buy eight barrels of powder as well, if we can get it from France," Simon added, raising a spoonful of aspic to his mouth. "Ammunition is growing more and more difficult to get."

"Well," Courtland quipped with a glib smile, "I

guess we'll just have to steal it from General Gage again."

Jack laughed. "That old goat has finally gotten wise to our tactics. More redcoats have just landed from Asia and every last cannonball in the colony is under heavy guard. I fear we'll be able to sneak no more from that source."

"Did you know we've built a town storehouse, Jack?" Peebles asked. "We've gathered enough flour, butter, molasses, rice, and beef to feed a small militia for a month or more if need be."

Jack frowned. "Perhaps you should remove everything, Simon, ask residents to hide it in their own homes. We have word that Gage has spies roaming around the countryside mapping the locations of warehouses so the redcoats can confiscate the contents."

Courtland watched a servant enter with another bottle of Madeira and waited until the fellow had retreated again. "I heard it said that two fellows dressed as day laborers stepped into a Concord tavern and inquired for work last week," he said conversationally. "They spoke the King's English too well and were instantly suspected. The landlord grabbed his musket intending to fill them with shot, but they slipped out a back door."

"By God!" Peebles swore. "If we were to catch a damned British spy here in Swanston we'd hang him from the highest tree in the common and let the vultures pick his bones."

"One would think Gage would chose his spies more cleverly," Virtue interjected, dipping her fingers into a dish of candied violets. "Why doesn't he use women and send them out as maids? Why, when I think how much gossip my Polly overhears . . . Of course, she keeps everything under her cap. Otherwise, Stepfather would know exactly how much I spend on bonnets and close up his purse." Dimpling, she flashed her rhapsodic smile at the sour-faced man.

"Tories won't find it easy to remain here," Susannah commented in her cool voice, ending her long silence. "They're taunted mercilessly for their loyalty to Britain. Indeed, the Saundersons packed up and went to Boston just yesterday."

"Aye. And arguments turn into fisticuffs almost every night at the tavern," Simon added. "Lines are being drawn. Tempers are at snapping points."

Such talk continued over the course of dessert, and although Chaynoa usually absorbed every word spoken about the volatile times, she found herself inattentive, her thoughts drifting as unpredictably as clouds. She had tried not to show abashment over the panoply of food and luxury, the likes of which she had never seen, but the fact that she sat at such a feast gowned in silk and ribbon, her tightly laced corset molding her into a figure as modishly erect as the other two women, astounded her. She almost feared to eat or speak lest the dream be shattered.

During the course of the evening Courtland's mother had not addressed her once, nor had Simon, beyond a formal nod of his powdered head, but in spite of their coolness and her unaccustomedness to the company of such important people, exultation lay just beneath the surface of Chaynoa's quiet mien. She had triumphed. She had climbed the hurdles they had initially presented and was fast becoming a part of their esteemed society. Soon she would be hostessing her own gatherings.

Through the flames of the candelabra she observed Courtland. Since their quarrel in the clearing yesterday the strain between them had not lessened. She knew that she had erected an armor of sorts against him; because she could not lie in his arms at night and let him be satisfied, and because she needed to keep her guilt at bay, she had directed her energies toward winning a place in the community. But she was beginning to think that she would exchange it all just to see Courtland look at her the way he had when she had first arrived at his house in a tattered rag.

"What's that racket outside?" Virtue asked now, turning her head toward the darkened window. "It sounds like singing."

Peebles arose from his chair and strolled to the window to investigate, drawing aside the fringed velvet drapes. "Why, 'tis a group of townspeople carrying torches. They seem to be walking alongside a wagon . . ."

In a scraping of chair legs, all the guests rose, Jack and Courtland moving to aid the ladies while the voices of several dozen people drifted through the window.

"What are they doing, Stepfather?" Virtue asked excitedly. "Is that someone riding in the wagon? 'Tis so dark I can't tell."

Simon threw open the casement and, amid a rush of cold September air sharpened with the scent of burning pine, exclaimed, "Good lord! 'Tis a man they have tarred and feathered."

"Tom Shandy," Courtland murmured, bending out to better view the dramatic procession that crawled up the road. He had gotten wind of the plan to humiliate the Tory sympathizer last night at the tavern.

Everyone gazed down at the poor wretch, who, limelit by the blaze of torches, sat manacled in the cart wearing his painful black coating of pitch and goose feathers.

"This sort of thing is becoming more and more common in Boston," Jack said with a shake of his head. "The patriot mobs call it 'humbling the Tories.' "

"Well, they should be humbled," Susannah declared with the dispassion usual to her nature. "If you ask me, they're nothing but cowards afraid to fight a war."

The exuberant townspeople with their bobbing rushlights passed the house shouting loudly and singing off-key. Someone in the mob glanced up to see Simon and his dinner guests observing from the window, and yelled, "To freedom! To independence! To hell with Gage!"

"To freedom!" Jack returned with an upraised fist.

Virtue, concerned with politics only as far they related to household and social matters, but eager to support her betrothed's cause, echoed his enthusiasm, and leaned so far out the window that her lace-edged petticoats showed. "Humble the Tories!" she shouted.

The singing increased in volume until it became nothing more than tuneless bellowing, and the fervidness of this new patriotism that blew over the land like a fresh and unquelled gale so infected Chaynoa that she, too, thrust her head out the window. Then in a burst of heartfelt sentiment that surprised not only herself but all the others standing near, she cried, "Humble the Tories! Send the redcoats home!"

"You're truly one of us now, Chaynoa!" Virtue exclaimed, squeezing her shoulder. "No one can doubt that."

Beside the two women, Courtland clenched his jaw and stiffened.

Chapter 18

As the coach passed through the city gates of Boston Courtland gazed through the window at the low, cold townscape, his thoughts troubled. Jack had invited the Days for a visit to his home, with the double purpose of providing chaperonage for Virtue, who pleaded to escape the rural climes and experience the excitement of the city.

Beside Courtland, Chaynoa craned her neck as if not to miss a single sight. She had never set foot in a city before and he could tell by the tensing of her clenched gloved hands that excitement beset her at the prospect of such a treat. Even her initial worry over a separation from Hahnee, who was in the tender and judicious care of Iris Oakchurch, had receded.

"So many bells!" she exclaimed as they turned onto the rough cobbled pavement of High Street and heard the churches proclaim the hour in exultant tones.

Jack smiled. "The one that has a low, sad peal is King Chapel. And hear the sour one? It belongs to New North. The high dignified chime is from Christ Church. Their bells open and close the market every day, and on Sunday they call the townsfolk to worship. Christ's is the highest steeple."

Amid the divine clamor handbells rang on every corner, wielded by hawkers advertising strange wonder cures, shoe shines, or the imminent serving of a delicious meal at the Bunch of Grapes Inn. Cowbells tinkled on the necks of lumbering bovines as lads drove them toward the common, and shop bells dinged with the passage of hurrying patrons, all while the harness bells of a hundred carriage teams danced their own jingling melody.

Boys blowing tin horns and beating drums drummed up business for tailors, milliners, goldsmiths, bakers, apothecaries, and jewelers, while oystermen cried, "Oys! Oys! Buy any oys?" Other fishermen competed with hoarse shouts of, "Fresh haddock, cod, mackerel! Come and buy at the head of the ferry ways!"

Scurrying between them, dodging the gaily painted carriages with sleek plumed horses, black chimney sweeps toted brooms and filthy blankets full of soot, yelling, "Sweep o' sweep! Sweep o' sweep!"

Chaynoa looked all about in wonderment, the odors of rum, tar, and packed humanity blending with the tang of the white-capped sea, which lapped rhythmically at the long jutting wharves. The coach had turned onto Ship Street, a crabbed, century-old lane snarled with carts, drays, and wheelbarrows, and their driver had to abruptly haul back on the lines to avoid collision with a bespectacled headmaster conducting a tour for a straggling line of schoolchildren. While they were stopped, a vile odor drifted through the coach window, prompting Virtue to clap a hand to her nose.

Jack laughed. " 'Tis Seneca Oil. See the Indians selling it there on the corner? They dip a blanket in

an oil spring, then wring out the noxious stuff into
bowls, which they try to peddle as a cure for rheuma-
tism."

"People actually buy it?" Virtue gasped.

"Believe it or not, they do. They smear it all over
themselves, I'm told."

The coach moved on, passing the wharves and
warehouses of the city. Long Wharf, closed now that
the port was empty of any ships save the British
man-of-wars riding anchor a few leagues out,
stretched gray and desolate in its abandonment.
Many of the once busy shops along the wharf were
boarded up as well, and visions of the myriad tall
masts, hailing from every port in the world, that had
once vied for space at the industrious docks remained
only a ghostly memory.

"The most peculiar wonders used to be on view
here," Jack said with a tightness about his mouth.
"Polar bears, tigers, outlandish machines, even a
pickled pirate's head in a jar. And"—he added, raising a brow at Virtue—"life-sized fashion dolls wearing the latest vogue from Paris. Mrs. Hiller managed
a marvelous waxworks on the next block, too, with
lavishly dressed kings and queens in her historical
display."

He looked across at Courtland. "The pinch is
being felt here. The wealthy are not much affected
yet—inconvenienced perhaps—but not straitened.
But the poor . . ."

Courtland had noticed the signs. While the ladies'
eyes had been filled with jewelry gleaming in shop
windows and fashionable ladies sauntering in silk, he
had glimpsed queues of grim-faced people waiting to
receive food. He knew from Jack that a Donation
Committee had been established to dole out contributions pouring in from the countryside, charity

meant to aid the sailors, mechanics, carpenters, and warehousemen out of employment. He knew too that the recipients of this benevolence were asked to work in return, clean the city wharves and streets, or do repairs. And recently the town selectmen had created hundreds of jobs in the brickyards, an effort financed by cash contributions generously given in order to keep the city afloat during the British occupation.

With assessing eyes Courtland had also noted the sea of army tents that covered every vacant field in Boston, and the cannon mounted upon the surrounding hills, an undeniably formidable sign of the military presence in this town. Countless soldiers in scarlet tunics strolled the streets, stoically ignoring the oyster shells and sea coal furtively hurled at their backs. And when the coach rolled past Province House, where Tories and British soldiers congregated to socialize, he saw a knot of officers idling on the steps, laughing as if their spirits were high in spite of hostile local resentment. Without a doubt, Boston was the only place in Massachusetts where Parliament's laws were able to be enforced, the only place where Gage was in control.

Courtland had written to the general regarding Jack's invitation and, hopeful of Courtland's gaining access to a Sons of Liberty meeting in Boston, Gage had granted permission. Captain Day's regiment had been ordered under penalty of severe punishment not to acknowledge an acquaintance with Courtland if they encountered him anywhere in public. And since he had only been in Boston two days prior to his departure for Swanston, there was little chance he would be recognized by anyone else.

As the coach turned back in the direction of Boston Common toward Jack's house, a peculiar thudding sound, perfectly timed and in rhythm, came to the passenger's ears. The tramp of nearly a thousand boots rang upon the cobblestones to snappily barked commands and, unbeknownst to the others, it was a tramp Courtland recognized well—and strangely missed.

The two women leaned toward the window to get a better view. Facing the near side of the coach, parading down the adjacent street, marched long disciplined lines of British soldiers, their bayonets agleam above dashing cocked hats while drummer boys beat an even cadence below the colorful silk of their fluttering banners.

Virtue's mouth fell open. "Will you look at them—their lines seem endless!"

"Three hundred and seventy parade every day," Jack drawled, folding his arms across his chest. " 'Tis Gage's way of showing us his strength. I can tell you the tempers of our citizens are at a boiling point with his effrontery. We suffer the sound of marching or target practice constantly."

"Oh! Close the window, Jack, dear," Virtue complained. "And draw the blind down so we aren't forced to see any more of those detestable redcoats. Besides, the November air is freezing."

Jack did as she requested and solicitously drew her fur-lined cloak more snugly about her shoulders. At the sight of his tender attentions Chaynoa lowered her eyes to study the brown serge gathered across her lap. The gown was another gift from Virtue. Even if she could have found ample fabric in the ever dwindling supplies in Swanston—and assuming Courtland could have afforded to pay for it—there had not been time to have a traveling suit of her own made up before the trip. It was odd, Chaynoa thought, how her feelings had changed regarding Virtue's charity. At the Peebles's home several weeks ago she had felt like a princess swathed in the borrowed beige gown, but now she struggled against the experience of a poor relation. No doubt part of her discomfort derived from Courtland's reaction to the borrowed garments; she had caught the look upon his face when his sister, like the agent of some benevolent society, had carried in the gift. He had said nothing, but his eyes had glittered with what could have been offended pride.

She frowned, for it seemed many troubles ripped at the delicate fabric of their strained relationship. The memory of the most recent incident made her shudder. One evening Courtland had come in from a thunderstorm to find her in the kitchen and, wordlessly, as if unable to help himself, he had walked behind her and pressed his lips to the back of her neck.

She had started, and then, as if fear were an enemy to be conquered, she had closed her eyes and endured her husband's touch, let him slide his hand inside her chemise and cup her breast, praying desperately that she could let him carry through. As she stood rigidly and forced herself not to push his hands away, tears had streamed from her eyes. But Courtland had sensed her silent struggle and his fingers had fallen away from her quivering body abruptly. With shame, she knew that her cringing compliance had been more daunting to his manhood than any passionate outburst. And since that night, he had not laid a hand upon her. Nor had he spoken a word beyond the stilted conversation necessary to everyday living. His evenings were all spent at the tavern, and as Chaynoa lay listening in the attic night after night, distraught and sleepless, she never heard the tap of his boot heels on the stair until well after midnight.

Now her eyes slid askance to regard his hands,

encased in snug tan leather, where they rested atop
his thighs. She saw the edge of his shirt ruffle peeking
out from beneath the turned-back cuff of his surtout,
she counted the covered buttons at the knee of his
breeches . . . one, two, three, four . . . He had been
quiet during the journey, and although he had not
leaned forward once in his seat to view the passing
scenes, she knew his eyes had missed little. She wondered what thoughts he turned over in his mind, for
when she risked a glance at his face, his jaw was
clenched. Was he thinking of her?

Presently they arrived at Jack's home, which
proved to be a commodious brick one situated across
from the nearly fifty-acre common. Her first impression as she was ushered inside was favorable; the
residence was not so large as the Peebles estate, but
quietly elegant with marble mantels, teakwood pan-
eling, and inlaid floors.

Jack's father, as overweight as his son was spare,
greeted them exuberantly, and his sister Priscilla
rushed forward to meet everyone with a warmly
demonstrative touch. Chaynoa thought her the most
beautiful woman she had ever seen with her glossy
red hair artfully styled to best enhance its natural
curls, and her cream polonaise gown dipping low to
display overabundant curves. The widow possessed a
quick infectious smile that brought an answer to the
lips of those who glimpsed it, and her high white
brow was classically rounded and intelligent.

When her eyes alit upon Courtland's chiseled face
and tall frame, they widened perceptibly, so that the
jade-green irises appeared surprised, or satisfied. In
turn, Chaynoa noted, Courtland seemed to regard
her with the avid though carefully unobtrusive appreciation men reserve for conspicuously sensuous
women.

With grace and a talented knack for encouraging lively conversation, the fair Priscilla ushered them into the dining room and presided over a tasty noon meal, and afterward, when they all sat together in the parlor sipping cherry wine, asked her guests about their plans for the afternoon.

"I should like to take Chaynoa to North Square to shop," Virtue declared. " 'Tis becoming so tedious trying to buy anything in Swanston these days."

"Well," Priscilla answered, "most of our shops still have a fair selection of goods. Many people are strapped for money and dare not squander it on anything other than the bare necessities. Heaven only knows what will happen in the months to come. Better go and enjoy yourselves while you can. 'Tis cold out, so dress warmly, and I shall have tea awaiting when you return."

"Tea . . . ?" Jack inquired with a teasing lift of a brow. "You are serving tea, dear sister? Have you become a Tory?"

"Oh, Jack! You know 'tis only Labrador tea."

"That vile stuff you brew from herbs? Ugh! Spare us and serve coffee instead."

Priscilla laughed unself-consciously, joined by the others, and, after offering everyone marzipan from a silver dish, turned her attention back to Courtland. "And you Mr. Day?" she inquired with her bright head atilt. "With the ladies off shopping and Papa and Jack busy at their warehouses, what will you do?"

"I have business to see to, but 'twill only take an hour or so. Would it be an inconvenience to you if I returned here afterward?"

"Oh, of course not! You are our guest. Spend as much time here as you wish. I fear you shall have to endure my company, however," she said with an eloquent gesture, "for I have decided to be a stay-at-home today."

" 'Twill be my pleasure to enjoy your company."

Chaynoa drew on her gloves and stood to let the servant drape her cloak over her shoulders, waiting for Courtland to acknowledge her departure. But even when she bade him goodbye and took Virtue's arm to go, her husband did not escort her to the door, but only rose and inclined his head before returning his attention to Priscilla.

Distressed by her husband's ever-growing remoteness, Chaynoa's spirits did not renew themselves when the coachman handed her down at North Square. The square, which was really a triangle, sat one block inland from the waterfront, and therefore caught the sea winds, whose chilly gusts played havoc with cloaks and hats. Despite the chill, pedestrians bustled about the marketplace, creating a swirl of color that blended with swinging shop signs, polished brass, and gleaming bow windows. Old North Meeting House rose at the apex of the triangle, flanked by shivering trees which hung on to the last shreds of their orange foliage like modest maidens clinging to tattered camisoles. Country people, many speaking only German, sold vegetables out of two-wheeled carts, their horses unharnessed for the day and pawing at tethers while farmers' slaves trudged past loaded down with grain sacks. Lively boys herded flocks of fat turkey while yeoman in leather breeches displayed hens, hams, and firkins of butter in rickety wagons.

"Prices seem reasonable here," Virtue commented as they wended their way through a noisy maze of cages packed with quail, partridges, and pigeons. "Turkeys are two shillings, butter is six shillings a pound, veal three shillings a pound. But Jack says fuel is exorbitant. He says the house will be cold this winter. Of course," she added with a sour expression. "I've no doubt the redcoats will be warm enough. Jack says they buy up all the fuel and much of the best produce."

Their breaths frosty puffs in the air, the two young women hurried past a silver shop displaying sword hilts, baptismal basins, teapots, and dog collars, and, veering left, headed for a fashionable milliner's Virtue often patronized.

"Here it is!" she said, pointing.

They turned and nearly collided with a British officer exiting the establishment with a huge box in his arms.

"I beg your pardon," he apologized, and, removing his hat with its edge of silver lace, swept it before him in a respectful flourish while holding open the door. "Allow me."

Virtue lifted her chin and raked disdainful eyes over his elaborately trimmed tunic, and, addressing Chaynoa, spoke with scornful hauteur. "Let us go to the shop next door, dear, so we don't soil our shoes where *his* have trod. Snake in the weeds!"

"Grass," Chaynoa whispered, and with an aplomb no less dramatic than her friend's, swept her skirts aside while the maligned English soldier chuckled amusedly behind them.

When the girls returned to the Bretton house a few hours later, Virtue complained of a headache and trailed upstairs, leaving Chaynoa in the vestibule peeling off her gloves. As she dragged the hat from her head and felt warmth return to her tingling toes, she heard laughter, male and female mingled, which floated from the rear of the house. Quietly she wandered toward the sound in search of Courtland, and through an open door glimpsed her husband and

Priscilla standing beside a merry fireplace, coffee cups forgotten upon the mantelpiece while they perused a newspaper Priscilla held open in her hands.

Courtland stood close to his alluring hostess, his head bent to see what she pointed out upon the page. His teeth flashed as he laughed at some remark she made, and Chaynoa realized it had been a long while since she had heard the sound of his pleasure.

For endless moments she studied him unobserved, and saw him through suddenly changed eyes, eyes that fully realized the charm and the virility of the man in black broadcloth and white ruffled stock. Strange, she thought, that she had never seen him this way before, as other women must. She supposed she had always viewed him as a kind of protector from a storybook, an invulnerable sort of being with feelings not as strong, not as important as her own. As he smiled at the other woman now, she realized he was a person who needed just as she needed, who responded to care and attention just as she did.

Unable to suffer another moment of the scene, Chaynoa fled up the stairs, and when she had closed the door to the bedchamber and gone to peer at herself in the mirror, a new realization struck her. For the first time, through his very remoteness from her in recent days, Courtland Day had become a flesh-and-bone being to her, unimagined and . . . desirable.

Chapter 19

"You know, of course, that the East India Company nearly went bankrupt in '73. They had forty million weight of tea stored on the Thames back then, a seven-year supply. So what does England do? She gives the company the monopoly on the American market."

Boris Bretton, Jack's father, buttered his bread in disgust and shook his powdered head. "Did King George really believe we would endure it passively?"

The Days sat around the Bretton's elegantly laid table enjoying roast mutton and discussing the hot political topics that occupied the tongues of every Bostonian.

"What does that mean exactly?" Chaynoa asked, wanting to understand the causes that hurled the country toward conflict. She felt comfortable conversing with Boris Bretton, even if she did not feel at ease with the glances his worldly, widowed daughter threw in Courtland's direction like lures cast to some coveted animal of game.

"It means that England reduced the export tax by threepence so that the East India Company could undersell its competitors here in the colonies. The devil of it is, she taxed the tea on this side of the

Atlantic so that *we* should have to make up for the lost revenues out of our own pockets."

"Aye, Chaynoa," Priscilla further explained with a nod, "England appointed a handful of consignees—only *certain* merchants who could sell the tea—which put all the other tea sellers out of business. Horribly unfair. So we simply boycott and buy coffee instead. All except for the Tories, of course."

Chaynoa wondered if Priscilla was really speaking to her with condescension, or if she only imagined it.

"These days the Tories enter those British tea shops at their own risk," Jack commented, stabbing at a bite of mutton on his plate.

Courtland said, "I hear the Sons of Liberty are on the rampage here in Boston, tarring and feathering countless people loyal to the Crown."

Jack's usually amiable face hardened and he spoke bitterly. "That's right. If we can't send the redcoats back to England, we'll persuade the Tories to go."

A silence fell, during which everyone seemed to eat with more energy, spearing cooked carrots and pickled beets as if the morsels were enemies to be slain. While Boris wielded his knife he cocked his head to one side and contemplated Courtland across the table. "Speaking of redcoats," he said slowly. "We have one in our home."

Courtland's vitals tensed but his face remained expressionless. "Indeed . . . ?"

" 'Tis that blasted Quartering Act," Boris explained, attacking a bite of his mutton.

Courtland raised a brow. "You mean Gage's order that private citizens must house his soldiers until the British barracks are complete?"

Boris laughed. "Aye. Our carpenters refuse to build the blasted barracks, you know. Word is, Gage is bringing workers over from England to do it. But they won't finish before winter, and his soldiers will be freezing in their tents—those that aren't defiling our homes with their presence, that it."

Priscilla set down her wineglass. "We have one of those despicable Jack Puddings living right here in our home. Can you imagine? Ah, well," she added with a breezy laugh, "at least we take our revenge where we can. We've given him the smallest bed-chamber and refuse to take meals with him. He must eat leftovers with the servants or eat not at all."

"What's a Jack Pudding?" Chaynoa asked, for she had never heard the term before.

"Why, a British officer, of course," Virtue said. "Isn't that an appropriate name?"

Chaynoa smiled and nodded while Boris laughed above his wineglass and Courtland dabbed his mouth with a napkin.

Servants came in to clear the table and remove the damask cloth, revealing a more delicate one beneath, upon which were then set plates of cheeses, nuts, and a chocolate trifle, along with fringed napkins, clean glasses, knives, and spoons. A small trolley bearing decanters of port, claret, and sherry was rolled in and positioned beside Boris, and when each gentleman had poured a drink for himself and the lady next to him, conversation resumed.

"What is the officer's name?" Courtland asked.

Jack looked up at him. "What officer?"

"The one living in your house. If I should run into the scoundrel in the hallway some morning I'd like to know who I'm addressing," Courtland explained with a glib smile.

Boris growled, his mouth full of trifle. "He's Lieutenant Jeremy Eastham, arrogant as the day is long. Always talking about his father's estates in Yorkshire. Stumbles in drunk most of the time." He waved his laden fork. "I swear, if we do go to war, we'll face a half-foxed army. Ha! The damned redcoats probably won't be able to stop playing cards long enough to fight!"

Courtland felt his choler rise at the insult and for once could not suppress the dangerous need to argue. "They're bored," he said.

"What?" Jack asked.

"Bored. They're bored. And edgy now that Gage has forbidden them to carry their sidearms outside of the barracks in case they should be provoked and fire into a crowd. It wouldn't be an easy thing to have stones hurled at your head every time you stepped into the street, and have no way to defend yourself."

Every pair of eyes at the table turned upon him in curious regard, and Courtland knew that the hard, bright edge of condemnation had marked his voice. But he would not apologize.

Priscilla broke the awkwardness of the moment in the way of an accomplished hostess, her face as gracious as the cameo pendant nestled between her breasts. "I can see you're a man who can view both sides of an issue fairly, Mr. Day. I've always admired such a trait. Sometimes we feel so strongly about a topic that we become too narrow-minded. Don't you agree, Jack?"

Her brother sipped from his glass of port. "Of course."

"I know you're fair-minded, dearest brother," Priscilla said with a glowing smile. "Now, I shall take the ladies into the parlor while you gentlemen smoke and finish your port."

The ladies withdrew, and as Courtland looked askance at the two patriots lighting their long slender pipes with an ember from the hearth, he saw that their faces were as impassive as granite. He wondered if his pride had just spoiled his chance of winning their confidence, and the chance of gaining a coveted invitation to their secret society. He wondered, too, what would happen when he chanced to pass Lieutenant Jeremy Eastham in the Bretton hallway some morning.

That night Chaynoa could not sleep. She lay abed listening to the unfamiliar sounds of the city, of the town crier calling out the hour and weather, of the ceaseless clop of heavy hooves. The night did not even appear as dark as it should, for outside her window a street lamp glowed, its large glass globe lit earlier by a clattering fellow carrying a can of oil and a ladder.

She did not know where Courtland lingered, why he had not come to bed, or how she would react when he did. Could she lie beside him in the shadows, share a bed with him for the first time, still and mute, wondering at his thoughts while the rift between them widened silently into a gulf? Even if he were to lie no more than a few dark inches away, Chaynoa knew he would not touch her. She doubted he would ever touch her again.

Turning over upon her side, she plucked restlessly at the sheet. Where was he now? She had not been able to remain in the parlor another minute and observe her hostess as she took down book after book from the case and discussed the contents with Courtland. The pair had reviewed many stories, strange and wonderful tales Chaynoa had never heard before, and then they had examined a new volume of poetry, which Priscilla had recited in her soft well-modulated voice. Her comments were punctuated by her prompting smile, and Courtland grinned often in response.

Was he still downstairs with Priscilla now, sitting beside an intimate fire while the coffee cooled in the silver pot, speaking of people with strange names like Shakespeare and Swift? Chaynoa waited and waited, her eyes staring at the shadow play upon the wall, but he did not come, and desultory, she listened to footsteps ring upon the cobbles outside. Their thudding sound increased, grew very near, as if at least a dozen men sprinted down the road in heavy boots. When she heard shouts she sat up in alarm and tried to make out the bellowing demands echoing off the brick walls below.

Glass shattered suddenly, and, throwing back the quilts, she ran to the window, but had only a view of the dark common while the disturbance seemed to be occurring at the building across the street.

Slipping into a wrapper as she ran, she hastened down the stairs to find Courtland and Priscilla already poised at the open front door. They were watching an unruly mob of men who swarmed around the residence next door hurling rocks through the windows and shouting. Each of the villains had his face blacked and wore a white stocking pulled low over his brow, and two members of the frightening assembly rattled the door violently as if to yank it off the hinges.

"What are they doing over there?" Chaynoa cried.

Courtland barred her way with his arm. "Careful. Stay back. Glass is flying everywhere."

Horrified by the chaotic scene outside, she failed to understand his lack of action. "Shouldn't we do something to stop them? They're destroying that house next door. Perhaps they intend to murder the people inside."

"There will be no murder," Priscilla said composedly. "My father and brother are involved. They're doing what they must do with the Sons of Liberty. The old rascal who lives there has been buying English goods and selling them in his shop. We've known him to be a Tory for some time, and his moment of reckoning has come."

In nightdress and cap the victim had been dragged out into the cold while his molesters invaded his house, and, by the sound of it, smashed up the furnishings with no mercy at all. A few minutes later the disguised Liberty Boys dashed out of his door and into the night, their fists raised triumphantly while their shoes crunched upon broken window glass. The street lamps illuminated the white stockings pulled over their faces in an eerie way that seemed to transform them all into tall destructive ghosts.

" 'Tis over," Courtland said tightly, his eyes still fastened on the forlorn old figure wandering confusedly in the cold. "You ladies go back to bed. I'll see what's to be done."

Without another word he left them, striding to the street where he took the frightened gentleman by the arm and guided him gently through his battered front door, which still gaped crookedly upon its hinges.

Chaynoa watched him pick up the old man's night cap and set it atop his head. With a strange, unbidden clarity she recalled the time Courtland had come to her cottage loaded with food, then recalled his stay in the Swanston jail on her behalf, and his unfailing patience with Hahnee. When Priscilla turned around to go to bed, cold and weary, she remained at the door determinedly, vigilant and watching, waiting for her husband.

She failed to hear the rear door of the house open and close, but when unsteady footsteps thudded behind her all at once, she started and wheeled about.

A man faced her in the uncertain light, and she instantly discerned the glint of pewter buttons and the gleam of a cutlass hilt sheathed at his side. Because there had been so much talk of war and bloodshed at dinner, and because the hatred of Gage's troops had settled determinedly in her breast—heightened now by the act of violence just witnessed—she stepped back in instinctive fear; the uniformed man looming over her seemed to represent the whole British army.

"Hey, you're not the red-haired beauty of the house," he drawled, "but someone new." Stepping close, he reached out as if to touch her loosened hair, laughing when she cringed. "My God . . . I've never seen hair so long."

"Nor or you likely to again if you lay your hands upon my wife."

Jeremy Eastham did not fail to recognize the voice of his superior officer, the man he loathed, even if he was too bleary-eyed and the room too dark to clearly discern Day's visage. He almost opened his mouth to address the captain by name, but his benighted brain cautioned; Lieutenant Eastham would not be flogged to death for revealing Day's identity. In the last few months he had made it his business to discover the captain's mission in Swanston, and knew precisely what he had been assigned to do there, although gaining access to that well-guarded information had cost him plenty. He did not know that Day had gotten himself a wife in the interim, but found the news exceedingly interesting, and wondered if Gage had been informed.

"My apologies," he said with an unctuous, unsteady bow never meant to be respectful. "But . . . it *is* lovely hair."

Courtland stepped forward to seize him by the arm, and Chaynoa took the opportunity to disparage the man, her usual reserve giving way to a burst of indignation. "You drunken bloodyback! What they say about all of you is true. I hope the patriots send you back to England!"

"Chaynoa!" Courtland snapped. "Go upstairs."

She did as he bade, climbing the steps in reluctance, glancing worriedly over a shoulder to see the two figures in the vestibule facing each other in a hostile way.

Once upstairs, she stood restively at the window gazing down at the common and its sea of army tents, which appeared as pale perfectly aligned rows of triangles. Dawn approached and a few soldiers began to emerge, stretching their arms before rudely relieving themselves in the shrubbery.

Chaynoa turned her eyes away in disgust, and analyzed her sentiments regarding this army who threatened the peace of the colonies. Although she would have liked to claim a care for politics, she knew her feelings had much more to do with personal interests. She had come to love the white clapboard house on Queen's Road, love the stout kitchen with its copper pots and stone hearth, the rocking chair which soothed her cares at the end of every day while she sat watching Courtland write. She had found a place there in the village, and she did not want to leave it; she wanted the warm days of every summer to touch her as she knelt in the garden, she wanted the cold evenings of every winter to be kept at bay by the hearth fire and Courtland's solid presence. But what if this army with its endless supply of well-equipped soldiers were to clash with the colonials, start a long and bloody war, march through the countryside burning and looting until little remained of what she knew? What if they destroyed the house on Queen's Road, and Courtland went away to fight?

As if the idea would strangle her she raised a hand to her throat and swallowed.

Although the sun peered over the edge of the tree-tops now, she did not bestir herself to dress. The night's disturbances had shaken her composure, unbalanced the tenuous safety of her world, while Courtland's growing detachment undermined the security he had always provided before. She yearned to see him step through the door, yearned to run and lay her head upon his shoulder and feel his arms go round her, the tension dissolved, the strife gone, and safety returned. She yearned to have him vow never to leave her, never to admire again with his gray eyes any woman but herself.

But when he did enter the room a moment later, she could not bring herself to go to him, to plead for his arms, for her desire was not greater than her fear of rejection. She saw that his expression was shuttered, and he scarcely glanced her way as he opened a clothes press and removed a fresh suit of clothes. He obviously did not intend to stay with her and rest.

She felt ill at ease in his presence, yet determined to force feelings to the fore. "Did you convince that despicable soldier to go to bed?"

He gave her a strange look over his shoulder, an unpleasant look. "Yes." The word was short and clipped.

Stung, she turned to the window again and contemplated the tents below, where redcoated men, huddling in the cold, sat about on camp stools eating rations.

"Why don't they just go home?" she said scornfully, waving a hand. "Just pack up and leave us alone."

Across the room Courtland stilled, his fingers pausing on the buttons of his waistcoat. And as he looked at his wife's slender form outlined by the bloodred light of morning, his eyes narrowed all at once, as if she had become a complete stranger, someone he was not even slightly acquainted with anymore. Who had she become?

Unreasonably, he condemned her all at once for failing to sense who he was, for failing to respond to him in any way save that of a servant hired to care for him impersonally. It infuriated him that he could want her so much while she wanted him not at all—except for security, or to maintain her precious place in respectable society.

Yanking off his wrinkled dinner waistcoat, he threw it across a chair, and with cool sarcasm answered her question. "They don't leave because this country happens to belong to their king."

His cruel tone provoked Chaynoa and made her contentious. "No, it doesn't—it belongs to the people who labor to carve a decent existence out of it. It belongs to the people who live here."

Courtland laughed derisively. "You mean to Jack and to Boris and to Virtue, and to those gentlemen in knee breeches down there on the street? Did the Indians believe that when you lived with them? Did they believe that even though *they* were the ones carving out a decent existence at the time, the Europeans had a right to it? Should all of us leave now and give it back to the natives? That would validate your argument, wouldn't it?"

Color rose in her face at his unsparing attack, and with angry eyes she watched him open the wardrobe and remove a clean coat.

"Conquering the weak and stealing their land is what the world is all about, Chaynoa. 'Tis what it's always been about, and always will be. You're more naive than I think if you believe otherwise."

She stared at his face as if searching to find someone she knew in the guise of a stranger. "I have never heard you speak so harshly."

He stepped close and gazed down at her, his mouth twisting into a discourteous smile while his eyes held hers squarely. His voice was woundingly direct. "That's because you don't know me. Nor have you ever sought to."

She held his gaze for a full moment, seeing in his eyes coldness and resentment and something else she could not name. Although she struggled to find one, no rebuttal came to her lips; she could not deny his words, and her eyes were the first to slide away.

Courtland pivoted, and in a silence so violent that his wife could hear its energy in the way that he undressed himself, he removed his shirt and breeches. She bit her lip and kept her back turned, listening to the swish of fresh linen as he tucked his shirttail into his waistband, listening to the whisper of his coat lining as he thrust his arms through the sleeves. The two of them were married, and yet, such strangers that she could not even turn around and look at him while he changed his clothes.

Out of the corner of her eye, she caught his reflection in the mirror, and watched while he knelt and began to polish his boots with a quick, furious hand. When he had finished that task he went to the shaving stand and ordered his hair with a comb before taking up his razor to shave. She noted that he used his left hand to perform the ablutions, and the detail caused a memory to prick her all at once. She had always respected his privacy before, never pried into his business or into the elusive mystery that sometimes seemed to surround him, but now, insensitive of his need for secrecy, she blurted a question in retaliation. "Who shot you the day you stumbled into my cottage? Why were you wandering about the woods bleeding to death?"

The sound of his shaving ceased, and water slowly dripped off his wet hand to splatter in the basin. When he answered his voice was quiet and inexplicably chilling. "You once accused me of having ghosts locked up in my past. Well, it should please you to know that you were right. I do have. But much to your misfortune, I'm going to keep them locked up, keep you in suspense—at least, until I'm forced to do otherwise."

"What do you mean?" she demanded.

His eyes glittered and he wiped his jaw with a towel, straightened his stock, and buttoned up his jacket, all with no haste. Then he pressed the latch of the door, and, still ignoring her question, added, "And when I *am* forced to do it, God help us both, for it will be one damned disastrous day."

Chapter 20

The next day the sky clouded and snow began to fall. Courtland stood amid its hissing descent, his eyes focused upon the four British battalions encamped upon the common. His own regiment was not there, but quartered at the Distillery in West Boston, and he felt a sudden unbearable restlessness to rejoin them, to quit the sham into which he had become embroiled and return to the honorable position he had earned for himself.

Despite the cold he had earlier removed one of his gloves, and his cold fingers turned a small silver ring over and over in an absent rhythm. It was a wedding band he had purchased this morning for Chaynoa, and as he contemplated its unbroken circle and the dull light its metal reflected, he wondered why he had bothered.

Far better to be disencumbered, free. In binding himself to her, in loving her—and he *did* love her—he had created a great tangle in both their lives, and when the unraveling finally came, the shreds of their relationship, still fragilely woven, would be undone.

His eyes strayed to the ground, to the puddle at his feet, and he pondered the ice-glaze that rigidified its surface, feeling as if a similar, but more formidable frost lay between himself and Chaynoa, one he did not know how to melt. He had tried patience, compassion, kindness, all to no avail. And when those methods had exhausted themselves he had tried to take her in his arms and force the ice-glaze to shatter. But it had not, and now as he remembered her the night he had held her in his arms, stiff and shivering with tears streaming from her eyes, he felt disgust. It was an emotion which, even if unfair, was honest. She had been right in her prediction; her scars were too deep for him to heal, and they had outlasted his patience.

He sighed, trying to think of other matters. Last night, much to his surprise, Jack had taken him to a house in Brattle Square where the Sons of Liberty convened. He had listened carefully and learned a few important secrets, but felt little resulting sense of triumph. Each day he relished his mission less and less, his enthusiasm waning with the difficulty of betraying men with whom he socialized and dined, men who had bestowed their trust and who were loyal to a cause they believed worthy.

After the meeting, he had sat alone in a tavern half the night, thinking, weighed down with a despondency that assaulted him on several fronts, and for the first time in his marriage, seriously and assessingly, he contemplated infidelity. He was a healthy man with no lack of opportunities for bed companions, both in the lower and upper ends of town. A serving maid at the tavern had offered herself, flattering his bruised male pride. Then this morning Priscilla had contrived an opportunity to pass him in the hallway, and he had known that were he to create an opportunity, she would spend an afternoon with him in pursuit of physical adventures.

He wondered if his life was to be spent this way,

weighing the risks, the guilt, and the pleasures of unfaithfulness before returning each night to his own hearth and to the woman he loved but who could not love him.

He pocketed the ring and replaced his glove, sliding it over his cold fingers while hearing footsteps rasp over the light dusting of snow.

"Captain." Jeremy Eastham's red tunic shone bright as blood against the grayness of the morning. Glancing around to make certain of their privacy, he affected an apologetic smile. "Permission to join you, sir?"

Courtland eyed him, feeling no enthusiasm for his company. He nodded coldly.

Jeremy stepped close, his hands clasped together behind his back. "My apologies for the other night, sir. I was full of rum and had no way of knowing that she was your wife, of course."

"Of course," Courtland replied with no forgiveness.

The lieutenant stared out beyond the tents to the artillery companies as they began target practice on the common. In between the rounds of musket fire he spoke irritably, soldier to soldier, as if needing to vent his discontent. "Yesterday Gage asked the town selectmen if we could attend church service in Faneuil Hall, and the bastards refused their permission—they were disinclined, they said, to worship with any one wearing a red coat. Bloody hell, I'm beginning to wonder who gives Gage his orders—King George or the pompous fools here in Boston."

Courtland raised a brow. "Still anxious for war, Lieutenant?"

"Anxious for something. God, 'tis dull here. And frustrating. We're forbidden to carry sidearms, you know. And if an alarm occurs at night we've been forewarned to march to our posts without loading our muskets. If we're attacked in darkness we can only defend ourselves with bayonets. What sort of commander leaves his men so vulnerable?"

"How is morale?"

The lieutenant lifted his shoulders. "There's a deal of grumbling in the ranks. We're having to dig our own fortifications because these damned colonial laborers refuse, no matter what Gage offers to pay them. And the forage money the general promised us hasn't materialized yet. But confidence is still high. Our men know that there will be no contest between these backwoods yokels and His Majesty's Army."

"And you believe that?"

Jeremy observed the captain's impassive profile. "Of course I believe it. Don't you?"

" 'Twill not be as easy as Gage and the rest of you judge."

As if he had just heard a traitorous statement, the lieutenant countered slyly, "A few in our ranks are deserting. I hope your . . . forced stay with the Swanston colonials hasn't changed your sentiments, too, Captain."

Although his tone remained unruffled, Courtland's eyes flashed a warning. "Need I remind you that I'm still your superior officer, Lieutenant?"

Jeremy bristled and his face grew red. With effort he kept his voice controlled. " 'Tis just that I couldn't help noticing that your wife is quite a patriot. *Sir.*"

Courtland swung around. "You're dismissed, Lieutenant Eastham. And since you profess to suffering a dullness of routine, I'm assigning you to fortifications duty. You may begin now."

* * *

Priscilla had planned a social evening, and Courtland found himself more enthusiastic about the occasion than he might normally. He was restless, filled
with ennui, and had to admit that the colonials knew
how to enjoy themselves, how to dance and dine with
none of the stiff trappings and insincere propriety of
the London fetes which he had attended.

The Brettons had no ballroom but they had
removed the furniture from their parlor to allow
room for dancing, and in defiance of the shortages of
luxury items imposed by Courtland's comrades-in-
arms, a buffet table stood well stocked with food in
the dining room. Indeed, the mood of the guests
seemed expectant, and with a disturbing presenti-
ment Courtland wondered if these people, too,
sensed that the political tension would soon explode
and allow the future course of their country to clearly
emerge at last. The demarcation between causes grew
daily more defined and stretched, and although neither side relished war, both accepted its eventuality,
and both only procrastinated the inevitable in order
to better prepare for it.

Amid feathers of falling snow, guests arrived, the
frosty air of their entrance chased away by blazing
fireplaces and the hot mulled wine dispensed from
silver urns. The gowns of the ladies were the colors of
the last of the autumn leaves swept away now by the
first breath of winter. Damask, velvet, and satin glim-
mered with diamond beads of melted snow as it reflected flames of candlelight.

Chaynoa had not yet come down, and Jack intro-
duced Courtland to each guest, joined by Priscilla,
whose baroque shoulders and breasts rose like a
fluted column out of a gown no less bright than her
hair. When she brushed close he smelled her liberally
dashed perfume and saw the sheen of moisture on her

full lower lip, his body reacting with a strong natural response. Indeed, it seemed wherever he glanced, plump breasts, soft arms, and swan-curved necks adorned with trembling jewels assaulted his senses, until he felt hot in his wool jacket and a little mad with the compulsion of his fantasies.

Several gentlemen engaged him in conversation, a servant offered him a brandy, yet he glanced repeatedly at the stairs, anxious to see his wife.

At last she descended with Virtue, swathed in velvet the color of a summer forest. Although he had not really been able to afford it on a captain's pay, he had provided money for the dress, wanting to see his wife in no more castoffs. He was gratified to see that her hair was not piled modishly over one of the ghastly cow-tail heddus rolls used by the other women, but simply plaited in two gleaming ropes coiled at the back of her head, the front smoothly brushed to accentuate the line of her brow. She wore no powder or lace gloves, and no jewelry, for he had given her none yet. Her satin slippers, embroidered and topped with pink rosettes, were her only real concession to vanity.

His wife's simplicity amidst so much artifice stirred Courtland, and he waited until she met his eyes, wanting her to read his admiration. But in the darkness of her gaze he found only rebelliousness and hurt, left over from his curtness toward her yesterday. He was surprised and deflated, for he had not believed her prone to petulance.

She did not join him, but looked away and went with Virtue to Jack's side, so that he was left alone in the center of the vestibule.

"Are you going to get yourself inoculated?"

Courtland realized he was being addressed by an

elderly gentleman wearing a Ramillies wig and a puce waistcoat. "I beg your pardon—"

"Advertisement in the *Evening Post*," the fellow repeated, sipping his drink and rocking on his heels. "Some doctor from Constantinople claiming he can prevent smallpox with the prick of a needle. Do you believe it?"

"Aye," Courtland said absently, his eyes following Chaynoa across the room. "I was inoculated in Europe last year."

"You don't say? Didn't make you ill?"

"No, it didn't. Excuse me." Preoccupied and annoyed that his wife seemed to have no intention of seeking his company, Courtland hailed a servant and ordered a glass of whiskey. As he tossed it down a moment later, he watched Chaynoa chat with Jack. She moved with ease amidst people now, speaking in her quiet but attentive way, which gave her a peculiar selective allure that seemed especially appreciated by the male gender.

"Did you know Gage ordered two more deserters executed today on the common?" Boris asked, sidling up to him with a plate of food in his hand. " 'Tis rumored that he never pardons them. Hah! I suppose all the redcoats would desert if he didn't make examples of them. There's plenty of land to be claimed in America, after all. A resourceful fellow could make a new life."

"If he were so inclined," Courtland replied irritably.

"Precisely. And many chaps are." He crammed a bite of seed cake in his mouth. "By the way, have you heard Gage's latest decree? Beginning next month, Bostonians who are not sworn Tories will not be able to travel freely out of town. One must go to military headquarters and apply for a permit, state why 'tis necessary to leave. Damned tedious business. We won't tolerate it long, I can tell you."

Nodding now and then, Courtland listened tolerantly, the talk of Gage and his army heating the room while the evening slowly passed.

It was midnight before Chaynoa retreated upstairs after graciously bidding her host and hostess good evening. Courtland watched the trailing hem of her sacque gown slither from step to step as she ascended, and gulped the last drop of his whiskey in his glass. In a half hour or so he would follow, speak with her, attempt to sort through the complicated net of their relationship. He would kiss her more tenderly and less urgently than he had before, persuade her to yield, and once she had, all would be well between them. A physical bond would be sealed, one unrefutable and lasting, and it would help their marriage withstand the blow of the secret he must reveal. Afterward, he would take her hand and slip the silver ring over her finger as a sign of his devotion to her.

Most of the guests had departed. Only a few unescorted gentlemen determined to drink every drop of rum in the house remained, and as he conversed sociably with them, Priscilla approached and pressed a brandy to his hand insistently.

"Mr. Day," she said, smiling up at him so that he saw her mouth move smoothly over her teeth. "Do go to the library and fetch my fan. I swear 'tis stuffy in here despite the cold outside. I left it on Papa's desk, I think. Or perhaps on the mantel."

Courtland found himself still staring at her mouth even after she had stopped speaking. His eyes flickered over the skin of her throat and downward where the cleft between her breasts created a dusky line that disappeared inside the ruching of her gown. The scent of her flesh distracted him.

He had had too much to drink, he realized. Nevertheless, he continued to sip his brandy while he wandered into the library, which was empty and warm—hot, in fact, he decided, twisting his neck against the tightness of his stock.

Priscilla's fan proved invisible, lying not upon the cherrywood desk or on the marble mantel, and he roved irritably about the room in search of it, checking the bookshelves and chairs to no avail, wondering where in the devil a woman would lose such a thing. His head throbbed from too much drink, and just as he was about to retreat empty-handed, Priscilla entered the room, and, with no self-consciousness whatsoever, shut the double doors behind her.

He looked at her in the appraising way of a man who recognizes a woman unoffended by bold male scrutiny. "I couldn't find it," he told her, the words sounding thick and slow.

She came to stand so close he could see the dusting of powder on the ridge of her collarbone. "Find what . . . ?" she whispered.

Good lord, Courtland thought, she would make love right here, right now if I asked. He was experienced with women like Priscilla, and while that experience functioned as a warning, it also served as a seductive reminder. " 'Tis stifling in here," he murmured, going to the window and forcing open the sash. He leaned out and breathed in the bracing cold.

Behind him, she laughed, then walked forward in a swish of rich fabric. "The gentlemen are engaged in a game of whist," she confided as if they were conspirators. "And the ladies have all gone to bed."

An exciting sense of danger aroused Courtland suddenly as he looked into her inviting green eyes, and he reminded himself that he was a man who enjoyed danger and had gone too long without it.

Here was a woman who enjoyed it, too, and she was drunk, maybe not as drunk as he was, but comfortably relaxed.

When she reached out a hand and slid it over the lapel of his jacket Courtland knew that it was the lady's habit to consummate her flirtations. He considered the pleasure, unused to denying himself for the sake of compunction, and with no conscious decision to do so, found himself kissing her all at once, his action so rough and selfish he felt on the level of some rutting animal teased too long in the field. His frustration seemed to burst and grip him violently, drench him with the heat of need, and he felt lost within the flattery to his maleness that only a yielding woman could provide.

Priscilla grabbed his hand and pressed it to her breast, and he groped, slipped his fingers inside her gown to grasp what she would offer. Her own hand crept beneath his jacket and over his waistcoat, between the buttons of his shirt, and he ground his teeth in a yearning for pleasure.

His conscience, half ignored until recently, struggled with his physical longing and shouted at him to reason. With his head thrust against the curve of Priscilla's scented neck, he hesitated, but realized he did not want to stop . . . did not want to stop . . .

She pulled his jacket off one shoulder, and with effort he drew away, pushing aside her insistent hands while shaking his head as if to clear it. "We've had too much too drink . . ." he muttered, forcing his eyes from the breasts he had fondled. He glanced about to find something to cover her with, and spying a tapestried rug on the sofa, cast it over her shoulders.

"You needn't go," she said with no trace of anger. "Indeed, if you prefer that we go to my room—"

"You're very charming, Priscilla, but I prefer that you go there alone just now."

He was hardly more composed a moment later when he stumbled upstairs and threw open the door to his bedchamber. Chaynoa sat at the vanity brushing out her hair, still gowned in the green velvet, and the embroidered slippers peeked out from beneath her hem like two stamens from an opened blossom. Her hair was spread in curling bouquets over her shoulders and her lips were as pink and tender as two parted petals.

She stared at him as if he were not quite sane, and as Courtland caught a glimpse of his reflection in the mirror he realized her reaction was not unjustified; his hair fell over his brow, his clothes were rumpled and his face was flushed with his recent encounter.

"Chaynoa . . ." Surely, he thought, every ounce of his frustration conveyed itself in those three short syllables.

But she stood up as if prepared to sidestep him, and he moved closer and held out his hands in appeal. "Did I tell you that you're lovely, were the loveliest woman downstairs tonight? I don't think I've told you enough. I should tell you more."

He knew he was doing badly and, blinking, tried to focus his eyes upon her face. She was afraid. She was afraid of him just as she always was. He remembered the ring, and with every good intention fumbled in his pocket, kneeling unsteadily at her skirts, clutching them in his arms, marveling at the softness a month's wages had bought, thinking how green was the color, as green as the woods where he had found her.

Her hands were clasped restlessly at her waist, and he reached up to still them, draw one apart from the other like two intertwined vines. They were ice cold and the thin silver band slid easily over the knuckles of her left hand. He closed his eyes and buried his face in her warm skirts again. "You need a ring," he whispered huskily, "I never got you a ring."

Her hand moved, touched his hair, stroked it, and the gesture spurred him into a hard, melting pleasure. In one swift but unsteady jerk he stood up and seized her mouth with his, ignoring the stiffening of her limbs as he used the weight of his body to press her to the wall. As he had so many times he imagined her freed from the gown, pictured the shape of her calves, the texture of her waist beneath his hands, the fall of her hair spilling over his arms as he drew himself into her.

His hands felt so heavy and clumsy he did not bother unfastening the tiny buttons down her spine, but jerked the gown loose, fending off her efforts to impede him, ignoring her cries as she strained to push him back.

I'll force her, Courtland told himself, *just this once I'll force her, and afterward I'll rock her in my arms and tell her how much I love her . . .*

"Courtland!" she cried. "Courtland, for God's sake, don't do this—not like this! Not like—"

Chaynoa battled him in earnest now, turned her head from side to side to avoid his mouth, writhed beneath his hold, twisted her wrists free when he sought to pinion her. Their mingled breaths were harsh creature noises in the darkness, the sound of their struggle violent. She scratched his chin with her nails and pummeled his chest, finally sliding down to her knees and scrambling away before he could snatch her back.

Courtland reeled, suddenly too drunk to stand, and braced his throbbing head against the wall. He was alert enough to realize two things: his wife had run away from him, and he had nearly committed a forceful act that would forever have divided them. He was sorry, he wanted to say he was sorry. But instead, in an outpouring of impassioned anguish, he balled his fits and slammed them against the wall, shouting, "I can't stand what you're doing to me, Chaynoa! I can't stand it a day longer. Do you hear me? You've got to stop what you're doing to me! For God's sake, how can you make me fall in love with you and then act as if you blame me for it!"

But she put her hands to her ears, shut out his voice and left him, running downstairs to the garden exit of the house where she snatched a gentleman's cloak off a peg before slipping out into the dark wilderness of the city. The sudden cold did not daunt her; she felt a part of it and stopped in the still, ice-riven miniature garden to breathe it in. She could still hear the echoes of her husband's voice and put her hands over her ears to shut out the sounds of its anguish.

But still she heard it and, as if to flee the hoarse plea of a strong man fallen into desperation, ran. The snow had ceased, and the church spires were inverted icicles pointing to a frigid heaven where the moon reigned and eerily outlined the frost-sculpture of the city.

Leaving cloud breaths behind, Chaynoa hastened to the gate, whose frozen wrought iron burned her hands, and, slipping through, entered the street with its mottled cobbles. The road lay empty, the houses slept, and the street lamps were myriad moons in a row. Her heart hammered with her husband's cries, and she began to run madly with no destination in mind, needing only to be free of his words, free of walls and fences so she could think.

She found herself on the common, and shuddering

at sight of the ghostly tents, turned her back and went toward the waterfront, searching for comfort in the rhymes of the surging tides. But the sea spread itself before her in the form of a remote, unsympathetic void, and while she stared into its nothingness memories of the woodlet home and its loneliness assailed her.

After a while her feet grew so wet and cold she had to retreat. But she refused to reenter the house. She returned to the garden and, finding a secluded site beside a row of sheltering yews, sat down, huddling in the heavy cloak with her feet tucked beneath her gown and her hands thrust in the pockets. Then with her eyes closed she tried to summon the echoes of her father's people, tried to feel the solace of nature, the spirits of the living things around her. But they would not come to soothe her and lend direction as they had always done before. She had abandoned them long ago for another way.

And so she waited for dawn, knowing what she must do when it arrived.

Courtland was asleep in a chair beside the window when she returned to the room. His long legs were sprawled, relaxed, and one arm dangled to the floor, the sleeve pushed up. A broad sword of early sunlight angled in through the panes and banded his chest in citron. His jacket and waistcoat were thrown carelessly upon the floor with his stock, and his shirt was half-unbuttoned and wrinkled beneath the arms. Below his tumbled hair a frown marred the space between his brows, as if even in slumber his mind was not at ease. With a vague and unpleasant surprise, Chaynoa realized that he was no less vulnerable than she, no less capable of pain.

Her slippers were silent upon the flowered carpet as she approached him, and when she was close enough, her hand trembled as she extended it toward the point of his cheek. His head was tilted at an angle, resting against the red leather of the chair back, and she breathed deeply, touching the rough, warm plane of his face, the lean place above his jaw. As her fingertip moved, she had the odd notion she touched a reclining marble god created by an ancient storyteller.

Courtland's eyes opened, red-rimmed but beautiful. The sun slanted across and illumined the clear irises, turning them almost blue, almost the color of a perfect heaven. He blinked as if such pure light hurt them, and stared up at her face.

Without a word Chaynoa moved her hand to his mouth, to the well-molded lips which were slightly apart, then brushed his hair off his brow. His eyes stayed fixed to her face, narrowed, brightly hard with distrust and weary anger. Undaunted, she braced her arms on either side of his chair and slowly stooping down, touched her mouth to his.

He did not move as she kissed him with her inexperienced lips, but kept his hands upon the arms of the chair, unresponding, tense with the expectation of disappointment. Her fingers traveled to the buttons of his shirt, which she twisted to unfasten, and when the garment gaped open below the collar and she slid her fingers inside to touch the bareness of his skin, the muscles of his belly contracted in anticipation.

She stepped between his legs and slid to her knees, and in wonder he looked at the top of her warm dark head where the sun made it gold, then closed his eyes as her mouth trailed over his chest in a path.

Before resolve abandoned her, Chaynoa then un-

tied the front of her gown and bent her body so that
the nakedness of her breasts came against his. The
pure sun streamed over them, melded their flesh together with moisture, and Courtland reveled in the
clear, sharp pain of the moment, hearing his breath
and hers, only dimly hearing the pulsing march of
soldiers' feet outside. She pushed the shirt off his
shoulders, then slid her fingers down to find his hand,
which she raised to her lips and, after kissing it,
pressed to the bareness of her breast.

Courtland touched her there with reverence,
looked in her eyes for leave to do more, which she
gave with a grave lowering of her lashes. Beneath his
hands, her gown descended to the floor in a shivering
river of green, followed by lacy clouds of linen, atop
which two silken slippers fell, one turned upon its
side.

He stood up, and when she placed her hand at his
breeches with intent darkening her eyes, he stayed
her from what she would do. Slowly he moved backward with her to the bed, which was an untouched
rectangle of bright white centered in a room without
shadows. He looked at her unclothed form, more
lovely than the one created in his imagination, and
knelt down to bury his head at her waist, touch her
thighs with his hands, slide his fingers down her legs
to her slender feet and back up again.

He did not pull her beneath him and cover her with
his weight; instead, he lay down upon his back and
lifted her atop his own body, and when anguish
crossed her face, he murmured gentle words to stay
her apprehension.

And in the melted gold morning Courtland lay
beneath Chaynoa, breathed, moved, and gloried in
his wife's knowledge of what it was he needed. He
cried out, letting himself be eased, relinquishing his

whole being to the terrible, splendid rage of pleasure . . . even if she would not.

A few blocks away, Jeremy Eastham sauntered out of the headquarters of General Gage, replacing his hat with a smile that was almost obscene in its satisfaction. Inside, the general summoned an aide with a wrathful flourish of his hand. "Get the personnel portfolios from my desk and bring them here," he snapped. "I shall have to send another man to Swanston. And if that bastard Courtland Day has betrayed me, he'll go to London and be hanged for it!"

Chapter 21

They spent the day together, walking the snowy streets of Boston, smiling in spite of their frozen cheeks, and eating pastries in a tavern along with cups of sugared coffee. Chaynoa had never felt such lightness, and not even the hard-faced men in red uniforms who patrolled the streets with bayonets dampened her happiness. She was loved by a good and protective man, and she realized that nothing else in her limited and unusual life had ever sent her spirits winging quite so high.

She recalled their lovemaking with a certain forced detachment, but with an appreciation for his tenderness, for when he had grown too urgent and she had stiffened, he had checked himself and waited until she could reach out for him again. He had never loomed above her or pressed her down. In the bright warm room he had understood, anticipated the direction of her fears and altered the acts of his lovemaking to help her through the culmination, after which he had cradled her in his arms and whispered his satisfaction.

"We had better go back to the Bretton's," he said now, opening his surtout and wrapping it about her as they tracked through a new veil of snow. "You're cold."

She had been admiring a basket of puppies a ragged child sold on the street corner, and turned away at her husband's suggestion, resting her head against his shoulder. When they arrived at the iron fence enclosing the Bretton home, a man detached himself from the line of hedges and stepped forward.

"Courtland Day?"

"Aye?"

"A letter for you, sir."

Although the envelope was not addressed in Gage's hand, Courtland knew it could be from no one else. "Er—Chaynoa," he said, glancing about. "Why don't you go on in? Put your feet by the fire and warm yourself. I'll be along in a while. Go ahead," he prompted with a smile.

When she had walked up the steps after glancing over her shoulder once to receive his reassuring nod, Courtland addressed the courier. "Am I to reply?"

"No, sir. I was told these were orders."

"Thank you."

After the man walked away Courtland fingered the envelope with no perturbation, assuming it contained orders to return to his regiment. That meant Chaynoa would have to be told tonight, told who he was and what he had been doing in Swanston. She would be surprised, of course, she would . . . *It won't matter. She'll take it in stride. She'll be proud to find that she's a captain's wife.*

He tore open the letter, his eyes narrowing as he read, his stomach tensing in dismay. These were not orders to return to his regiment, but orders instructing him to make a tour of countless towns and villages stretching from Massachusetts to New York for the purpose of infiltrating patriot meetings. It was a tour that would take him all winter to complete.

He stared at the snow falling upon the pavement and thought of the ironies of life, of the unexpected impediments that always came to thwart the even-keeled course of a contented existence and make it disjointed. With a smile of bitterness he refolded the letter and turned around.

Chaynoa was perched upon a stool before the hearth humming softly to herself when he entered the bedchamber. Her shoes and boots were peeled off and cast aside, and her petticoats raised above her knees so she could warm her feet before the roaring blaze. "Come and join me," she said happily. "Your nose is more red than mine. Oh, what is that?" she asked, suddenly noticing the basket in his hand.

Wordlessly he set it down and retrieved the contents.

"Courtland! 'Tis a puppy from the litter on the corner!" She took the little dog in her arms, putting its squirming body to her fire-flushed cheek, and laughed with delight. "You went back to purchase it for me?"

He nodded and gave her a smile that did nothing to chase away the grimness of his eyes.

"Come and sit beside me," she invited again, patting the warm floor in front of her stool. When he knelt, she released the puppy and slipped her arms around his neck, whispering, "Thank you."

He held her, his chin resting against the top of her head, and felt his joy from the day, from their earlier lovemaking evaporate into a gloomy morass, for he knew happiness was not an easy specter to call back once it had flown.

He dreaded what he must say, and to delay the

inevitable moment asked a rhetorical question. "Do you like the pup?"

"Oh, yes! You know I do. Hahnee will adore it as well. He's even more partial to animals than I am."

"Perhaps the dog will be company to you this winter."

"This winter?"

He stared into the fire and, assembling his story, delivered the deceit in guilty unease. "That letter—the one the man delivered down on the street—it concerned my financial affairs. I have to leave tomorrow, travel down south on business."

Chaynoa drew back, one of her thin hands still resting atop his shoulder. "I'll go with you."

He looked beyond her stricken face to the orange embers and the black wreckage of charred wood that had fallen through the grate. "I'm afraid I have to go alone."

"Why?"

" 'Tis best. But I'll escort you and Virtue back to Swanston first, then be on my way. Hahnee can continue to look after the stable while I'm gone, and I know you can rely on Iris or my sister for anything else you may need. We'll have to depart Boston in an hour. Can you be ready?"

She stared at him and, because she was disappointed and failed to understand his obdurate evasion after the intimacy of their day, grew distant, absently sliding his ring on and off her finger. "It's urgent then . . ."

Courtland nodded, feeling her suspicions grow. "Aye. 'Tis urgent."

"What sort of business is it?" she asked with a studied casualness that belied her sharpened interest.

He forced a smile. "Nothing that need worry you. But will you be able to manage in Swanston without me? If not, I could ask Jack to let you stay on here—"

She shook her head impatiently, dismissing the diversionary question, then lowered her lashes and turned away from him on the stool. "You'll be gone a long while."

"The winter. But I—" He paused, regarded her profile, unable to resist laying his knuckles alongside her cheek and stroking its softness. "I don't want to go, Chaynoa," he breathed. "I wouldn't go if I had a choice in the matter. But I'll be back. I'll never leave you. Do you understand? I'll never leave you."

Her arms came around his neck again and she embraced him tightly as if to hold him from going. He stroked her head and murmured that he loved her and, before he could be swept away by his own desire, stood and quickly gathered up the candles around the room. The day had grown gray, and after lighting the wicks, he placed candlesticks in every corner, knowing that darkness, that being touched in darkness, was a part of Chaynoa's terror.

When the glow of a half dozen flames made the room softly radiant, he sank down with her upon the carpet beside the hearth. Her billowed skirts made a striped sumptuous cloud beneath his head, which he had laid upon her lap in an interim of sensual enjoyment heightened by the desperate ache that always precedes the separation of lovers. He held her for long moments in this way, his arms wrapped about her waist and his hands still, until she relaxed and let him kiss her.

Then, after a log crashed and sent a shower of bright sparks spiraling up the chimney, he eased her back and began to caress her, knowing it would be the last time in many months. He waited until she slid the gown from her body in her silent, grave way, watched the amber of the fire touch the native brown

of her small but womanly breasts, watched as she
drew down the white foam of petticoats to reveal a
dusky belly and deerlike legs. Unpinning her coil of
hair, she sat upon her heels as he removed his own
clothes, waiting solemnly with the long braid twining
over her shoulder, her eyes black and glistening, the
scent of her skin the scent of earth. He lay back with
his head upon her pillow of skirts, and she came to
him, pressed her fingers to his open mouth while he
slid his palms over the firm tawniness of her breasts.
With tenderness he lifted her atop his body, and she
shifted, placed her hands upon his chest and half
closed her lids so that her lashes cast long obscure
shadows over her cheeks.

As snow clung like thistledown to the windowpanes and the fire hissed in the grate, she denied him
nothing of her body, and although he vowed his love
again and willed her to do the same, she did not
surrender to him the words he whispered so needfully
to her, nor did she cry out, when, with his face twisted
in passion, he gasped her name aloud.

The winter passed, but it passed upon creeping,
frost-bitten feet that left icy tracks over silent fields
and riverbanks. Although nature was oblivious to
anything save its own mysterious cycles, the country
split in two. In the province of Massachusetts one
was either a patriot or an enemy, and was labeled
such with no consideration of past friendship or fa-
milial connection. To escape intolerable treatment,
Tories poured into Boston from the villages even
while the poor of that city slowly starved, and dysen-
tery swept through both civilian and military ranks
with equal favor. The troops blamed the plague upon
their inadequate quarters, adding one more com-

plaint to a vast list of others continually submitted to their beleaguered general.

In the streets of that tension-fraught town the patriots growled at the king's troops and the king's troops growled back, punishing citizens who encouraged deserters and executing those captured deserters before public firing squads. Riots were common; once, in a particularly bloody foray, city watchmen used their hooks as weapons and British officers retaliated with drawn swords, hacking off noses and fingers with no discretion. In order to divert his restive men and direct their energies, Gage sent them into the country on eight-mile marches wearing full battle gear, and with an absence of respect they tramped over stone walls and through grain fields provoking the helpless rage of farmers who already faced the hardship of a poor harvest.

The Continental Congress resolved to stand up to Britain, and village politics became an underground business fraught with feverish preparations and countless antigovernment plots. Mobs kept the courts closed in protest of Parliament's oppressive Acts, and the Sons of Liberty tightened their ranks in response to disturbing rumors that British spies roamed the countryside in search of secrets.

In Swanston, men began signing up for militia duty, although the ranks were slow to fill, for wages were only one shilling four pence, and laborers could earn nearly double that amount on the farms. The town organized two companies of minutemen and one volunteer troop of horse whose men were required to have a musket, bayonet, knapsack, cartridge box, and thirty-six rounds. While they drilled on the common in slush and snow, and studied their manuals of arms by firelight, stores of supplies were amassed and hidden in every house and business, arriving often in ox carts filled with dung or packed in candle boxes to divert British suspicion. Town guards were posted at the crossroads to alert citizens of any distant glimpse of a scarlet tunic, and false alarms sent hysteria rippling through the streets like wildfire.

And still, Courtland did not come home. Chaynoa clung to the white clapboard house as one clings to a dear treasure threatened by some unseen but lurking thief. She kept it perfectly, waiting for the day when Courtland would return and sit at his desk again, sup at the table with her, trudge in from the snow smiling and ruddy-cheeked. She needed the security of his nearness, for she had drawn her own inner strength from it, and without him she felt like a nestling on its first tentative flight. But as the months passed, her wings inevitably matured, and so did her independence in both thought and judgment.

Courtland wrote to her erratically, and Iris read the letters aloud until Chaynoa could decipher the scrawled lines herself after diligent lessons with Robbie. To be able to read the words her husband had penned gave her immeasurable joy, and many afternoons she sat beside a frosted windowpane in hopes of seeing a messenger tramp down the road with a letter in his pocket. Never did Courtland send these infrequent correspondences by post, nor did he provide her with a forwarding address. She wondered at his secrecy, and the burn of unassuaged curiosity vexed her until the burn kindled into a raw resentment. He had abandoned her when the country hurtled itself toward war, when food was growing scarcer and rumor more alarming. Before he had left, she had even lain in his arms and pleasured him in utter abandon in order to bind him to her more irrevocably, and still he had gone away. What business would be so important?

At least Hahnee seemed content in his own inscrutable world, although with the hindrances of his poor brain and mute tongue she never really knew his state of mind, but only received hints of it through his childishly candid actions. He tended the horses conscientiously, and on bitter nights she coaxed him to come inside the house and sleep beside the fire, enjoying his familiar company, loving the sight of his funny, twisted face, which to her was more endearing than ugly. During Christmas he had rescued two raccoons from traps, but as she had nursed them back to health, he had forgotten them. Her brother had a new diversion that winter.

In an imitation of the militia men he saw drilling on the common, he paraded around the house with the old musket, which was harmless, for last summer Courtland had removed its firelock so that Hahnee might keep it safely for his own play.

"He's a man," Courtland had told her when she expressed her concern. "Let him feel like one."

Chaynoa did not lack for occupation. She worked about the house and eagerly accepted invitations to quiltings and socials, fully ensconced now in community affairs, helping sew uniforms and assemble cartridges for the militiamen. She exchanged recipes with other wives and was called upon with increasing frequency to bring her basket of cures and tend an ailing child. She delighted in holding Sadie's infant and secretly wished for one of her own. She believed that the last vestige of the woodland creature she had once been had fled forever, and was glad, unaware that another had found that creature beautiful.

The pup Courtland had given her had grown to be a sad-eyed spaniel, one she called Rembrandt when

Iris told her it was the name of a great artist. She hoped the name would please Courtland and make him laugh. It did. But not until the snows had melted and the crocuses pushed forth their white, sleep-wrinkled heads from the thawing ground. Once more the earth had quickened and come alive, and although it proclaimed a season of promise with its unusual warmth, every heart feared that the blood of its countrymen would soon mingle with that of its enemies and christen the new green life.

On a shimmering day in April Courtland rode his horse to the front gate, and, after dismounting with the eagerness of a long-detained voyager, strode quietly to the front door, wanting to savor the moment of his homecoming, to notice every image and scent that made it extraordinary. He could scarcely wait to see Chaynoa; during the length of his absence she had come to represent all the best things he had ever sought to steal from life.

The door was open to permit the breeze and he entered noiselessly, seeing the furnishings just as he had seen them every night when he had summoned up their shapes and held them in his mind before the image of Chaynoa escorted him into restless sleep. He had continually feared for her well-being, and had sought the news from Boston at every stop, prepared to throw Gage's orders to the wind and return to his wife if conflict erupted.

Now he could hear her moving in the kitchen, and walked quietly to the doorway. In an instant he absorbed the entirety of the domestic picture: the bundles of drying herbs and wild flowers hanging from the rafters, the jars of purple preserves lined on rows of new shelves, the familiar pewter arrayed on the cupboard, loaves of bread in baskets, the butter churn in the corner next to a Guinea straw broom, a shirt to be mended draped neatly across the rocking chair arm. The pup, now grown, snoozed beneath the open window where the curtains billowed, and two raccoons peeked from behind a stool.

Just as he had seen her do once before in a time long past, Chaynoa was dipping candles. She wore the simple muslin gown, and her movements were as practiced as ever, so smooth that the long brown braid scarcely swayed. Her back was turned, but he could see her neck, her ear, the loose curls at her nape where perspiration beaded. The wax smelled earthy and hot, and he noted how the slender candles quickly paled in color when she raised the rod from the kettle. He took a breath. In that moment life seemed whole, unstinting, and perfect.

Chaynoa turned. At first she only stared at him with disbelieving eyes. He wanted to step forward and sweep her into his arms, but checked himself and waited for her to respond, wanting to find in her eyes an emotion that matched his own.

He did not. And yet, she let the candle rods fall to the floor and threw herself against him with a little cry. "Courtland . . . oh, Courtland! I thought you'd never come back!"

"I told you I would," he said smiling. "Remember?"

She nestled her head against his shoulder, and he caressed her hair in long adoring strokes before lifting her chin, then kissing her mouth. She complied, responded with ardor at first, but after a few minutes slipped out of his arms and put a small but determined distance between them.

Courtland sensed restraint in her manner, and at first surmised it stemmed from the awkwardness over their long separation, but after examining her face more closely, decided she was angry with him over the amount of time he had been away. In the way of a wronged wife she sought to make him suffer a little before unbending, and he resigned himself to speak of casual matters until she gave up her stiffness. "You and Hahnee have been well?" he asked.

She retrieved the candle rod from the floor. "Aye. We've managed fine. And you?"

"I fared well. But tell me the news of town—surely there's much for me to catch up on."

"Only the business of war. Everything revolves around talk of it. But I'm sure you read the papers while you were away."

Her tone was cool, and he felt a quick resentment over the unfairness of her attitude. "What has happened here at home while I've been gone?" he asked, keeping his tone light. "What have you done with your days? While I was away I often pictured you working here in the kitchen, or in the garden. Obviously you worked very hard. A man couldn't ask for a more pleasant house to come home to."

She poured a mug of cider, set it down before him, and answered with an indifferent shrug. "I did the same things I always do."

"Am I not to be forgiven?" he inquired with a quiet directness.

"Forgiven . . . ?" she repeated, turning her back again. "Forgiven for what?"

"For going away."

She stilled and, putting the candle rod down, turned to look at him with a serious, straightforward regard. " 'Tis not the going away, Courtland. 'Tis your secrecy over it. You surely don't consider me so naive that I would believe your contrived excuses."

For a moment he contemplated her with equal gravity. "If I swear to tell you everything very soon— as soon as I have leave to do so—will you come and sit here beside me, will you let me hold you? I've dreamed of it, Chaynoa," he confessed. "As often as a man can dream."

She considered him as if to gauge his sincerity, and then in a rush of quiet remorse came to him, opening herself for his embrace and clinging to his shoulders with all the pent-up anxiety of many months. But she did not kiss him.

"What do you call the pup?" he murmured against her ear, wondering with a niggling disappointment if she would always have to be coaxed into his arms this way.

"Rembrandt."

He drew back to search her face. A sweet smile curled her lips and brightened her eyes, and she put her arms around his neck, pressing her cheek to his until the edge of his disappointment slowly melted away.

Before the afternoon of his homecoming could fade into twilight Courtland banished the last of Chaynoa's resentment with his natural charm, so that when he finally grasped her hand and drew her out of the kitchen, she allowed him to lead her up the narrow stairway to bed.

They came together while the day slowly waned, their long intertwined limbs turned pale by the last rays of a descending sun, their dark heads bent together in a renewal of unshared but fevered passion. Courtland had bought her a bracelet, a circlet of plain but good silver for which he had traded his pocketwatch in Albany, and as he put his mouth to her breast again, he slid it meaningfully over her wrist, hoping in vain to hear the words she had never given him.

Chapter 22

"We have a British spy in Swanston," Chaynoa said over breakfast two days later.

Courtland's hand tightened around his coffee cup, but he kept his voice composed. "Really? I didn't notice him hanging from the highest tree on the common when I rode in."

She laughed. She was making cheese and smoothly shaped the curds in the cheese press with her thin, practiced hands. " 'Tis just an idea Iris and I have. No one else seems to take us seriously. He works for your stepfather around the estate—gardening and painting and the like. A plain young man, but he has sharp eyes, and he snoops."

"Snoops?"

"Aye. Lurks about watching people and asking odd questions. No one tells him anything of significance, of course. His name is John Freeman."

Courtland helped himself to another slice of bread and carefully spread marmalade over it. "When did he come to Swanston?"

"A few days after you left. He trudged through the village with a bundle over his shoulder and went door to door asking for work."

"Did he come here?"

"Nay. Now that I think on it, ours was the only house on Queen's Road at which he didn't stop and inquire. I wonder why?"

"He probably heard the gentleman who lives here is fiercely jealous."

"Oh, Courtland."

She laughed again and poured him more coffee, but his responding smile was absent, his thoughts suddenly troubled and far away.

Hahnee came stomping into the kitchen a moment later with the ancient musket thrown over his shoulder, his chin up, and his right arm held as straight as a rod. In a loud clomping of boots he marched around and around the room in an imitation of the town militiamen, and then with a clumsy but admirable effort performed an about-face before standing at attention beside the hearth. Chaynoa had dyed his jacket blue like the patriot uniforms, and on the days the militia exercised he proudly paraded around the common behind them, earning indulgent grins instead of the jeers he had once received.

"Incline left!" Courtland ordered now, knowing how Hahnee delighted in following exercises from the manual. "Prepare your arms! At ease!"

The feebleminded young man managed a fair mimicry of most of the maneuvers, and Courtland rose to give him a slap on the back together with a few words of high praise. "You're a good soldier, Hahnee. Probably better than half the officers in General Gage's army."

"Courtland . . ." Chaynoa said with a soft, secretive smile. She went to open a trunk beside the hearth and drew out a bundle wrapped in muslin, which with curious reverence she unfolded. A jacket, beautifully sewn and dyed the same blue as Hahnee's, was soon revealed, and she thrust it out at Courtland with a grave understanding of noble male duty. "I—I guessed that you'd want to join the town militia since all the other men are," she said. "They've been telling me all winter what a brilliant officer you'd make. After all, you're a natural leader, and no one can fire a musket as well."

Her eyes softened as she stroked the soft blue wool. "Of course it frightens me to think of you putting it on—everyone knows there'll be a war sooner or later. But . . . I'd be very proud to see you wear it."

Courtland stared at her. The thought of this eventual predicament had entered his mind, but not the possibility that his wife would come to care so much about it. He could see that in his absence Chaynoa had completed her metamorphosis from the girl he had rescued from innocent isolation, to an integral part of the Swanston community. Because she had wanted to be a part of it, and because it seemed the right and natural thing to do, he had helped ease her into the ranks of the stiff-backed matrons who so discriminately ruled the village. And now she was one of them. *She was one of them.*

He looked into her wide, radiant eyes as they stared at him expectantly, and the noose that had rested passively around his neck for months and months seemed to tighten as if jerked by invisible but malicious hands.

" 'Tis a fine jacket," he managed to say with forced gratitude, taking it from her outstretched hands while mustering a smile. "But, I thought I'd wait awhile to join the militia—after all, I've just arrived home. Isn't it natural for a bridegroom to want to spend time with his wife?"

Natural or not, fate and his own necessary but damning dishonesty contrived to rob him of that luxury of time.

Later that afternoon he sat writing at his desk, composing an impatiently worded letter to General Gage that was to accompany a revised list of the arms and ammunition hidden about town. Last evening he had gleaned the information from the Sons of Liberty meeting, and it now lay in his top desk drawer awaiting dispatch.

Suddenly he heard the bell of the meeting house toll, and as he listened, the frequency of the tolls increased to the peal of an urgent alarm. He threw down his quill and strode to the door, throwing it open to look up and down the street concernedly.

Townspeople poured out of their houses and shops or ran from the fields in response to the call, their faces anxious with the ever-present fear of an expected British attack. Courtland fetched his pistol from his desk, and as he thrust it in his belt, Chaynoa clattered down the stairs with laundry falling from her arms.

"The bell!" she cried. " 'Tis an alarm!"

"Stay inside," he ordered without glancing up.

"What is it?"

"I suspect a British regiment has been sighted on the road. I'm on my way to find out. Wait here until I return." He sprinted for the door.

Chaynoa threw down her bundle of laundry and hurried to the window, wondering with gripping dread if war had at last begun. As she passed Courtland's desk her skirts stirred a paper there, causing it to sail off and flutter at her feet. Distracted, she snatched it up, the letters *G A G E* leaping out at her with such clarity that she paused to stare at them. The letter she held was written in her husband's flowing hand:

Your Excellency General Gage,
    It is my unhappy situation at this time to be

expected by the People of this and neighboring towns to enlist in the Colonial militia, which Your Excellency knows has been organized by antigovernment factions and openly prepares for war with our own King and Country.

Although I am bound and ready to do my Duty to my King, I find the idea of donning the uniform of the Enemy repugnant, while at the same time I am alert to casting possible suspicion upon my motives, which would be perceived as cowardly were I to refuse Enlistment.

I beg leave to return to my regiment in Boston immediately. After nearly a year of Duty in my current capacity I believe I have furnished all the useful Intelligence possible and can be of no further Service in this regard.

> Yours and His Majesty's Faithful Servant,
> Courtland Day, Captain,
> 4th Regiment of Foot

To Chaynoa the world and everything in it seemed suddenly unreal; nothing but the pinpoint of light hurtling through her brain like a comet through a tunnel held her consciousness. The letter fell from her fingers and seesawed to the floor, where its downward sway created an agitated contrast to the utter stillness of her limbs. For long moments her mind was unable to absorb the significance of what she had read, and grappled wildly with the impossibility.

Then, energized all at once by a terrifying need to confirm the truth, and at the same time praying that the truth was not as it seemed, she fumbled with the unlocked drawer and seized upon the engraved spyglass.

4th Regiment of Foot.

As if turned suddenly to molten metal, it tumbled from her hands and rolled in a whirl of brass across the floor. A stack of papers lay in the open drawer, and she yanked them out, uncaring that she tore the edges. One read:

30,000 pounds musket balls and cartridges
100 reams of cartridge paper
256 tents
Firearms and green carriages made at Watton's mill.
Holsters, belts, saltpeter, beef, pork, all stored at public warehouse. Medicine chests stored in meeting house. Thirty-one hogshead of wooden ware stored at Oakchurch house—detail on map . . .

The sound of shouting and the persistent angry peal of the church bell did not penetrate her senses; her brain was numbed to everything that existed outside the gray haze of her discovery. Only her husband's footsteps ringing against the planked floor arrested her. He entered the room, his tall form blocking the light from the window, and with dull eyes Chaynoa looked up and saw his gaze focused upon the papers clutched like a crumpled but still deadly weapon in her hand.

"4th Regiment," she whispered thickly. "The King's Own . . ."

He said nothing.

"A royal corps." She spoke in a monotone, with labored deliberation, as if it were necessary to voice her husband's treachery in order to believe it. "Men chosen for their aggressiveness and skill in fighting. I heard Jack speaking of them once in Boston. He said that they were the best of what the enemy would use against us . . ."

In some part of his being Courtland knew that the end of a fragilely built but warm passage in their relationship had come, knew that no matter what words he chose to say, they would be unheard in the hollow chamber into which the two of them had just converged.

The church bell clanged in persistent fury, and with an effort he shook himself out of his thoughts. "Four companies of British regulars are advancing," he said quietly. "Their intent is to confiscate arms. Have we anything hidden in this house?"

She looked at him, and upon her face a most condemnatory smile served to further rend his hope. "Another for your list to the British general, Captain Day?"

"There's no time for us to gore each other with words, Chaynoa. What have you hidden here in my absence? Tell me quickly."

She raised her chin and flung words at him like retaliatory bullets. "The cellar is full of cartridges. There is cartridge paper in the attic. Will you use them in your own musket and *aim* it at us, Captain?"

He ignored her, turning on his heel and striding out of the house to join the chaos upon the street. Chaynoa followed in his wake, and with a calm but determined demeanor took up a stance at her front stoop, prepared to defend her home even if her husband would not.

Three mounted British officers trotted down the lane accompanied by companies of foot soldiers marching three abreast with muskets held at their shoulders. They marched to the sound of drum and fife, and that ominous rhythm, combined with the resplendence of their red column, created a vision that was terrifyingly intimidating.

Women trotted from their houses with children clinging to their skirts, crouching behind their gates to stare with paralyzing fear at the enemy. And the town militia, running with their arms half thrust in the sleeves of their blue jackets, clutched their weapons and looked outraged at the effrontery of the British invasion; at the same time they appeared to be at a complete loss over what action to take, for there were fewer than three dozen militiamen while the British ranks swelled to more than a hundred trained veterans in full battle gear.

With an insolent lack of haste, a lieutenant approached the Days' house and pulled his horse up short, directly addressing Courtland. "Are you Captain Day?"

Courtland stepped forward, and the throng of townspeople turned their heads to stare at him with a mixture of confusion and disbelief. He glanced at them, seeing every man and woman with whom he had ever dined, shared ale, or danced. "Aye," he stated grimly, but without a trace of shame. "I'm Captain Day."

A stunned hush fell over the crowd, and the lieutenant regarded their gaping mouths as if he enjoyed the abashment of these dull colonials who had just learned their trusted neighbor was an officer in the British army. "I carry a dispatch for you, Captain," he said, removing a packet of papers from a cylindrical leather case. "You're to return to Boston within twenty-four hours and report to General Gage himself. His Excellency has provided me with a list of arms and ammunition and the various locations in this town where they're supposedly concealed. 'Tis the list you compiled yourself on the ninth day of

November last. But frankly, Captain, the list is considerably beneath the general's expectations, and Private Freeman here has indicated that since your return to Swanston you've had ample opportunity to update this report."

Courtland observed the fellow John Freeman who Chaynoa had so astutely suspected. He wore the clothes of a working man and stood at the head of the officer's horse giving Courtland a level regard that was not quite disrespectful, but unmistakably knowing.

Even as Courtland met his pinning stare, he thought of the paper lying upon his desk, the one that could leave an entire village of men, women, and children defenseless if relinquished to the proper hands. His eyes shifted to the men of his own army; above their brightly decorated uniforms their young fresh faces suddenly seemed closed and foreign, unaffiliated with him in any way. In contrast, behind their perfect ranks the earnest sunburnt countenances of his neighbors frowned, and he moved his gaze from the blur of their visages to his wife, who stood upon the threshold of the place where the two of them had lived. Her eyes bored into his, penetrated them, while she held her breath like all the rest.

With futility he realized that the boundaries between patriotic obligation and emotional loyalty were never clearly drawn; and yet, somehow, he must find a place to draw a line between the two of them now.

He turned to the lieutenant. "If Private Freeman knows more than I about the hidden stores then let's invite him to share his information."

The officer pivoted in his saddle. "Private?"

With unease the young man shifted his feet, then hesitated a moment, glancing from the officer to

Courtland and back again. "I can't tell you," he admitted at last. "But I suspect Captain Day can."

"Do you accuse me of being negligent in my duties as an officer, Private Freeman?" Courtland inquired coolly.

The fellow reddened at the challenge, then looked up at the lieutenant as if for encouragement, and when he failed to find it, declined to take up the gauntlet. "No, sir. I do not."

"Then it would seem, Lieutenant," Courtland stated, "that the list you hold in your hand is complete."

The officer glanced at John Freeman as if to seek his confirmation, but the fellow only pivoted on his heel and stalked away, the sound of his footsteps followed by a low murmuring from the crowd.

The next instant would ever remain in Courtland's mind as the one moment in his life he would change if he could, regardless of the cost to himself or his destiny. Hahnee, dressed nattily in his blue jacket, galloped around the corner of the house, and playing some game dimly fashioned in his child's mind, aimed his inoperable musket at the long line of British ranks.

At the rear flank of the column stood an alert young soldier, who, acting upon an instinct, lifted his primed Brown Bess and fired in defense of himself, even as Courtland squeezed the trigger of his pistol in a desperate attempt to save the life of Chaynoa's brother.

But when the double reports had echoed off the clapboard house, both the soldier and Hahnee lay still upon the ground.

Screams of terror rent the air and weapons on all sides were immediately drawn; only the calm and authoritative voice of the British lieutenant diverted further bloody disaster on Queen's Road.

With a chilling cry of denial, Chaynoa draped herself over the body of her brother, while, across the road Courtland knelt to cradle the head of the young soldier he had slain. Confused, people shouted for the surgeon and ran into their houses for medical supplies, and through the disorder, Courtland looked desperately across the yard for his wife.

Still bent over Hahnee, her hand stroking his motionless face, Chaynoa glanced up and met her husband's gaze, and what Courtland saw in her eyes struck him. *She blames me.*

Even while he watched, the space between them seemed to deteriorate into a vast wasteland, one silent and empty, whose endless miles were unnavigable by anything other than grief.

Night had fallen over the white clapboard house. In the shadowy parlor the body of Chaynoa's brother rested in innocent nobility, laid in a simple unlined coffin around which a half dozen candles flickered like well-meaning but ineffectual sentinels. He wore the same blue jacket in which he had died, for Chaynoa had insisted upon it. No one had come to the house; she had tended her brother alone after Courtland quietly carried in the casket, and not one word—cold, cruel, or indifferent—had she uttered since. When he had tried to touch her, offer comfort, she had thrown off his hands.

Now she sat before the cold kitchen hearth and rocked to and fro in a slow, persistent rhythm that Courtland thought would drive him mad. Two candles sat upon the trestle table, but only one was lit, and its feeble but resolute flame fended off the night alone. He felt as if he would explode with the emotion roiling inside his chest, and still searching for the words for which he had searched in vain all night, he stepped forward.

"It was my duty," he said.

He knew he had uttered the words, he had heard them, but they were like stones cast into a deep well by a stranger's hand. "It was my duty, Chaynoa. I was *ordered* to do it."

The rocking ceased. But she neither turned around nor moved a finger, and he could see only the top of her head where it rested against the chair back. She answered him in a low, rancorous voice that gave him no quarter.

"If it is a man's *duty* to betray his neighbors, if it is a man's *duty* to betray his family and his wife, then you, Captain Day, have done it admirably. You deserve to feel proud."

Courtland did not know which was more excruciating, the blame or her dispassion. But he did know that she would say no more tonight, and that she would accept no comfort from him over Hahnee's death.

A coldness settled over him, the numb coldness that sits at the threshold of despair. Surely she could feel his agony, surely it was such a palpable thing that its dark smothering wings stirred the very air around her. But if it did, she displayed no empathy even though he gave her uncounted moments to do so. "Chaynoa—"

"Don't speak to me!" she screamed. "Don't say another word to me, damn you!"

He stalked toward her, ground his foot down upon the rungs of her chair to stay it, and spoke through his teeth. "I'll say plenty! You have given me no chance to support my actions, not a moment to explain, and you've behaved toward me as if I were not your husband but an enemy. You have no idea what war is really about, and you seem to have forgotten that there is another side to it other than your own. Out of respect for your brother I'll hold my tongue about what happened this afternoon until tomorrow. But then you'll be made to listen to what I have to say, make no mistake about that."

Swinging around, he left her then, going to his study and slamming the door. And for the remainder of the terrible night he sat there with his head between his hands, thinking, regretting, listening to the *creak, creak, creak* of the rocking chair until it echoed in his brain.

Early the next morning Hahnee was buried. No one of the village attended the funeral except the minster and his family, and finally, limping painfully but stoically up the hill, Iris Oakchurch arrived on the arm of her grandson. With the aid of the Reverend Reynolds, Courtland lowered the coffin into place, and while they wielded shovels and covered it with dirt, Chaynoa returned home without him.

A while later he entered the house and, wasting no time, confronted her, his voice stripped to hardness by her coldness. "We leave for Boston in an hour. Pack your things."

She stood in the parlor removing her black bonnet from her head. He would always remember the particular tilt of the brim, the way her thin hands stilled upon the ribbons to leave one loop draped over the point of her shoulder.

"I will not be going with you," she said with a chilling quietness.

"What did you say?"

She pivoted, her face as smooth as a mask. "I have

no intention of leaving Swanston. I have no intention of going anywhere with you."

The corner of Courtland's mouth raised, and he replied with a quiet sarcasm that seemed the only alternative to a savage retort. "You are my wife. Or have you forgotten?"

With a slanted, unwavering gaze she looked at him. "I am the wife of a Swanston liveryman."

"You are the wife of a British officer!"

She walked to the window as if to escape his nearness and his anger, as if needing to put a physical distance between them in order to illustrate the emotional one. "No, Courtland," she said sternly. "I am not. And I never shall be."

This turn of events, her cool comportment and resolute words stunned him, left him speechless. But he knew he had to say something to keep the conversation alive, for once silence fell between them, all that he wanted would be lost. "What about our feelings for one another?" he demanded. "Are those to be thrown away just because you don't happen to like my choice of profession, just because I was required to keep silent even when I longed to tell you the truth? Do you believe it was easy for me betraying those people? Do you believe it was easy deceiving you?"

An acid smile curved her lips. "I suppose it was easy enough to allow you to carry it off."

"Dammit, Chaynoa! What do you intend to do then? Watch me ride off down the road, for God's sake?"

"I never said that I loved you, Courtland!" she cried, throwing her bonnet to the floor. "I never said it!"

Her passionate outburst of honesty struck him, and all at once he felt as if he had just fallen from a great height and lay breathless and disoriented, flat on his back. He answered through his teeth, his tone cruel. "You're right. You never said it, did you?"

He saw that his cruelty had hit a mark, but it was a useless victory, for the game had ended yesterday, in the street.

"I have made a life for myself here," she told him flatly. "And I don't intend to give it up in order to traipse around after the despicable British army, living in makeshift camps with a pack of whores. Did you think I wouldn't mind?" she finished with a sneer of scorn.

He spoke slowly, with equal contempt. "Aye. I thought you wouldn't mind."

"Then you were wrong."

"It seems that I've been *wrong* about a lot of things."

The brass spyglass Chaynoa had dropped on the floor yesterday had never been retrieved. It still lay shining dully in a pool of sunlight, and she regarded it now with a significant raise of her brow. "I could say the same."

"Then why don't you?"

"Very well. What you represent is hateful to me, utterly hateful. And the fact that you were sly about it too—a traitor—destroys all the regard I ever had for you."

For a long moment Courtland observed her in disbelief, as if he could not accept either her contemptuous words or her own betrayal of him. His eyes narrowed, grew pitiless in their examination and in their unsparing accusal. Without uttering a single word he reminded her what she had been when he discovered her, and what he had done to change her life, all because he had cared to make her happy.

"I'll go and pack," he said with a hard gleam in his

eye. His lip curled with bitter mockery. "And you, my love, can stay here and defend your country."

After he had saddled his horse and left it at the gate he returned to the house one last time. The place seemed crushingly silent, so silent, he thought, that every piece of furniture appeared different than it had before, sterile instead of warm. In his study he packed his papers in a satchel and fastened it, and as he was going through his desk drawers his hands brushed against the stack of watercolor paintings. For a while he stared down at the pictures, meticulously brushed images, that, for years, he had prized above any other possession in his life. They seemed silly all at once, things that a child might cling to far away from home, and with a wry smile, he tossed them across the desk.

He found Chaynoa sitting in the parlor. The curious little carvings Hahnee had fashioned lay in a jumble upon her lap, and she fingered them while staring blankly out the window.

"I have left money for you on the table," he said quietly. 'Tis all I have presently, but more is due, coming to me when I arrive in Boston. 'Twill be quite a sum. Enough to purchase—" He paused. "Enough to purchase a house. I'll send it to you so that you can remain here, if that is what you wish to do." He did not wait for her to reply, but picked up his satchel and went out the door.

Just as he reached his horse and pulled the reins loose from the post, her footsteps sounded behind him, and with a quick, absurd hopefulness he glanced around.

But she had stopped at the porch, only intending to watch him ride away, and with an ironic smile of self-mockery he gathered up the reins. As he swung his leg over the cantle the east wall of the white clapboard house caught his attention. Slashed across the clapboards, written in mud by some malicious hand, were the words "Capt. and Mrs. Jack Pudding."

Alerted by his expression, Chaynoa glanced around to read the epithet herself.

For long moments the two of them stood staring at it, and then their eyes met and held. Courtland dropped his satchel and strode across the yard, shouting at her when she would have darted inside the house, ordering her to wait.

"For God's sake, Chaynoa," he exclaimed urgently. "Come with me. They will crucify you here."

Slowly, with a kind of rigid resignation, she untied her apron and began to use it, rubbing off the ugly smears of mud. "They've done that already, once. I survived it. And I will again. I will not leave."

"What are you holding on to, Chaynoa?" he demanded. *"What?"*

She paused to regard him, her voice husky and passionate, her eyes asparkle with tears. "I am holding on to my life, Courtland. To my *life*—the one I always dreamed of having, the one that is decent and safe. The house is all I have left of it."

"You have me," he accused, his face hard with unforgiveness. "You have me!"

"No, I don't!" she countered vehemently, turning toward the house. Then she paused, and the last words she flung at him, the last look she gave him, cut him to the soul. *"The British army does."*

Chapter 23

As one door closed, another opened unexpectedly
upon Courtland's return to Boston, and with the
sense that his whole world was crumbling about his
head even while he watched, he stepped across the
threshold.

He stood in uniform in the center of a vast courtroom whose dimensions were barren of anything except inhospitable benches, impersonal drapes, and
other grim-faced men decorated with lace and epaulets. There seemed no colors in the room at all, save
dullest brown and vivid scarlet, and a cold sun
streamed in through the vertical windows to empha-
size the only movement in the space, dust motes floating directionless through sunbeams. Occasionally a
ray glinted off a cutlass hilt or off the high gloss on
a boot, and once or twice someone coughed with
half-choked embarrassment.

His steps precise, an official strode forward and
spoke in tones so stentorian that the dead air vibrated. "This is a General Court-Martial of which
General Pigott is President, called for the trial of
Captain Courtland Day of the 4th Regiment of Foot,
who is accused of conduct unmilitary and—"

Although Courtland's eyes were fixed upon the

stripes of a British flag suspended from the ceiling, he did not see it. It was strange that he cared so little about the possibly dire outcome of the proceedings going on around him, at which he was the center. He was detached from all the ritualistic ceremony that would determine his future, and thought with an inappropriate humor how his life had always seemed pushed or pulled by circumstances into which he had been inadvertently plunged, as if a series of accidents had been planned by a force determined to keep him stumbling down a preplanned path.

The stripes on the flag blurred, and superimposed upon them, he saw the image of a woman. He saw the features of her face and form in such minute detail, that for a moment she actually seemed real. In a swish of muslin she entered the courtroom and quietly slipped into a seat, unnoticed by anyone else. She had removed one of her gloves, and a silver ring flashed upon her finger when she folded her hands in her lap. Her dusky cheeks were flushed with concern and her eyes deep black with love.

". . . thirdly, of firing a pistol at and killing Private Patrick Spendlow of the 23rd, Royal Welsh Regiment, who—"

Like a shred of fog that vanishes with sun, the image shattered, and Courtland realized that he had willed Chaynoa to be there with such concentration that his chest still heaved with the effort. But she was not there; in the rational workings of his intelligence, in the deepest passages of his heart, he knew she was not.

The first clash of what would prove to be a long and costly conflict had occurred at Lexington and

Concord, and a full-scale war loomed upon the horizon like a monster just rearing its head.

The hours of Chaynoa's life passed in an empty solitude. Her triumph over prejudice had dissolved, along with the warm net of social acceptance once cloaked about her shoulders. Iris Oakchurch remained loyal, but even that venerable lady's fidelity could not induce the matrons of convention to reestablish Chaynoa into their social favor. Even Virtue dared only a few surreptitious visits to the white clapboard house, for she was too protective of her own position in the hierarchy of decorum to risk putting a stain upon it. Chaynoa was the wife of a British officer, after all, and worse than that, an officer who had infiltrated both the village uppercrust and the confidence of its fathers without a qualm. They asked each other how his wife could not have known, how she could not have been a part of his scheme. And as they asked, they remembered her past, just as they had conveniently forgotten it when it seemed to their advantage. They had called themselves magnanimous then; now they called themselves patriotically righteous.

But Chaynoa doggedly clung to her home, living in it as if it were a safe cocoon. In the days after her husband departed, she had dropped a curtain over her emotions in order to avoid examining them too closely; and yet, occasionally that curtain parted just enough to give her a brief and painful vision of the man who stood behind it.

Once, just after he had left, she had forced herself to step inside the room that had been his office, and had seen the watercolor paintings deserted upon the desktop like broken pieces of an old dream. They were a most poignant sight, for she knew well what they had represented to their creator. As she stared

down at the faded but beautifully brushed hues, she
felt as if she stared into a naked heart, and the sight
was so wrenching that she gathered up the pictures,
and with great care packed them away.

Her days passed uneventfully until Jack Bretton
appeared on her door step unexpectedly.

"Jack!" she exclaimed, inviting him into the parlor. "How good of you to call."

The young man's face was serious, his manner
awkward, as if he did quite know how to address a
woman who had been abandoned by her husband
under mortifying circumstances. He declined a chair
and remained standing stiffly in the center of the
room before removing some papers from his coat. "I
thought you should know," he said simply.

She searched his eyes and then glanced down to
peruse a few lines of the document.

Record of the General Court-Martial for the
trial of
Captain Courtland Day.

It is the Opinion of the Court that the said
Captain Day is guilty of failing to advise the
Commander in Chief of the full and comprehen-
sive list of colonial ammunition stores in the
township of Swanston as ordered; secondly, of
failing to reveal the whereabouts of said stores;
and thirdly, of drawing his pistol and killing
Private Patrick Spendlow in the presence of
Officers . . .

Chaynoa paused and glanced up at Jack with
stricken eyes.

"I obtained these records with difficulty," he explained. "Although the trial was to be kept secret

from the public, it was quite sensational in military circles and lasted for days, so that news finally leaked out." He lowered his voice as if embarrassed for her. "It seems General Gage, in exchange for certain favors, dispatched your husband here to spy upon us. If he carried out his duties satisfactorily Day was to receive a promotion and enough money to purchase a piece of family property in England."

Chaynoa sank down onto a chair. "And he was found guilty of all three counts? What was his sentence?" She was too frightened to read the words herself.

"He was found guilty of unmilitary conduct—a vague charge, but one strong enough to penalize him. At least the evidence regarding the first two counts was not substantial enough to stick. John Freeman had seen Courtland enter the Sons of Liberty meeting and knew he would have access to a complete list of stores, but as Freeman had no physical proof of negligence in the matter, the Captain was let off with no more than a slap on the wrist. Of course, Day was convicted of the murder of the British soldier, but the Court considered the fact that he was attempting to defend his brother-in-law, and was lenient. Nevertheless Gage maintained his suspicions."

"And Courtland's sentence?" she repeated.

"Light. He was suspended for a month. But Gage refused to give him either his promotion or the promised bonus. So if Day expected to return to England and live out his life on some prettily situated piece of property, no doubt he is disappointed."

"No doubt . . ."

Jack turned his hat over in his hands and, after a moment of clumsy silence, gave her his regards and turned to go.

"He could have betrayed us," Chaynoa blurted

before he could reach the door. "He could have told them everything." She pulled open the top drawer of Courtland's desk and removed a sheet of paper, which was the only one remaining there.

"This was in his desk the day the British came. I saw it. 'Tis a complete list of every military store we have in Swanston. He could have given it to the officer, Jack. But he didn't. He spared us that."

"I know," Jack said quietly. "Everyone in Swanston knows. How ironic that Day's act of clemency will be to the eventual cost of his own men." He shook his head. " 'Twould not have been an easy decision for any man to make under the circumstances."

"No . . ." she echoed faintly. " 'Twould not have been."

A few weeks later Courtland Day tethered his horse to the railing in front of the Stirrup and Iron Tavern. The dinner hour had passed, and he knew the taproom would be filled with townsmen enjoying their rum and their heated talk of war in the usual habit. He was in uniform, his cutlass hanging at his side and his boots spotless. Boldly he strode into the room, and his sudden and startling entrance suspended every word of conversation. A pottery bowl fell from a serving maid's hand and shattered on the floor.

"Gentleman," Courtland said, nodding with exaggerated civility. "I hope the evening finds you well, and that the ale is no less potent than it was when I enjoyed it with you." He ignored the resulting glowers and pinned a stare upon his stepfather, who sat with the selectmen over a game of cards.

"I have come on business, Stepfather," he announced, sliding a rolled paper from his tunic and tapping it against his palm. "This is a Writ of Assistance. It grants me permission as a representative of His Majesty's Government to inspect the warehouses situated on your property." He tossed the paper across the table, scattering cards. "Will you accompany me or shall I go and perform the search alone?"

The old man sputtered, then slowly eased up from his chair, yanking his pipe from his teeth and regarding his stepson with both contempt and a sudden naked fear that paled his florid features. He glanced about at the other townsmen, who gave him sympathetic nods but made no move to interfere lest they be targeted with the same threat. All of them knew about Writs of Assistance, the royal device originally designed to catch colonials who evaded paying customs duties on smuggled goods. These days the document was used as a convenient excuse to inspect property without having to state a specific object of search. Despised by the Americans, it had become one of the reasons to fight King George.

Peebles straightened and ground out, "I will accompany you, of course."

"Good."

Without waiting, Courtland mounted his horse and cantered toward his stepfather's estate, where news of his arrival quickly spread through the house and brought Susannah Peebles hurrying out to find him.

Courtland did not address his mother, but guided his horse to a large brick warehouse behind the stables where he dismounted and removed his musket from the saddle. With the butt of it he smashed the bolt that secured the thick doors of the structure, and flung them wide.

The interior light was dim, but the vast number of

wooden crates stacked halfway to the ceiling was visible enough, along with the black letters stencilled on the sides of every one: EAST INDIA COMPANY.

Simon appeared, puffing with exertion and fear, and Susannah trailed behind to stand uncertainly in the doorway, staring at her son with her mouth gaping unattractively.

Unmoved, Courtland regarded the pair. "I'd bet a whole month of my captain's pay that the good people of Swanston would be interested to know that their most esteemed citizen is hiding several thousand pounds of British tea on his property." He raised a hand and indicated the crates while addressing his stepfather. "Is that what keeps my mother in silks?"

Her ususual cold serenity evaporated, Susannah grabbed his sleeve, and Courtland realized it was the first time since his return to American that she had touched him. He supposed that the fear of losing her luxuries was the only thing that roused Susannah to true passion, and the notion brought him not only loathing but a certain oppressive distaste when he realized that he had sprung from the loins of such a woman.

Her fingers squeezed his sleeve, and her voice was breathless from the horror of her possible loss. "You don't intend to go and tell them . . . ?"

Courtland gave her a long regard, realizing that for the first time in his life he was able to view her through the unclouded eyes of a man. "No," he said flatly. "I don't intend to tell them."

"Why?" Simon demanded, laying a hand upon the bridle of his horse which he would mount. "Why would you go to this trouble and then throw away the opportunity to ruin me?"

Courtland swung a leg over the saddle, tugging the

reins free of his stepfather's hand. "For Virtue's sake," he said. "Only for the sake of my sister."

They watched him go, watched him rein his horse toward Queen's Road. And then with furtive haste the Peebles scrambled back to the warehouse, slammed the heavy doors and safely bolted them.

It had been a long and tiring day, and yet the prospect of her empty bed scarcely appealed to Chaynoa as a welcoming conclusion to it. She wondered if all the days of her life would be just like this one, filled with necessary tasks done only for herself, and ending with the company of a dark room packed with shadows.

When a quiet rap rattled the front door she started, for no one but Iris and Robbie came to call anymore, and they always came round the back. With an unsteady hand she set down her candlestick and hastened across the vestibule.

Her husband stood upon the threshold with night behind his back, dressed in all the elaborate splendor of his country's uniform. The silver lace over blue facings, the red waistcoat rich with pewter buttons, the white breeches and black boots all combined to make a picture of noblest manhood. He looked taller than she remembered, and broader of shoulder, but these slight alterations in her imagination were not as disturbing as the change in his eyes, which seemed to gaze out at her from the gravely handsome and unmoved face of a perfect stranger.

She had known in some secret corner of her heart that he would come back to see her one last time, but the reality of his presence now found her startlingly unprepared. Shaken of her self-composure, and even of the dispassion she had drawn about her like a shell, she stammered a greeting and trailed into the parlor as if on feet no longer connected to her body.

Courtland quietly closed the door, and, without removing his hat, which was an obvious signal that he did not mean to stay long, followed her into the room, where they stood together like two long-ago-introduced acquaintances at a loss for conversation. As the seconds passed, a cold glass wall, transparent but unshatterable, seemed to rise up out of the floor between them and divide the parlor in half.

While Chaynoa regarded her husband with a consuming scrutiny in order to store up the details of his appearance and peruse them later in the inner chamber of her loneliness, his own eyes seemed loath to touch her face. Memories of his past kindnesses suddenly flowed back to Chaynoa in a poignant tide, but it was only later, upon reflection, that she realized Courtland Day had performed for her many miracles.

And now he performed a last one, which he slowly, wordlessly produced from his waistcoat pocket. It dangled from his fingers, a heavy tracery of old silver that had once adorned an aristocrat's neck and crossed an ocean before passing through many unlikely hands. After its long years of entombment it was black with need of polish, but the unmatched craftsmanship of its filigree still evoked a certain old-world charm that seized the imagination.

Chaynoa trembled, her hands outstretched in the way of a novice touching a newly unearthed, sacred relic.

"I took a squad of men to the clearing and had them dig it up," Courtland explained quietly, and now that his wife's eyes were lowered to the necklace he looked his fill at her. In that instant all the months of the past suddenly began to fall away like petals from a flower stem, and he saw her again as he had once seen her, shy and guileless, her doelike eyes full of trustful admiration. Just for the moment he refused to remember that she had ever looked at him in any other way. Just for the moment he wanted to believe, to pretend, that she had loved him.

"The necklace should buy you a good life," he heard himself say. "The kind of life your mother wanted for you." He genuinely hoped that it would, for he could not bear to think of her living a shabby or difficult existence. And yet with a dismaying jolt, he realized that he would spend the rest of his life wondering . . .

He cleared his throat, fighting to push through the agony of the moment. "You should consider moving south. 'Twill be safer in New York or Philadelphia than in these villages surrounding Boston."

"I know." She was clutching the necklace, and its links cut into her hands, but since the physical pain drew the edge off the other emotions she closed her fist more tightly. She could not look at him; his last kindness was too great, and her voice came through her lips as a whisper. "I know. But I'll stay here regardless of the danger. 'Tis where . . . 'tis where I'm happiest."

That his wife was able to say she was happy when his own life was utterly devoid of that commodity caused Courtland a pang of bitterness, and he did not trust himself to speak.

Chaynoa stared at the buttons on his tunic, at the Roman IV surrounded by a wreath. It made her think of his other life, and she wondered if he was the brilliant officer everyone in Swanston predicted he would be. A sense of unreality befell her, and the polished pewter buttons grew unfocused. She wanted to say she was sorry about their life together, wanted to say it desperately, but the opening up of that wound was too great for her courage.

"I heard about . . . about your court-martial trial," she stammered at last. "Jack told me. I'm sorry, sorry that you'll not be able to buy back your home in Devonshire. I—I know how much it meant to you."

Her sympathy, expressed when he was most vulnerable to it, made Courtland's heart swell, and he had to take a quick breath and look up at the ceiling in order to stop the prickling behind his eyelids. "There were papers with the necklace," he said, removing a fragile bundle of parchment from his waistcoat. "Just as you suspected, they incriminate Julius Twiggs. He was engaged in unscrupulous business dealings with my stepfather. One of the papers deals strictly with Peebles, as a matter of fact, and with your permission, I'd like to keep it. It could do him harm, you see, and for the sake of my sister—"

"Of course," she almost cried, grateful to be able to grant him any favor, no matter how small. "Take it. 'Tis yours to do with as you please."

"Thank you." Although Courtland would have liked to delay the moment of their final separation by hours, by days, he knew a quick severance was better. He remembered the silver ring and bracelet suddenly and looked for them. But she wore neither. It seemed a sign.

"Well," he breathed, his voice husky. "I must go now. 'Tis a long ride back to Boston."

He moved away, but paused at the front door and stood staring intently at the white panels while delivering his last words with his back turned. "I wish you the best, Chaynoa. I have every confidence that you'll do well. You're an extraordinary woman, a survivor, and you know what it is you want from life." He hesitated and took a breath, his confession difficult.

"I was unfair to you—I ran with the hare and hunted with the hounds, as they say. My only hope is that you won't think of me with too much bitterness. I . . . I'll always remember you with honor."

Unstrung by his unfailing gallantry, marveling over his lack of coldness under the circumstances, Chaynoa swallowed. She stared at his back, at the epaulets on his shoulders, at the blue cuff of his sleeve, at the silver lace edging his hat. Their shapes were unnaturally sharp, so vivid that her eyes burned with them all at once. She wondered what had happened between the two of them, why she felt such a sudden splintering explosion of pain in her breast. Was he experiencing it, too?

With a desperate need to know, she searched for a sign. But his shoulders were square and his spine stiff, his hands relaxed at his side.

And then, she saw his head lower, slowly and gravely, and the movement was such an eloquent posture of grief that Chaynoa almost wept in response. Guilt assailed her. She flew to him, knelt at his feet, and grabbed his hands, cradling them and pressing them to her lips in a gesture of tenderest respect and farewell.

Courtland drew her to her feet, and in equal regard lifted her fingers to his lips, which, with gentle formality, he kissed one by one.

For the fist time since he had come into the house Chaynoa looked fully into his eyes then, into the gray irises below the fine black brows that had regarded her once in the way of an impassioned bridegroom. And she saw that the long dark lashes dripped with tears.

As if afraid she would remark upon it now that he had been so weak as to reveal his emotion, or afraid she would mutter something that would only make the moment more excruciating for them both, Captain Day released her hand, and sketching a deep and honoring bow, left her.

Behind him she clung to the door frame as if she would collapse without it.

Chapter 24

"Our relief must now arise from driving General
Gage, with his troops, out of the country, which, with
the blessing of God, we are determined to accom-
plish, or perish in the attempt . . ." These were the
words proclaimed in May by the Massachusetts
Committee of Safety.

After the first meager but fateful spill of blood in
Lexington and Concord the previous month, the
British and the Americans faced off, and now stood
poised with their clenched fists raised and their teeth
gritted, ready to spar.

On June 12th, to the utter rage of its patriots,
General Gage had proclaimed martial law in the
town of Boston, and the number of occupying redcoats had swelled to five thousand as the *Cerberus*
sailed into port carrying Generals Howe, Clinton,
and Burgoyne. In retaliation, rebel regiments gathered hurriedly at posts established everywhere on the
outskirts of the captive city, and although ragged and
ill-equipped, they were ten thousand strong and
eager to fight.

Chaynoa's thoughts were always centered upon
Boston. While she mechanically pulled weeds in the
garden she thought of conditions there, and at night

when she lay staring at a moon-chased ceiling, her
hand straying with inexplicable anxiety to the barren
place beside her, questions whirled in her mind.
*Where is he? Is he well? What will happen when he
marches off to war?*

The villagers of Swanston were hoarding food-
stores, and some menfolk packed up their women
and children and sent them to New York and farther
south out of harm's way. But Chaynoa stayed. Nothing could tear her away from the white clapboard
house that had come to represent the last shred of
permanence in her life.

An illness had struck Iris Oakchurch, and the en-
feebled ancient lay like a weathered rag doll bound to
her bed. Chaynoa sat beside her one golden spring
afternoon while the sparrows trilled outside, holding
her twiglike hand with its crisscrossing of purple
veins and speaking in hushed tones about the future.

"My niece from Albany is coming . . ." Iris said.
"She will see me to the end and then take Robbie
home with her. Pray God she is not caught in the
midst of battle. I know in my bones that ere this
month is out we will hear cannon fire and the cries of
many men. Lord help us all." She closed her translucent lids and shook her head with its cobwebbing of
white hair while her fingers squeezed the girl's with
all the strength they still possessed. "And you, child
. . . ? What will you do?"

Chaynoa stared out through the window beyond
the petunia scented garden, beyond the fields to the
fringed edge of black-green forest, whose mysterious
depths seemed no more than a dream of childhood
that drifted back to haunt her every now and then.
"I'll go on with my life, Iris. Just as I've always
done."

"Your husband is with his regiment in Boston now?"

"Aye. In Boston . . ."

"Ah." Words came from the lips of the old woman in short airy puffs. "There's no knowing where he'll be sent when this war begins in earnest. You may never be able to find him again. If you wait."

Chaynoa turned her head and looked into the face wrinkled with wisdom. "If I wait . . . ?"

"Do you care for him, child?"

"Of course, I *care* for him."

"Do you love him?"

Chaynoa closed her eyes, pressed down suddenly by a great, crushing weariness. When she began to speak, her voice took on a dreamy lilt that suggested the recollection of some faraway vision both unexpectedly sweet and heart-rendingly mournful. "I thought so once . . . last summer. I was watching him from a distance. He was cutting hay, moving through the fields—I can see him now—his hands upon the scythe, the sun upon his hair, the way his shoulders strained beneath his shirt. The shirt was white, I had washed it the day before . . ."

She broke off, and the lilt faded away to leave her voice gravely perplexed. "There was a part of myself that held back from loving him, Iris—a part that didn't want to trust itself to his hands. It retreated into a cold hollow little place inside my heart every time he tried to call it out. I didn't want him to have it—I wanted no one to take it away from me."

"Do you think it was your heart, dear?" the old woman asked, as if that organ were some removable thing that could be taken from the body and held apart.

"Yes. And, Iris, it was guarded by utter rage. Protected by it." Suddenly energized, Chaynoa rose up from her chair and paced to the window, where she took up a tense pose. "On the same day I discovered who my husband really was, Hahnee was killed by a British soldier—one of Courtland's own *kind*. I was enraged, and the rage grew and grew until I thought I would die from it. I couldn't look at Courtland, I never wanted to look at him again. And when he told me it had been his *duty* to betray us all, to lie to us even while he shared our lives, I wanted to strike him. How I yearned to strike him!"

She slammed a hand upon the sill and wheeled to face her friend. "And I knew if I got up from my chair, I *would* strike him, I would fly at him and use my fists upon him like a wild animal. I wanted to hurt him, longed to hurt him that night!"

She sank down at Iris's bed and laid her head against the sheet, and the sage stroked her hair. "Perhaps you should have . . ." Iris said in her uncondemning way. "Perhaps you should have let the rage loose. You have held on to it too long. It has been your savior . . . and it has been your warden, too."

Chaynoa whispered, "When Courtland returned with the necklace, when I looked at him standing in the parlor dressed in the enemy's color, I felt . . ."

"Felt what?"

She sat up. "Other than Mam, he was the only living soul I ever truly trusted, Iris. And he betrayed me. I lived with him, married him—married a *British soldier*—someone I had learned to despise. And he let me do it, he never told me. I had to discover it myself. And it devastated me, hurt me as if he had stabbed me with a knife."

"He was honoring something greater than himself when he came to live among us, Chaynoa," came the firm reply. "He was honoring that uniform. Good men wear red coats, too, you know."

The old lady sighed and closed her eyes. "Ah, well, whatever you decide to do, I'll not worry, for I know you'll clear whatever hurdles life throws your way. You're brave, more so than any of the rest of us who have always lived sheltered existences ruled by social trivialities and frivolous fears. I think you have discovered that our way of life is not the one you really want. Haven't you, dear? Haven't you . . . ?"

Chaynoa knew in her heart that it would be the last time she would ever stand inside the white clapboard house on Queen's Road. She took nothing away from it except her bag of treasures, which included Hahnee's carvings, the porcelain figure Virtue had given her, and Courtland's watercolor paintings. With great reluctance she had relinquished her pup to Robbie's eager arms. The raccoons she had loosed in the woods, and the horses in the livery had long ago been taken away by some agent of General Gage, who had also claimed ownership of the house. She could have traded the filigree necklace to keep it; but she had not.

As she wandered through the rooms of the silent house, she did not disturb the arrangement of the furnishings, except for one small item. The whimsical needlepointed sampler hanging on the kitchen wall she took down from its peg, and once more read the words, " 'Tis double the pleasure to deceive the deceiver."

Quietly she laid it upon the trestle table, facedown, and then walked out of the house.

She hiked toward Boston, catching a ride now and then upon supply carts that trundled behind a colonial militia company marching toward an outpost. When the afternoon sun reached its zenith and she was only a few miles away from her destination, a faint rumble vibrated the air.

"Thunder," she said to the driver of the cart. "Perhaps we'll have rain, be relieved of this heat before we get to Boston.

The man cocked his head in order to listen. "That ain't thunder, ma'am. It's cannon fire."

"Cannon fire?" Fear seized her as she imagined some bloody skirmish taking place on the Boston Road, and she listened with increasing dread as the roar of cannon boomed more often, punctuated with the higher pitched sounds of mortar and musketry fire.

But nothing—not even the haze of smoke wending toward the distant clouds—could have prepared her for the sight she witnessed as the cart topped a rise and provided a panoramic view of Boston, its beaches, and the Charleston hills.

"My God . . ." she breathed, putting a hand to her brow to shade her eyes. "What's happening there?"

The man beside her drew the horses to a halt, narrowed his gaze to view the scene, and announced simply, "War, ma'am. War is happening there."

She stood up in the cart. On the western end of the peninsula the town of Charleston was in flames, its burning church steeples creating pillars of fire that rose above the scenes of battle occurring on the hill. British ships positioned in the ferryways between the two towns spat steady streams of fire across the water, as did cannon positioned at the batteries. And countless barges filled with redcoats floated toward the Charleston shore for landing.

Already long lines of British soldiers marched beneath the brutal sun in their slow and rhythmic step, climbing the rise known as Bunker Hill, where patriot defenders hastily dug earthworks and crouched behind fences with their muskets poised. The handsome-coated red tide of two thousand men—the finest infantry in the world—wound through the tall, waving green grass in perfect ranks, their white cross belts, lace, buttons, and bayonets agleam. The tall hats of the Grenadiers bobbed while the arms of fusiliers strained as they pulled cannon into position, and dashing officers shouted orders that blended with the awful thunder of the fire.

Like an audience at some elaborate play, spectators blanketed the landscape and stood on Boston rooftops watching the grand and awesome battle unfold, wondering with dread where in the melee their loved ones struggled.

Wondering the same, Chaynoa stumbled from the cart and ran to the edge of the rise. She saw the first British line, wearing full battle gear in the smothering heat, reach the entrenched colonial defenders. The patriot muskets glinted just before spitting out a deadly volley of fire, which in only seconds mowed down the redcoats in an awful massacre. Countless fusiliers fell as the assault continued mercilessly, collapsing in piles atop their slain or wounded fellows, some attempting to retreat only to be shot down on the beach by another rain of patriot bullets.

Chaynoa cried out at the horrible sight and, running back to the cart, clutched the arm of the driver. "The King's Own!" she screamed above the rumble of cannon. "The 4th Regiment—do you know their uniforms? Can you see them?"

He squinted. "Looks like them following what's left of the fusiliers up the hill."

She turned horrified eyes to the new line of British soldiers fighting their way up in an attempt to breach the patriot trenches. They stumbled over heaps of bodies as their own ranks quickly succumbed to a hail of fire, and though their officers shouted hoarsely, trying to rally the confused ranks, the sight of the slaughter proved too much for the stunned recruits.

"Courtland!" Chaynoa cried, putting her hands to her face, straining to see details in the chaos as she imagined him wounded or dazed.

Bodies lay everywhere—in the grass or in the shallow reddening water off shore, grotesquely contorted, half covered with thick oily smoke as the relentless rounds of firing continued, pouring forth from ships' guns and cannon. The screams of men pierced the air, and behind it all, the burning buildings of Charleston collapsed.

The redcoats made standing targets for the patriots who lay protected behind their earthen walls, and before long, the British numbers were so depleted by the continuous murderous volleys that they were forced to retreat in a wild, undisciplined mass.

The ill-equipped and ragged rebels leapt for joy, triumphant, scarcely believing that routing the famed British army had been so easy. Chaynoa could hear their exultant cries and see them waving their muskets at the distant crowds. She turned her head toward the beach, shading her eyes to see the British.

Down below, the enemy regrouped their straggling and decimated companies, and, leaving behind the hundred pound battle packs that had hindered their agility before, moved to attack again. Sheets of fire cloaked the forefront of the battle, and although she strained to see the foray, Chaynoa could only catch glimpses of the British barges full of wounded and dying redcoats as they were ferried back to Boston. She was in a fever of anxiety, seeing hundreds of men lying scattered over the hill like scarlet slashes. And yet, the British battle drums continued to beat an

urgent, demanding cadence, and the soldiers perse-
vered, marching forward in endless lines, most to be
slaughtered. Their numbers and their casualties were
staggering, their screams audible even as far as Chaynoa's standpoint.

"When will it end?!" she yelled at the driver, seizing his arm again. "When will they stop?"

He shook his head, speculating direfully. "When
there's nobody left to fight. When they're all dead."

Finally, after a quarter hour the patriot musket fire
grew more sporadic beneath the steady onslaught of
the enemy, and the remaining British ranks, realizing
their foe's ammunition was near depletion, rallied.
With their own Brown Bess muskets emptied as well,
they surged forward over the hill like maniacal
avenging devils, their bayonets flashing, their primeval battle cries loud enough to rival the mortar fire.
A ghastly interim of hand-to-hand combat ensued
while desperate men struggled against desperate men.
The Americans had few bayonets and could only
fight with the butts of their muskets or with clubs or
stones as their enemies leapt over the breastwork and
assailed them in a murderous rage, but fight they did,
like savages to the death.

A cloud of black smoke and dust hung over the
massacre, and the crowds of spectators stood in para-
lyzed silence, praying, some falling to their knees in
anguish.

" 'Tis over," the driver pronounced in a hoarse
voice. " 'Tis over, and the British have won the day.
But at what price . . . ?" He pulled out his pocket
watch and released the catch, shaking his head slowly
in incredulity. "Only two hours and hundreds of men
are dead."

The words jolted Chaynoa out of her daze. She
stumbled across the rise with her bag of belongings

over her shoulder, then ran down the road toward
the quieting battle scene, gasping for breath in her
terror. All around her others did the same, desperate
to find their loved ones, stumbling and pushing, sob-
bing incoherently.

In a stupor she climbed over broken stone walls
and shoved past others crowding close, her long
skirts swishing through tall trampled grass matted
with blood and flattened with bodies. The ghastly
odor of death and scorched earth and battle smoke
clogged her nose, and everywhere the hoarse screams
of dying men created the most nerve-shattering
sound on earth.

When she reached the edge of the battlefield Chaynoa had to stop for breath. For long moments she
stood frozen, utterly stunned as she slowly turned her
head to take in the entirety of the horrendous sight.
"Thousands . . ." she gasped woodenly. "There must
be thousands lying here . . ."

Bleeding, twisted bodies, most of them in red
coats, littered the hill, heaped in twos and threes in
places, eerily cloaked in shreds of smoke. Their long
muskets, goatskin packs, cocked hats, cartouche
boxes cluttered the field, so that between the debris of
war and the bodies, Chaynoa's numb feet could
scarcely progress. Bile rose up in her throat and she
bent over double, vomiting in the grass.

When she straightened, her eyes fastened upon a
young blackened face staring up at her in the stinking
haze, its temple pierced by a bayonet. Another body
lay close, next to her bloodied shoe, the abdomen
gaping open from a mortar wound. "Oh, God . . ."
she moaned, bending over, heaving again.

Sweat rolled from her brow, wet her gown under
the arms and between the breasts, and she reeled,
struggling to stay conscious. "Courtland . . ." she

whimpered, the name of her husband wrenched from her throat in a noise no less plaintive then the other cries.

Chaynoa began to stumble over the ground, her eyes stinging so badly she could scarcely see the vague, crouched figures of wailing women draped over the bodies of loved ones. She fell, and crawling on her knees began to look into every powder-blackened face lying on the ground, yanking her skirts away from the countless redcoated arms that stretched out, beseeching her for help. A suffocating heat emanated from the ravaged earth in undulating waves, and she staggered to stand again, her feet half sinking in the sticky clay.

"Courtland!" she screamed, shutting out the moans of the dying, dimly noticing the busy surgeons who briskly directed litter bearers through the labyrinth of fallen red tunics and gray smoke. Far below, on the water, she could see the barges ferrying their dying human cargoes to Boston, then returning by lantern light for another load.

Twilight approached and the still smoldering buildings of Charleston backlit the gruesome stage, so that Chaynoa felt she staggered through the passages of an earthly hell ringed by brimstone and tortured souls. As she hunted vainly through the sea of suffering humanity, as she callously ignored clutching hands in her search for only one pair that were particularly fine-made, rage began to build inside her chest. She felt that her surroundings possessed no rational meaning, and groped for an understanding of how, in the space of two hours, a hillside of green orchards could be strewn with nothing but the wasted fruit of good men.

Her shoe snagged upon a half buried musket, and she fell with a jolt to the ground; for a moment she lay still, disoriented, her hand throbbing. The edge of a small object had embedded itself in her palm and she turned it over, wincing, trying to distinguish its fuzzy shape. When a surgeon moved past with a lantern, shouting orders, his light aided her, glinted off the pewter button stamped with a Roman IV.

"His tunic . . ." Chaynoa mouthed the words dazedly. " 'Tis a button like the one on Courtland's tunic . . ."

She struggled to her feet, terror-struck, certain the button she held was his. Suddenly every ghostly grimacing face resting on the mangled ground called to her, and she screamed, hysterically trying to search them all. The hill was dark with night, and except for the smoldering fires and the light of bobbing lanterns, she could not discern the features of the casualties without stooping down and scrutinizing them. Once, as she frantically cradled a man's head between her trembling hands to examine it more closely, she sobbed with relief, for it was too young and too fair to be the one she sought.

She sank to her knees, overwhelmed, lost, her mind utterly unstrung by the scenes of carnage, and by the fear she felt. When she saw a British soldier walking toward her, one whole and alive, she cried out and lurched forward to seize his sleeve, bawling Courtland's name, begging him to take her home. But the eyes staring back at her were not gray and familiar; they were the unresponsive eyes of an exhausted stranger.

She looked at the grimy face of the soldier stupidly, and her hysterical rage seemed to increase, burgeon, blend with an older, more primitive one. Wildly, she dashed forward over the hill, avoiding the scattered remains of war, zigzagging through bodies, knocking aside a surgeon's arm when he begged for her help.

She staggered on to the shore and, wading in cold knee-deep water, leaned over to peer inside the bobbing barges overloaded with sprawled men.

"My husband!" she screamed at the weary, indifferent ferrymen who made to shove off with their poles. She grabbed the jacket of one. *"Where's my husband?"*

Her cry fell upon deaf ears, for every wife and sweetheart wandering directionless over the hills was crying the same despairing words.

For hours Chaynoa trudged about with the other women, hearing the wails of those who had found grim news, hearing an endless roll of carriage and coach wheels as Tories drove over the dark pitted road from Boston to haul away wounded British officers, or as patriots transported their own dying men. Horses draped with bodies snorted and shied, and the sound of British axes and picks as they resolutely stabbed at the hill in order to refortify the costly prize, served as a solemn reminder that war was far from finished.

"Captain Day . . . ?" she cried once, seeing a young soldier in a familiar uniform staggering toward her supporting a wounded man. "Do you know Captain Day?"

He stopped in weary patience. "Aye, I've heard of him, ma'am."

She seized his ripped sleeve. "Where is he?"

"Sorry, I haven't seen him since the first attack. Most of his company's dead—he may be too." Dully, he hobbled on. "Gotta go now."

Chaynoa followed, her feet dragging, her skirt weighed down with seawater and filth. Her endless, monotonous, and now hoarsened appeals for her husband prompted no reply from the sluggish figures she passed, and she despaired, pausing a moment to wipe the perspiration from her reddened eyes.

At the bottom of the hill a burial detail had already begun. In darkness relieved only by a few flickering lanterns, exhausted British soldiers dug an endless line of graves for their fallen fellows, who, except for the officers, would lie forever unmarked.

Chaynoa focused upon the specterish, slowly moving figures. The sight of a tall man wearing a silver laced hat and officer's epaulets pricked her dulled senses, and for long moments she watched him stab the earth with a shovel, then put his foot to it, before mechanically throwing the earth aside. He spoke to no one, but performed his grim task with his head down, the dim light reflecting off once-white breeches and a torn tunic begrimed with powder smears.

Chaynoa's heart lurched. She stared longer. Wonder began to surge through her body slowly, and with the wonder, the remnants of her long-held rage exploded. Gasping, she lunged forward with her arms outstretched, and when she reached the officer, fell against his chest and began to pummel it with her fists, crying fierce and incoherent words she did not hear, but which she experienced excruciatingly in her soul.

"Why did you *leave* me?" she screamed, her face flushed with rage. She pounded his shoulders, clutched his collar. "How could you? You said you never would! *You said you never would!*"

The shovel fell from his hands with a thud. A low sound came from his throat and he enveloped her in arms shaking with weariness and astonishment. He said nothing at all. He could not speak. He was too overcome all at once by the benevolence of God, by the miracle that had seen him through the gruesome day, and by the miracle that now pressed herself against his heart.

Chapter 25

Together they trudged through the hazy, other-worldly streets of Boston, over which not only blackness had fallen but an eerie pall that harrowed the soul with its oppressiveness. In an incongruous and almost noiseless glide elegant carriages and farm carts rolled over the cobblestones together, along with any functional vehicle, carrying dead and dying men to hospitals or homes. Every sound seemed hushed. Even the low, anguished keen of lamenting mothers and new widows was strangely diminished, Chaynoa thought—or perhaps her senses were only numbed to the spirit.

The wounded were taken to makeshift hospitals in the almshouse, the churches, and an old factory opposite the granary, and people stood in their lighted doorways watching the terrible parade progress, occasionally running out to give a drink to a thirsty casualty or to offer a strip of linen for a wound.

When Chaynoa and Courtland arrived at the Distillery where Courtland's regiment was quartered, he opened the door to his small spartan room and ushered her inside without speaking. Then he lit a lantern, and after setting it aside went to stand by the

window, where he stared out at the melancholy view
for long moments.

"There were only four of my company left . . ." he
muttered in a dull voice, more to himself than to her.
"Only four out of thirty-nine."

Chaynoa knew he had not yet shaken off the clinging horror of the battlefield; nor had she. Walking to
his side, she gently eased off the once-proud coat,
drew it over his arms and laid it atop a chair. And
then she dipped a towel in the washbasin and wrung
it out, and, looking tenderly at his haunted face,
wiped away the stains of battle.

But before she had finished the task, he stayed her
hand, and, gathering her in his arms, pulled her to the
narrow bed. "Just lie beside me . . ." he whispered
shakily, touching her face with a hand bruised and
lacerated from fighting. "Just lie quietly beside me."

She did, and with a low moan he laid his head
upon her breast, put his arms about her waist and
closed his eyes, listening to her breathe. "Don't
move," he whispered. "Don't move."

"I won't."

He sighed, and for the short remainder of the terrible night, stayed in her arms, sleeping the dull and
stupefying sleep of an exhausted warrior.

Before dawn, while the street lamps still burned,
forgotten by the watchmen, Courtland arose and
washed himself, and although he moved quietly in his
ablutions, Chaynoa awoke when the place beside her
cooled and alarmed her senses.

"Good morning," he whispered so she could locate
him in the darkness.

She adjusted her eyes and discerned him, shirtless
and barefoot, drying his hair with a towel. "Is anything wrong?" she asked, still befuddled, unable to
shake off the remnants of her brief but heavy sleep.

"No, but I must leave soon. There's much grim work to do—it'll take days just to bury the dead." He shook his head. "When I think of the numbers, remember how many fell . . ."

"Even now it seems unreal," she murmured.

He shrugged into a shirt and slipped on his boots, shaking off the depression of the moment with a half smile. "You'll need clean water—I'm afraid I've dirtied what's in the basin. There's a pump outside. I'll go fetch some there and be back in less than a minute."

Although his voice was heavy Chaynoa could tell that his usual dauntlessness was fast restoring itself, and she felt cheered.

When he returned, she bathed her face and hands with an almost frantic eagerness, amazed how the simple condition of being clean could revitalize overburdened spirits.

Across the room Courtland unwrapped a loaf of bread which he declared to be a couple of days old but still edible. "Sorry I haven't got any butter or marmalade to make it more palatable. But there should be coffee sellers out on the streets as soon as it's light." He gave a pained smile. "Too bad we haven't some of that sweet cream you used to serve with my coffee every morning."

At his allusion to their life together in the house on Queen's Road, Chaynoa halted her washing and glanced up. His eyes were regarding her levelly, and in them she read his regret, which he expressed far more eloquently through silence than he could have done with any apologetic words.

"Do you mean to stay?" he asked suddenly.

She stared at him through the blue shadows and, with chagrin, realized that he was genuinely unsure. Did he think she had only come to Boston out of

duty or obligation, and now that he was safe, would
return to Swanston again. "Oh, Courtland," she
cried, dropping the towel and crossing the room. In
a rush she threw her arms about him, pressed against
his length, and buried her face in the hard inner curve
of his shoulder.

He embraced her with anguish, and in a burst of
confession, breathed his doubts against her ear. "I
only wish you felt for me what I feel for you, Chaynoa . . . Yesterday on the hill I kept thinking of it,
kept wishing. 'Tis strange, but sometimes in battle a
man's thoughts are far away, his emotions detached,
centered somewhere else even while he's fighting for
his life. If I fell, I wanted to know that you had loved
me—"

"I do!" she cried, taking his face in her hands,
kissing his jaw, his ear. Then, finding his mouth, she
murmured, "I do, Courtland."

With his own mouth he parted her lips while she
moved her hands down his chest, touched his ribs, his
tautening belly. After a quick intake of breath Courtland pulled her closer, and, sliding her gown from her
shoulders, freed her breasts, bending to press his lips
between them, kiss them. She ran her hands over the
ridge of his shoulders, over the curve of his back,
wanting to rediscover the strength and warmth of
him, borrow from it, merge with it.

He pulled her to the bed, where their coming together was urgent and undisciplined, as if they both
strained to deny the mortality they had witnessed on
the hillside, yearned to seize peace and wholeness
where and when they could. And, for the first time,
when Chaynoa begged him to do so in a hasty whisper, Courtland poised himself above her waiting
body, and his flesh met hers with a thrusting, aggres-

sive tenderness that, at last, conjured up no specter born of past shadows.

He loved her with all the unbound vitality of a young man cleaving to his bride, and bound the marriage. And where, before, Chaynoa had been silent, she cried out now, her need matching his own at climax.

Afterward they lay together, motionless, appreciating the feel of the other's warm and comforting presence, both refusing to think of the future. Neither spoke; in the unbroken perfection of the moment they did not feel the need.

At last, having delayed his duties as long as he dared, Courtland reluctantly rose and donned his clothes, dressing in the first violet rays of dawn. "I may not return here until very late tonight," he said. "Will you be all right alone?"

"Can't I help? Isn't there anything I can do?"

"The hospitals will be grateful for every pair of hands today." He took hold of her fingers and kissed them before searching her eyes in concern. "But the sights will be terrible there. I heard a surgeon say that the poorer equipped colonials used nails and rusted metal in place of musket balls. The wounds are ghastly ones."

"All the more reason for me to offer to do whatever I can. I'd like to help *your* men—your own regiment." The words were spoken softly, her vow of loyalty to her husband, and Courtland pulled her to his chest and held her there.

A few minutes later when he opened the outside door, he saw a woman hastening across the street toward him, waving a hand to catch his attention. "Courtland!"

He narrowed his eyes, trying to see through the early morning haze and the faint gray smoke that still drifted from the ruins of Charleston, thinking surely that his ears had deceived him, for the woman's voice had possessed an astonishing similarity to his mother's.

"Courtland! I'd like to speak with you, please."

Susannah Peebles emerged from the dirty pearl obscurity, less elegantly clad than usual and looking travel-worn, but her carriage still stiffly erect and high-held, her tone as genteelly imperious as always. "Can we speak alone somewhere?" she asked.

Courtland struggled to stifle his surprise, wondering why in heaven's name his mother was traipsing about these besieged town streets alone, seeking out a British officer in his British barracks.

"Mother—"

"Where can we go?" she interrupted, and when two wounded fusiliers in powder-stained uniforms trudged past, one supporting the other, she swept her skirts aside, obviously not intending to give Courtland a reason for her unexpected appearance until he had provided a semblance of privacy.

"My quarters," he said, jerking his head in the appropriate direction.

"Take me there."

If she was surprised to discover Chaynoa in her son's austere, shadowy room, Mrs. Peebles gave no sign of it. She glanced about the unprepossessing space devoid of luxury or any chair, and, as if disquieted by the need to stand in the midst of such inhospitable surroundings, finally took up a stance by the washstand.

"Virtue and I have come to stay with the Brettons," she announced without preamble and, raising a brow, gave Courtland's red tunic a distastefully significant glance. "Jack insists we're too vulnerable in the country, too unprotected from British attack.

If there hadn't been so much chaos in Boston, we would never have made it through the town gates this morning."

Neither Chaynoa nor Courtland responded, and in the resulting seconds of awkwardness Susannah opened the black netted purse she carried looped over her wrist and drew out a small leather-wrapped package. With difficulty, she met her son's eyes. "No doubt you feel I've been a poor mother to you, Courtland—neglectful, indifferent at times. I'll confess to that failure, if you like, but I won't apologize or make excuses, and I certainly won't attempt to explain. However, I would like to try and make amends for it—for the past. Simon is in agreement with me."

She extended her hand, almost airily offering him the package. " 'Tis a goodly sum of money. It should help keep you in comfort during this horrid war, and then set you up somewhere afterward. I suppose you'll go off to England," she finished with an indifferent sigh. " 'Tis what you always wanted, after all."

Courtland stared at her, the outward features of his face devoid of expression, but in the innermost depths of his eyes a tinge of sorrow lurked, for he realized that had she made the same simple offer years ago, when he was still a boy and could have loved her, he would have accepted it gratefully. "Keep your money, Susannah," he said after a moment's pause, his voice tight, deep in its manliness.

An unattractive smile curved his mother's mouth at his rejection of her gift, but in her cool unruffled way, she persisted, "You have a wife to keep."

"And I will keep her with what I earn."

"Have you decided to be unbending?"

"Merely self-sufficient, as I have always been. As I was raised to be."

Susannah tilted her head. "Very well. Now that I see there is no forgiveness in your heart, no desire to come to terms, I shall bid you farewell." The package disappeared inside her purse. "Goodbye, Courtland."

Thinking oddly that there had been a kind of hasty relief in Susannah's last gesture, Chaynoa escorted her as far as the street, where the woman hesitated and, with measuring eyes, scrutinized her daughter-in-law without any particular show of softness.

"Will you accept the money?" she asked. "The life of a camp follower won't be an easy one, even for you, and the cash would provide a few luxuries you won't otherwise be able to afford on a captain's salary. Conceal it from him if you must, but accept it. In such times as these, I'd never allow pride to get in my way."

Chaynoa thought privately that pride had ruled the whole course of Susannah Peebles's life, but she did not comment upon it. "Courtland has made his decision and I'll not dishonor him by going against his wishes," she said.

"Then both of you are fools." The older woman jerked on her gloves, and, avoiding the funereal stream of carriages still making their gruesome rounds, stepped purposefully across the street, leaving Chaynoa to stare after her with a thoughtful frown.

"Why did you refuse her gift, Courtland?" she asked gently upon reentering his quarters a moment later.

He was settling his hat atop his head, and his expression beneath its shadow was hard and set, unrelenting. "Because she only offered it to me out of guilt."

"What?"

"Aye. Before I left Swanston I had the opportunity to ruin Simon's name, to run it through the mud, in fact. But, for my sister's sake, I decided against it. By giving me money, my mother sought to ease her conscience over the whole affair, over all the other times she has turned her back upon me." He lowered his head. " 'Twas the only reason she came today."

There was no bitterness in his voice, only a resigned acceptance of his mother's character, and a little sadness that, no matter how valiantly he tried, he could not quite manage to conceal.

When he moved to stand near the window, Chaynoa joined him, and together they watched as the red edge of a new sun peered over the town, a town that wearily prepared itself for a trying and costly siege.

"What will happen here, Courtland?" Chaynoa asked, laying her head against his shoulder. "What will happen now?"

"A very long war, I'm afraid," he said with no relish, stroking her hair. "But at least we'll be together through it."

"And afterward? Will we go to England after it's over?"

He released a long breath and pondered her question with a kind of painful and disillusioned introspection that seemed to try his spirit. "I don't know. I'm no longer sure there's anything there for me, Chaynoa. I've begun to wonder if the dream I held for so many years isn't just that—a dream that reality could never match. Sometimes I think we imagine things in glowing pictures just to soothe ourselves, to get us through times we couldn't otherwise endure—or simply because we know the reality will never be tested. If I saw the place in those pictures again—the real place—maybe it would look different to me, maybe I wouldn't feel the same about it anymore."

Chaynoa left his side to fetch her bag of belongings, and, pulling out a drawstring purse, removed an object from it. The sun sparked off its now polished surface and made silver lace of its filigree. Draping the necklace across her husband's palm, she closed his fingers over it tightly, put both her hands atop his, and whispered, "Go back and see then, Courtland. Do what you must here, and then let us both return to Devonshire and find out if what you say is true." Eagerness lit her face. "Let us test the dream."

Courtland enfolded her in his arms, and nodded. He even promised lovingly to do as she suggested, clenching the filigree in his hand, realizing with a kind of relieved dawning that he made the vow only for her sake, out of respect for her desire to make him happy.

He had already found the dream. It was real. It was vital. And he held it in his arms.

Epilogue

He had bought her a rocking chair. It sat before a stone hearth built at least two hundred years ago, and in it, with loving wonder, she had rocked their first born son, and soon would be rocking another downy-haired mite, probably one with particularly keen gray eyes.

The house was just as she had imagined it to be, just as warmly time-weathered and magically enduring as the faded watercolor paintings had suggested, and it possessed a soul that welcomed any who crossed its worn slate threshold. Fittingly, its surrounding landscape undulated in variegated shades of perpetual green softened to gentle blurs by the mist that rolled in with dawn and returned again each night as she tucked the baby in his heirloom cradle.

She arose now, smiling maternally at her child napping on his quilt, and went to look out the tiny leaded window, very English, which she had always fancifully likened to a transparent mosaic fashioned of diamond chips. Through it she saw her husband crossing the fields with a team of plow horses, saw him glance up at the sky as if to judge the accuracy of the almanac's prediction, and, when he found the heavens clear, she heard him whistle a tune that made

the horses prick their shaggy ears and swish their
tails. He was tall, trim, and broad shouldered, more
handsome than ever, she thought, with the harmony
of life settled comfortably over his features and the
tranquil reflection of Devonshire in his eyes. Dressed
in working corduroys and top boots, the mud of the
fields upon their good sturdy leather, he tethered the
team in the yard, his hands not as nimble as they had
once been, but still useful, thank the Lord. At the
close of the war in Yorktown they had been injured
by mortar fire, and, as fate would have it, never
healed well enough to allow him to paint again with
the same deft strokes he had once effected with such
ingenious skill.

But the fields and the hard honest work they provided seemed compensation enough to his spirit,
those, and the firelit evenings with his family, and the
pleasure he found in her arms at the close of each day
when they ensconced themselves beneath a mound of
down quilts in the old, creaking four-poster upstairs.

She ran out to meet him now, following the convo-
luted path overlaid with crushed seashells, breathing
air fragranced with the perfume of her blooming
white roses, which looked blue now in the descending
dusk, and waved the letter in her hand to catch his
attention.

"What do you have there, love?" he asked, throwing an arm about her waist before stooping to deliver
a hard, quick kiss to her cheek. "Another letter from
Virtue?"

"Aye."

"What does my sister say?" In a leisured stroll he
started walking toward the house with her, his arm
riding her waist, his hips brushing the flowered print
skirts let out to cover the ripeness of her fertile belly.

He groaned. "Please don't tell me the letter is filled with nothing but fashion news again."

Chaynoa smiled. "She says they have named the baby George—after their president of course—not our king."

Courtland laughed.

"Priscilla has remarried—thank the saints." Chaynoa lifted a brow and murmured the words with an exaggerated pleasure that made her unabashed mate grin. "And Jack's business is flourishing," she continued, "doing so well that he is taking on a partner now Boris has retired. Since her husband is becoming such a popular pillar of society now, Virtue insists she will have to make another trip to London soon to order fashionable gowns. The Boston dressmakers just won't do—they have no flair, no style, no idea of *bon ton,* you know."

"Oh, of course, of course they don't," Courtland agreed with feigned gravity, opening the kitchen door and escorting her inside, where he removed his hat, scooped up his sleeping son, and, gently cradling him in his arms, put his lips to the dewy, pearl-colored brow overlaid with wisps of minkish hair.

" 'But I will not patronize that odious dressmaker in Bond Street again,' " Chaynoa read on with the proper amount of dramatic expression. " 'He cheated me dreadfully last visit, used such cheap lace and shabby velvet that I have had to give the whole lot of his inferior gowns to my friend Gertrude. He is a shameful fake, a masquerader, a positive snake in the weeds!' "

"Grass!" Courtland said in a perfectly timed chorus with Chaynoa. "Grass, Virtue, *grass.* "

The baby awoke to the sound of their hilarity and Courtland nuzzled his cheek, still chuckling. "She never could get that right. If I corrected her once, I must have corrected her a million times. Poor Jack."

Chaynoa smiled and, putting the kettle on for tea, paused to reflect upon the twists and turns, so unpredictable and fortuitous, that had carried her here like a vessel propelled by a strong wise wind. Of course, the filigree necklace had redeemed the stone farmhouse, but it had not purchased the happiness that dwelled inside its walls. Courtland had done that.

All at once Chaynoa laid aside the tea canister and threaded her fingers tightly through her husband's, so that he gave her a curious regard, which she answered fondly with a smile learned long ago in a tangled wood. It was a place far removed from the velvet fields of Devonshire, of course, but a place never quite forgotten, especially on evenings like this, when Grandmother Moon peeked through the window knowingly, and the scent of a long green river seemed to fill the air with wonder.

Author's Note

While the village of Swanston and its inhabitants are entirely fictional, I made every attempt to accurately reflect the political and emotional climate of Massachusetts during the time period just prior to the Revolutionary War. I am indebted to Ablah Library, Wichita State University, and the Wichita Public Library and its interlibrary loan program for excellent resources.

I enjoy corresponding with readers. You may write to me care of Zebra Books, 850 Third Avenue, New York, New York 10022. Please enclose a self-addressed, stamped envelope for a reply.

Previous books include: ANGEL FIRE
LOVE'S SECRET FIRE
and ARABESQUE.

FROM AWARD-WINNING AUTHOR
JO BEVERLEY

DANGEROUS JOY   (0-8217-5129-8, $5.99)

Felicity is a beautiful, rebellious heiress with a terrible secret. Miles is her reluctant guardian—a man of seductive power and dangerous sensuality. What begins as a charade borne of desperation soon becomes an illicit liaison of passionate abandon and forbidden love. One man stands between them: a cruel landowner sworn to possess the wealth he craves and the woman he desires. His dark treachery will drive the lovers to dare the unknowable and risk the unthinkable, determined to hold on to their joy.

FORBIDDEN   (0-8217-4488-7, $4.99)

While fleeing from her brothers, who are attempting to sell her into a loveless marriage, Serena Riverton accepts a carriage ride from a stranger—who is the handsomest man she has ever seen. Lord Middlethorpe, himself, is actually contemplating marriage to a dull daughter of the aristocracy, when he encounters the breathtaking Serena. She arouses him as no woman ever has. And after a night of thrilling intimacy—a forbidden liaison—Serena must choose between a lady's place and a woman's passion!

TEMPTING FORTUNE   (0-8217-4858-0, $4.99)

In a night shimmering with destiny, Portia St. Claire discovers that her brother's debts have made him a prisoner of dangerous men. The price of his life is her virtue—about to be auctioned off in London's most notorious brothel. However, handsome Bryght Malloreen has other ideas for Portia, opening her heart to a sensuality that tempts her to madness.

Taylor-made Romance from Zebra Books

WHISPERED KISSES   (0-8217-5454-8, $5.99/$6.99)
Beautiful Texas heiress Laura Leigh Webster never imagined that her biggest worry on her African safari would be the handsome Jace Elliot, her tour guide. Laura's guardian, Lord Chadwick Hamilton, warns her of Jace's dangerous past; she simply cannot resist the lure of his strong arms and the passion of his *Whispered Kisses*.

KISS OF THE NIGHT WIND   (0-8217-5279-0, $5.99/$6.99)
Carrie Sue Strover thought she was leaving trouble behind her when she deserted her brother's outlaw gang to live her life as schoolmarm Carolyn Starns. On her journey, her stagecoach was attacked and she was rescued by handsome T.J. Rogue. T.J. plots to have Carrie lead him to her brother's cohorts who murdered his family. T.J., however, soon succumbs to the beautiful runaway's charms and loving caresses.

FORTUNE'S FLAMES   (0-8217-5450-5, $5.99/$6.99)
Impatient to begin her journey back home to New Orleans, beautiful Maren James was furious when Captain Hawk delayed the voyage by searching for stowaways. Impatience gave way to uncontrollable desire once the handsome captain searched *her* cabin. He was looking for illegal passengers; what he found was wild passion with a woman he knew was unlike all those he had known before!

PASSIONS WILD AND FREE   (0-8217-5275-8, $5.99/$6.99)
After seeing her family and home destroyed by the cruel and hateful Epson gang, Randee Hollis swore revenge. She knew she found the perfect man to help her—gunslinger Marsh Logan. Not only strong and brave, Marsh had the ebony hair and light blue eyes to make Randee forget her hate and seek the love and passion that only he could give her.

Available wherever paperbacks are sold, or order direct from the Publisher. Send cover price plus 50¢ per copy for mailing and handling to Penguin USA, P.O. Box 999, c/o Dept. 17109, Bergenfield, NJ 07621. Residents of New York and Tennessee must include sales tax. DO NOT SEND CASH.